THE
RISE
TRILOGY

USA TODAY BESTSELLING AUTHOR
ASHLEY ZAKRZEWSKI

No part of this book may be reproduced or used in any manner without the author's consent. This is a work of fiction. Names, businesses and likewise are all product of the author's imagination.
© 2021 COPYRIGHT ASHLEY ZAKRZEWSKI
All rights reserved

Rise of the Blood Lust

Rise Book #1

USA Today Best Selling Author
ASHLEY ZAKRZEWSKI

1
Envio

As my eyes flutter open, I quickly gaze around an unfamiliar room. The last thing I recall is driving home from a college party with a couple friends, and then semi lights beaming into my retinas as my hands dart in front of my face.

Where am I? How did I get here? It is eerily quiet, until the ringing inside my head makes me grimace. *Am I dead?* It is a rational analysis, but this isn't what I anticipate the afterlife to look like; it's too dull. Could this be hell? I've never been a religious person, so it could be... This could be my hell.

There is a disastrous thirst spawning inside me as my stomach tenses. *How long have I been here?* My breathing accelerates as I sit up, opening my dry mouth to call out, but remember all the scary movies I've seen. Screaming out is never a good idea. If anyone is here, maybe I can escape before they know I am awake.

As my feet swiftly hit the arctic concrete floor, the room starts to swallow me whole. Impulse takes over as my feet as they scamper across the sandpaper-like floor to see outside. A small dingy window provides a look into the desolate hallway. As my face touches against the glass, screams begin bouncing off the walls. What the hell is that?

I cover my ears wincing. The voice is coming from inside my own head, and the outcries won't stop. *Aah – it hurts. Make it stop!*

The flickering lights harmonize with the voices, and time is kept by my hammering heart with erratic little bursts. My eyes close, immersing myself into another room far worse than this one. This room is darker, and blood on the floor...

"Don't fight." The deep voice is sinister. "It'll only make things worse for you."

I am seeing through this man's eyes, but how? A hysterical woman appears, pleading with him to stop. My head shakes, and just like that, I am back in that same unfamiliar room. Am I going mad? Even though my mind is still hazy, my gut tells me to run like hell. I place one hand on the wall and the other on the door handle, trying to open it as discreetly as possible. It is just the blood-soaked gurney and me trapped in this filthy room, and I somehow doubt dust bunnies are going to help me out of this situation. As I slip out and gently shut the door behind me, a heated breath hits my neck, sending goosebumps down my spine that keeps me in place. Slowly, I turn around to a man with reddish-yellow eyes staring back.

What is wrong with his eyes? My gaze flicks behind him. The gut-wrenching screams continue, a horrible background noise I can't escape. *If he is here, who's still hurting her?* I swallow uneasily.

Maybe I am dreaming. This is just a nightmare, and I am really in a coma at the hospital in Frankfort.

"Good, you're awake. Gotta snack waiting to be devoured," the man says, licking his lips.

I want to turn around, escape him, but my legs have other plans. They trail behind him toward the woman's pleas ricocheting inside my head. As I get closer, my bottom lip is raw, and her screams become even more boisterous. My eyes bang shut, not wanting to see the horrific sight again.

"Open your eyes and say hi to your snack," a man demands.

My stomach twists, catching sight of a woman tied up, hanging from a chain, blood still dribbling from a deep flesh wound on her neck. The eyes answer a lot about a person, particularly when they decline to make eye contact. Well, that's me, trying not to look at her. Something is fueled deep inside me, making me lurk closer and closer. I swiftly realize the fuel is her blood that smells gratifying and pure. It should revolt me to look at this poor woman, but instead, it excites me.

"What's wrong with me?" I demand, trying to prevent myself from thinking about how exquisite she will taste. "What did you do with my friends?"

The man peers over at me from across the room and says, "Don't worry about it. You'll be fine. Just need to eat something."

Eat? I know exactly what he is implying, but my abdomen tenses again. I've seen this plenty on television, but it's all a myth. Vampires. Vampires aren't real. My belly cramps, and the smell of the hot blood makes my mouth water, and that feels all too real. Secretly, I pinch myself to confirm this isn't a nightmare. *How did I get here from the crash?* It looks like an abandoned old hospital probably not been used since World War II.

I take a deep breath, trying to calm my hammering heart, and then risk a glance at the woman. Blood is coated across her neck, her face, as if someone has rubbed it in. Her eyes are wide and panicked in a too-pale face. *This is not happening*, I tell myself, coercing my gaze to the ground.

"Don't make me tell you again." The man's voice is gruff. He stands almost seven feet tall, his eyes illuminating evilly. "I know what you're thinking. You're worried that it's wrong or evil." He lifts his hands in a dramatic shudder, the sneer rich in his voice. "News flash, it's not. That's just humanity's take. I'm sure the rabbit feels the same way when a wolf needs a snack." He claps his hand on my shoulder like we are old friends. "And I know just how much you need one," he purred.

I find myself intently watching her again. Her blonde hair is matted, mouth hung open as she weeps, and the tear tracks left little pale streaks through the red.

I don't want to be a monster! But, oh... I lick my lips.

"Jakob, you want me to force him?" one of the bystanders asks.

"No. Just give it a minute. He'll do it. He's hungry. Aren't ya, boy?" he smirks.

Oh, yes. So hungry. I take a step toward the woman, nostrils flaring to better catch her scent. When I did, something almost animalistic takes over, and my body springs into action.

My feet race over to the woman, and the smell is overwhelming. I try to fight it, but I'm not strong enough.

"Come on, go ahead. I wanna see those beautiful baby blues turn into fiery yellow. She tastes good, I promise."

My nose rubs along her neck, soaking up the aroma as my newfound fangs penetrate her skin. The warm blood flows into my mouth, and the taste is much better than I anticipate. This only makes me want more. I fly into a frenzy, ripping my head back and forth, consuming all she can give me.

"Please! Stop!" The young woman cries out, but it is all background noise to the wonderful taste.

"Told you he wouldn't last long. They never do." Jakob laughs.

I am not myself. With everything in me, I try to pull away, but something else has taken over. It won't let me stop.

As I continue drinking from her, her fingernails dig into my skin, using her last bit of energy to try and save herself.

"I'm so sorry." I whisper into her ear, before taking the last of her.

The poor woman hangs motionless, and there is blood smeared all over my face and spreading on the floor. Remorse starts devouring me. I just took an innocent life and for what? So, I could become a monster? *What the hell was I thinking?* It isn't me. This wasn't me!

"See. They always give in, in the end." Jakob says, smiling at the other two in the corner.

"Why did you want me to feed on her?" I ask, confused by the quick turn of events.

"Because you're a Blood Taker now, boy. My property, and you'll do as I say. It'll all make sense in the next few days. Follow me."

Again, I try to stay stagnant, but my feet scurry after him. It is like my mind is no longer connected to my body, telling it what to do. Jakob is, as stupid as that sounds, like I am his own personal puppet on a string for him to pay with at his leisure.

It's pitch-black outside, the only light guiding our way is the sparkling stars in the sky. Jakob's in front of me, and the two others behind. Are they scared I will run? I can't say I haven't thought about it, but what good will it do me? There are three of them; I'd never make it.

"What are we?" I ask.

Jakob turns to face me. "Gods. Immortal creatures."

Without thinking, a laugh escapes.

"What the hell ya laughing about, boy?" He backhands me, leaving me on the ground.

"I was thinking more like vampires."

"Same thing. Soon humans will cower beneath us and act as slaves to our very being."

We walk for what feels like an hour when we come to a concealed tunnel doorway.

"Where are we?" I ask, my face wrinkles up at the stink. It's like a high school locker room—all unwashed bodies and sweaty clothes.

"Home, boy. We're home."

They open the iron gate that leads to what I think is a deserted tunnel, but splits into three directions. I can hear others farther down, laughing and fighting.

"You can follow down that path. It'll lead you to Pavel. He'll help you get settled in," Jakob says.

I couldn't move. Where am I? I will never be able to find my way out alone once I go down one of these paths. It isn't like I can turn around and dart out of here without being detained. *Don't even think about it, idiot. You might die if you try that.* Jakob didn't look like he would have any qualms with killing me.

"Go on, boy. Don't make me tell you again," he says as he thrusts me farther down the passageway.

Walking gradually, I can hear the laughter getting more pronounced. What the hell am I going to do? I can't turn around and run because it sounds like hundreds are up ahead. They will surely catch me before I make it too far.

I curve around the corner and stop dead, my lips parting. The sheer number of vampires is baffling; those closest to me look my way. Some have expressions of repulsion, yet others bore knowing smirks. The closest, a man, grins. His legs carrying him toward me.

"I'm Pavel. Here's our rec room. Most of our time is spent out here. It's getting kind of overcrowded, so we'll probably have to transfer some out to other locations."

"Other locations?" My eyes grow wider.

"Oh yeah, we have hundreds of them. You surely didn't think this was all," he says, looking around like I am crazy.

I shake my head, mouth open, and freeze. How many are there? Vampires have been roaming the streets undetected and humans have no idea. How could we be so stupid and naïve?

The rec room is filled with sitting tables, amongst other things and very much resembles a bar atmosphere. Some are playing darts, while others are playing pool. By looking at the men down here, you couldn't tell they are different except for their eyes. It seems most have been around each other for a while, no fights at least. Hopefully, I'll be able to fit in here.

"Are there no women down here?" I ask, leaving the rec room to follow him.

"Don't be silly. None of us need that distraction. Jakob wouldn't have it. We've got too much to do to be worried about carnal pleasures."

At first, I think he's kidding... Wouldn't having women make it easier to focus? Give the men something to look forward to coming home too? Or maybe they don't have the pleasure of feeling love?

"Here's your room. You'll be sharing with Lorenzo. The next one over is mine if you need anything."

Pavel seems normal, unlike Jakob. His smile disturbs me, not knowing if he is just putting on a show for the newbie. Maybe this won't be so bad.

"Hey," I yell after Pavel, "you wouldn't happen to know if my friends are down here too, would you?"

His face wrinkles, "what friends? As far as I know, you're the only new addition."

If my friends aren't down here, then maybe they lived. Will they look for me? My mind starts going through all kinds of questions. Who will miss me? How will my mom take the news? My stepfather won't give her much time to grieve, anyway. He likes everything to be done before he gets home from work, and if not, well a beating is on it's way. I've always wanted a life away from my stepfather, and maybe this is my chance. Monster or not.

This room is where I will be spending most of my time, surrounded by bleak walls, and two cots that sit on opposite sides of each other. A couple of books lay on a table, so I assume that is Lorenzo's side. Sitting on the bed, my hands clasp over my head, contemplating if I hadn't gone to the college party, would I still be human? After those last few seconds staring into the bright lights of the oncoming semi, my human life ceased to exist. This place is my home now, or so Jakob says. I'll be trapped here *forever*.

2
Jane

My life has never been unicorns and rainbows and never been good enough in my parents' eyes no matter how hard I try. My mother uses me as a pawn while I'm my father's favorite punching bag. I yearn to get away, praying every night I will make it to graduation before something more detrimental happens.

When I marched across the stage last night, tears well up in my eyes, knowing this is it. My chance to finally get away and never look back. Find happiness, that's all I want.

My parents didn't bother to attend my graduation. Rather than throwing me a party, my father beats me while my mother watches. She is just happy it isn't her. I never understood how someone can idly sit back and watch their daughter get beat into oblivion.

Many questions arise over the years, why she stayed, or why she made me stay all these years. I would have been better off in foster care. At least I might have been placed in a good home with people who didn't strike and scold me daily.

Jason went through my things and found my acceptance letter to the University of Kentucky. Honestly, I didn't plan on telling them about college, because they never thought I'd get a scholarship to be able to attend. My strategy is to leave one night while they are asleep and never come back. If I am lucky, they won't come after me. Things, however, will probably get immensely worse for my mother. Without me around to take some of the beatings, it will be solely her. How long will she survive?

Jason stands there, acceptance letter in hand, basically foaming at the mouth. I know what's coming, and there is no way out of this room.

"You think you're going to leave us? Huh?" He shouts as he hits me repeatedly, saliva spewing out of his mouth and hitting my face. "You aren't a little girl anymore. Get up and take your punishment like a real woman."

"A real woman? If you're a real man, you wouldn't be hitting me or my mother, you piece of shit." My hand speeds to cover my mouth, knowing I just did something I might possibly never come back from. I hit the floor and ball up in the corner of my room, trying to make my ribs and face inaccessible to his impending blows. It's all I can do. He is much stronger than me, so overpowering him isn't an option.

A couple of weeks ago, he cracked one of my ribs, but I wasn't allowed to go to the hospital. As sheriff, if the police are called, my father is the first to know. Everyone in the police department looks up to him for climbing the ladder so fast and having a perfect family. They didn't even know half of it. Our family is far from perfect. Every day we have to fake our lives to satisfy my dad. I always wondered how no one sees how dysfunctional we are. My mother isn't allowed to leave the house besides to go grocery shopping, and only if she is able to cover up any bruises he has given her.

I clutch my ribs, hoping another one isn't cracked. It's getting harder to breathe as I gasp for air. Why am I still here? I should have left last night while they were both asleep and never looked back.

When the blows and yelling finally halt, I open my eyes. Jason is nowhere to be seen, and with no hesitation, I grab a suitcase and start throwing necessities into it. Jason can't keep me here, and in the eyes of law I am an adult. He has hit me for the last time. My mother, Lorraine, just stands there without uttering a single word. It's both of their jobs to protect me, right? Instead, they both have only inflicted pain my entire life. What would my life be like if I had been honored with different parents?

One night, I dreamt of it. My life was dramatically different. My new mom and I were close and told each other everything. My dad, well, instead of punching me, sat down at the dinner table and asked how my day went after giving me an enormous hug. My friends, oh yes, I was allowed to have friends, would come over and spend the night. Oh, how I craved that to be true when I woke up that miserable morning, only to realize it was all a dream.

I hesitate, still clutching a shirt in my unsteady hands, my mind flying back to when it is a sippy cup in my trembling grip. Jason didn't restrain blows then, either. I swallow tightly, suddenly that three-year-old all over again. Closing my eyes against the memory, I take a deep breath.

My bedroom door opens, and there he is. I shove past him to find my mother in the living room. He attempts to hit me again, but I catch his fist and twist it behind his back. Enough was enough, and I refused to let him touch me again.

"Jane!" My mother gasps, her hands going to her mouth.

Maybe I should give her one more chance. "Mom, we can both leave!" I cry, my voice high and frantic. "Get as far as we can from him! Come on! Aren't you sick of this?"

In her eyes, I see flashes of memory: the time he split her head against the granite countertop, how she lay unconscious for hours. Another time when he shoved her into the wall, pummeling her until her eyes swelled shut and blood dripped from her chin. She slurped soup through a straw for days after that one. All the things I witnessed while being such a small child scarred me. "Come on," I plead. "Let's just go. Come with me!"

She bites her lip and drops her gaze to the floor – a floor she's been on too many times to count. "I'm not leaving my husband," she mutters, "He loves us both! We... we just need to do better. Be better!"

All these years, I have questioned if this is what love looked like, being beaten all the time. If it is, I want no part of it.

"Better? I've done nothing but bring home good grades, do everything he asks, and get beaten. What makes you think he'll ever change? This is your only chance. Take it."

In shock, I loosen my hold, and he yanks free and wheels to face me. His fist comes hard and fast at my jaw, and I collapse to the ground. My hand flies to my lips and comes away bloody. "Get your hands off me! After tonight, you won't ever see me again."

"Jane, stop acting out. You aren't going anywhere," Jason says.

Nothing he can say will keep me here. It is time to make my final exit. Forget about this place and all the bad memories that come with it. Give me a fighting chance of becoming someone productive in society.

"I'm no longer under your control. Or did you not realize that already? Don't expect to get a Christmas card from me or anything. I hope I never see your disgusting face ever again."

I race to the door, but it comes back flying in, propelling me into the wall.

"My, my. What do we have here? Two shitty parents that no one will miss, not even their own daughter."

A man stands before us, blood dripping down his chin and eyes that look like a demon. I shudder at the thoughts running through my head. His eyes only waver at Jason.

"Who the hell do you think you are?" Jason asks.

The man laughs then licks his lips. "I'm the guy who's going to rip you to pieces while you beg for mercy," he takes a step closer, and I watch, unable to look away, as Jason scrambles backward. "I bet she cried for mercy, too. Isn't that right? How's about I make you a deal, hmm? I'll give you as much mercy as you gave her. How does that sound?" His lips curve up into a smile that sends goosebumps rippling up my arms.

As the man walks toward Jason, I try to back up slowly to exit out the door, but two more walk in. They are even scarier than the first. Why are these men in our house? We didn't have anything of value – our TV barely works.

"Take whatever you want. Please, just don't hurt us," Lorraine screams.

I look at my mother balled up in the corner, arms covering her head, eyes peering out from between them. She is shaking so hard I can see it even from where I'm sitting.

The men share a look, then laugh. "We didn't come here for your stuff. We came here for you."

The first one who has never taken his predatory gaze from my father suddenly charges forward. Before I can blink, he has him pinned against the wall, his fist knotted in Jason's plaid shirt. His hands scratch at the bigger man's arms as he lets out a mewling cry of terror. Jason goes utterly still when the man leans forward and places his bloodstained lips right next to his ear. I can see them moving, whispering something, and then see tears trickle from Jason's eyes. I always thought it would be nice to see him take what he dished out – now, I only feel only a numb sort of shock.

"Wh-what are you?" He chokes out.

"Your worst nightmare. Not only do we love human blood, but we despise shitty fathers. Thanks to you, we'll be checking two things off our list tonight."

The man wastes no time grabbing his neck and biting him. All the while, Jason's screams are echoing off the walls while my mother sobs in the corner knowing she isn't far behind. The man's head is ripping from side to side with blood squirting like paint on a canvas. I can't bring myself to speak. My voice is trapped. Why should I try to save him? As horrible as it is, maybe this is karma showing him what an awful person he's been all these years. I am not going to beg them to take me instead, he deserves whatever is coming to him.

"Please! Stop," my father begs, but they just chuckle.

The man slicks back his black hair and tsked at Jason. "Now, we've talked about this, remember?" He purrs. "All the mercy you gave her." He cut his eyes over to me, his face streaked with the lifeblood of the man who's spent that very life hurting those he is meant to protect. His gaze rakes me up and down, and I feel the first strange tingle of a thrill. "And it doesn't look like you gave her any. Such a delicious shame."

And then his head bends over Jason's throat, his last words drown in the sounds of his own burbling gurgles.

Not a single tear is shed as the light goes out in his eyes. My mind is scrambling, thinking I am next. Fear washes over me as I try to formulate a plan to get out of there. They are much bigger than me, so there is no way I am going to outrun them. Still, I have to do something. I couldn't give up so easily. As soon as I see an opening, I race to the door, but one of the men grabs me and throws me back against the wall like a rag doll.

"Leave her alone!" Lorraine yells as the other two men are ravaging her.

These aren't men; they are vampires. I don't want to believe it, but it is the only thing that makes sense. Vampires are real?

"Stand up!" one of them says to me.

I stand up, obeying orders, anything if it makes my death less painful than theirs. He looks into my eyes and tells me to be quiet. Suddenly, I can't speak. I stand there while this creature sinks his teeth into my neck. He is gentler with me than my parents.

"What are you doing?" Another vampire asks.

"We can't kill her. We need her turned. Don't question me. Finish up here."

My head starts spinning, and I might have stumbled, but the vampire wraps a strong arm behind me, holding me up. What is happening? *Needed me... turned?* My thoughts swirl groggily in my head. *Turned... turned... not going to die... wasn't this dying?*

"You're going to sleep for a while," he whispers against my neck, dragging my attention back from the edges of unconsciousness. Dread settles ice-cold in my gut. "And then you'll wake up feeling brand *new*."

3

Envio

As soon as the girl fell unconscious, I pin her against one side, nip my thumb, and close the wound instantaneously. *She's even prettier in person*, I think before brushing a strand of her thick black hair to the side. This is the woman I have been seeing. She will save us.

Jane will never have to live in fear again. Once she feeds, no one will mess with her, especially back at the bunker. She will be our secret weapon, a natural revenge seeker like myself.

"Lorenzo, Pavel! I'm heading back," I yell to the others. They are taking their time feeding from the mother. I glance down at the young woman in my arms, at the swelling near her mouth and the blackening bruise near her eye. *I hope it takes her a long time to die*, I think viciously. Parents are supposed to protect their kids from getting hurt, not inflict the pain themselves. My desire to make them pay for what they made her endure all these years, only made me want to stay and watch her suffer. Yet, I need to get her fed, and that has to be my priority.

Jakob will be waiting for her arrival, and he isn't the most patient vampire. He has a policy that we aren't to turn women, but that changed when he learned about what I can do.

The girl is a lighter burden than my thoughts as I stride toward the bunker. With the battle against the Guardians looming, Jakob is getting more and more volatile. His temper is on a hair trigger, and it seems like I am always the one setting him off. *Even though it's not really me*, I think. We are constantly recruiting more candidates to join us, but we need young ones. They prove to have a burning desire to please their sire, to prove their loyalty and usefulness.

Jakob is someone no one wants to piss off. Not only is he our leader, but he is maniacal. We've been searching for a vampire named Samuel and still no luck. Many have been killed for their failure, but so far, I've been lucky.

"What are you doing? And w-who are you?" A voice erupts out of nowhere.

I stumble as the girl's reedy voice breaks through my plotting. In shock, my grip loosens, and she hits the dusty ground with a thump. Shit! Normally, they didn't wake up for a couple of hours after being turned. Jane is turning out to be less normal than I expected.

"Sorry. You just surprised me," I say, holding out a hand to help pull her to her feet. She stares at it for a long moment before pushing it to the side and standing on her own.

"I don't need any help from you." She brushes off the dirt from her jeans and out of her hair. "What are we doing? Walking on a barely lit road in the middle of the night?"

I brush off her question with an appreciative look. I like spunk especially from women. "I'm Envio."

"Okay, then a different question. What did you do to me?" she says, holding her head. "Why did you come to my house?"

"We'll talk about it later, once we get you fed."

I could tell she is trying to fight the urge, but it isn't that easy. When you are in between being bitten and the first feed, the lust is overpowering. Once you give in to the bloodlust and let it consume you to the point of taking a human's life, it usually controls you forever.

Is that something I really want for Jane? The life she has lived, isn't that enough violence for her? These thoughts need to go away, because the last thing I need is Jakob doubting me. I've worked too damn hard for him to keep me around and be trusted. Without his trust, I'd be dead within a matter of weeks.

"Why did you kill my parents?" She stops walking and crosses her arms. "I'm not moving until you tell me."

Honestly, that is a conversation for another time and above my pay grade. Jakob wants to be the person to explain everything to her, and he won't be happy if I take that away from him.

"I had a dad that beat me every day," I say, neatly side-stepping her question. "When my mom finally left him and married my step dad, I thought I was in for a better life. You know, the kind the other kids at school had." Out of my periphery, I catch her nod of understanding. "Didn't happen. He may have been worse than my real dad. For a long time, I didn't have the strength to do anything but take it." I bare my teeth. "Hearing what was going on in your house... I'll kill any abusive asshole I can get my teeth into. Especially for those that hit women."

When I look at her, the depth of my connection to her only grows. The way her long black hair hangs to the small of her back and her deep-blue eyes sparkle from the stars. Hell, even her skin, still pale, looks flawless. I can't imagine why her own father would do something like that. The more I look at her, the more I doubt that this is the right decision. Shouldn't she belong to the Guardians? With someone like her, they can finally beat Jakob.

"What is that smell?" Her nose crinkles. "Smells like a farm..."

"They don't all smell bad. Some are downright delicious," I laugh. "Are you ready to eat?"

The apprehension of her face tells me this is going to be harder to sell. I think back to when I turned, and the things swirling around in my head. Vampires aren't real. Only now, I know they are. "Listen... I know this comes as a bit of a shock... vampires being real and all... it'll take some getting used to... but we gotta get you fed."

"What if I don't want to?" She replies, looking at me through her lashes. "I don't know if I can kill someone."

If I know she isn't coming back with me to Jakob, I could show her a different way, but as of right now, I have no idea if she can be trusted. Showing her how to feed without killing could be the signature to my death warrant. "Just let your instinct take over... that's all you have to do. It gets easier, I promise."

"What—do I do?" I hear the nervous tremble in her voice, and the neon lights of the bar reflect red in her eyes as she gazes up at me. "You'll know exactly what to do," I step closer, allowing my lips to brush up against her ear. "When you're surrounded by the blood pumping." I use my fingertips to trace a line down her delicate neck over the carotid artery. She shudders beneath my touch, and I smile, exposing wickedly sharp fangs. "Your instincts take over..."

She licks suddenly parched lips, and I remember that same desperate thirst before my first feed. The gut-wrenching hunger, the need... The smell of her desperation is delicious.

"Come on," I say, using a firm hand on the small of her back to urge her to the door. "Let's just go in there and have some fun."

The bar is especially packed for a Thursday night, which proves to be a great time to feed. The goal is to get in and out before causing too much attention. With the war looming, the Guardians can be anywhere.

"I'm not sure about this. I don't think I can kill anyone. I'm not like you."

She is more like me than she realized. The human instinct is to stay alive, well that's mine too. If I must kill a few to stay alive then I will. Being under Jakob's watchful eye, I have to blend in to bide time until I can switch teams. Who knows, maybe Jane and I can work together, but how could I tell if she is someone I can trust? Only time will tell.

A drunk guy comes up to her and asks her to dance. As she follows, her eyes shoot back to me with her mouthing, I can't do this.

I stay close to keep an eye on her, and find an empty stool to order a beer. Oh, how I wish that is me swaying behind her, feeling her body against mine. This vampire thing isn't all bad, but the fact Jakob has a rule about there being no women in the bunker, makes it hard to get my needs fulfilled. That makes me think about all the other vampires, and how they must feel the same way. Is she really safe going back there? The only woman surrounded by hundreds of men. My hesitation grows the more I think about it.

"How's the newbie?"

I have never seen this vampire before. "Oh, she'll be fine. We just need her to feed so we can finalize her recruitment. Right now, I'll let her have a little fun before she kills. It won't take long for her instincts to kick in with all the blood pumping in here. You wanna join?"

The man smiles and counters, "Let's go get the rest of the recruits. They would love to get in on the action. We could take all of these humans down without breaking a sweat."

"I'm sorry, I didn't catch your name." He isn't a Blood Taker which can only mean one thing. *A Guardian*. Simply have to play it cool until I can escape. They never go anywhere alone which means there are more waiting outside. We should've never stopped here. If I didn't get back to the bunker with Jane, he would surely kill me.

"It's Stephen. Let's go."

I follow him without hesitation because there is no need to cause a scene.

"So where are these recruits?" I ask, looking around knowing there aren't any.

Two more vampires approach me. Both appear to be at least in their mid-forties.

"What are you doing here, Envio?"

"How do you know my name?"

"Oh, your maker and I go way back," he says. "Maybe he's mentioned me? Samuel?"

My gut ices with fear. This is the man Jakob is so eager to get back. He is with the Guardians? Why didn't he mention that? There is something else Jakob is withholding, and I can't wait to figure it out. The reason he withholds that Samuel is their leader is because that will make the others want to find him even more.

Samuel takes an aggressive step forward. "Why are you here? This isn't your place. It's ours."

I cast a furtive glance around. *Outnumbered. Alone. Stupid. Stupid, careless mistake*, my inner voice yells. My shoulders square and chin lifts in defiance. *If I'm going to die today, I'm not going to make it easy.*

"Liz, go find the girl he was with. She'll need our help," Samuel demands flicking his head toward the bar. His attention shifted back to me. "Because I'm not one of you. I'll give you one chance, an opportunity for redemption that I gave a few others. You can join the Guardians and fight. Not that I expect you to say yes."

I've been biding my time until I can join them, but not now, Jakob would savagely kill me and make me into an example. He could have someone watching me right now. I can't afford to take the chance. If there is one thing he can't stand, it's traitors. I've seen him murder for way less. "Not gonna happen. My loyalty lies where it always has, to Jakob." My body fuels with adrenaline knowing what's coming next. Samuel won't let me leave here alive, but I won't go quietly.

Without hesitation, I ran up on Samuel first. The only thing that might save me is my recent feed. There are two of them, but I am fast. I jump on Samuel and start whaling on him. Stephen comes behind and pulls me off, only to receive the blows himself. They have no idea who they are messing with right now. They aren't going to be able to kill me. I bash Stephen's head into the concrete, leaving blood trailing on it. Samuel is still on the ground, fighting to get back up. A prime example of why we recruit younger vampires.

"Have you seen me?" I ask, pumping my fists into my chest. "You thought you could kill me? Just the two of you? Next time, come better prepared."

My intentions aren't to kill them. That will take away any chance of the Guardians winning this battle. My sliver of humanity depends on their win, and my tether to Jakob being severed.

 I run off into the night, lucky to still be alive, but didn't know for how long. When I show up without Jane, he might just kill me and all this would have been for nothing. My feet scamper toward the bunker, wondering if this is my last night to live?

4
Jane

I'm just about to take Envio's advice, when an older lady approaches me and introduces herself as Liz, urging me to come with her. Does this lady really think I'm going to leave with her? I have no clue who she is.

"Where's Envio?" I ask, looking around for him. "He just up and left me? Seriously?"

She shakes her head. From the looks of her, she isn't sure what to say. "Well—Envio had a choice to make. The outcome is up to him. Same with you. However, I don't believe he informed you of the decision. So, before you feed, let's get you up to speed."

Do I trust this woman? She seems different from the vampires that killed my parents.

"I know you've had a long night, but there are some things we need to discuss. Like lots of changes in the coming days. Some are going to make you very uncomfortable. I'll be here to guide you if need be. Do you have an idea about what I'm talking about?"

I nod.

"I'm not your enemy. Just here to help ya once you make your choice, that's all."

"What choice is that?"

Liz fumbles her words, "Umm... Well, you have two options. Complete the transformation and change into a vampire, or you can choose not to feed and die."

Die? My head crams up with so many thoughts and feelings, I can't even speak. What kind of option is that? Isn't our survival instinct to do whatever it takes to stay alive? I get rid of one evil only to be a slave to a new one. What is it about me that attracts this bullshit?

"So, to live, I have to feed? There's no way around it?"

Liz shakes her head. "Unfortunately, no hun."

Tonight has changed my life at the drop of a pin. Tears well up, and I can't hold them back. Why did they have to choose my house?

"You don't have to make your decision right now. Once you decide, let me know."

Great. On top of everything else. A sudden image of the gore back home flashes up in my mind's eye. *Not like I can go back there.* My gaze drops to the floor. I'd wind up in jail on top of everything else.

"End of the week?" I mutter. A sharp pang in my stomach reminds me why I have that deadline. "I don't even have a place to stay." For a long moment, the sounds of the thumping bass and background chatter of the bar are my only response. This decision seems too big to make on a whim. I'll need more details like what being a vampire will mean for me. Could I still go to college? Even thinking about that at a time like this makes it seem trivial and stupid. I am trying to decide between living or dying, and the first thing that comes to mind is college. I shake my head, feeling ashamed. I've been trapped by parents all my life, never really allowed to do anything that normal kids did. No friends, no sleepovers, and for sure no boyfriends. Right when I can finally get away from it all, Envio chooses my house.

"Well, you can stay with me for now, since you don't have any place else," Liz offers, her voice gruff and a little awkward. To cover the kindness, she adds, "It'll make it easier on all of us, having you close. If you choose to feed, there's a way to go about it without killing."

My eyes fly up to meet hers, and my brows lift so high I feel certain they slid right up into my hair. I study Liz—the laugh lines around her mouth, the crow's feet at the edges of her blue eyes. She looks safe enough. Then again, this sweet-looking grandma is a vampire. So. There's that. Liz waits quietly, the only sign of her impatience a faint thinning of her lips. *What choice did I have?* I give a mental shrug. "I'll take you up on that, thank you."

"This way, then," Liz says, showing another flash of impatience in the way that she spins so quickly for the door. Maybe being here is as hard on her as it is on me. Another wave of hunger salivates my mouth, and then the cramps begin. As I follow her out the door, I cast one last glance around for Envio.

"Found her," Liz is saying to two men when I return my attention to her. "I've explained her choices. She's going to come home with me."

I look up at these two men, tall with broad shoulders. They look like bodyguards. *Are they hers?* "Excuse me, who are you?" I ask, my eyebrows raised. My gut is telling me I should run far away, but I don't.

"Samuel and Stephen. Glad to see she got to you before you fed."

"Where's Envio?" I ask, feeling abandoned after he makes such a point of turning me.

"He got away. Probably headed back to tell his leader about me. I'd expect a visit soon from him," Samuel says, staring at Liz like he is telling her something mentally.

Why am I so upset by this? I've known him for what, an hour. Envio turned me into this creature and didn't give me the same choice as Liz. Maybe he would have if I stuck it out a little longer.

―――

For a vampire, Liz lives quite well. Her house is Victorian with beautiful white pillars holding up her porch, the house painted eggshell white. The fact it is old gave it even more character. As I make my way inside with the door, it squeaks open to the living room. It's laid out with expensive-looking rugs and art. Each room of the house is bigger than the last.

"This'll be yours. I'll grab some freshly washed sheets and put them on the bed while you take a shower. I'm not sure if these clothes will fit, but they'll do."

After my shower, I stare into the mirror for a long moment. I didn't look all that different... Unable to help myself, I bare my teeth at my reflection, checking for fangs. Then, feeling a little silly, I shake the excess water from my hair and get dressed before heading to find Liz. She will be the one to answer my questions, and I have so many.

In the living room, her eyes and mouth are open. My legs cross the room in three strides.

"Liz?" I say, shaking her. Her head drops forward, hair falling about her face, but she doesn't answer. Nor does she blink. "Oh, God. Liz!" I push her head back up against the couch cushion. To my horror, as soon as her head falls back, blood trickles from her nose. "Oh, no. No, no, no. What the hell is happening? You can't be dead; you're a freakin' vampire! Come on! Liz!" I mutter, shaking her again. Why did I care so much about this lady?

Abruptly, she sucks in a loud gasp, blinking rapidly, obviously disoriented by... well, whatever the hell just happened.

"Oh, Liz! I was worried sick! What was that?" I snap.

"I... I'm sorry," she says, stumbling over her words. After a few more groggy blinks, she tries again. "I'm sorry. I should have warned you. I..." She blows out a harsh breath.

I run to the kitchen and grab a damp washcloth to put on her forehead. "Not to sound rude or ungrateful, but that scared the crap out of me. Is that normal for you?"

If I am going to be staying here, then I need to be forewarned.

"I thought you were dead. Which now seems stupid given what we are, but does that happen often?"

"I'm sorry to have frightened you," Liz sighs, mopping her forehead with the rag. "I honestly didn't even think to mention it. My turning came with an added gift." The way she spits the word makes it sound more like a curse. "I have all the vampire traits one would expect. I also have visions and no control over them."

"Well..." I trail off, trying to process this latest information. "You were bleeding," I say finally.

"It's part of it," she assures me while reaching into the purse sitting beside the couch and pulls out an old receipt and a pen. She scribbles on it for a second, then hands it to me. "This is Samuel's number. If it happens again, don't be scared. Just call him. Okay?"

I clutch the slip of paper in a tight fist and nod. Suddenly, I am hit with an overwhelming wave of exhaustion. Something must have shown in my face because Liz leans over and pats my leg.

"Go have a rest. I know you're tired."

Numbly, I get to my feet and go to my room.

For the next several days, I stay in my bedroom. As I stare at the walls, the flashes of my parents' murders keep creeping into my mind. Envio can't be all bad, could he? He had every opportunity to kill me but turned me instead.

I sit there, taking in the lilac paint on the walls and the flower wallpaper borders. This must have been a kid's bedroom previously. The bed is only a twin and doesn't leave me much room to spread out, but I'm not one to be ungrateful. The bedroom is much bigger than I am used to. I sit down at the beautiful white vanity sitting across from my bed and brush through my thick black hair. Suddenly, I want to chop it all off. A fresh start to mark my new journey with whatever decision I make. Jason never let me cut my hair; he said it was unladylike. I look around for scissors but see none. I'll just have to wait.

Liz tries a couple of times to get me to come out, but I just want to be alone with my thoughts. I have a decision to make that literally is life or death. The problem is, my stomach is growling, and I feel weak. It's time to get my questions answered and make a decision. There isn't anymore time to put it off if I want to live... whatever that means as a vampire.

I come down the stairs, to find her in front of an old wooden bookcase that wraps around the outside walls filled with books. I notice her name on one of the spines, Elizabeth Cameron. She's an author, interesting choice of career for a vampire. It makes sense for her to do work where she can be home. Visions popping in out of nowhere could be hard in an office setting, not to mention the complication of being a vampire. Do they hold regular jobs just like humans? Pay taxes? The questions in my mind are just piling up.

"You write books?" I ask, wondering what made her want to pursue that kind of career. I find it fascinating. My favorite subject in school was always English, but the most I'd ever written is a short story, never embarking on the journey of writing a full-length novel. It must be stressful and take a lot of courage to let thousands of people read and criticize your work. The mere thought terrifies me.

"Actually, I wrote books before I got turned." She gives a sad shake of her head. "Now, I have to write under a pseudonym, so my children can't track me down. I'd love to see them but didn't want to have to explain why I wasn't coming around anymore. They wouldn't understand."

She's right. What excuse would she be able to tell them? Keeping her distance is the better choice for her family, but not for her. From her gaze at the floor, I can tell she is missing her family deeply. I wish my mother felt that way about me. You know, motherly love. I always came second, with Jason being first. For a long while, I thought something was wrong with me, that I couldn't make her happy or proud, but as I got older, the realization came that she just didn't care for me like she should. Lorraine only cared about one thing, Jason. Anything to make him happy, even if that meant beating me senseless. It just didn't seem to phase her, being stuck as a battered woman for so long.

She never once tried to leave him, and that utterly shocked me to my core.

"Did you make that bedroom up for them?" I ask, remembering the lilac room with the small bed for a child.

"Yes. When I first moved here, I believed one day my family would be able to come visit. When things between the Blood Takers and us were settled. When I left, my daughter was pregnant. I made that room for my granddaughter."

I can't fathom the pain she must feel of never being able to meet her grandchild. This newfound life of hers hindering her chance to be close to those she loved the most.

"Have you ever gone out that way and peeked? To see how they're doing?"

She shakes her head. "No, I don't think I could handle it. I wouldn't be able to stop myself from approaching them."

Seeing this side of Liz truly shows me that she is different from the others. It inspires hope that I can be more like her instead of the ones who killed my parents. Ruthless and evil.

"Let's go. I'll go with you. You should at least get to see your family. Make sure they're doing okay." I say, reaching my hand out to her.

"I don't know. I don't think it's a good idea," she says, shaking her head, backing away from me.

"Come on, it is." I say grabbing her hand to walk her out to the car.

She starts up the old beat-up Toyota Camry and takes off. The closer we get, the more nervous she becomes.

"I don't know… we should go back."

I sigh, "I won't let you do anything… or even get close. But you're going to see your granddaughter tonight, so stop fighting me on this and drive."

We come to a sudden halt, and my body jerks forward toward the dash. "What are you doing? Trying to get us killed?"

"That's their house," she says, pointing her wrinkled finger.

They live in a small brick house with a brightly painted red door. The living room has windows, but the blinds are up so we can see inside. Liz gasps as a young girl runs across the living room. Her face lights up like a Christmas tree.

"That's her. That's my beautiful granddaughter," she says, tears falling down her face.

Over the next hour, we sit and watch as the little girl hops, skips, and jumps around the living room, moving from mommy to daddy's lap. They look happy, and Liz is able to see that. When the light turns off and the blinds are put down, that's our cue to head back. "I just want to hold her, see her personality develop, let her know that Grandma loves her..." She says, wiping the tears, and putting the car in drive. "Maybe one day... we could be together again." The drive back is spent in mostly silence, but occasionally, Liz will tell me a story about her daughter. Things she remembers from before she was turned. The memories will keep her sane, even if she can't ever hug them again.

When we pulled back into her driveway, the need for space is evident, and didn't want to push. "I'll give you some space," I say, opening the door, climbing out, and shutting it as softly as I can. My feet climb the front steps and go inside. I am sure the trip makes her very emotional, but it's worth it.

The trip makes me think about the things I never had before. If mom was still alive, she'd never feel as Liz did about her child. Some women were never meant to be mothers, and she was one of them. Young girls talked about having kids one day, playing with baby dolls preparing themselves for one day having a child, but not me. The last thing I wanted to do was bring a baby into this world only to mess it up. My thought was if my mom was that screwed up, there's no guarantee I wouldn't end up the same way. Every child deserves better than that. They deserved people who love them unconditionally. That love I would do anything to experience.

5

Envio

My fingers beat out a nervous rhythm on my legs as I near the entrance to the tunnels once again. *Jakob is not going to be happy.* Still, a little thrill runs through me at the thought of Jane escaping with the Guardians. Not good for me, not good for the Blood Takers, but... I shrug to myself. *Good for her.*

My loyalty to Jakob is strong but dwindles more every day. Every time I feed, give into the urge, I can feel myself slipping. I don't want to become a monster. My vow is to never become like Jakob. I still have some human emotions, but I keep them under wraps. He can't find out I didn't fully transition. Through the transformation, I zealously guarded a kernel of humanity buried deep inside myself. My will to remain me, at least on some level, is too strong to be overcome, even by the bloodlust. Even by Jakob.

My lip curls in utter distaste at the mere thought of my maker. The only kills I enjoy are the abusive assholes. That part is true. It's hard to maintain both sides, sort of like leading a double life. I would give anything to be with the Guardians, but Jakob has too much control over me.

I wish my maker was anyone else. Why did it have to be him? I am compelled to give my life for his, to keep him safe, and for what? So more people would die. Every day, I hope that an opening will become available and someone will take Jakob out. Once he is out of the picture, with me far away, so I'm not compelled to save him, I'll be free. Slaughtering won't be a part of my life anymore. Until then, I do as Jakob says without any pushback. I can't risk him realizing I am not staying true to his cause. If he ever finds out, I will surely have a slow and painful death. Jakob is sadistic—his favorite playground is the mind, but he isn't slow to torture the body, either. The more followers he gets, the more his ego swells.

My stomach churns as I near the tunnels. Images of the horrors that befell the last vampire that "failed" Jakob flashes across my mind —and their failure had been far less complete than mine.

Could we even win without Jane? The two parts of me warr at the thought. If we didn't, but Jakob survives, what will my life be worth? I snorted. Not much. Then again, if we did win, who would I even be? Could I keep that kernel of self safe if we won this war? I shudder. Then I take a bracing breath and push the door open, stepping into Jakob's office.

He is lounging against his desk, a thick folder in his hand. He glances up when I walk in. His face lit briefly with a manic excitement as he peers around me into the darkened hall, obviously expecting Jane to follow me in. When the hall remains empty, Jakob's gaze flies back to me, his eyes narrow.

"Where is she?" he hisses.

You know, I've never noticed how many tiles there are on this floor, and I take up a sudden, serious study of the ground. "The... Ah, the Guardians got her. It was all I could do to get away; I would have died if I'd tried to get her back then. I—"

"Then you should have damn well died!" Jakob yells, rising to his full height and tossing the folder on the desk. "At least then we could say your death was worth something! Instead, you come dragging back here, tail between your legs, stinking of failure!"

"We'll get her back," I say, fighting to keep my voice even. "We just have to come up with a plan." *Or you must come up with a plan. Because I'll see her back here only over my dead body.*

Even here, in this awful place, I can feel her presence; she is the first warm tendrils of sunshine on a winter morning, the softest gleam of hope, and I will protect that at all costs. The tiny piece of humanity within cheered at this sudden drive to protect instead of destroying.

"We'd better get her back, you worthless…" He turns and stalks over to the concrete wall.

With one sharp move, he punches it, and a little cloud of dust and crumbles of concrete rain down to the floor. My stomach clenches.

"This fight will be hard enough without your screw ups," Jakob continues, wheeling to point a finger at me. "We need her. You knew we needed her! You're the one that had the damn vision!"

And I am. Three days after my first feed, I have a vision of a beautiful woman with flowing ebony hair and eyes the pure blue of a summer sky. She is fierce, a warrior princess, with Guardian blood staining her mouth and the world burning around her. She is perfect.

At first, I hoped to use this newfound gift to do good, to harm Jakob's organization and to bring peace back to humanity. *Yeah, all right, Superman*, my inner critic growls. Again, my negative emotions are overshadowed by a wave of giddiness. This time, I recognize it; the emotion isn't me at all. It's Jane.

"I know I was," I say, my tone placating. "And we're going to see that vision fulfilled. I know it." Another flush of emotion from Jane, and I have to bite back the smile that threatens. Because now is not a good time for that!

"You had better do more than know it," Jakob snarls, his eyes snapping with fury. "You'd better see to it. In the meantime, you'd better see to some recruits. The last batch you brought in won't be nearly enough. Especially without that girl."

"I'm on it," I say with a quick nod. That is as much dismissal as I am going to get from Jakob right now.

So, I push down both Jane's joy and my own dread and back out of his office. I despise recruiting. The bloodlust is addictive, and the further I slip down that road, the less chance Human Envio has of ever bringing me back to myself. To keep it in check, I try to let Lorenzo and Pavel do most of the killing.

And I never turned anyone. Not before Jane. She is my first.

Her face in my mind brings a warmth and connection that even my begrudging loyalty to Jakob can't touch. *I'll see her survive this war if it kills me.* The certainty is my death may be exactly the price of her life.

As I head back to my room, a rush of sadness comes over me. It is like my heart is being physically tugged on, and I wonder what Jane is so sad about. Did something happen with the Guardians? Is she safe? As much as I've heard about them from Samuel and the others, there are good, and actually want to keep people alive. We share that goal even if they didn't believe, but one day they would. Someday, in the future, I will be able to show them that I am not your typical Blood Taker and this is all done out of help to them. Everything I do is to help them win this war, not Jakob.

Pavel walk past my room, and then comes back. "Where's she at?" He asks, looking around. "I didn't see her anywhere."

"The Guardians got her... it was close, almost didn't make it back myself..."

He sits on Lorenzo's bed. "Damn, and it must have went okay with Jakob since you're still breathing, huh?"

"I guess you could say that... we'll have to find her... if not my death is coming..."

Pavel nods, getting up from his bed. "Glad we stayed behind... her mother begged and pleaded the entire time... and as you requested, we took our sweet time before taking the last drop..."

She deserved to suffer after everything she put Jane through. I didn't know Jane's story, but mine is similar, and I know how something like that will affect us for our entire existence. If it is up to me, she will never be hurt again, and someday she will learn what being loved is like, truly loved.

My abuse started around age three, and pretty much continued my entire life. And like Jane, my mother stayed with my father for years. I endured so much pain from that man, and so did she until enough was enough. One day while he was at work, she packed up our stuff, and never went back.

A year went by with no abuse, and I finally thought I might actually be able to have a normal childhood, like all the other children, but that didn't last long. She started seeing a new guy, and he seemed nice enough at first. Coached my soccer team, took me to games, and really made an effort to spend time with me, but once they got married, everything changed. It was like a shift in personality, and the beatings began for both of us.

She stayed with him, and to this day, they were still married. Although, I wouldn't say happily, but my mother seemed to get complacent just like with my father. We both deserved better, but when you have someone constantly telling you that no one else would want you, you start to believe it.

This is the reason I have such a connection to Jane, knowing we have gone through similar childhoods, and as bad as mine was, hers was probably worse. Seeing her with bruises on her face, it struck me to my core, wanting to prevent something like that from ever happening to her again.

6
Jane

After a couple of hours, I go downstairs to check on Liz. Nothing stopped her from visiting them from afar, and she needs to know that they are safe and happy.

"How ya feeling?"

She closes the book in her hand, and shifts her attention to me. "Thank you... I would have never gone if you hadn't pushed me."

"I just wanted you to know you could trust yourself... and that grandbaby of yours was adorable. They looked happy..."

"Yes, they did..."

Sitting on the couch, I want to ask some more questions and find out how this is going to work. The trust is building and she will answer my questions without sugarcoating. My decision has to be made soon, but I need to know everything before making it. Being a vampire will change things, and not in the direction I pictured before Envio walked into my house. "Can—Can I ask you some more questions?"

Liz nods, "That's what I'm here for... Big decision to make... but it's all yours."

"I just... I mean, you're different from them. The others, I mean.

The ones who came to my house. They were..." I trail off with a shudder. "Savage may be an understatement. But you, you don't seem that way at all. What's the difference?"

A smile creeps up on her face. "Well, dear, that's simple. I have been meticulous about feeding and how much. If you do so, then you can control the urge. Those men can't do that. Once you give in to the bloodlust, truly give in, then you become a different person. It shuts off the humanity inside you. The ones like me are called the Guardians. We stay true to our human side as best we can and don't believe in slaughtering."

"Well, Envio didn't slaughter me. He just turned me. Why did he do that?"

It's the question still buzzing inside my head. He had every opportunity to kill me, but he didn't. Why? Something about him makes me trust him, even though they've made it clear I shouldn't.

"That's very unlike them. Maybe he had orders he didn't share with you," she says, making me question Envio's motives. Could she be right? If so, what would those orders be?

One thing is for sure, I didn't want to become like the others, savage and evil. I want to remain as human as I possibly can. If staying with Liz helps with that, then so be it.

"So, if I choose to feed, then I could become like you?"

Liz nods. "Of course. I'll help you along the way. If you listen and stay cautious, everything should go fine."

What if it didn't? What if I can't resist the urge and become one of them? What then? My head sways as I try to make a decision, hands shaking from the nervousness of what will come to be. Death isn't an option. After everything I persevered through with my parents, there is no way I am giving up that easily. I want to experience things, like love and friendship.

"When do I feed? How long do I have?" If becoming a vampire keeps me alive to experience those things, then I'd do it.

"If you're sure, we can go now. I'll take you to a place where most of us feed," Liz says, her eye winking.

"Yes, let's get it done..." I reply, attempting to mentally prepare myself for this change while we walk out of the house and down the street. It's not like I know what it's going to be like, or how I will feel afterward. The main hurdle would be drinking from someone. Could I?

We stop in front of a bar, a couple blocks away, and inside are plenty of strangers who smell horrendous. I hope the smell gets better; right now, it's not appetizing at all.

There isn't anyone outside to card, so Liz finds us a table but doesn't order drinks. I assume she knows how young I am. The bar is filled with mostly women dressed in provocative wear and a lot of makeup. Dear Lord, how long did it take them to get that crap off their face at night? Jason never let me wear makeup; he always told me I was beautiful the way I was. Sometimes, I would sneak into my mom's makeup when they were asleep and experiment. My makeup never looked as perfect as these women. Practice makes perfect, I guess.

"Let me give ya some pointers. The easiest place to feed is a bar. As a woman, you just get a guy to dance with you, then ask them to go somewhere private."

"There might be a hitch in this plan. I can't dance... like at all." I sigh. Out of everything, why did this plan have to involve something I loath. I flash back to my seventh-grade dance that my dad let me go to. He didn't give me a choice which I still think is weird, but now that I think back, it was probably more of a punishment. I sat in the corner of the room the entire time. Never even touched the dance floor. Not again.

"You'll do fine. Just move from side to side. Once you have someone, ask them if they want to go somewhere quieter, like the bathroom," she says, starting to giggle.

"The bathroom? Why would anyone want to go to the bathroom?" I ask but quickly realize what she's insinuating. "I'm not that kind of girl. Far from it. I don't think I could pull that off."

Liz laugh. "Don't worry. I'll be right here. It's easier than you think. You aren't going to do anything with him. Once in the bathroom, look deeply into his eyes directly and tell him to be quiet. This will make him listen to you and stay quiet while you bite and feed."

"Deeply into his eyes? What does that do? What's to keep him from screaming bloody murder, alerting everyone in the bar?"

"It stuns them for a couple of minutes. When you're done, nip your finger and apply some blood. It will close right up. He'll never even know what happened."

Confidence isn't something I've ever had. I'm more of a fly-on-the-wall type. This is way out of my comfort zone. I take a deep breath. *You can do this.*

I get up from the table and walk out on the dance floor. The song the DJ boots up starts with an easy, thumping rhythm, and I sway. Taking a deep breath—it's now or never—I lift my arms above my head and add a sensual swivel to my hips. A pair of heavy hands descend on my waist, and it takes all I have to shoot a smile back over my shoulder, instead of yanking them away. The man behind me bears striking green eyes and floppy brown hair; he's cute, in an endearing sort of way.

From the way his eyes rove my body, "cute" is not what he thinks of me. He probably thinks he's about to get lucky. Poor thing has no idea what he just signed up for.

My stomach rumbles. *It's time to get this party started.* I turn into his arms and grip the top of his shirt, bringing his face close to mine, and my lips to his ear.

"Mm," I purr. He smells delicious. "Want to go someplace quieter?" The thirst lends me confidence, and I pull back with a saucy grin. When the guy chuckles and gives a little nod, I use my grip on his shirt to tug him off the dance floor, never taking my hungry predatory gaze from his face.

"The bathroom? Are you sure you want to do this in there?" His face is wrinkled.

Instead of answering, I pull him inside and lock the door behind us.

"What's wrong with being in here?" I ask, running my thumb over his throat. I could hear and feel his pulse, plain as day, just waiting for me. Begging for me to take a sip.

"Hold on, darling. Don't you want to talk a bit first? I never met a girl around these parts that moves as fast as you."

"Be quiet. This won't hurt," I say, gazing into his deep-green eyes. His face goes blank, and I take that as my cue to feed.

I sink my teeth into his neck and instantaneously moan. It is like being handed chocolate and being told you could have an endless supply. It tastes like southern comfort food after a breakup with a boyfriend. I couldn't stop. *I want it all...*

"Jane? Is everything okay?" Liz bangs on the door.

I try to answer, I really did—all that comes out is an incomprehensible moan. In the next second, my mind's back on the heat and the thick pleasure sliding down my throat. He stays still beneath me, and I knot my fingers in his shirt, sucking more firmly.

"It's been too long!" Liz's voice is sharper, more frantic. "You have to stop, or you'll kill him!"

As soon as her words are spoken, they are lost in the rush of another swallow. Then the door is slamming inward, bouncing back off the wall, and Liz is yanking me. I growl, a fierce, territorial sound.

"What the hell are you doing?" Liz snaps, finally managing to tear me off him.

As soon as I am, the spell is broken. "Oh, God, I'm so sorry! I don't know what I was doing!" I gasp, suddenly aware of how pale he is, how blank his stare. "I'm so sorry," I repeat, fumbling with my thumb to close the wound.

"I told you. The difference between us and the Blood Takers is we stop before giving in. You can do it, but it takes self-control."

We both walk out of the bathroom, leaving him behind, and start back to the house. I can't speak the whole way and go straight to my room. What if Liz didn't show up when she did? Who would I be? I can't believe I came so close to losing it. Would it be like that every time? My chest rises and falls still pumped full of adrenaline from the feed. How could Liz even look at me after what I just did?

"What am I..." I start talking, walking down the stairs. "What am I going to do next time? I'm not strong enough..." As I stride into the living room, and breach the doorway, I see her slumped over in her chair. *Not again!*

"Oh! What do I... the phone number! Where is that receipt?" I sprint back to my bedroom and yank open the top drawer of the nightstand. There, nestled at the top, is the receipt. The name Samuel and the number are there in Liz's sprawling script. I dial with shaking fingers. He answers on the second ring.

"Samuel? This is Jane. Liz said to call if... oh, God, she's passed out again, and she said to call you, and I'm calling you and please, can you hurry—"

"I'm on my way." Then the dial tone is ringing loud in my ear.

I wonder if this happens often, Liz's visions. They seem to come at the most inopportune times, and if they are frequent, then I need to know what to do when it happens. I can't call him every time.

I pace the porch, biting my fingernails, waiting on him. That's when I realize I know nothing about this man. When things settle back down, I would need to ask some questions about him and the other gentleman from that night, Stephen. Are they Guardians?

His Ford Focus screeches into the driveway, and I practically leap at him. "Finally, you're here."

"Anthony, stay in the car." Samuel raps the top of the car and heads my way.

I fight back a sob of sheer relief. "What do we need to do?"

"How long has it been?" Samuel asks, taking the steps two at a time.

"I don't really know; I just came out to talk to her about..." I wave off my explanation. "I found her about thirty minutes ago."

He gives a short nod as he yanks the front door open, and makes his way inside the living room. Samuel takes her hand, and begins whispering something to her that I can't make out.

"Go outside... I can feel your nervousness from here..."

Of course, this is now the second time since I have lived here that she is found unconscious. He might be used to this sort of thing, but I am not. He needs to remember that.

I stand on the porch, shaking my head at the intensity in which he speaks to me. He's very authoritative.

The car door swings open with a creak, and the other man climbs out. He's tall. Handsome, too, some part of my mind recognizes.

"My name's Anthony," he says, sticking out a hand. I shake it as he continues. "Nice to meet ya. How's it going in there?".

"I don't know," I admit.

"Well, what say we pop in there and see then?" he says, eyebrows wagging.

"I thought he wanted you to... you know." I wave toward the car.

"Better to ask forgiveness than permission," Anthony whispers loudly, eyes twinkling with good humor. "Come on." He pulls open the door and ushers me inside with a hand on the small of my back. Butterflies take wing in my stomach. They vanish when we round the corner into the living room.

"I saw someone," Liz is telling Samuel. He is knelt in front of her, his hands helping her shaking ones to grasp a glass of water. *Did we even drink water?*

"It's all right," he assures her. "Think. What did you see?"

"A girl. A girl that's going to ensure our future. We have to find her!" Her gaze turns on us, wide and panicked. "She's going to save us!"

Samuel's brow furrows. "How do we find her? What's she look like?"

Liz wrinkles her nose. "She has a small scar on her face, but it's quite small. You would have to get close to notice it. It's like a chunk of her lip has been taken out. You must find her first. Hurry!"

"Liz, I need more. Besides the scar. What does she look like?"

"Bright red hair, fair skin, and emerald green eyes."

Is she serious? That isn't exactly something you could input into google and get a match of less than a couple hundred thousand girls.

"Any idea where she might be?" He asks, waving his hand around, begging for more information knowing the task she's giving him is going to be difficult.

"I saw a sign for Falls City Hall. You must hurry. If they get to her first..."

"I won't let that happen... I'll do some research and start looking tonight."

Samuel waves me over to the side, "Make sure she gets some rest. The visions take a lot out of her, and sometimes she can be stubborn. Call me if anything happens..."

He's going out on a mission to find a red-haired, emerald green-eyed girl, with a chunk missing out of her lip. Sure, that isn't going to be hard to find. There are probably only a hundred thousand girls with that color hair and eye combo. Piece of cake.

"Let's go, Anthony. I gotta get you home, and start looking..."

They walked out of the house, and could hear the car screech out of the driveway.

Who is this girl? What did she mean save us?

7

Sasha

"Time to get up, girls. You don't want to be late for school," I say in a low, calm voice so as not to startle them. The last thing I need is for them to wake up grouchy.

I go to the closet to get their outfits ready while they slowly wake up out of their trance. For Rebecca, I pick out a yellow summer dress and pair it with white sandals. For Sarah, a pair of Bermuda shorts and a classic black t-shirt with tennis shoes. Rebecca loves wearing dresses, and for the life of me, Sarah would never wear them. To each their own, I guess.

"Seriously? You must get up. Let's go," I say in my sterner voice. They can't be late to the bus again, or I'll be late to work.

Once I finally hurry them out the door, I take a quick shower and get dressed for the day with my khakis and work shirt that are too small for me. I head downstairs to help run my family's store. It's not what I planned to do after high school, but my family needs me. Instead of hiring help, I filled in when needed. They can't afford to hire an actual employee due to the drop in business lately.

I pause on my way out the door to pick up my favorite picture. It's Drake and me, one of the last good pictures we took before he left for college. Bright-green leaves filled the trees behind us, and he was laughing that openmouthed belly laugh I love. I touch his face almost reverently, my lips tilting into a little smile at the memory. The park had been so crowded that day! Kids everywhere, and others like us, high school sweethearts, holding hands and trying to squeeze every moment out of this final summer, reveling in the bittersweet knowledge that everything was about to change. I knew it would be one of our last days together until he came back from college.

On impulse, I kiss the tip of my finger and put it on his cheek. Then I put the picture back up on the dresser, shoving aside the pang of longing, and I hurry down the steps to work.

At twenty-two, I'm completely inexperienced with men and how to keep them around. My dad, Joseph, says I have too much personality. I guess it's because I love to speak my mind and didn't care what others think. He once told me I need to act more like a lady. To label me as outspoken is an understatement. Men can't handle my mouth. It's hard for me to take things seriously, but even more so when I'm nervous. I've insulted my date without even realizing it too many times to count.

My dream was to go away for college, but my parents couldn't afford it. My grades were phenomenal, and I could have gotten a scholarship, but I knew how important it was for me to be here. *The things we do for family.*

As I walk into the store, already dreading the day ahead of me, I switch over the open sign and unlock the door. The aisles are overflowing with products, and many things are out of place. We have hundreds of items in the stockroom but nowhere to put them. Business hasn't been so great this month, but my parents did give me permission to try something new. I put an ad in the local newspaper that every customer can get ten percent off their purchase of fifty dollars or more. It seems to help because within a couple of minutes, six ladies have come into the store, browsing the shelves.

"Can I help you find anything, ma'am?"

"Oh no, darling. I've been shopping here long enough to know where everything is," the older gray-haired lady responds.

I continue tidying up the store in between customers. The ad turns out to be a success. My parents will be happy to see the influx in sales today. My high school math teacher always said, "You would be surprised what ten percent off could do for a sinking store."

I will thank her for giving me the idea. My parents love this store and can't bear to lose it. It's the legacy my grandparents left them when they passed. The chain stores opened in the next town over and stole most of our business.

The bell jingles as someone walks into the store. "Can I help you find anything?" I ask, still cleaning up the aisles.

A familiar voice replies, "Milk?"

My heart drops to my stomach. I want to run up and give him a big hug, but a lot can change in the three years.

"It's in aisle two," I reply.

He's been to the store a million times and knows where everything is shelved. I take in the sight of him, trying not to let him see how it impacts me. My cheeks are suddenly flushed, and I can't contain the smile on my face.

"How's being back?"

Drake grins. "Great, now that I got to see you. I've missed you. It's been a long time."

I try not to blush but can't help it. The one person who has always understood me is Drake. We grew up together. When I was four, his mom bought a house down the street from our store. I had gotten a new tricycle that day and rode it around the street. That's when I saw him. He was playing in his front yard but stopped when he saw the shiny new bike. As we grew up, we got closer. I couldn't hide anything from him even if I tried.

"You married yet?" I ask, turning to put a box of cereal up on the shelf to hide my blush. Deep down, I hope the answer is no, better yet that he isn't seeing anyone.

"Nope. Definitely not."

I hope he didn't hear my little sigh of relief.

He stands there fumbling around with his keys, staring down at the floor. I never thought seeing him again would be so awkward.

"Can we go to dinner sometime? Doesn't have to be tonight, but sometime soon before I go back to campus?"

"Yeah, how about tomorrow night?" I reply, glowing.

I can't believe he just asked me out. Secretly, I have been waiting for him to graduate so he would come back. Maybe we can pick up where we left off. He still has one year left of school but back visiting his mom during the break. He attends University in Frankfort which isn't too far away.

He glances at his watch. "I wish I didn't have to wait. Tomorrow, it is. See you later, gorgeous."

"Uhh - Drake? Don't you need milk?" I say, pointing to the refrigerator aisle.

"Oh yeah - you're right. My mom would kill me if I came back empty handed. You hear about the storm coming in tonight?"

"Yeah, shouldn't be hitting within the hour. Hopefully it doesn't get too bad. You know how I hate storms."

I follow him to the register, and ring him up. "You don't have to make up excuses to come see me. No need for milk next time." I smile, and laugh a little.

Drake leaves, and it's time to lock up the store. I head upstairs afterward to get into some comfortable clothes. The uniform khakis are a size too small, but I didn't want to complain since I can't afford to buy new ones.

My heart flutters as I hear sirens wailing outside, opening the door to find my parents in a panicked state.

"We need to go! There's a tornado not too far from here."

I can't move. Ever since I was a child, I tremble at the thought of storms. Tornadoes are even worse; they cause so much damage and take people's lives. How is everyone not afraid of them like I am? Around my sisters, I have to be strong. Rebecca and Sarah run up to me and grab my hands.

"I'm scared." Rebecca says, squeezing my hand tightly.

My parents work a lot, so they think of me more like a mother than a sister. Somebody has to step in and fulfill the role. I'm the person who gets them ready for school, feeds them breakfast, and helps them with their homework every day.

Johnna is running around frantically trying to gather things. My hatred for storms comes from my mother. When I was younger, if there was a thunderstorm, we were at the shelter. It made me terrified of any kind of storm. I hold my sisters' hands tightly and lean down. "Everything is going to be okay. We've seen a few storms. Nothing is going to happen. I promise."

There is not much to choose from in downtown Louisville. Once my mother gathers up everything she deems necessary, we head across the street to Falls City Hall. It isn't like we have many buildings on the old main road to choose from to seek shelter. Most of the buildings were built in the 1800s and didn't appear to be in good shape.

While walking over, I could tell my sisters are getting frightened, but I lean over and smile. "Everything will be okay once the storm passes. I'm right here."

Right now, it appears I'm the only calm one. Inside, I'm secretly panicking. Above us, the sky's dark, and the rain is coming down like bullets piercing our delicate skin. Our shoes are soaked and our toes are numb. The wind's howling as the storm grows closer and closer, and the tornado sirens are blaring their warning for everyone to seek shelter immediately.

We get into city hall and at least two hundred people are huddling in groups. How many people can this building hold? It's the newest building in town and deemed the safest in the wake of a tornado by the mayor.

"Please stay calm. It should pass over us shortly, and then we'll be able to go back to our homes. Until then, no need to cause panic," the mayor announces.

We bow our heads to pray since faith has always been a big part of our family. We never miss a Sunday church service. We can hear the howling of the devastation outside, houses getting ripped apart, and people screaming. The next thing we know, what sounds like a derailed train is upon us. I cover my ears; it's so loud I swear my eardrums are bleeding. Rebecca and Sarah huddle together with my parents, and then the worst thing imaginable happens. The roof collapses on top of them, just inches away from me.

The room echoes as the debris keeps falling all around me. It's silent for a few moments, but I assume it's from the shock. Then all hell breaks loose.

All around are the screams of people in need of help, babies crying, and all I can think about is my own family. Are they okay? *God, please!* I pray desperately, sheltering my head with my arms. Smoke and dust and the screaming wind leave the entire scene rank with terror.

"Mom! Dad!" I cough, peering out from beneath my arms. "Girls!" I wheel in a circle, squinting against the grit of falling debris and powdered Sheetrock.

I finally caught a glimpse of my dad's bright-yellow shirt on the ground. In a blink, I'm on my knees beside him, clutching at his shirt.

"Dad! Daddy," I cry. He mumbles, his lips barely moving, but I can't hear him over the chaos. I flip his hand over and feel with cold fingers for his pulse. It's faint, erratic. "Oh, God, please!" I fumble at the piece of ceiling pinning his torso down. As it shifts, red stains his shirt, spreading quickly.

I lay my head down on his chest, blinking back tears. My heart is thundering in my ears. "I can't move it, Daddy. I'm so, so sorry."

My head stays there on his chest. I try once to look up and find the rest of my family. One of my sister's shoes lay next to a massive chunk of crumbled ceiling.

They are gone. All of them. Just like that.

"I promised them," I mumble brokenly. "I said everything was going to be alright. I promised them!"

Rage boils in my heart, abruptly brimming over the edges, then spilling over into a hot fury.

"I begged you, God!" I yell, my voice joining the general melee. "I begged you to save them! We've never missed a service! What did we do to deserve..." I shove my palms against my flooding eyes.

My father's dying right in front of me, and there's nothing I can do about it. I hold his hand for what seems like seconds, until he takes his final slow breath as the life slips out of him.

Why did he have to take my entire family? Why didn't he take me too?

I start compressions on Sarah, then blow into her mouth trying to bring her back. After many sets performed, there's still no change. Seeing their blood-covered torsos is one of the most horrific things I've ever seen. The image will forever be burned into my head.

The crying ensues again as I realize they didn't even have the chance to leave their footprint on the world yet. I will never hear my sisters' laugh or my parents say I love you again. I'm frozen in place, not wanting to leave their side.

There's still falling debris coming down everywhere. I need to get everyone out and help those who are alive. My emotions won't get the best of me. Starting to remove debris from people who are pinned beneath and still alive, I notice a man across the room helping people, performing CPR. The piece of the roof on top of this young man is too heavy for only me to remove. Maybe he can help. I yell for assistance but get no response. So, I try again, but louder. He still didn't move. I jump to my feet, intending to go get him, but... *Wait. What's he doing?* I tilt my head, and my eyes narrow.

"Sir?" I shout, not believing what my eyes are witnessing.

He turns around with blood coming out of his mouth, merely feet away. Where is the blood coming from? Is he hurt? Looking down, the woman's neck is bleeding. That's when I realize this man is *feeding* off the injured. My screams echo off the remaining walls of the city hall. No one notices because of all the screams going around the room. I'm the only one witnessing this tragedy. Did he have anything to do with the stories? They spread like wildfire across Kentucky of people going missing and then showing up in the streets with their blood drained and slaughtered. Could it be? Is that man one of them? I'm standing there watching him drink the poor woman's blood. There are only three others helping the injured. The number of dead bodies is overwhelming. I stand as still as I can, taking more slow deep breaths. He has short black hair and dark-brown eyes. The hair stands up on the back of my neck. What's he going to do? He starts to come closer, and with every step, I panic.

My feet are cement blocks, too heavy to lift to be able to get away from the impending doom coming toward me. I whimper, but no one notices the pair of us—me standing there, terror churning in my gut, and him stalking toward me with all the predatory danger of a panther. It's like my body isn't listening to my mind. I pull my head back as far from his reach as I can get with my feet locked in place. He grips my chin firmly and forces me to meet his dark eyes. "Don't worry now. This won't hurt a bit."

8

Sasha

My eyes flutter open to deep-green walls I've never seen before. Where am I? I rise up out of bed and search for something to defend myself with, anything. I rifle through the closet, dresser drawers, nightstand, and nothing. There are no contents inside any of the furniture. Did anyone even live here?

I hear footsteps coming down the hall, so I fly back to the bed and squeeze my eyes shut, pretending to be fast asleep. *Please don't kill me.*

"I'm not stupid. I know you're awake. Come on, now. We've got things to talk about," the man says, faintly amused.

"Wh—what could you possibly need to talk to me about? The fact you kidnapped me, my whole family being dead, or that you're a monster?" I say, rising. There goes that mouth of mine.

He walks closer, and I knee him in the groin without hesitation. The monster grabs his nether region and groans but not for long. I try to make a run for it, but he's too fast. How's that even possible? I had the fastest record for running a 5K in track and seldom found anyone able to beat me.

He grabs my arm and jerks me around to face him. *Ow!* Every hint of humor has drained from his features, and they are hard and stern. "Don't make me tell you again," he warns. "We're going where we can talk. Now, come on."

He keeps his grip on my arm, too tight to be entirely comfortable, and pulls me toward a bright, cheerful kitchen. Still, the sounds of the screams echo in my ears, along with the noisy clash of still-falling debris. I wince. At first, I think I am just hearing them from before, but no, that's happening right now!

"Mm, you can still hear them, can't you?" he says with a smile on his face.

I look at him blankly, my pulse pounding. How the hell did he know what I could hear?

"Side effect of the change. Amplified hearing. We're miles from there." He pauses, taking in my shattered look. "Lot of things are going to be different now. I'll help you get through it."

Don't worry, this won't hurt a bit. With his words, the memory of his teeth in my throat float sluggishly to the top of my mind.

"Did you drug me?" I croak, my throat sore from the dust and screaming.

"Of course not!" The man looks affronted. I narrow my eyes, trying to ignore how it increased the throbbing behind my temples.

"Who are you, then?" I ask, one eyebrow raised.

"My name's Samuel."

"That's not what I meant." From his wry expression, he knows what I'm asking. "Maybe I should have said, what are you?" I wrap my arms around myself and add, "I saw what you were doing to that woman."

"That woman?" He arches a brow. "Oh. I see. That poor girl was dying. I merely hastened her end."

"Yeah, anything to help her out," I replied acerbically. The smirk that quirks his lips infuriated me.

"Rather two birds with one stone situation, don't you think? I was hungry; she was dying. This saved someone else the discomfort of a feed, eased her own pain, and gave me lunch all in one."

I push back the rush of anger at his blasé attitude toward an innocent life. "There was no need to hurt her more."

"Dying a painful death, yes. I only helped relieve her pain faster. To me, that was the noble thing to do."

"So, in answer to—"

"Ah, yes. I believe you know exactly what I am." He smiles. "But allow me to set your mind at ease. I'm one of the good ones."

"There are good ones?" I snort, wondering where I even found the courage. Perhaps because I have nothing left to live for? Maybe because if God saved me from a tornado that wiped out half my town, no way he's feeding me to a myth. I shrug to myself.

"Not many," he allows. "But—"

"And," I cut him off, relishing in my newfound bravery, "the way to tell if you've met a good one is if they rush someone's death and then bite you in the middle of a town-wide tragedy?"

"That's one way," he says with a little wink. "After all, if I wasn't one of the good ones, I would've killed you already—along with anyone else left alive after that tornado. There wouldn't be a single human left in that building. You can bet on that."

My lips thin. "And how many others did you save?" I say, making air quotes with my fingers.

"Just you, I'm afraid," Samuel says with a shrug.

"Then what made me so special? Not only did you save me, you brought me home. I must really be something."

For a long moment, he studies me. Then his face softens with pity.

"I saw what happened to your family. I wanted to give you a better life. Another chance."

"A better life? How can you give me a better life?" I snicker.

All I want was my family back. Maybe press rewind and never go into that city hall. Although, not sure our chances would have been any better had we stayed home.

"I already did."

My head shakes, trying to comprehend what he means. How

could he provide a better life for me? Being a vampire isn't a better life, not if it means feeding on innocent people to stay alive.

"I turned you. Now you won't age, and you can enjoy life for as long as you don't make enemies. Remember that!"

Turned me? *Side effect of the change*, I hear his earlier comment again.

"Turned me?" I say aloud. "Like..."

Samuel looks supremely smug.

"Yes, you're like me now. You'll not age. You can enjoy your new life, your fresh start. Go wherever you want, do whatever you want. Be whoever you want."

"But... my family..." I stammer, trying to picture picking up and leaving everything I'd ever known. There's no way I could do that. *Who would run the store? Where would I go?*

"I didn't take your family from you," Samuel says kindly. "But they're gone, nonetheless. I know your grief won't fade quickly, but it will be easier if you leave here."

This can't be happening! I just lost my entire family, and now I'm a freaking vampire? This is too much for me to comprehend. My mind's doing circles. I bob my head, trying to clear it, when I hear more screams. He must be telling the truth, or I wouldn't be able to hear the people from the other side of town.

My whole life has changed in the last couple of hours. What am I going to do? Right now, I need to focus on my family.

"I need to go back. To My Family... They need to have a proper burial at least. I can't just leave them there on the floor like trash. I'm not a monster. Well, I guess I am now, but not in that sense."

He pauses and turns his eyes toward me, studying my face with uncomfortable scrutiny. Pity softens his gaze.

"You're not a monster. Let's go take care of your family," he replies, his voice tight and slightly disapproving.

We walk back to the city hall to help the injured. Samuel drives the wounded to the hospital while I wait for the emergency responders to escort more victims out of the debris. Once they are all picked up, we make our way back to my house.

"See, I can control myself. No one ended up dead after all. All the injured are safe at the hospital. Aren't you proud?" he says dramatically with a huge grin.

Did he want a medal or a gold star for behaving himself for a couple of hours?

As we pull up to my house, there's only minimal damage from the winds. The front window of the store is shattered, and pieces of glass are strewn about, mixed with boxes of cereal and spilled cartons of milk. Cans of soda lay all around, and bags of chips have been torn open. I step over an unopened box of diapers and cross over to the staircase. The door is blown shut, but when I pull it open, it becomes apparent that the damage is limited to the downstairs.

I move slowly up the steps, and my mind flashes back to all the times I'd rushed my sisters down them to get to school. Memories flood my mind. "Hurry up, Sarah! We're going to be late again!"

Or the night of prom. "You look beautiful, Sasha," my dad says, pride in his voice as I pause at the landing, radiant in my dress.

My throat tightens. I push the door to the apartment open. As soon as the comforting smell of home hits me, I sink to my knees. Samuel stops behind me, shifting awkwardly in the doorway.

"They're never coming back," I say, my tone flat.

"No."

I break down and sob. Samuel tries to console me. "Don't touch me," I yell, pushing him away.

"I'm trying to help," Samuel says, backing off.

I can hear him off to the side, shifting from foot to foot.

"I'm going to bed; leave me alone."

I spend the rest of the night in my sisters' room. Remembering their laughs, special moments we had together, and crying into my pillow. My heart is heavy with regret.

The next day is even more horrifying. I receive many phone calls and visitors, but I don't want to speak to anyone. It's like a constant reminder of them being gone. I know they are; no need to keep reminding me. It's the polite thing to do, to tell people you are praying for them when they lose someone, but it's frustrating, nonetheless. My phone rings right before I turn it off to silence the calls.

"Sasha, I know you're going through a lot, but we need you to come down to identify the bodies since there were so many in the tragedy."

I want to throw up. The last thing I want to do is see them like that. My eyes flash back to their bloody bodies lying there. Tears begin to fall again, and I just want this to end.

"Can't someone else do it? You know them; you can't just identify them yourself?" I say hastily.

"I'm sorry, honey. I would if I could. Can you come down today?"

I groan. "On my way."

After everything, that's the one thing I want to do the least. I already have nightmares from seeing them like that in the city hall, but this. This is different. This will be the last time I will see their faces, dead or not. I try to make myself realize it's a blessing to get to see them one last time before the funeral. It didn't work.

I walk into the living room where Samuel sits reading a book on our couch. My couch. "Hey, I need a ride. Can you take me?"

He lays the book down and follows me to the car. I give him directions and dread getting there.

"We're here," he says, frowning, "Do you want me to come in with you?"

This needs to be done alone. My shoulders rise and fall as I take in a deep breath before opening the car door and getting out. The walk up to the front entrance makes my chest tighten. *Did I have to do this? Could I do it? You must.*

As I enter the morgue, my chest only grows tighter, and I fall short of breath. A lady appears out of nowhere. "Hello, can I help you?"

"Yes, I'm here to identify my family," I say, starting to tear up. *You can do this. Keep it together.*

"Oh, honey. I'm so sorry for your loss. Wait here."

I hear some shuffling going on in the next room, knowing exactly what she's doing on the other side of that wall. I close my eyes.

"Okay. We're ready. Follow me."

I follow behind the pretty blonde lady into the next room with four tables. They are on there. I know it, but maybe this has all been a long dream and we are all safe.

She pulls the sheets up just far enough where I can see their faces, and I lose it. My tear ducts loosen, and it's like Niagara Falls running down my cheeks. They look pale and so dead. No life left in them. I cover my eyes, not wanting to look anymore.

"You can go now, darling. That's enough."

I run out of there like someone is chasing after me, not stopping until I'm safely inside Samuel's car.

"Are you okay?" he asks, putting his strong hand on my shoulder. Instead of knocking it off, I embrace him. He seems shocked at first but then gives in and hugs me back.

"I'm sorry you have to go through this. You're not alone. I'm here," he says, trying to comfort me. I let him go so he could drive us back home.

"I'll let you have some space," he says as we walk in, and he picks up his book.

I hear the alarm go off in the store. Who the hell could that be? I walk downstairs to find Drake at the door. I forgot about dinner. There's no way I can go tonight. My mind's like putty. I wait for the butterflies to twirl in my stomach at the sight of him, but even they are still. "I... ah... just wanted to come check on you. I heard about your... I mean gosh, Sasha, I'm sorry."

He moves to hug me, but I press a firm hand against his chest. "Nothing will bring them back."

All I want is to hear their laughs or have them bother me one last time. Sure, my parents were hard on me, but they raised me to be the woman I am today. My sisters adored me and always said they wanted to be like me when they were older, but now, they would never have that chance. It was taken from them. But why? Why couldn't he have just taken me instead? They hadn't even made their mark in life yet. *You took the wrong ones, God.*

"You're right. Nothing can bring them back, but you are here, still breathing. Even though it's hard to understand, everything happens for a reason. We have to believe that it's part of a bigger plan."

I know he's just trying to help me feel better, but it's not working. I'm happy he cared enough to come over here to check on me. Too bad nothing could ever happen between us again. Things have changed, and he wouldn't want me now. Not a monster; who would want to be with me?

"Listen, I know we were going to go to dinner, but I just don't think it's a good idea. You still gotta go back to college, and my heart can't take you leaving again. It's not fair to either of us."

My heart's heavy, but doing the right thing. Stringing each other along only makes matters worse.

9

Jane

Envio's voice sounds talking to a tall, scary looking man. How am I seeing this? It's like I'm seeing through his eyes and can't look away. Did I fall asleep?

"How have you still not found her?" The man's pacing around the bleak room.

Is he talking about me? They are looking for me?

"Jakob, it's not that easy. She's not with Samuel anymore."

How did he know I'm not with Samuel? He must be watching me. What would I do if he found me? There's no way I would go back with him, especially to the man standing in front of Envio right now. He has plans for something, and I want no part of it.

"I'll take care of him... you just worry about her..."

"She could be anywhere..."

Jakob picked him up by his collar, feet dangling inches off the ground. "Fucking find her... she can't be left alone... if the Guardians..." He puts Envio back down. "Just find her. No more excuses. Don't make me send Pavel and Lorenzo out for her."

What did Jakob want with me? Liz is right. Envio did have an ulterior motive when turning me. I'm now questioning everything, maybe he isn't different from the others. He just put on a show for me that night, making me believe he's a good guy.

Suddenly, I am back in my room and my feet hit the cold hardwood as I run into Liz's room. "I...had a vision... or something."

"What are you going on about?" She asks, sitting up on her bed. "Since when do you have visions?"

"I saw Envio and Jakob... talking about me. How is that possible?"

She explains that sometimes we can see through our maker's eyes. You never know when it's going to happen. How did I not know about this? I still have so much to learn.

"So, can he see through me?"

"No, it doesn't work that way. Only we can see through our makers. They can feel us, like our emotions, but that's it."

If Envio could see me, then he would find and take me back to Jakob. Then what would Jakob do with me? I have no idea what his plan is, and am not willing to find out.

"So, how are you feeling? It's been two days... you had me worried."

"No need, sweetie. My visions drain me, some more than others..."

I asked her what the deal is with the vision the other day. What did she mean that girl will ensure our future? There's still so much I didn't know about this life, the people in it, and just vampires in general.

"She's gonna be the one that helps us win the battle..."

What battle? Nobody had mentioned one. "Against?"

"The Blood Takers... it's bound to happen, especially if they kept slaughtering at the rate they're going... the media surrounding it was only pointing closer and closer to something paranormal and eventually the humans would pick up on it..."

She explains that a man named Jakob is their leader, a masochist who plans on making humans slaves to our kind. They have no qualms over killing innocent people, and even take pleasure in it.

This is the man Envio is following? No way. He just didn't seem like that type of person.

"So, when you say help us, you mean the Guardians, right?"

"Yes."

They are a group of vampires that don't believe in what the Blood Takers are doing. They want to save humanity and live alongside them in peace, but the others make that difficult. Every day more are killed, and they are to blame for that.

"And what about Samuel? Anthony?"

"They are part of it. Samuel is our leader."

It seems only fitting. The way everyone follows his orders. "So, this girl is supposed to be like... our saving grace? How do we know she won't screw things up or make it worse?"

"My visions are never wrong. I saw very clearly the end of this battle. We were victorious with her standing at the front."

Samuel's out trying to find her, and who knows if he will have any luck. He didn't have a bunch to go off of. What are they going to do when he finds her? Bring her back here?

Questions just kept looming out of mouth, one after another. Yet, she answers every single one in quick succession. Samuel has two boys back in Frankfort with him. Stephen and Anthony. The boy I met the other night when Samuel came to help with Liz.

"He seems sweet." I say, waiting for her to give me something about him.

"He's a different one... really wants to be like his brother... just wants something to do."

She gets up from the bed, and starts heading downstairs. "We need to feed tonight... or at least I do. Need to replenish."

My last feed rushed back to my mind, remembering how horribly that went. Am I ready to try again? At least Liz will be with me. I can't trust myself. "I'll go with you, but I'm not hungry." I lie, because telling her the truth seems like too much right now.

We get dressed, and walk down to the bar. The inside isn't as packed as last time, but probably because it's a weekday. Only meant less people to choose from. I sit down at a table, and Liz heads off to find her drink.

Being alone makes me skittish, especially after seeing through Envio. His leader's downright terrifying, and I hope I never come in contact with him. But it also leaves me with questions. Is Envio truly as bad as they say? They have never been alone with him, or even probably had an actual conversation. Sure, I get it. He's a part of the Blood Takers, and that's enough to make them hate him. But not enough for me.

My eyes search the bar, and Liz is nowhere in sight. She must have found someone, which means we will be leaving soon. Maybe I should feed when she gets back, at least attempt to try. Liz will watch me carefully this time. I glance around the room, seeing if anyone piqued my interest, when someone sits next to me.

"How are you?" Envio asks.

My body starts to shake. He found me. "Please - don't hurt me."

His hand falls on mine, "stop... there is no need to fear me..."

I can read his face, like he's appalled I'm terrified of him. "I saw your conversation with Jakob... you're here to take me back to him... I won't go..."

Envio's head sways, "not in the slightest bit... there's a lot you don't know about me... but my intention is for you to stay with the Guardians."

I hear him clear as day tell him he will find me. Is he really trying to lie to me right now? Plus, why would he want me to stay with the Guardians? They are enemies.

"Listen, I can't stay long... but pass something along for me... Samuel needs to prepare."

I remember back to Jakob saying he would handle him. His plan is to come after Samuel. How did they know each other?

"Jakob will be coming for him... and when he does, you don't need to be there. He won't stop until you are found..."

Why is he helping me? The Guardians? This isn't anything like the man Liz and the others described to me. They are obviously wrong about him. "Why are you protecting me?"

"Jane, I'm gonna be honest with you... but only with you... I don't want to be a Blood Taker... I'm not like them..." He didn't get to finish before Liz heads my way, and he leaves.

"I'm full. We can go now."

My mind's processing everything Envio just told me. So, he didn't want to be with them, and might very well be a good guy. No one would give him the chance to prove himself. Maybe one day.

Jakob will come for Samuel, and there isn't anything anyone else could do about it. He needs to be warned, and quick. The real question looming in my mind is why he is coming after Samuel specifically?

"I need to tell you something..."

Liz's eyes widen when I tell her Envio was just here. "Why? You shouldn't have let him leave... he knows better than to come to our property..."

"Stop for a minute and listen. He came to warn us that Jakob is coming after Samuel." Agitation sets in because she won't let me explain without interrupting me.

"Why would he come to warn us? That makes no sense. He's a Blood Taker, what good would that do him?"

"I think you and the others don't give him enough credit. Maybe he's not as bad as you make him out to be..." I could tell by her voice that she didn't believe Envio.

"We knew Jakob would find us eventually. Let him come for us."

10
Sasha

A couple of days have gone by, and Mrs. Atterby, a longtime customer, arranged the funeral to be held today. I slip on a long black dress but not ready to say my final goodbyes. That would mean it's real. Samuel has been by my side the entire time. *Surprisingly.*

"I know you aren't ready, but it's happening whether you're there or not. You'll regret it if you don't go," Samuel says firmly.

Instead of adding another emotion to my plate, I head to the funeral.

When we pull up to the cemetery, a lot of people are there to honor my loss. Most of them are regulars to the store. They know the Bowers family most of their lives, even watched us grow up from infancy.

The funeral begins, and we take our seats up front.

"Our town mourns as we gather here today. Not a one among us has survived this tragedy unscathed. Joseph, Johnna, Rebecca, and Sarah Bowers were among those taken from us too soon, and we honor their memory here today. I know they'd be touched to see so many of you here."

As the funeral progresses, many people stand up and say kind things about my family, but then it's my turn. I take a deep breath to fight back the tears, trying to compose myself as I walk up to the podium. It grows silent as they wait for me to speak. I try, but nothing will come out. Closing my eyes to calm my nerves, no matter what, I'm speaking on behalf of my family before they are laid to rest forever.

"Thank you all for coming," I begin. A sea of faces stare up at me expectantly. I swallow thickly before continuing. "Thank you for being with us. Not just now, as we put my..." I hear a few murmurs of sympathy. "As my family is laid to rest. They were... well, you all knew them. Rebecca was a firecracker—she lit up a room just by walking in." I give a little snort, something between a sob and a laugh. "Sometimes it was by accident, but the room was definitely brighter for it." There's a smattering of laughter.

"She was passionate, and she stood up for what she believed in. A few days before she... before, she told me there was a girl at school being bullied. Someone told her the girl had talked about suicide. Rebecca wanted to help, wanted this girl to know she was loved." I meet a few eyes in the crowd. "My worst regret is that I never asked that girl's name, and Rebecca never got to tell her that she mattered."

My throat tightens, and my eyes brim. *But, Sarah...*

"Sarah was only nine. She was too young to understand that there was evil in this world." I risk a pointed glance at Samuel. "And like all kids, she thought she was going to live forever." I duck my head. "She wouldn't have lived forever, but she should have lived a lot longer than this. I know that there's supposed to be some bigger plan. I know everyone says that they're in a better place. But they should be here with me." My voice cracks, and I have to stop.

Long seconds tick by while tears stream down my cheeks, and the audience sits in silence. "I'll never forget Sarah's humor and wit. Do you remember when she put a frog in Mrs. Tate's desk?" I shake my head, trying to keep the flux of emotions shoved down enough to at least finish this.

"I know I'll never forget it!" Mrs. Tate pipes up with a choked laugh. I return a watery smile.

"My family's memory will stay with me for as long as I live." *You'll not age.* "I can't imagine how I'm going to cope with their loss, but... if they're at peace, if they're in a better place..." My voice breaks again, and Samuel steps to my side and puts a possessive arm around my shoulders.

"Thank you all for coming," he says, his voice carrying even to the back. I gust out a shuddering sob. "Sasha needs her privacy and your understanding in this trying time. Thank you all for your support."

As he ushers me out, I hear the muffled whispers. I couldn't summon the energy to care.

Once we get back home, I realize I haven't eaten in almost a week.

"The longer you go without eating, the harder it'll be to resist the urge." Samuel says, watching me hold my stomach.

"I knew you were going to bring that up eventually. I can't feed on anyone here."

There's no way he is going to get me to feed on someone in my own town.

"We can leave. I don't live far from here. You won't know anyone there, plus it will help with your transition. There's so much for you to learn before you can be by yourself."

I didn't have anything keeping me here. With my family gone, all I have left is the store and I decided to hand it over to Mr. and Mrs. Atterby.

If on my own, I won't survive long. In some weird way, I trust Samuel. A bond has developed over the last week. He could have bolted a week ago, but he stayed to help me through the toughest stage of grief.

"So, what's the difference between you and the others?" I ask.

Samuel sighs. "I don't believe in killing. You don't have to kill a human to survive. They are *how* we survive. Big difference. I haven't given into the bloodlust. I take what I need from a human to survive, and that's it. The others, they take it all while enjoying it. They don't care whether it's a child or an adult. I've seen them kill toddlers before."

I decided to go with him to Frankfort but just long enough to learn the basics. A suitcase sits on my bed to fill with my essential items like family memorabilia, clothes, and other basics. There are a lot of things I didn't want to leave behind. He understands. Frankfort is only an hour's drive. We head out onto the road and leave everything I know behind. Even though I'm not happy with Samuel for turning me, he did it with good intentions. Maybe this is my second chance at life. But it won't be the same without my family to share it with. I fall silent, and more memories flood my mind.

11

Samuel

Our drive is spent mostly in silence. Sasha is still grieving, and she needs time. Honestly, I thought it would have taken more convincing for her to come back with me. One thing I know, our bond is strong even though it has only been a week. Her emotions hit me like a train. The pain, guilt, and denial. There's no way I could leave her.

With her family gone, there will be a void inside her, but the Guardians can help fill that void. We could be her family now.

I feel bad for withholding the truth, but how do you tell someone their destiny is to become a vampire? What rational human being is going to believe that? I have to lie until I know she's ready to hear it. Once she sees what we are up against, Sasha will understand. She might not appreciate her destiny, but she will at least understand the evil behind it. Plus, Liz would be better at explaining her vision. All I know is she's damn lucky I found her and not the Blood Takers. She couldn't be the only one with this ability. Unlike Liz, they might be able to control what they see.

Before I was turned, my life was of a family man. I married my high school sweetheart right after graduation, then I went on to receive my degree in mathematics. My wife gave me two beautiful children and stayed at home until they were old enough to go to school. Alicia decided to use her degree in marketing to help local law firms gain new clients.

Everything changed when I was taken. On that day, my kids no longer had a father or Alicia, a husband. They were all alone. I knew once I turned that staying away was the only option. The pain of missing my family hurt every day, but I couldn't ever go back. I wasn't the same man I used to be; inside me was darkness.

Darkness that I didn't let consume me. If I did, my eyes would be like theirs. There was only one physical difference between us and them, our eyes. As Guardians, we kept our natural eye color. Blood Takers took on an evil shade of red.

I had to make a new life for myself somewhere new once turned. I stopped in Frankfort on a journey to California and just never left. I joined the police force and slowly worked my way up to becoming the new sheriff. Before I had been turned, police work was never something I wanted to do, but afterward, it made sense. As a police officer or sheriff, we found out about crimes first. That meant I would know if vampires were in town or had been in town for that matter. Over the last couple of months, the attacks had become more frequent, which meant either it was rogues or the Blood Takers paying a visit. Once I saw Envio, I knew the Blood Takers couldn't be too far away. That only confirmed my suspicions.

"How did you get turned?" Sasha asks.

My eyes widen because I haven't told that story in a very long time.

"The man that turned me no longer exists. You sure you want to know? It's not a good story."

"Yes, please."

I sigh. "Well, let me start with before I get turned. Rumors were going around about people going missing. They weren't sure what was going on with the disappearances. I knew immediately when I came face to face with Jakob Dietrich that he was the cause. He was trying to find a way to stop the aging process or slow it down. That was when he started abducting families using the blood of the children to inject into the adults. Thousands and thousands of them. All the vampires alive now are because of him."

"Someone had accidentally created vampires. And by injecting the blood of children? How's that possible?" Sasha asks.

I continue. "Over the course, the body mutated it, and I started to crave human blood. At that point, I was no longer human, but I had to have human blood to survive. Now, there are thousands of them, maybe more. Our species began because of an experiment that went wrong. The process was painful. The vampires that get turned into an actual vampire are lucky. It's nothing like the process I had to go through. I wouldn't wish it on my worst enemy."

I hate rehashing the story. Every time I tell it; I cringe until the end. It makes sense for her to ask questions. She's young, impressionable, and a new vampire. I would be worried if she didn't.

"What was the process like for you?"

"I won't go into that. Don't ask," I reply. I've been asked by many but only one knows the pain firsthand: *Liz*. We are both made the same way. Neither of us spoke about that night. Gut-wrenching screams, lust coming over me, and Jakob egging me on to feed.

"Jakob is a psycho. Once—."

"Wait. Is? I thought you said the guy that created you was dead?"

I frown. "I said the man that created me doesn't exist, not that he died. He's turned. But he's not one of the good ones." I wait for her to process that. When she didn't comment, I continue. "Once he figured out what was happening, he did nothing to stop it. Although I'm not sure if there's anything Jakob could have done once the process started. He subjected the world to this misery. Once we started the process, none of us could go back to our families. We knew we would hurt them if we did. The Blood Takers come for anyone that's been turned. They try to recruit everyone into their group."

"Where did he get the idea that kids' blood would help stop the process?" Sasha asks.

"No idea. Jakob said it has something to do with all the mutations in the food we eat and the medicines were prescribed."

I have an idea of what's going through Sasha's mind after hearing the news. Vampires wouldn't exist if not for Jakob. This, in turn, meant she would still be human. Her silence showed how overwhelmed she was with all the information.

My mind takes me to what's happening in Frankfort. People going missing or showing up slaughtered on the streets. As sheriff, I'm determined to get to the bottom of it. My fellow officers always dismissed it as wild animal attacks, but I know the truth. It isn't like I can tell them. Mere humans would never understand.

My hope: Stephen's ready for his role of protecting Sasha. He has been my protector since I turned him. Instead of being forced, it;s always been voluntary. He always felt like it was his duty. That's going to have to change, I mused. Sasha needs his protection more than I.

We didn't know if anyone else knew about her. So, we have to err on the side of caution.

"Stephen will be showing you around Frankfort. He's one of our best and around the same age as you."

She didn't respond, just kept staring straight ahead at the road. Her face is still pale, which only makes her emerald eyes pop more. The window is down, leaving her long hair to flap in the wind as she considers what I tell her. She seems oblivious to my scrutiny.

The more I look at her, the more my concern grows. She's pretty, but I hope that won't complicate things between Stephen and her. He's never been a womanizer; that's his brother Anthony.

Anthony wants so badly to be human again, but it can never happen. Most of his nights are spent locked in his room sulking. Occasionally, we could get him out. The only thing he wants is revenge for their parents.

"Let's roll the windows down and enjoy the rest of the drive. We're not that far away now." I say, done answering questions for now. She needs to process everything, and that would take time.

I pull out my phone, and dial Stephen. "We'll be arriving in ten minutes. Please update Liz."

Stephen knows what's expected of him with her arrival. She couldn't be let out of our sight, bad things would happen if the Blood Takers ever found out her fate. Surely, she would be targeted and killed. We couldn't afford that. Our species needs salvation and she's the one who can give that to us.

We all need time to prepare her for what's coming. This next year will be critical to saving humanity; our primary focus is getting her, and the others trained.

Many questions cross my mind immediately. Has she ever even been in a fight? Did she know how to defend herself? If not, training will have to start immediately.

The car screeches into the driveway, Anthony and Stephen waiting to greet the newfound Savior.

"Sasha, this is Stephen and Anthony." I say, slamming the car door behind me.

Stephen shakes her hand gently. "It's a pleasure to meet you."

"Seriously? What kind of handshake was that? Are you scared to hurt me?" Sasha scoff.

"I... apologize," He says. "Please, let me show you to your room."

We all head inside, Sasha following us, when I step back to allow her to admire it, she shoves past us and slams the door just inches from Stephen's nose. Well, I never told him the job was going to be easy.

"Well," Anthony says, clapping his hand on his brother's shoulder with a smirk, "bet that's not how you saw that going."

I jerk my head in invitation to follow. They follow me into my bedroom on the opposite end of the house. Liz explains Sasha is particularly important to our future, but she has a choice to make right now.

"Maybe we should not give her the option," Anthony says, shrugging his shoulders and sitting down on the bed.

I don't know if I could live with myself if we didn't. Everyone should have the opportunity to make the choice for themselves. If we didn't give her the choice, wouldn't that make us just as bad as the Blood Takers? Savior or not, we can't force her into this life, or we'd be just as awful as them.

"We can't just not tell her!"

"The real question," Anthony cuts in before I could say anything I would really regret, "is what we do if we give her the choice, and she opts not to feed."

"I have to say, I've spent some time with the girl, and I think she'll do the right thing by us. She's grieving the loss of her entire family right now. They were killed in a tornado that hit. So, we need to be kind to her during this time, boys."

We fall quiet, and for several long minutes, there are only the soft sounds of breath and creaks of leather when someone shifts.

"Ach, all right," Anthony says finally. "Go get her."

I knock on the door. "Hey, can we talk to you out here, please?"

12
Sasha

What the hell did they want to talk to me about? I just freaking got here and want some quiet. A growl sounds and I open the door.

When I walk out, I feel like I'm walking onto a stage; every person is staring at me. The tension in the room is taffy thick. *Oh, God. I just got here, for crying out loud! Give me a break.*

"Can we make this quick? Planned on hanging out in my room for a while." I say, rolling my eyes.

Stephen's jaw flies open, "We just want to talk. It won't take long. Take a chill pill, will ya."

"After being bitten and turned, there's a choice for you to make. Ask all the questions you want for us to help your decision," Stephen states.

"What decision?" I ask, panning the room of men. "What are you talking about?"

"It's simple enough," Anthony says. He leans up against the door-frame, close enough I brush against him as I walk in. He cocks his head to the side, clearing his throat while gauging my reaction as he continues. "If you want to live, you need to feed. Like, on a human. If you choose not to feed, you'll die."

"Because that's really a choice... Tell me more about the... what did you call them? The Blood Takers."

Samuel fills me in on some things about them, but there's so much more I would like to know. Did they have a plan to stop them? What are they doing to prevent more casualties? What is their plan?

Samuel nods. "What would you like to know?"

"How do we stop them?"

I don't have anything to live for right now, but I can protect the humans from them. Someone needs to. If not, a lot of people are going to die. That could be my reason for living. My turning into a vampire will have meaning.

"We call ourselves the Guardians. Training will have to be done, but I think we can take them out eventually. It'll take time though." Stephen says, stroking his chin.

I nod my head, taking in the choice I have to make. Could I really feed on humans? I close my eyes; I can't fathom it. "Let me go back to my room and think about it."

They shook their heads and I walked back to my room, slamming the door behind me. It's plain, but I didn't mind. I had to share a room with my sisters since they were born. My head hit the pillow, and I closed my eyes envisioning myself feeding on an innocent human, cringing at the mere thought of it. My stomach flip flops. Could I be a vampire? Death scares me; my life will be over. There would be no coming back. Once I feed, will I regret it?

I flip over on my stomach with my face in my palms, trying to decide. Did I really have an option? I mean I get to make the decision, but who would choose death?

I jump up from the bed and go back to the living room. "I'm not sure if I'll regret it, but... I'll feed. Or I'll try. If I can't go through with it, then I guess my decision will be made for me." I inform them. "But... I want to find a way to take out the slaughterers. Whatever you call them. It's the only reason my feeding makes sense. Okay?"

"Well, we were thinking about going now. It's been a couple days for us. You wanna join?" Stephen asks.

"I've got to feed at some point," I say, shrugging my shoulders. If I can make a difference, and help save innocent lives then I'm making the right decision. From what they are telling me, the future of humanity seems bleak and if things continue the way they were, it wouldn't be long before they cease to exist.

I grab my jacket out of habit, not that I need it. The spring air outside is perfect. The smell is overpowering, and I take in all the different scents. The pollen, freshly cut grass, and bonfires wrestled with my nose. It's amazing all the things I can pick up. When I open the car door, Samuel's hand appears on my shoulder.

"No need. It's only a block over. We'll walk."

I'm not going to argue since I haven't been able to spend much time outside lately, between taking care of my sisters and running the family store. I shudder, my mind bringing back the image of my family lying dead on the city hall floor.

"You okay?" Stephen asks, stopping beside me. "You look like you're about to be sick. We don't have to do this tonight, if you would rather wait another day."

"No, I just got a mental picture of my family. It needs to get done. Let's go." I say, not skipping a beat and catching up ahead to Samuel and Anthony.

As we approach the bar, I stop dead in my tracks. Am I ready for this? The thought of humans being killed and being able to help put a stop to it makes me realize it's exactly the right choice. No more doubts. *Let's do this.*

I follow the men into the bar and take in the scenery. Women are hanging all over the men sitting at the wet bar, surely wanting to rack up free drinks before leaving them high and dry. None of them are getting lucky tonight. A smile crosses my face and Samuel notices.

"What ya smiling for?"

I nod in the direction of the bar and he laughs.

"This table will work." Anthony says, sitting down. "Let's figure out the game plan."

"How's the senses?" Samuel asks, his eyebrow raised.

He knows why my face is turned up. They didn't smell good. In fact, they smell awful, like rotten meat left out for days. The bartender brings our shots Anthony ordered, and I didn't waste any time throwing mine back. It'll calm my nerves.

"Be careful, liquor affects us strongly. You only need one," Stephen says.

As I stand up, losing my balance, Stephen catches me.

"Careful. You don't want to break something," he says, easing me back upright.

There's a man in the corner watching me. I can't believe my eyes. Out of all the places, I see him here. I turn around before he recognizes me and asks how to proceed. It's not like I know anything about feeding on humans.

"So how does this work?" I ask. Was it supposed to come naturally to me?

"You pick whoever you want, but you don't just bite them. You gotta wipe them first. That'll make it, so nothing's remembered."

I watch the others feed one by one for pointers on what to do.

"What if I do it wrong?" My insecurity is setting in.

"You probably will, but we'll be here to help you. Just take him to the back side of the bar where there aren't many people. This way we can contain it if it gets out of hand," Stephen replies.

It's now my turn and my stomach is growling. I search around the room, trying to find a young man. Over and over, my eyes skim over cute guys, finding my gaze drawn only to him. Our eyes lock as he makes his way over to me. *Shit*. What the hell am I going to say?

"Sasha, what are you doing here?" Drake asks.

"I moved here. What are you doing here?"

"I live down the road. I go to college here, remember." He laughs.

The eagerness to feed is coming over me. I can't feed on Drake. Could I?

Smiling, I take his hand while he accompanies me to the dance floor. It makes me think of our prom. I was so eager for that night, wondering what would happen. Drake was a gentleman and always had been. He spun me around while we talked.

"What made ya want to move here?" He asks, clasping my hand in his and swaying across the floor.

I put my head on his shoulder, "A family friend lives around the corner actually. I came to stay with him for a bit. Thought maybe a change in scenery would help."

He kisses me, "I'm so sorry about your family. I can't imagine what you're going through. If you need anything, ever, just call me."

I can hear the blood pumping through his veins and can't wait any longer. The sharp gut-wrenching pain starts.

"Are you okay?" Drake asks me, his hand on my shoulder.

"Would you like to go somewhere quieter?"

He takes my hand as I lead him to the back. This is it. There's no coming back from this. Once I drink his blood, I will be a full-fledged vampire. Staring into his eyes, I mutter, "This won't hurt a bit."

"What are you doing? Get off me," he says.

It's not working. Why? I gaze over at the others sitting at the table, just motioning for me to continue or try again. What am I going to do if this didn't go right? It's *Drake*, not some random stranger, but they didn't know that.

After a couple of tries, it finally works. Stephen has been watching just in case I mess up. I never knew the taste of blood would be so enticing. My fangs help me drink the delicious substance flowing from the wound, probably more than I should. I am drinking my first love's blood, and it tastes like chocolate-covered strawberries.

Samuel snuck up behind me and growled into my ear. "Stop now. You've had plenty."

I didn't want to stop. It tastes so good. The pain in my stomach starts to subside, but I want to keep going.

"Sasha, stop right now!"

As I continue to drink from Drake, he shakes me. I am in a trance-like state, only worried about feeding. Stephen forcefully pulls me off him.

"What do you think you're doing? You're gonna drink this poor guy to death. You don't want to do that, do you?"

Out of the trance I come, and my eyes lock on Drake's. What have I done?

I smile, putting a little crimson from my thumb on the wound. "Thank you for the dance. Let's catch up sometime."

"You did great. Way better than my first time. For starters, you should never go out to feed by yourself. At least as a precaution, take one of us with you," Stephen explains.

Walking out of the bar, the guilt consumes me. I never saw myself as someone who didn't have self-control. What the hell happened back there? I almost became one of those vampires, the ones that killed innocent people. They weren't kidding about how easy it can be to give in.

"What's going on?" I ask, hearing two of them whispering.

"Nothing that concerns you," Samuel replies.

Obviously, I can make out what they were saying, the Blood Takers. They are here? My heart skips a bit. Samuel starts talking about jumping town for a bit. Why would we leave? Isn't the point to get rid of them? We should stay and fight.

"We just got here. Are we really gonna leave?"

"I don't need you meeting the Blood Takers right now. They aren't exactly our best friends," Samuel replies.

We head back to his house and get in the car.

"Do you hear that?"

"Yes," Samuel replies.

"Aren't we going to help them?"

"No, we can't right now. If someone's screaming, then it's already started," Anthony replies.

I'm not going to listen to them. The whole point of me feeding is to help protect the humans. My new vampire legs run as fast as they can toward the screams, stumbling across a young woman slumped over in the alleyway.

"Please stop!" She begs.

"Why don't you leave her alone?" I ask in a high-pitched voice.

"I don't feel like it. She's my dinner. Go find your own," the vamp replies.

Maybe I shouldn't have intervened.

"She giving you trouble?" another chimes in.

"Actually, she is. Get rid of her."

Before I know it, the vamp is attacking. I forgot that with this new life comes new abilities, but my punch didn't even phase him. He kicks me in the chest which sends me flying into a dumpster. *Ouch!*

Out of nowhere comes Samuel and Stephen to save me. Obviously, they didn't think I can handle this on my own.

It sucks that they are right. I rub a hand over my throbbing head.

"Stay away from them," Stephen yells.

They work together to tear the vamps apart. It takes them both to get the Blood Takers down. They are much stronger having recently fed. After pulling their limbs apart, they light their bodies on fire. *That's how they kill vampires? Fire?*

"I could have handled it on my own, guys," I say, teeth clenched, trying to save a little face.

"It didn't seem likely. You're too young to take on a Blood Taker. They have the advantage, not you. We are nothing compared to a recently fed Blood Taker. Remember that." Samuel says sharply.

We are so caught up in our conversation, we forget about the young woman sitting ten feet away, sobbing.

"Who are you?" she asks.

I hurry over and drop to my knees beside her. She skitters back a little, her face pale in the moonlight. "No one important. Are you okay? Did he bite you?"

"No, you stopped him."

The woman glances at me with a questioning look in her eye. I'm sure she has many questions about us, but right now, I can't answer them.

"We can't just let her go. She's seen too much," Stephen says to me, wiping her so she wouldn't remember a thing.

"Are you okay?" he asks her.

"I'm fine," she says, looking around, and walks off into the night.

I feel good for helping an innocent woman. Who knows what could have happened if we didn't intervene?

―――――

"Are we almost there?"

I've been staring out the car window for what seems like hours, watching as trees and cars flashed by. Every minute seems to take at least three. I sigh. I've never really been a fan of road trips, especially ones that are spent in complete silence.

"We could at least talk," I say. "I mean... how many more are there?"

"Like us? We have many across the country. I don't know exact numbers, maybe five thousand or so. Not all vampires fit into the Guardian or Blood Taker category," Stephen say.

"And the Blood Takers?"

"No idea. They turn people every day, and their numbers grow. On the other hand, they're violent, and they scrap a lot, even among themselves."

I never would have guessed there are that many vampires out there.

"They turn humans frequently and then after, slaughter their entire family so they'll remain loyal to their cause. Vampires shouldn't have to hide, but they could be smarter about it. If they keep turning humans at this rate, then eventually humans would cease to exist. No humans to feed on would mean we wouldn't survive. They don't think about that though; they just see blood everywhere and the thrill of someone begging for their life to be spared."

"How did you get turned?" I ask.

"That's not something I like to talk about much," Stephen replies, his hands tightening on the wheel. "It was awful. My brother and I saw our parents slaughtered. The Blood Takers either didn't know we were there—which would be weird, our hearts were beating plenty loud enough—or we were too small for them to bother with. We snuck out to the back alleyway, and Samuel found us there."

Anthony chimes in. "Samuel gave us the option. He could turn us, and we could help rid the world of these vampires, or we could leave. Of course, you can see we both got turned. We wanted to get revenge for our parents."

I can tell they both look at Samuel as a father figure and sre grateful for the new life they'd been given. "How do you like being a vampire?"

"It's got its advantages like never aging, speed, and abilities. Blood Takers give us a bad rep though."

Humans might not be so scared if the Blood Takers aren't draining and slaughtering people left and right.

We halt in a driveway in front of a beautiful Victorian house. An older woman walked outside to greet us along with a young girl with long black hair.

"Hello, I'm Liz, and this here's Jane."

"Thank you for letting us stay here under such short notice." I say with a smile.

When we get inside, I feel the awkwardness in the room like crickets. Liz and Jane are both staring at me. Why is it everywhere I go people just stare?

"Hey, can you show me where I'll be staying?" I ask Liz.

I follow her to the back of the house where my room is. The bed is much more comfortable than Samuel's house. As I lay down, I overhear someone crying in the next room. At first, I'm going to leave it alone, not my place. It's not like I really know these people yet. I try to mind my own business.

"Everything okay?" I ask, knocking.

Opening the door, Jane's sitting on the bed with her face in her palms.

"You okay?" I ask again as I place my hand on her back.

"I'll be okay. Everything's just so new to me. I wish I could see my family again. Which makes no sense because they were the worst parents ever. How could I miss them? All my life I'd begged to get away, then they're taken and it's like I still grieve them."

I understand where she is coming from missing her family. I would do anything to see mine one last time. The pain will never subside. It would always be with both of us.

"Talk to me. Tell me everything. I'm a good listener."

Jane sobs. "They killed my parents right in front of me. Ripped them apart like snacks. I had to sit there and watch. I can't stop the images from flashing in my head every time I think of them."

"I'm so sorry. I couldn't imagine."

"I beat myself up because why should I miss them? They never did anything but cause me pain for my entire life. Broken bones, bruises, and scars. They did that."

There's a knock at the door.

"Yes?" I answer.

"Everything okay in there?" Stephen says, opening the door.

"We were just talking."

"About what?"

"Losing our families, if it's any of your business," Jane replies.

"It'll haunt us forever, but one day we'll get our revenge," Stephen comments.

We need to get out of there, clear our minds.

"What do you say we go do something?" I suggest.

I follow Jane out of the room, who then grabs Stephen and Anthony. We all want to be anywhere but there. All the painful memories are floating around in our heads.

As we leave Liz's, the four of us walk down the street.

"I can't wait to eradicate those assholes. I wish we were ready." I say, glancing at Stephen.

"We'll get there. Believe me, it's gonna happen soon, which is why we need to get trained up. They're a lot stronger than most give them credit for, and they use it to their full advantage."

As we come across the bar, there are men outside smoking with women hanging all over them. I snicker, disgusted at how open everyone is with affection. I sure the hell didn't want to have it shoved down my throat everywhere I go.

As soon as we order drinks at the bar, the conversation starts flowing.

"Can you imagine what our lives would be like if we were human right now?" Stephen asks.

"Emotional. Heartbreaking!" I reply.

"Well, that's part of being human. Even as a vampire, we've got emotions," Jane comments.

"Yes, we do but the Blood Takers, they've lost it all. They only know hunger," Anthony says.

Jane chimes in. "I'm glad I met you guys. It's nice to have some friends that understand the frustration of losing their family. I'd love to come back to Frankfort with you guys. It's not that I don't like it here, but I'd like to be around people my age."

"I wouldn't mind, but we would need to clear it with Liz and Samuel," Anthony replies with a smile. "Samuel should be back tomorrow for us."

13
Envio

"The three of you are going out tonight. Have some fun, but find some recruits. You know the drill," Jakob says.

"Anything in particular you want us to look for, boss?" Lorenzo asks.

"Well, if you go to Frankfort, see if you can find Jane while you're there. Other than that, just have some fun."

I hate recruiting but Pavel and Lorenzo love it. There's no emotion left in them at this point. The only reason they like recruiting is because they get to scare and kill people. Sometimes it kills me that I have to associate myself with these vampires, but didn't have a choice. The Guardians will never trust me, and Jakob will find me anyway. I didn't want them to die because of me, especially Jane.

Ever since that night, I wonder what it's like for her to be with them. Maybe she isn't meant to be with the Blood Takers. Honestly, with Jane and Sasha being with the Guardians now, they stand a great chance at beating us if they play their cards right. Jakob will never admit it, but we have vulnerable spots.

If I can trust Jane, which I hope I can, then some information will do them good. Yet, I have to be careful with what I share and with who because one slip up could get me killed. I didn't do all this, and stayed with the Blood Takers just to die. There's a point, helping the Guardians win.

As we near the exit from the tunnels, I know what's going to happen. I have to prepare myself for it every time. Lorenzo is a nasty creature who loves to feed on young women. His looks probably help him get close until they notice the eyes. He's tall, slender, and Italian. Pavel likes men the most. He loves degrading them of their masculinity and making them feel small. I never quite understood why, but I guess everyone has their own thing.

I let them lead the way back into Frankfort, knowing who will be there. The last thing I want is for them to find Jane, but I can't tell Jakob no. *Please don't let Jane be out tonight.*

Loud music is coming from the downtown strip. It's a Friday night, and being a college town, so many would be at the bars and drinking heavily. Easy targets. Lorenzo and Pavel will want go there. We never came back with many recruits because those two loved to slaughter. Most of the time, they didn't even try to recruit, and eventually I figure Jakob will catch on, but he didn't seem to care much.

As we near closer to downtown, Pavel comes to an abrupt halt.

"Listen, how about we don't recruit tonight. Let's just have some fun. Show them what we are capable of. The Guardians won't know what hit them," he says, a vindictive smile on his face.

The Guardians? Their plan is to go after them, without Jakob? He won't be happy about that. I couldn't object without raising suspicion, but the last thing I want to do is go along with that plan. "How about we just go have some fun and leave a mess for them to clean up?"

As we come up on the bars, many are outside. Lorenzo and Pavel take it upon themselves to make friends. You would think our eyes would scare them off, but sometimes I didn't think they even notice, probably too drunk. I try to keep my distance, but not so much to make them question what I am doing. They have big mouths, and won't hesitate to tell Jakob anything.

Lorenzo finds a younger girl, probably nineteen, outside with her muscular boyfriend, which catches Pavel's eye. It's sometimes interesting to watch and see how their ideas pan out. They like to have fun with their victims. Most of the time, it ends brutally. It never gets easier watching them take an innocent life. I couldn't wait to get away from this side for good. Help people for a change.

"How are ya, sweetheart?" Lorenzo says as her boyfriend goes inside.

"I'm alright."

Her boyfriend will only be gone a minute. He better hurry.

Pavel follows the boyfriend inside. He likes to start by befriending them. It makes the ending much more satisfactory.

"Hey, whatcha drinking?" he asks as the boyfriend leans against the bar waiting for his drinks.

"Tequila shots," he answers plainly, not giving him any attention or eye contact.

That's exactly what he wants. Pavel loves macho guys. They always beg the hardest after being broken down and realizing how weak they are. It reminds me of my obsession with abusive assholes. They always beg the hardest, even though they didn't give their victims the same choice.

As the boyfriend receives his drinks, Pavel follows him back outside, meeting his girlfriend and Lorenzo. Interested to see how this one pans out.

"What the hell's going on?" he asks, handing his girlfriend her shot and putting his arm around her.

"Oh, nothing. Your girlfriend here was just asking if I wanted to come back with her."

His arm quickly leaves her shoulder as he turns around and punches Lorenzo in the mouth. "What the hell's wrong with you? She's not going anywhere. Get the fuck away from my girl."

They pretend to walk away then wink at each other. It's time. As they pounce on them, the bystanders quickly start running inside or in the other direction, seeing the blood splatter on the concrete steps.

The rumors are true about how brutal Blood Takers are, and this is proof.

"You aren't getting away that easy, sweetie," Lorenzo says to the young girl as she cries.

He pulls her head back by her ponytail, and his teeth sink into her neck. His strength is so great; her head has come off onto the pavement beside him. That didn't stop him from feeding; he just continues. He isn't going to waste any of that precious blood.

Pavel is breaking every limb in the boyfriend's body as he feeds on him.

"Please...stop...why...are...you... Doing this to us?" he yells, gurgling on his own blood.

"Fun. It's fun to see how weak and puny you humans are. It makes me laugh. You always think you're so macho, until you meet us."

When Jane sees what they have done, it's going to make her question me. Everything I've told her has been the truth. I don't want to be a Blood Taker anymore, but I have to choose my timing carefully. Jakob will come after me, and the first place he'd look will be with the Guardians. I have to keep Jane safe as long as I can, and that can only be done from within. So every day, I bite the bullet and fake my way through living as one of them.

Jane would understand once I have the chance to explain everything, until then her perception of me will only change as long as they are out doing things like this in the streets of their town. Sure, the Guardians aren't prepared to take us on yet, but it will only be a matter of time.

14
Samuel

There have been hundreds of missing persons within the last few months, and no leads. At least to the human world. I know who is responsible and will get justice. Patience is key in this particular fight with evil.

"Sheriff, we've got an emergency. Something's happening downtown. We got multiple calls of people being attacked on the street."

They're here. I run to grab my gun and head straight to the door. "Come on, boys, we need to head out there now. Radio the rest to meet us there."

I jump into my police car, turn the sirens on, and speed off onto the road. The Blood Takers love easy bait, and this is a college town. Luckily, they have me as Sheriff. Loyal to a fault to the people that elected me to keep them safe.

As I approach downtown, bloody carcasses are everywhere. It has only been fifteen minutes after the last call came in. They are long gone. Blood splattered all over the street and buildings nearby, even on some of the cars. Why would they do it so out in the open? Almost like they are trying to send a message.

As I step out of the car, with my deputies not far behind me, I have to come up with something. This is going to raise even more suspicion. In the past two months, we've had a hundred people killed in downtown Frankfort with no leads. The statements we've gotten, even though they're true, everyone else passes them off as crazies. Honestly, I am surprised humankind hasn't figured it out already. I guess since they are taught to believe in stuff they can only feel and see, it will be hard for them to believe it could be vampires.

Three of my deputies show up, halting to a stop. Their mouths drop stuck in place, witnessing the horrid sight. This isn't the first crime scene they've been to, but the first one of this magnitude.

"Sir, what do you want us to do?" A beam of sweat trickles down Deputy Shawcross' forehead waiting for instructions.

"Contact the coroner and radio back to the station with an update," My feet ushers across the rocks, crunching underneath my boots, to the patrol car surrounded by bodies.

As I canvas the scene, my eyes land on an older man draped over a stool inside the bar. The man is watching me, maybe he knows something.

The bell above the door jingled as I went inside, walking straight up to the older man. "Sir? Sir, are you all right?"

"I s-s-s-saw 'em," he slurs, about the time the rank smell of alcohol slaps me in the face. My nose wrinkles. No one is going to believe a word he says.

"What'd you see?" His hand reaches out for help getting down, and I oblige. His dark hair is slick with grease, and his beard is frizzy with little bits of food in it. A drop of liquor is suspended at the corner of his lips. Nausea roils in my stomach. "Tell me what you saw."

"Them three boys over there," he gestures wildly around the room. "They were everywhere."

"Three boys? What did they look like?"

"Oh," he drops his head into his hands and peers out at me like a child afraid of the dark. "They were crazy and bigger'n a mountain, 'cept one wasn't bigger, and that girl..." He moans and shakes his head. "And yellow eyes!" he adds, his voice raising to yell at the end.

Well, I muse. He's too drunk for his testimony to count for much. But he confirmed my suspicions.

"Sir," I say firmly, "we're going to need you to come down to the station and fill out a statement. Come on, now." I grunt under his weight as I help him stagger to his feet.

As I walk outside to hand him over to Shawcross, I see him. His eyes peer at me, and then he starts to run away like a coward.

"Deputy, take him down to the station and get his statement filed." I barely finish my sentences before I take off after him. Instead of running away, he's waiting for me around back.

"Tell me I'm not seeing who I think I'm seeing," I drawl with a predatory grin. "Tell me you're not so stupid as to return to the scene of one of your own crimes? Haven't you ever watched any crime shows?"

As I rack my head around him being here, I know he isn't stupid enough to come back here without there being a reason.

Envio's eyes narrow. "I didn't do this. This was Lorenzo and Pavel's doing. I'm not the enemy here."

I snorted, *did he really think I'd believe that he was a good guy?* No one on their side is good for anything besides slaughtering innocent people.

"You're telling me that you live with the Blood Takers, you eat like the Blood Takers, but you're not a Blood Taker?" I point with my chin toward his face. "Your eyes give lie to that, friend."

"I know it looks that way," he said, his hands lifting. "But I'm telling you how it really is, and I can be a huge help, if you'll let me."

"Get the hell out of my town and stay gone. I don't want to see you back here again. Help or no help. Be sure to tell your leader, we're coming for him."

It isn't long until Envio is gone with a huge mess left behind.

As I make my way back to the front of the bar, one of my deputies is talking to a couple of women.

"I saw a man, black hair, maybe six feet tall." The deputy was writing everything down. "He attacked a man while one of the others attacked his girlfriend."

The more information she gives the deputy, the more that will make it into an official statement. I have to be careful. "Did you see what caused all the blood?" I ask, pointing to the blood splattered everywhere.

"You'll think I'm crazy?" Her eyes dart at the ground. "I already feel crazy enough."

"Try me?" The deputy answers.

"Well, it looked like he bit them. But that doesn't make any sense, right? He must have had a knife or something." The woman quickly starts backpedaling, not even believing her own story.

"Well, I can't put that in a statement if you're unsure of what you saw, ma'am."

The woman stares at the ground again, "I understand. I'm not sure what I saw anymore."

I pull Deputy Shawcross to the side. "I've got to go pick up my nephews. Think you can handle the rest of the statement?"

"Of course, sir."

I head back to my car, and start the drive back to Liz's house. I'd make it right before dawn. The kids are safe there, and the Blood Takers didn't find Sasha or Jane, so the plan is successful. But, how long are we going to be able to keep them from the Blood Takers?

15

Jane

Arriving back in Frankfort, the town's in panic mode. Bodies are lying in the streets with people crying over them.

"Why didn't you tell us?" I ask Samuel.

Instead of answering, he parks the car. "Let's get out and help. It'll look weird if the Sheriff isn't around."

Samuel is the sheriff here. Bet that comes in handy when they come into town slaughtering his people. He can keep the humans eyes off us for as long as he can, but if this keeps happening, it's only a matter of time before they catch on. They can't be oblivious forever, and eventually Jakob will do something to make us known.

"You okay? Can I get ya anything?" I ask a woman hovering over her husband's body.

"No, I'll be fine. We need to catch the people who murdered our families. This can't go without punishment," the woman replies.

They ransacked their town and are now messing with our livelihood. The coroner is on the scene and bagging up the bodies one by one. We need to protect this town, but we can't do it alone. If we can take the Blood Takers out one by one, then it wouldn't be a problem, but they almost never run around alone from what Stephen has said.

"Are you okay?" Anthony asks.

"I'm fine. I'm just so sick of these Blood Takers already. How could they do this to your town? Do they have no respect for our kind? Something needs to be done!"

"Our kind?" Anthony asks wryly. "It's their kind now, Jane."

"But that's beside the point. I agree, something must be done. And believe me, we're trying! What would you have us do?"

He turns an expectant look on Sasha—after all, isn't she who the vision shows, leading us to victory?

"Hell, I don't know. Something, anything! We can't just let this continue. Humans don't deserve this. You must agree with me since you're not one of them yourself!"

The better question is how are we going to help the humans? We can't get the Blood Takers alone; there are too many. Maybe we can try to get some of them to come to our side. Samuel mentioned some are forced into this lifestyle to save their families. They should be the target.

At the rate the Blood Takers are going, humans will be extinct within a decade. The Guardians need to be the barrier of protection. We feel emotions like sympathy; Blood Takers did not. Once you wear a pair of fiery eyes, your humanity is lost.

Stephen is sent out by Samuel to retrieve the latest batch of recruits so he can address them about the situation that happened in Frankfort. As the leader, he needs to keep everyone up to date on our plans.

"Thank you all for coming. As you know, our area was attacked, and lots of lives lost. There's no doubt in my mind this is going to cause hysteria, and we need to put an end to this. Who is with me?"

They all know what needs to be done, just need someone to make them stand up and fight.

"We'll need to get more recruits. Are you up for going out tomorrow possibly?" Samuel asks me.

"Of course, whatever you need me to do," I reply.

Anthony looks like he's on a mission, but waits patiently.

"Hey, what's up?"

"I just wanted to see if you were interested in getting a drink with me?" He asks.

"Sure." My eyes have been on him since the first night.

The first couple of minutes of our walk are spent in silence. Neither of us know what to say. "So…"

"How do you like it here?"

I shrug. "I like having people my own age around. It provides a little comfort."

We walk into the bar and grab a table. Sitting down, a smile crosses his face that proves to be infectious. I want to get to know him, and not listen to the things Liz or anyone else has told me. Maybe they are wrong about him too.

After a couple of shots, we're confiding in each other and laughing hysterically, swapping stories of before being turned. It's nice to be able to sit down, and just talk to someone my age. Liz listens, but it's not the same.

I explained to him what happened with my parents. Pity shows in his eyes.

"I can't believe your parents did that to you. Your own parents. I'll never complain about my parents again."

I want him so badly to wrap his arms around me and tell me everything is going to be okay. He's the first boy I ever had the privilege of going on a date with, or well I don't know if Anthony is considering this a date. Whatever, I've never been alone with a boy besides Envio when he turned me. The way he looks at me, I can understand why girls are always so giddy when talking about their dates.

"I won't let anything happen to you," he says as he takes my hand.

"Why would you care what happens to me?" I ask, looking down at the floor.

He pulls my chin up. "You're worth more than you think. I won't treat you like your father did. You deserve so much more. Believe that."

He's being so kind, and that's something I'm not used to, especially from men. Jason never treated me like this, or even showed an ounce of care for me my entire life. Yet, Anthony has only known me for a week and already sees my worth. I didn't want to leave this bar. His company is soothing, and the conversation's easy. I didn't feel rushed or judged.

"So, what about you? What were you like before you got turned?"

"A senior. Best friend banged my girlfriend. Football. Not really much to say."

"Can I hear about your parents?"

"I'd rather not. The Blood Takers murdered them, but I'll get my revenge someday."

He's broken inside, like me but didn't want anyone else to see. Liz is wrong about him. Anthony just wants someone to recognize him, instead of his brother getting all the glory. Samuel does seem to favor Stephen, that much is clear.

"We'll get revenge for our families. I know it."

After several more hours of much-needed conversation, it's time for us to head back. Inevitably, the others will be wondering where we are. On the walk back, I slowly get closer to him and slid his hand in mine, as I held my breath. I fear he'll pull away, but instead he gives my hand a squeeze.

Tonight has proven to be one of the best nights of my adult life. It's my first experience of liking someone and feeling that chemistry is like, and I can't wait to see where it leads.

Walking down the street with my hand in his, I realize that even though I'm a vampire now, there are things I can still experience.

"So… not to be weird… but was this a date?"

"I thought so. Is that okay?"

"Definitely." This is my first date. Jason didn't allow it. He didn't want me getting close to anyone. Always a loner in school, that was how it had to be. I couldn't disobey him because there would be consequences. But, he wasn't alive to hurt me, and can't do anything about tonight.

We walk back to Samuel's in silence, just enjoying each other's company. Tonight, we have learned so much about each other, and it brings us closer. It gives me a glimpse into the man he is, and how wrong the others are about him. One day, they will see him for who he really is.

As we near the door, I can't help but wonder if we will be going out again. All my life has been spent looking at the ground, not wanting to bring attention to myself. Never wearing makeup or doing anything to my hair made things easier to go unnoticed. Now, I'm free. I can embrace being a woman.

"I had a great time tonight," he says with his hands in his pockets.

"I got to know the *real* you tonight. Not the fake persona you put on for everyone else."

I didn't overthink, just lean in and kiss him.

"Good night. I'll see you tomorrow," he said as I slipped inside.

The next morning, the four of them are sitting around the coffee table, writing down plans. We all want the same thing. Justice. Revenge. I can't wait to get my hands on them and make them pay for all the suffering they've caused.

"What can I do to help? Need me to do anything?" Anthony asks.

Samuel scratches his head. "You feeling okay? It's not like you to ask. You've been acting weird the last couple of days. Everything alright?"

"I'm fine. I just want to do more. Anything I can do?"

"We need someone else to recruit. You think you can talk vampires into joining?"

"Probably. I could give it a shot."

He follows Samuel back to the table and joins the conversation.

"How many do you think we'll need?" Sasha asks.

"My guess..." He scratches his head. "Hell, I don't even know.

There's no telling how many are out there. The best we can do right now is try to get as many as we can."

"It'll be easiest if we start from the closest states and work our way out. The more we recruit, the more recruiters we can send out to find more," Stephen explains.

Anthony and I sneak out, knowing we need to feed before leaving tomorrow morning and head back to the bar.

"So, tell me more about yourself. Like before you got turned, what were your plans?" He ask, slapping down another shot.

"Well... honestly just to get away from my parents. Go off to college and try to experience all the things I never got to..."

"Like what?"

"My first kiss... dating... friends... I never got any of that." I can tell that right at that moment, he understands that he has been my first. It scares me to be vulnerable and tell him about this sort of stuff, but he's doing the same for me. Anthony didn't deserve to be shut out, because he's the first person to want to know more about me.

"So – I was your first kiss? God, I hoped it was perfect."

"No complaints here... except I'd love to do it again." I wink at him, as we enjoy our last drink before heading back. We have a long journey ahead of us tomorrow, and nobody knows how recruiting will go.

As we walk back to Samuel's, holding hands, my filter is lost. "I know this sounds weird, but do you think fate brought us together? I hadn't planned on staying with Liz much longer, but then you showed up. After that, I decided to stay in hopes of meeting you again," I say, looking at the ground.

"Look at me." He tells me, pulling my chin up so my eyes met his. "No need to look at the ground. And no, I don't think it's weird at all."

He leans in to kiss me, but suddenly wailing screams are coming from everywhere. Down the street, we can see Blood Takers heading to Samuel's. Around twenty of them. What are they doing back here?

We attempt to take a shortcut, but two of them stop us.

"Well, well, well. What do we have here? Trying to run away from the fun?"

One of them slips behind and throws me. My hands clench my sides from the impact.

"Leave her alone!"

Five vampires jump him, and aren't letting him up. "Stop! Leave him alone." They aren't listening to me, and limbs are coming off.

"Stay back! Don't! I'm not worth it!" Anthony screams. "Run!"

The last thing I hear before his body is in flames is my own heart-wrenching screams.

16
Samuel

Screams echo outside the house. I can hear Jane sobbing and then the door is kicked in and there stands Jakob.

"Samuel, you could've answered, but since you aren't polite enough, I'll have my men kill a couple more," Jakob says.

When he experimented on me, he didn't plan for me to survive, so when I asked questions, he answered honestly. Around twelve years ago, he was a family man. His son was the apple of his eye. On an unfortunate day, his son got in a car accident and wound up in a coma.

"What brings you back here?" I ask.

"You know why I'm here. For you."

The reason for his visit is to recruit me. He can't let me get away again. It already happened once, and he won't make the same mistake. I have learned to never underestimate him.

"You want me?" I try to act surprised.

"Yes, join us. I've been searching for you. You're one of the ones that got away and I can't have that."

Ever since the day I escaped him, he's been searching. Waiting for the day he found me. Running into Envio, and the fact that Jakob is here now, can't be a coincidence.

Sasha walks up to Jakob, but I put my hand out and shake my head. I can handle this myself. She didn't need to stick up for me. We need to protect her. The last thing we need is Jakob or any of the others to recognize her.

"I would never join you! You know that. You'll never have me as a part of your group!"

"Tsk, tsk," Jakob says, shaking his head dramatically. "I had hoped for better from you, Samuel. Didn't you hope for better, Envio." he calls back over his shoulder.

That yellow-eyed bastard. Envio shrugs with a grin.

"Ah, you can't win 'em all, boss."

"No. I suppose not." Jakob's gaze falls on Sasha, and he's on her in a moment. His fingers wrap tightly about her throat, and he leans in close. "What about you, then? Surely a pretty thing like you wants to be on the winning team, hmm?"

"I... would... never..." Sasha gasps. Even like this, her eyes spit fire. Jakob taps her nose with a finger, much like one would scold a puppy.

"Now, now, pet. Never say never." He smiles, and I feel terror run down my spine. Jakob shoves her back, and she falls on her bottom. One slender hand rubs the skin around her neck.

"I'll be back in a week, Samuel. Be ready to make the right choice, or the casualties will be on your hands. I do hope I'm being clear." He jerks his head, and all his cronies follow behind him.

Stephen looks around. "Where's Anthony? Jane?"

Suddenly I remember hearing her sobbing. "Let's go check on them."

When we walk outside, the scorch marks and blood on the ground next to her tell the story. A story none of us want to believe. Stephen screams, running to where Jane is covered in blood, and starts running after the Blood Takers, but they are long gone.

This is my fault. Jakob knows I won't give in to his threats. This is a message directed toward me. He will do whatever it takes to get me on his side.

We spend the next couple of hours grieving the loss of Anthony. I want to keep a close eye on Jane because I know they were getting close, and she's fragile. *Poor girl.*

Jane, though grief-stricken, isn't having it. "We need to stick to the plan. The only way we're going to get revenge for Anthony is bulking up our numbers. His death will not be in vain."

How many people must lose their families? We need to focus on the road ahead for Anthony's sake. Even though he wasn't much of a talker, we all knew his hatred for the Blood Takers. They took his parents away from him. Now, they have taken him from us.

"Stephen, you stay here. I don't think it's a good idea for you to be out there right now."

"The hell I am. They just murdered my brother!"

Sasha places her hand on his shoulder. "Jane can handle this. You showed her how to defend herself. Take some time. You'll need it."

I follow Jane outside. Failing isn't an option.

"Jane, the one thing you have to persuade with is the loss of life. They've been on a killing spree along these states, and vampires will know our secret is close to being revealed. Use this to your advantage."

17

Jane

As I get into my car and turn on the engine to start the recruitment search, a rap sounds at the window. I look up, and my jaw drops. *Him? Here? Now?* After what just happened... My stomach clenches, but I shove the grief back down. Rain pours down, and his hair looks inky dripping down onto his forehead. He swiped the water from his eyes and waited.

"Can I get in?" His voice is muffled through the glass. "It's freezing out here."

I suck my lower lip between my teeth and consider. Envio never seemed the vampire others portrayed him to be. On the other hand, he did stand by idly by while Anthony... I shake my head, scattering my thoughts. With a sigh, I unlock the door. He climbs in and shakes like a dog, water spraying everywhere.

"Seriously, you couldn't have done that out there?"

He laughs, the sound rich and full. His mouth has the same smug tilt to it now as it did when... The smoke burns my eyes and the acrid smell of burning flesh, of Anthony's... *Get a grip.* One thing at a time. Is Envio the enemy here? Or is he as lost as me?

"What do you want?" I ask, focusing my gaze on the steering wheel. I idly pick at my fingernail.

"To be like you."

My breath catches, but I can feel his sincerity flowing warmly across our bond. "I don't understand."

He leans in close and whispers in my ear, "I want to be a Guardian."

"A Guardian?" I arch a brow. "Considering last night... your people murdered one of them... You can see where there might be a problem... right?"

"I can," he admits. "But I'm prepared to do what it takes to prove I'm not like them. I deserted Jakob, so it's my death to go back. I've been waiting for a chance to see you, to show you who I really am."

He reaches out and puts his hand on my knee. Goosebumps ripple up my arms—from fear or pleasure, I'm not sure. "And the eyes?"

"Like any addiction, I have to work to fight the bloodlust. And around Jakob and the others, it's not like I could let them return to their normal."

"I wonder how many times you've used that line." I shoot a glance in his direction. He's watching me intently, his yellow eyes earnest. I look away again.

"Only on you."

"Only because you're hoping I'll swap sides."

"Oh, for the love," Envio pulled back. "I'm trying to swap sides."

"Even if I believe you, and I'm not saying I do," I say with a stern look, "the others won't accept you. Not after what you did." The familiar knot of grief settles in my stomach again.

"They might," he says. "Especially if you'll vouch for me."

"And who says I will?"

"I've got information they want. That you want."

"About what?" I turn a narrow-eyed glare his way.

"What they want or what you want?" At my expression, he grins. "For them, I'm willing to trade in secrets. I've been close to Jakob. No one else on your side can say that. For you—I know why I turned you that night. The real reason." He pauses, gauging my interest. At his words, my whole body tenses; my breath catches in my lungs, and my heart thunders.

"I'm willing to give you a tidbit in good faith," he murmurs. He reaches out and grips my chin lightly, his gaze tracing my lips with open hunger.

Almost against my own will, I give a little nod. He leans across the car and put his mouth near my ear. When he speaks, I can feel his breath moving the small wisps of hair there.

"I have visions."

"Visions?" I croak. A hot flush of embarrassment stains my cheeks, and I clear my throat. "Of what?"

"Of you." Envio's fingers strokes down the pale column of my neck, and my lips part on a gasp. "Of you as a great warrior, radiant as you fought the enemy."

Oh, I want that. To kill those who killed my family, to slaughter those who took Anthony's parents from him, to keep all the other boys and girls from growing up orphans... or never growing up at all.

Envio sits back in his seat. "Good faith tidbits are just that," he answered. "Tidbits."

I scowl. Of course, he isn't going to tell me everything. He'd be stupid too. There'd be no more leverage.

"Are you willing to vouch for me? I just need in the door. Then I have all the secrets I need to barter for my life and service."

"Let's say I'm willing to give you a chance to prove yourself. Right here, right now. It's recruiting time, and you're coming with me. Don't make me regret it."

Walking the streets of my old hometown is bittersweet. It's good to smell the cut summer grass, to feel the familiar breeze toy with my ponytail.

"You see those footprints in the cement?" My memory of the time when I had a friend flew back into my mind. It was a rare occurrence, so I couldn't forget it. It didn't last long once Jason found out, but was nice while it lasted. "When I was seven maybe, my parents were both working past supper, so we went down the street and ran through the wet cement. We figured they'd go over it again, but nope. Our footprints are still there."

"Wow, brave even at age seven. No surprise there."

Even though Envio didn't know anything about me, besides maybe what he has seen in his supposed visions, we both had the same type of childhood. We know the same struggles. "I wouldn't say brave. Jason had been furious when he caught me sneaking back in, but the pride I felt every time I walked past it was worth it."

He stops, sitting down on a bench, and patting for me to sit next to him. "Why didn't you come back here? People know you. You could finally have friends..."

Easier said than done, first of all, and even then, I am still a vampire. "My parents were murdered... the first person they would suspect would be me. Honestly, I don't think it's a good idea that I'm here now."

"You seem in the clear so far... but back to the task at hand. Finding vampires."

"This should be fun... your way of recruiting..." he said as we meandered past a coffee shop. "There's a lot less blood than their way."

"Are you telling me a vampire can get squeamish?" I tease, bumping his shoulder.

He snorts. "I'm telling you I don't like playing with my food."

"Do you all not care about recruiting?" I ask, suddenly curious. "Or is it all about the eating and the fun? Because there's an awful lot of you to not recruit."

"Oh, we're supposed to care," he says with a shrug.

"Then I'd think killing people is a little... mmm... counterproductive?"

"You'd be surprised how many people will agree to anything if it's their life on the line. Especially if they've seen their friends or family killed in front of them. Would you have chosen death?" he returns.

"Fair point."

Envio suddenly tenses. He lifts his head and takes a deep breath through his nose. "I do believe we have company," he says, jerking his head toward a postal worker hurrying down the street.

"Sir," I call, waving an arm. "Sir, could I talk to you for a moment?"

The man stops, though I can see the fight or flight all over him as we draw closer. As soon as we are near enough for him to get a good look at Envio—and his eyes—he bolts.

"Ah, hell," Envio curses. "Do you want me to catch him?"

"Definitely not," I say. "Assault and battery are not the way to get recruits. We're playing the Guardian way, remember?"

"Well, then we're going to have a bit of a problem," he says, pointing to his noticeable eyes.

"Do you think we can hide them somehow?" I ask.

"You mean like sunglasses?"

I shake my head. "That'd just look weird if we went inside anywhere. I was thinking more like colored contacts."

"We could try it," he says, his head cocks to the side in thought. Suddenly, he grins. "The color might bleed through, though."

I roll my eyes but can't stop the little bark of laughter. "Did you really just go there?"

"Oh, I so did. If I'm going to be forced into contacts, then I'm entitled to a pun about it."

I walk into an eye lens store and buy a pair of blue contacts. "Here, put these in. Let's see what damage it can do."

He slips them in, then looks at me. "So, what do you think? Do I look normal now?"

Without the blood-moon eyes, he's handsome. Not that he isn't with them. I am not sure anything could make him ugly.

"You look more normal," I say, laughing.

We continue my mission and finally recruit ten. It isn't easy, but Envio does a great job at talking them into it. He knows the Blood Takers and what they are capable of. The experience firsthand helps us out a lot.

Will the Guardians ever accept him? Not likely. Even when he tries to help by warning us about Jakob coming after Samuel no one believes him. Not so long after that, he shows up with his leader and they kill Anthony. Of course, he didn't kill him, but still. The people he's associating himself with, and that's all that matters to them. Is there anything that will ever change their mind?

Moving to Ohio and West Virginia, ten more are found. To be honest, there are few vampires, so the odds aren't in our favor. One of the recruits is an older woman, Darlene Wentworth. She decides to join to ensure her children's futures.

"From the look of things, this could only get worse. The Blood Takers need to be stopped before they take things any further and the world finds out about us. Humans won't understand the difference," Darlene says, walking back into her house to start packing.

From here, it only gets better. Between Virginia and North Carolina, we pick up seventy more recruits and are all set to arrive in Frankfort tomorrow. Thanks to Envio, I couldn't have done it without him.

As we head back to Frankfort, my mind isn't settled on bringing Envio back with me. The Guardians won't go for it, and something like this will need to be eased on them, not forced. I need to formulate a plan before I do anything drastic, but not really sure what that plan will be. Everyone needs time to grieve, and if Envio steps one foot near Samuel's house, he'll be torn apart and die the ultimate death without question.

"Envio, you can't come back with me. They'll tear you apart after what happened to Anthony."

"But I can't go back to Jakob… it's my death either way, it seems… I don't want to be that monster anymore. Please…"

"Do you have a phone?" His eyes are begging me not to leave him behind, and I didn't want to. "Put your number in mine. I'll keep in touch. Maybe we can both work together to prove to them you aren't the danger. But until then, you've got to trust me."

"We can't do this indefinitely," he warns me as I pull into a hotel parking lot. "If you can't think of a way soon, I'll have to approach Samuel on my own. I can't be running from both sides at the same time for long."

"I understand," I say, squeezing his hand. *When did his hand wind up in mine?*

He gives a wry smile, but I can feel his hurt. "So, I guess this is it, huh?"

"For now. I'll keep in touch."

Envio nods and climbs out of the car. He turns and leans against the roof, looking in at me. "I had a good time with you... reminds me of being human..." he says.

An abrupt rush of guilt floods me—*What am I doing?* He stands there while Anthony is killed! *But the Guardians say the Blood Takers have no human emotion left*, the other side of my heart whispers. And the hurt and affection in those eyes are real.

"Stay out of sight," I say.

He acknowledges my withdrawal with a terse nod. "Drive safe."

And then the door is shut, and I head back toward Samuel's house with success, guilt, and hope all draped over my shoulders.

18

Envio

Jane could be someone I can see myself falling in love with, and it isn't just the bond we share as me being her maker. Our childhoods and just understanding what the other struggled with because of that. My body is practically compelled to be close to her.

She's the only one that can see past the façade I play for Jakob, and see me. The man I have fought so hard to keep hidden deep inside, and that kernel of humanity for a moment like this one. If anyone can help me, it's Jane. There's no doubt about it.

My head rests on the pillow of the hotel bed, running through things I can do to get them to understand that I'm not the bad guy, when he takes over.

Jakob stands on the porch of a white house in the middle of a pretty subdivision with six Blood Takers waiting just off the front porch steps. I can feel his anger, and it's clear he knows that I ran. It's sending a tendril of fury through him as he tries to ignore it.

"Inside this house," he murmurs, "is Samuel's family. They'll leave here with us alive. Am I understood?"

I feel more than see their nods of agreement, though a couple shifts, a sure sign of their displeasure. Not that keeping them happy is his concern. The only thing he's worried about is using Samuel's family to get to him. A noble man like him can't stand by and watch his family be slaughtered. He'll leave with me then.

His fingers trace over the windowsill, remembering the many nights he's spent watching Samuel's family. The nights that Alicia, his pretty wife—oh, how he hated how everything Samuel had was so perfect. And then for him to be some bastion of righteousness for the vampires, too! — he gusts out another breath before allowing his mind to touch once more on those memories: of Alicia sitting up with her children, explaining that their daddy loved them, that he'd never just leave. The nights she'd burned dinner because she'd gone to the bathroom to cry so the kids wouldn't see. Then when she began to understand he was never coming home, how she'd become stronger. How she ran their home with single-minded focus, everything always shipshape.

Aydon is fifteen now, just the age a boy really needs his father. Amy is almost eighteen, and probably spends most of her time daydreaming about college and meeting her Mr. Right. Naturally, he'll be just like Daddy. Poor girl doesn't know who her daddy really is, but she'll find out shortly.

Jakob has been keeping an eye and spying on his family? He's jealous of Samuel, and want the life he had, but that will never happen. No one could ever love a vindictive masochist.

Jakob bares his teeth as he opens the door, going to Alicia's room first. A streetlight outside the window cast a faint white glow on her comforter. Her hair is spread out on the pillow, and she still sleeps tucked against another pillow, as if it becomes Samuel in her sleep. His lip curls in disgust. She still hasn't moved on? A beautiful woman like herself must have found someone interested, why sit around and pine over a man that isn't good enough for her anymore?

Seeing through his eyes, for the first time in a long time, really helps me see what is so wrong with him. He wants to feel love, and hates that Samuel has people who even after he abandoned them, still love him. Deep down, he knows he will never find anything like that.

In a blink, Jakob is up on the bed with her, kneeling over her prone body. She gets out the start of a scream, but his hand covers her mouth quickly.

"Oh, how I'd love to just rip out your throat, but the plan will only work if you're all alive."

Outside the bedroom, the others are ushering the kids to the living room. Their low sobs seem louder in the quiet of the night.

"Don't fuss now," He encourages her. Her breath comes in fast, shallow pants. "You don't know me yet. I know, I know. That's scary. But I know Samuel. I need you to help me help him. Understand?" His hand removes, and for a long moment, Alicia only whimpers softly.

"S-Samuel's dead," she stammers finally.

Jakob makes the obnoxious sound a buzzer makes.

He really is such an asshole, and sometimes I wonder if he was like this as a human. Surely, at some point in his life, he found someone to love him.

"Wrong! He's alive, and he needs your encouragement now. Maybe more than ever."

"You're a f-friend of S-Samuel?" she asks. A couple of hot tears leak down her cheeks.

"Friend might be stretching it."

He keeps a tight grip on her arm as he yanks her down the hallway. The others are ahead of the game—they've already taken the kids to the van.

I want so badly to be able to warn Jane, but this isn't something you can just wake up from. Once you are in their head, you're stuck there until it stopped. Who knows how long that would be?

"Please don't hurt my kids," Alicia cries as she stumbles along ahead of him. "Just take me. Please, please, just leave my kids!"

She has no clue who or what he is, and that's going to make the reveal of Samuel even more shocking. Would she still love her husband after she sees what he's become? That's he been around this whole time and never came back to her or the kids? *Doubtful.*

"Sorry, Alicia," Jakob smiles. "I may need more than just you, if he doesn't listen well the first time. There's only so many body parts a person can lose, after all." Alicia's cries swelled into little screams of terror. "If I were you all, I'd work on not irritating me. If you cooperate, you may get out of this mostly intact. If you don't, well..." he slices his thumb across his neck.

Alicia holds on tight to her kids until they are gagged and tied up.

"If you don't cooperate, I'll kill all of you!"

"Why would you want to kill us?" Aydon asks.

"The only reason I'm keeping you alive is Samuel. So, count your lucky stars right now."

My eyes settle on the floral wallpaper in the hotel room, and finally I'm back. I have to call and warn Jane. Her name pulled up on my screen and I hit the dial. One ring. Two rings. Three rings and then voicemail. *You've got to be kidding me!* I continued calling, but finally quit after ten voicemails.

Me: *Jakob is on his way to you... you need to hide... Lorenzo and Pavel are with him... if they see you, you will be leaving with Jakob tonight.*

My legs are restless, sitting on the edge of the bed, waiting for some type of a response whether text or call. After about an hour, I know she won't get the message in time, and most likely he's already there.

If Jakob gets her, I'll have to go back. Maybe I can come up with some crappy excuse he might believe to trust me again, and then get Jane the hell out of there. Or he would kill me, and then Jane would be left all alone.

I dial her number again, hoping that she picks up this time. *Nope.*

All I can do is sit here and wait to hear from her. If nothing by the morning, I'll go looking for her at Samuel's myself, no matter what the consequences might be.

19

Samuel

"Are we going to wait for them to show back up? We can attack them first. They'd never see it coming," Sasha explains.

Obviously, we can't do that without knowing where they are. If we are going to attack, then we need to be smart about it. A well-executed plan makes all the difference between lives lost and we've already lost too many.

I still feel responsible for Anthony's death, and don't want the guilt of anyone else's weighing on my shoulders. No others are going to die because of Jakob's want for me. Yes, I'm their leader, and they feel the need to protect me, but they should not lose their lives because of it. Not if I have anything to do about it.

When the door opens, I think it's Jane coming back from her feed, but then his voice fills the room.

"Well, well, well. Look what the vamp drug in." Jakob says, his lackies bringing three people in with blindfolds and gags. "I've got some fun surprises for you tonight."

They are taking hostages, now?

Jakob removes the blindfolds, and I froze. As I veer across the room, my wife and kids are on their knees. How did he find my family? Why the hell would he bring him here? The room suddenly seems like a vacuum, as if all the air has been sucked out the minute I meet Alicia's eyes. Years of betrayal and hurt haunt them, overshadowed by a more immediate terror. I open my mouth, but my tongue's cotton.

"Wh-what are they doing here?" I ask, trying to ignore the way my wife flinches at the sound of my voice. She thought I was dead, and now with her own eyes, it's proven to be a lie. How am I ever going to explain this to her?

"Call them my insurance that you'll see reason," Jakob purrs. "cause sometimes you seem to have issues with that."

"Leave them out of it," I growl, relieved to hear at least a little fire return to my voice. A fire is churning in my gut, and all I want to do is pounce on him, but I know if I do, then everyone will start fighting and someone would end up dead.

"Mm, no, I don't think so," Jakob shakes his head, all exaggerated sorrow. "You see, I went to so much trouble to get them for you! I'd hate to put all that work to waste. Wouldn't you, boys?" The vampires with him all give me vicious grins. I can feel the stares of the other Guardians as I sit, poised on the knife edge of two horrible choices.

"Jakob..."

"You're mine, Samuel. I made you. I own you. This is just to remind you of that." He whips a knife from his jacket and grips Alicia's hair in a meaty fist. "Choose. Which family do you want to save?" He leans down close to Alicia, and I feel my stomach freeze. "What was it he said, darling? Till death do you part?"

My eyes close, trying to figure out a way to save everyone, but it just isn't possible. The only way to keep this civil is to join him and leave everyone else behind. "Stop!" I hold out both hands, even as my wife's sobs come muffled through the gag. "Stop. Please."

"Ah, close, but please isn't the magic word I'm looking for here."

I tear my gaze away from Alicia, and I couldn't even bring myself to look at my children. Their soft, mewling cries are the only intruder upon the expectant quiet.

"Well? Come now," Jakob arches a brow. "What are the magic words?"

I drop my head. "I'll join you."

"No!" Liz cries from behind me. "You can't."

"I'll do it. Just give your word my family won't be hurt."

"Scout's honor," Jakob grins. "This family, at least." He winks at the Guardians standing around, faces pale with shock. I start out the door, intending to get them out of the immediate line of fire at least, but Liz grabs my arm.

"You can't do this!" Tears brim in those big brown eyes I love. I cup her face in my hands and use my thumbs to wipe them clear. "You can't leave me." Her voice cracks on the last, breaking my heart along with it.

"I don't have a choice," I whisper.

"You *do*! You do have a choice. Choose us," she swings an arm around the room. "Choose *me*!"

"I am," I say passionately. "I'm choosing time. Time for them, time for you. This is the only way. I know you'll understand." I drop a chaste kiss on her damp cheek.

"Please," she says, almost a groan. "Please don't do this."

"You have to win this fight for us," I whisper.

Jakob laughs, "Isn't that sweet? He's got himself a vampire girlfriend... and flaunting it in front of his human bride... how adorable..."

And then, before she can make me change my mind, I follow Jakob out the door, and help remove the gags from my family. I didn't know what to say to them. How do you explain something like this? *Sorry I've been gone, but I'm a vampire.*

"Take the children and never look back. I'll be fine," I whisper in Alicia's ear, wanting her and the kids to get as far away as they could before anything else could happen.

Jakob has other plans. He picks up Aydon and slaughters him right before my eyes, sinking his teeth into his throat and ripping it out, leaving blood gathering on the sidewalk where he stands.

Alicia falls to her knees, wailing at the sight of his blood trailing down the sidewalk toward her. I never wanted her to see any of this. She was supposed to go on and live a full happy life without me. I pounce on Jakob, sinking blows, one after another, but it isn't enough. There are too many Blood Takers. They pull me off him.

"Why?" I cry. "I joined you as you asked. You promised me that you would spare their lives."

"No human can know about us, isn't that the motto?" Jakob replied with a sly smile. "Come on... you had to know I wasn't going to let them live... not even you are that naïve."

"Don't you touch them; if you do, it'll be the last thing..."

His followers grab Alicia and snap her neck and throw her at my feet.

"You're next," Jakob says as he picks up Amy and bites her.

I know exactly what his plan is. If he turns Amy, then I will have no choice but to go with him to keep her safe.

"Wait. I'll go with you under one condition. Amy stays with Liz."

"What? Do you think I'm an idiot?"

"No funny business. I'll go willingly and join you, but only if she stays." I didn't think he would agree.

"Fine. It's not like the Guardians will last long once you're on my side anyway."

I walk back inside and approach Liz. "Please keep my daughter safe." When I walk out that door, it's inevitable that I will never be the same Samuel again.

20
Sasha

When the fight is over, we are left wondering what our next move is going to be with our leader joining forces with the enemy.

Amy is lying on the couch and hasn't moved for hours. The poor girl hasn't seen her father in years, and now he's gone again. I can't imagine the trauma. At least she isn't there to see her mother and brother be slaughtered by the Blood Takers.

We wait for her to get up, not wanting to disturb her. We have to be cautious of what we say, and how we handle this. Surely, Amy will have tons of questions.

Her body stirs, and my legs rush me next to her. "How are you feeling?"

"I'd really just like to be left alone."

"Listen, we're here to explain everything when you're ready. I'm sure you have questions that you'd like answers too."

There are plenty of things she needs to work through, like vampires being real, her becoming one, her dad alive and a vampire, and then him leaving.

Most of the others are still in shock. Honestly, most of them would have done the same thing if they were in his position. Samuel brought us together to take down the Blood Takers, and that's exactly what we need to do. Killing some of them in the fight is only the first wave. Everyone here needs to know we still have something to accomplish. Samuel joining the other side didn't deter us from our goal. The cause is very crucial to our survival, and we can't let this take us off our path.

As I stand up, my hands fall on my hips. "Listen, I know tonight didn't go like we expected it to. But Samuel brought us together for a reason. And he's trusting us to stick to it!"

"Because he stuck to it so well himself," Stephen says bitterly.

"Would you have done it differently?" I demand. "If he'd had Anthony or your parents, would you have said no and watched them die in front of you?"

"They died anyway," Amy says, her voice flat. "It didn't matter."

"You didn't die," Liz says. "And that matters. I refuse..." Her voice breaks, but she takes a breath and continues. "I refuse to think Samuel gave up his life for nothing."

"Exactly! He didn't do this for nothing. He did this for family. The best thing we can do for Samuel is stick to the plan. We're going to win this war, and Jakob's going to drown in the blood he has on his hands," I snarl the last.

Enough of this, I need to feed. "When I come back, we'll come up with a new strategy, one Samuel isn't as familiar with. Okay?"

There is another round of quiet affirmations.

Our bar—and hopefully Drake—is calling my name.

When I leave for the pub, my intent is to feed, but also to see Drake again. Even from down the street, I can smell him. His blood's aroma is sweet and pure. Walking into the bar, I order a drink but feel a wave of heat on my back.

When he works up enough courage to come over, he approaches and kisses me. I can feel his hot breath against my neck, sending chills down my spine. Right now, I want to think about anything other than the Blood Takers. Tonight has been awful, and the need to come up with a completely different action plan will take time. We can't take the chance of continuing under Samuel's plan especially since he joined the Blood Takers. He will probably be able to hold out for a while, but eventually they will make him give into the lust. That's why we need to be careful and precise.

"Where've you been?"

"I've been a little busy, but thought I'd come in and have a drink with you."

"I've been here every night hoping to run into you. I want to talk about our kiss," Drake says.

Crap, he remembered. I gaze into his eyes as we sway back and forth. No man has ever looked at me the way he does, with passion and lust. It would be easy to give in. Samuel warned me about getting close to humans, but right now, I couldn't care less about that. For years after he left, my mind wondered what it would be like to be with Drake again. Could we pick up where we left off and be as happy as we were before he left? Could he ever accept me as I am now? Somehow, I doubt it. How do you tell someone with no knowledge of vampires, that you were one?

Looking deeply into his eyes, I drink from his neck and heal it quickly.

He pulls me closer and say, "You're the girl I've been waiting for. No one else compares."

Butterflies flutter in my stomach; what girl didn't want to hear that? There's something that I have wanted to do for a long time. The one thing I didn't get to experience with Drake.

"Can we go back to your place? Catch up more?" I ask.

He nods his head and leads me back to his apartment a couple blocks away. I thought I lost everything and everyone from my human past, but here he is, standing in front of me. As much as I know it isn't ever going to work, it just isn't as easy to let him go.

"Why did you move here of all places?"

It's a valid question. "Family friends live here. I'm staying with them. I needed to get away. There was just too much hurt left there. I couldn't stand it."

I'm not lying. Being stuck in that apartment above the store would have driven me mad. I need to give myself a chance to be happy. It's merely a coincidence that Drake is here, right?

He leans in and embraces me; his warm body wraps around mine. As he lets go, I kiss him, gentle and soft. The one thing I miss from my human life is never having sex. Even with my boyfriend of multiple years. Here's my chance and with someone I trust. I stand up and slide off my shirt, straddling him, with my hands on his shoulders.

"We don't have to do this. You know I'm not pressuring you," Drake says, trying to make sure this is what I want.

"Believe me, I want it more than anything right now," I reply, then place a single kiss on his lips.

Drake lays me down on the couch, kissing my neck, while I run my fingers through his hair.

"Are you sure?" He asks, before unbuttoning my pants and sliding them down and off my ankles.

"Yes... stop worrying."

From there, we get to know each other on a whole different level. My senses are heightened, and I feel the ecstasy in every fiber of my body. Suddenly, I'm overcome with guilt for being here with him instead of back at the house.

"What's wrong? You okay? Did I do something wrong?" he asks.

"No, it's not you. I just had some bad things happen recently, and I can't get it out of my head."

I place a sweet kiss on his lips as I get dressed and head out the door.

Back at the house, Jane's curled up in a ball. "I just—I just can't imagine Samuel like them. Once Jakob makes him feed, he'll never be the same. He'll never be our Samuel again."

Our nightmare has become real. Samuel is gone, whisked away by the very enemy we are all trying to take down. I want to be mad at him, but I can't be. He gave up his life in exchange for his daughters. My heart is broken, but I understand.

Amy is all we have left from his human life. There's no way he's going to let that go. His job is to protect her, vampire or human. Those instincts don't just disappear. Embedded into us, the urgency to protect our children at all costs.

Liz sulks in her office, trying to pour herself into the manuscript that has been sitting incomplete for weeks. So much has been going on, but I know the deadline is fast approaching.

Why is she hell-bent on sitting at her house amidst this tragedy?

I head back over to Samuel's house where Jane would surely be. With him gone, Jane and I will now be responsible for it. I try to keep my mind off him. Even though it's harder than it sounds. The drive over makes it impossible not to think about Samuel.

He took me to his home, let me stay with him, and showed me how I could be a vampire without killing people. He showed me a better life.

21

Envio

I've only heard from Jane last night to check in after she finally received all my calls and texts, but it was too late. Just a simple call from her letting me know that Jakob has already been there, but nothing more. Hearing her voice on the phone only makes me wish she is laying here next to me. What is it that draws me to her? It's like electricity flowing between us, making my hair raise. Right now, I can picture her, lying down on her bed, her silky hair flowing while she browses a magazine. The way her lips barely part when she's thinking or paying hard attention to something. It's still beyond me why anyone would want to hit her, hurt her, or anything else. Hell, I just want to protect her and make sure she stays alive.

Somehow, I need to prove myself to the Guardians. I know exactly how. The Blood Takers surely are wondering where I am by now. Jakob didn't like it when his followers disappeared. He always thinks they are running off to tell the Guardians where they are hiding which is usually preposterous. I shrug. Well, this time he isn't wrong. I will tell Jane, but when it's the right time. Right now, it doesn't seem right. I'll keep the information to myself for now and fill her in later.

Envio: What are you up 2?

Jane: Lying in bed...trying to keep my mind busy from the catastrophe... how's it going there?

Envio: Need company?

I would love nothing more than for her to visit. Just being in her presence makes me feel like a better person. The person I want to be after all this is done. It's not like I want to join the dark side, forced is more like it. As I close my eyes, I can almost feel her soft hands caressing down my back and around my shoulders.

My heart starts racing. I have been alone for a week, with an occasional feed. If I did need to defend myself, strong is what I must be. Prepare for what can happen, always.

I look in the mirror and take my contacts out. I hate shadowing myself. Jane would understand. She knows I'm evil.

It feels like hours before I can finally sense her presence approaching. I open the front door before she even knocks.

"Hey, come in," I say, moving to the side to let the beautiful woman inside my hotel room. If anyone were to see this, they would get the wrong idea. Not that I'm opposed to bedding a beautiful lady. It's been an awfully long time.

Once I close the door, I can sense her nervousness as she looks around the room for a chair and notices only the bed.

"You can sit on the bed; I'm not going to bite." I chuckle. *Not that I didn't want to.* Jane cast a knowing look over her shoulder as she moved to the bed. Is it my imagination, or did she put a little extra sashay in those hips of hers?

"It's been a bit," I comment when she settles onto the bed—criss cross applesauce, as my mother called it. "Things must be busy over there."

A dark look appears in her eyes. "Well, you know Jakob paid us a visit."

"Who'd he kill?" Being by his side all that time, I know his presence always comes with a cost. There's never a time where someone didn't die. It's his signature scare tactic and always works.

"He killed Samuel's wife and son."

"I assume to get Samuel to go with him…"

"Yeah, Samuel joined him to save his daughter's life. They bit her, so she only has so much time. Her whole world came crashing down before her eyes, and she didn't even get to see the man her father was. The leader he was to us."

If he's with them now, does that mean that his earlier visions are null and void? Samuel would know the Guardians plans, and once Jakob turns him on his side, there will be nothing stopping him from spilling the beans. They need to work fast.

"So, have you guys come up with a new plan? Surely you aren't going to stick with the original plan that Samuel fleshed out."

A bright flush rises in her cheeks, and she shrugs one shoulder sheepishly. "We've been brainstorming," she says. One hand sneaks up and begins nervously twisting a loose tendril of hair. I just wait—her tension flowing along our bond, and the mix of feelings she has for me is exhilarating embarrassment, passion, anger, and affection. "We're preparing for a war, you know," she says, straightening her shoulders. The pointed glare I get shows she feels my amusement along our same connection.

"Ah, I see." I grin to take some of the bite from my next words. "And I couldn't be of any help with that."

Jane rolls her eyes. "Your kind of a nag, you know that?"

"If you're saying only kind of, then I'm not doing it right." I stalk over back to the bed, and she watches me come with desire and fear in her eyes.

The bed creaks beneath me as I settle beside her, and the tip of her pink tongue slips out, wetting her lips. I gently take the hair from between her fingers and tuck it behind her ear. "Don't you think we'd do better together?"

"I think we'd do better if you'd tell me where the Blood Takers are holed up," she replies, her voice breathy.

"Mmm, hmm." I shake my head. "You may accept me at my word, but I'm hardly giving up the only leverage I have."

"What happened to good faith?" she asks tartly.

"That was for you only, sweet."

"Sweet?" Jane arches a brow at me, and I return a wicked grin.

"If you'd ever tasted yourself, you'd call you sweet, too." I lean in close, relishing in the pounding of her heart. I lift her chin with my fingertips, tracing over those full lips with my thumb. Her mouth parts, and I resist the urge to slip my thumb into that welcoming heat. Instead, I slid my hand around and gripped her hair in my fist.

With a split-second pause, an offer for her to refuse, I claim her lips. The way she yields beneath my tongue sent fire coursing through me, and I feel my passion rise to meet hers.

"Sweet," I whisper when I pull away. Jane stares at me with sex hungry eyes, cheeks flushed, and lips swollen from my attention. "Better together, yes?"

She nods, somewhat weakly, and I grin.

"Good. Now," I lean around her to pick up the remote. "What ya feeling? Barring chick flicks, I'll even let you choose." I wink.

She blinks. Then she laughs, full and loud. If that sound could be bottled and sold, there'd never be a shortage of sunshine in this world.

"You're awful, you know that?" she says, punching my arm.

I click on the hotel television. "It's been mentioned. *Braveheart* or, oh, how about *Twilight*? I love it when they go all glittery."

She snorts. "I thought you said no chick flicks?"

"I'm choosing to think of this as... educational." I wink again, then I lay back against the pillows, pulling her down against my chest. "To show you what not to do."

"Now, hush. It's starting." Jane rolls her eyes but snuggles in closer, just as the beginning strains of music float out of the cheap, tiny speakers.

22

Samuel

Since coming back to this god forsaken tunnel with Jakob, all I can is hope and pray that Amy's going to be okay. After all, if not for family, I wouldn't have chosen to go with him in the first place, but the bond between a parent and child is far too strong to let her die because of my stubbornness. She deserves far better than me as a father. Liz and the others will keep her safe, if she chooses to feed. Did I want her to become a vampire? No, but also didn't want her to die either. Amy has a whole life ahead of her, and it has been stripped away by that masochist asshole. If giving up my humanity meant Amy and the Guardians have the chance to kill Jakob once and for all, then it'll be worth it. The last several years have been in anticipation of that final battle, leaving the Blood Takers without a leader would cause them to scatter or follow a new one.

At least with me on this side of the coin, I'm someone they will come to know and trust down here, and that could mean that when that day comes, I could get them to change their ways, follow new rules, and things could go back to normal. At least, that has always been my wish.

"You look like you're having entirely too much fun in here..." Jakob says, waltzing into my room with two woman.

He tries so hard to get me to give into the lust, but I've had years of practice. Yet, Jakob is smart and knows the only way he can get me to go evil will be to make me drain. "You know it, it's like a palace down here."

"Listen, you promised to come willingly, and right now you're being a pain in my ass..."

I sit in my room – the same room Envio apparently shared with Lorenzo – with two women begging to be let go. "I'm not going to kill them. They're innocent."

"Should I go back and get Amy? I thought we had a deal, but if you don't plan to keep it..."

I jump off the bed, "Don't touch her... it'll be your death and mine..." The only way he would leave her alone was if I give in, and did what I promised myself I'd never do for anyone. If I am careful, maybe I can save a sliver of humanity inside myself that Jakob won't be able to touch.

Jakob cuts the first woman's neck, making blood spew out, and run down her chest. The smell is intoxicating, and even though my self-control can resist it, there's no more time. I sink my teeth in, and drain her dry and that of her friend.

"There... you happy now?" I say, wiping the blood from my face.

"Only when you turn into the killer I know you can be... but I suppose that'll take time..."

My eyes roll, and I will bide my time until I can overthrow him. It'll be easier to infiltrate from the inside, but he won't be stupid enough to tell me anything of significance. All I could do is hope that I can gain some intel before the war begins.

"While I have your attention... there is something you can answer for me..."

"Okay, what?"

"Have you seen Envio? He just disappeared and that's not like him..."

"Not since the night you killed Anthony."

"Hmm... interesting. I was hoping you had kidnapped him, and that's why he wasn't back."

Why would Envio leave Jakob? He knows it would mean his death if he's ever found. Maybe he didn't want to be a part of this bloody disaster any longer. I can't say I blame him. How can anyone choose to follow this bastard? Kill innocent people for sport and pleasure?

Once Jakob leaves, I know it will only be a matter of time before the lust takes over me, and he will get any and all information out of me. It can't happen. If he finds out about Sasha, they will target here and the Guardians will lose. Hopefully, they are smart enough to think about that ahead of time, and in fact probably already have come up with a plan in case I tell Jakob about her.

―――

Over the last few days, I can tell how fast the change happens. I'm trying to hold on, but I don't know if I can fight it any longer. Today might be the last day I have any of my humanity.

I questioned my decision to join him, but knew it saved my daughter's life. Even if I turn into a monster, it's for a good reason. Nothing will push you to do something heroic more than my blood. She spent many years without a father, and the least I could do was show her I'm not the man she believed me to be, but a hero in the end.

The Guardians will need to bring their A game because Jakob isn't playing around anymore. Not to sound cocky, but with me by his side once the lust takes over, they will be a force to be reckoned with.

Jakob has us going to a local prison to recruit, and beef up our numbers before planning their next attack on the Guardians. At first thought, maybe a weird place, but it's Jakob, and a maximum-security prison filled with violent offenders. Changing a cold-blooded human killer into a vampire? Things are going to get bad and fast.

We get to the prison not far from our tunnel, and once there, it looks like a mob clustering around the gates, the air rank with violent excitement. My stomach churns, but for the first time, I didn't know if it's excitement or horror. The men next to me shift hungrily, but their gazes are fixed on Jakob, waiting for his signal.

"Remember," Jakob calls out. "These ones are for keeping, not killing. If I see any blood spilled that I've not cleared, heads will roll." He pauses, staring down those closest to him. "And by heads," he adds with a friendly smile, "I do mean yours."

Everyone waits for Jakob to give the signal. Our instructions are to get them to join first, and if they refuse, kill them. The guards look perplexed. Two hundred Blood Takers stand in front of their gates. Guns aren't going to hurt us, but they don't know that.

The guard yells, "It's not visiting hours, go home."

No one listens, but once the signal is given, we rush the gates. For a prison, it's sad to say, it didn't take much to bring the fence down.

Once we are inside, we kill all the guards and staff. No exceptions. We aren't here for them. Jakob wants the violent offenders.

As the walk-through of the prison begins, we recruit along the way. The hardest part is the yard filled with inmates. The inmates outnumber us, but we have strength on our side. When they see our clothes covered in blood, they scatter across the yard. This makes me laugh. Here we are inside a prison of violent murderers and they are running. For some reason I expected them to welcome a fight. Most of them are probably used to what we hear, people begging and screaming for mercy. We didn't give that to them.

Jakob stands up on a table. "Nothing to fear. We're here to offer freedom. No punishment, no judgment, and a lifetime of power. You can join and live or refuse and die. Your choice."

Jakob and I both know that these felons will want power. Who would turn down being free to kill whenever they want? We didn't even have to twist their arms and walk out of there with seventy-five recruits.

I haven't revealed Sasha yet, but it's only a matter of time before my humanity's completely gone. Once it is, Jakob will be able to get it out of me by loyalty. I still want the Blood Takers wiped out even if that means me with them.

Leaving the prison, it looks like a slaughterhouse. No way the news isn't going to find out about this. An investigation will happen. Jakob's smart and made sure no cameras caught anything, and there is no one left behind to give the cops any information.

Jakob wants there to be a war between vampires and humans. Proving vampires are the superior species is his number one priority. His belief of humans is for one thing: food. One day, vampires would be the rulers, and humans will be their slaves. The Guardians might be too scared to push the boundaries, but Jakob isn't.

Even in my thinking, I can see myself changing, feel myself slipping.

"Forgive me, Elizabeth," I whisper to the cool night air, wishing the breeze can carry my words to my love.

23

Sasha

"Sasha?" Stephen calls through the door. "We need to talk to you." The door opens wide, and I stand there, a mess in my pajamas, red hair frizzing around my face like a halo.

"Okay?" I say, brows lifting. The sense of urgency in his voice leaves me nervous. What could have possibly gone wrong now? Can't anything ever go right?

"If you'll join us in the living room?" He turns around, and starts walking away.

"What's going on?" I really don't like surprises or bad news. Hopefully, it's neither because I'm really not in the mood today. We have enough going on, and trying to find solutions for those problems.

"You might want to sit down." He gestures toward the chair.

Shaking my head, I say, "I don't want to. You're scaring me. Just tell me already."

"We've been keeping something from you." Liz speaks up.

"What?" The irritation is apparent in my voice, and this lead up crap they are doing is really unnecessary.

"A couple of days before Samuel found you, Liz had a vision," Jane chimes in.

"Okay? What's that got to do with me?"

"Her vision was of you. You were leading us to battle against the Blood Takers with thousands of Guardians behind you. You saved our species and humanity by eradicating them."

I didn't speak for a few good minutes, looking at them with a blank stare. "You've been keeping this from me? Why? Why wouldn't you just tell me?"

"We didn't want to pressure you, but now that Samuel's gone, we must act like the Blood Takers already know your secret." Stephen replies.

"What do you mean?"

"He might tell Jakob about you. If he does, they'll be back and in full force to take you out."

"Is that why you've been following me everywhere? In case they found out?"

"Yes, I swore to protect you, no matter the cost. You don't understand how important you are to our cause. We can't let you get hurt."

I start shouting and cursing while pacing back and forth. "You mean, you knew all this time and haven't said a word? Who the hell does something like that?"

"Yes, but only to protect you. We couldn't tell you before we thought you were ready. We didn't want to overwhelm you, in case you ran off."

"I'm sick of everyone treating me like a child. I deserved to know this from the beginning. At least I would have known I was here for a specific purpose."

"I'm sorry. I truly am. You can't tell anyone. The only people that know are Liz, Samuel, Stephen, and I. We need to keep it that way. The fewer people that know, the better. Remember, it's all about keeping you safe." Jane says.

"Screw you. I can't believe this. I need a drink."

Not wasting any time, I storm out of the room and head to the bar. I need to see him. As my footsteps sound on the concrete, my mind races because Drake might not be there. He keeps my mind off the crap going on. As I enter, the hinges on the door squeak. "Can I have a shot of whiskey, please?"

I scan the bar but don't see him anywhere. Maybe something has come up. I shake my head and walk toward the door.

"Dang, where ya going in such a hurry?" he asks with a devilish smile.

"Well, actually, I was waiting on you," I retort.

I immediately roll my eyes, knowing my mouth needs to shut. *Leave some mystery to you, girl.*

Drake grabs my hand and leads me inside to a table. He's my weakness. "So, can we talk about what's been happening? I just wanted to make sure everything's okay with you."

"I'll be alright. Just a lot of things going on. I'll be leaving town for a little while."

His face turns upside down. Did that upset him? I can't give him too much information, so explaining it to him won't be a good idea. The less he knows, the better. I gaze into his eyes, hug him, and feed quickly. "I know tonight was short, but I'll be back soon. Meet you here on Tuesday around nine. See ya then?"

"Wouldn't miss it." He replies with a grin.

As I walk back to Samuel's house—well, my house now—the others are there.

"I have great news," Stephen says. He wouldn't meet my eyes. *Coward.* "Ian and Lawrence just got back; they found the Blood Taker camps in Arkansas."

"How many were there?" I ask. It's the most logical question to ask.

"Indiana has the fewest. We're looking at probably seventy-five. If we're going to hit soon, that would be our best chance. We should take them out before they can turn or hurt anyone else," Jane explains.

She's right. We need to hit them now, when they will least expect it. Stephen sends out a mass message to the recruits, making them aware of the hit.

Stephen: We need to leave within the hour and meet up in Little Rock. We're going to obliterate the first home. There's only said to be 75. Let's get them before they hurt anyone else. Check in when you arrive.

Jane, Stephen, and I load up and began our journey. The tension is high ever since Stephen has told the truth. Pissed didn't begin to describe my fury, but I won't let it affect my role within the Guardians. I will still fight to eradicate the Blood Takers. That's the most important thing to me right now. Everything else is on the back burner until this is over.

Our plan is to hit them at night, while most humans sleep. The home is out in the country, so there isn't much worry about bystanders getting caught in the crossfire. The less human casualties, the better.

We meet right outside the woods that surround the edge of the property which sits on about three acres of land with a forest around it until you reach the clearing. The clearing is filled with vampires, Guardians. This is the start we have been waiting on. We have to hit them fast and with an element of surprise.

We split up, half going in toward the front and the rest through the back of the woods. They never even see us coming. Vampires are being flung onto the ground, ripping each other to pieces. I jump into action on the first vampire in my way. Teamwork makes this a lot easier too. I jump on top of one and hold it down while Jane rips his limbs off. Screams are coming from every direction. There are so many fighting that I can't keep track of who is getting killed and who is still alive. They keep coming and coming. We double their number. It isn't always going to be this easy. One after another, we keep taking them out and burning their bodies, careful not to take any chances of them living once we leave.

Wave after wave, more arrive, and they are ripped to shreds. Some even beg for their lives, but they know better. After everything we have seen their kind do, there is no way any of them are getting out of this alive. No mercy.

As the Blood Takers numbers keep dwindling down, it's easier for us to see how many are dead. The clearing is filled with bit and pieces of bodies on fire throughout. The smell of burning flesh burning my nostrils.

After a few hours, around a hundred Blood Takers are dead.

We lost ten Guardian recruits in the attack tonight, but all for a good cause. Everyone knows the possibilities when joining the fight. It isn't going to be easy. Everyone needs to stay at the top of their game and pay close attention. One little mess up could cost their lives.

We move on to the next home in Fayetteville, Arkansas. It has more than the last. Estimated with one hundred and fifty, we will still outnumber them. Our thirst is excruciating, and we need to feed to gain strength before the attack, stopping at a bar on the strip before heading to take care of business.

Honestly, we are still all high off the last attack. It feels good to finally be doing something, finally. It's far overdue. All of us have lost so many loved ones to them, and it's time for some payback.

We sneak into their territory and hit them hard. Only this is far worse than the last. They are stronger and faster which tells us they have been alive longer than the others. I look to my right and see Jane fighting off a particularly vicious-looking Blood Taker. He's big, easily twice her size—and her focus is not on him, but behind him.

Elderly Darlene is stumbling backwards, mouth slack with terror, clutching at the place where her left arm had been. Blood sprayed from her shoulder, and I feel bile rise in my throat. *She should have stayed home!* Tears join the sweat and blood on my cheeks. I try to fight my way over to her; on my right, I can see Jane doing the same. We meet over her body and share a horrified look. Suddenly, Jane's spine stiffens.

"We fight for her," she yells over the chaos, sticking her fist up in the air. "We fight for all the lives lost! For Darlene, for vengeance!" And then she screams as she tears back into the fray. It's ear-splitting, bloodcurdling, and even the most ruthless Blood Taker, even the timidest Guardian, pauses in its wake. She rips into the nearest Blood Taker, teeth and blade and fury. Crimson sprays her face like war paint, and madness thrives in her eyes.

"For vengeance!" I cry, my fist rising, as I too rejoin the fight.

The remainder of the battle passes quickly, and we finally stand victorious over the fallen bodies. I look around at my fellow Guardians. The ones that are left looking haggard but proud. *Good. They need their pride, now more than ever.*

24
Sasha

Refreshed and energized, we make our way to our final battle for now, Fort Smith. Every single Guardian has a reason to be in this fight, whether it's pure revenge or hate. That keeps them on their feet and ready to fight again.

What will we do if we cross paths with Samuel? Would we be able to put him down? It's so fresh in our minds. He won't ever be the same person, the person we loved.

"Sasha, are you okay?" Jane asks.

"Why?"

"I know we have plenty of other things to worry about, but what if we run into Samuel?"

It's a valid question as I have thought of it myself.

"What do you mean?"

"What if he's there?" Jane asks.

"Then we do what we must. Our mission is to take out the Blood Takers. He's one now. End of story. If he has scorching eyes, then he will be torn apart and set on fire, same as all the others."

Jane's eyes widen. "Are you serious? He gave you a place to live, mentored you. How are you so quick to kill him?"

"He's not Samuel anymore. So, stop thinking of him like he is."

Jane shifts in her seat uncomfortably. I cut a sideways glance at her.

"What?"

"He might be. The same man. Or not the same man, but more the same than you think. I think... I think it may be possible to come back from the bloodlust."

For a moment, I just sit in stunned silence. When I finally speak, my voice is quaky, uneven. "How can you even say that? After what we've been doing for the last forty-eight hours, how can you say they're anything like us?"

"I'm not saying they all are," Jane says defensively. "I'm saying it's possible that Samuel is. He didn't go to their side because he wanted to. He went to their side because he had to. He'll be fighting the bloodlust, not embracing it."

I snap my jaw shut and turn my attention back to the road. The rest of the car ride is spent in silence. It's an hour drive from Fayetteville. None of us really know what to say to each other, so silence is the best option.

Jane starts whimpering beside me.

"What's wrong with you?"

"I just can't believe we're doing this. I'm not crying because I'm unhappy. It's more of a being nervous. What if I die today? Or you?"

I scoff and pull over onto the shoulder of the interstate. "Why would you even say something like that?"

"It could happen. We lost Anthony. Who's to say I'm not next?"

"Listen, none of us are going to die today. Don't you dare say anything like that again," Stephen interjects.

Why is she thinking like that? Being so young, she's one of the best fighters in the Guardians. Jane's fast, strong, and dedicated. That only makes her more dangerous.

"We will stay close to each other. Watch each other's backs. Nothing's going to happen to us today," I reply.

Who am I trying to persuade, myself or Jane? The last of the road trip is spent in silence . The silence is good though since it gives us time to mentally prepare ourselves. Prepare for the worst. If we did, in fact, see Samuel here today, we need to make sure we would be able to take him down. Emotions aside, he is not one of us anymore. It might have his face, but not his heart. His loyalty is to Jakob now. No matter what Jane thinks. I look at her again. She's staring out the window, her chin on her fist. *She won't be willing. She needs watching in this next battle.* I resolve to tell Stephen my fears, but from the starstruck look on his face, I doubt that he will be willing to second-guess his warrior princess.

Pulling into Fort Smith, all of us storm out of the car to stretch our legs. Rogers Avenue has a strip of bars downtown. The Blood Takers apparently own and operate all of them. My guess is it makes it more convenient to feed. The bars are filled with drunks, and no one would see a thing.

We can't just burn the bars down. There would be too many bystanders. A plan needs to be put in place. Hitting each bar together didn't pose itself as an option. It gives them too much time to warn the others. The element of surprise is the only way it will work.

We find a small diner to discuss the details and plan after finding a map of downtown to show us the layout of each bar, entrances, exits, etc.

"I have a bad feeling. How are we going to do this?" Jane stutters.

I didn't pay attention; I'm too busy trying to formulate a plan with Stephen. How are we going to do it? Send a team to each bar, hit them all at the same time? We have no idea how many are inside each one. That isn't an option; that's a suicide mission.

"Let's call Monica and Ian. They were in the military. Maybe they can organize the best way to do this."

Stephen texts them to meet us at the diner and about half an hour later they show up.

"How can we help?" Monica asks.

"We need to formulate a plan. We figure with your military experience, you could help us come up with a good strategy," Stephen explains.

They shake their heads in agreement. Ian looks at the map while Monica talks to me.

"What would be the most effective strategy for the outcome we need?" Monica asks.

"The obvious result is killing them all without hurting any bystanders."

Friday night is the busiest night for bars. We would need to know how many were at each one. Surveillance could work, but we would need someone who could blend in.

"What about Kimberly?" I ask. "She looks like a college girl ready to party. If she could get inside and gauge how many we'll be dealing with, then we could come up with a more strategic plan."

That could work. I'm not sure Kimberly will be up for it though. I wave over Jane. "Do you think Kimberly could go undercover in the bars? Give us an estimate before we attack? She's the one that would blend in the most."

Jane laughs. "Maybe. It might not go well though. She gets nervous easily."

After a discussion with her, Kimberly is wired up and taking deep breaths.

"I'll be okay. I can do this. I can," she kept saying to herself. "I've never gone undercover before, but I can see why I was picked."

Everyone shakes their heads and wishes her luck.

"Testing, testing. Can you hear me?" Kimberly says into the microphone attached to her bra.

We can hear everything going on.

"Go ahead, beautiful. Girls like you shouldn't ever wait in line," the bouncer says.

"I'm inside," she whispers.

Kimberly continues to talk while inside the bar, giving us little pieces of information. "I'm staying close to the humans so they can't sense me. I count ten in the bar. No count for upstairs. I'm going to buy a drink, so I don't look suspicious and head to the next one."

We can hear her thanking the bartender, then she struts her way out to the next club, her heels clicking on the pavement.

"This one's dark. Going up to the bar."

We can easily tell when she goes inside because of the blaring music.

"Why do you look so down?" She asks.

"My wife just left me," the man says.

"Oh, honey, buy me a drink. Let's talk about it," Kimberly says in a flirty voice.

After spending about five minutes helping the guy feel better, it's on to the next one.

"Guys, there are guards at the entrance and exit. I think they know," she says softly into the mic.

What's going on? All we could hear was music and shuffling sounds.

"Can you hear me? They know. They know I'm here!"

"Kimberly? Can you hear me? Hello?"

The mic goes silent. I keep repeating myself until finally I can hear again.

"What brings you here?" a man asks.

"You mean to a club? I imagine the same reason everyone else is here. To have a good time."

He chuckles. "You smell like vampire, but don't look like one of us. Why are you really here?"

A static noise takes over the mic, which means Kimberly can't hear me.

"I already told you that. Can I go now?"

"We're coming!" I scream over the mic.

"Unfortunately, you're lying to me. I don't take kindly to liars."

I signal the group to go in. We ran through the club up to the top. The door swings open, and we try to save Kimberly, but we are too late. Her flesh is being torn from the bone. Kimberly cries out knowing she's about to die when one of the men lights a match and throws it toward her.

As much as I want to save her, the mission isn't complete without killing them. My attention is directed to the last three Blood Takers in the room. Hungry for revenge, I tear them apart and set fire to them with Jane's help.

I glance over at Stephen, who is kneeling over Kimberly's corpse. There's no bringing her back. We failed her tonight. I wish I could go back and come up with a different plan. One that means Kimberly would still be alive, but time machines aren't invented yet.

"You couldn't have known this was going to happen," Stephen says, placing his hand on my shoulder.

"Yes," I say brokenly, "I could."

25
Drake

It's only Monday night, and I'll see her tomorrow, but I can't wait. There are so many things I want to get off my chest. Fate keeps pushing us back together, and I will not deny it again.

The only problem, did she feel the same way? How would I tell Sasha I want more? How can I break the news that her persuasion never worked on me, and I know her secret? Hopefully, she'd realize they could trust me.

Standing in front of her door, I raise my hand to knock when the door swings open.

"What are you doing here?" Jane asks.

"Can I speak to Sasha?"

I glance behind Jane and see Sasha sitting awfully close to a guy on the couch. My heart plummets. *Maybe I don't know all her secrets after all.*

"N-never mind," I blurt. I stick my hands in my pockets and turn away from the house—away from Sasha—and hurry down the steps. *After all this time...* I shake my head, memories turning as bitter as ash on my tongue.

"Hey, wait!" I hear footsteps pounding after me. "Drake! Wait up!"

I can't bring myself to face her, but she grabs my arm and pops into view, anyway.

"Why'd you leave?"

Because you were sitting cozy with another man?

"they preoccupied you," I say instead. "I didn't want to interrupt."

"Preocc—." Suddenly, she laughs. "We were just going over some plans, Drake. It's not like *that*."

"You guys looked pretty chummy," I say carefully, choosing to study the green of the grass rather than the green of her eyes.

"Drake." She grabs my face in her hands and pulls my gaze up to hers. "Stephen and I are *so* not like that."

"You may not be," I shrug mulishly. "He definitely wants more."

Sasha rolls her eyes. "Don't be dramatic. Are you telling me the green-eyed monster got you?"

"Someone with green eyes has me," I mutter. Sasha just laughs.

It's now or never.

Deep down, I want to believe her, but Stephen obviously feels differently by his body language. A man can tell. Stephen wants more from Sasha.

"I need to talk to you about something. It's important. Can we go back to my place for a bit?"

Her eyes get huge before she responds. "Sure, if it's that important then Stephen can wait."

She walks beside me to my apartment. It's getting closer to summer, and you could tell by the warmer nights. When we make it inside, I turn on the air to cool it down a bit while she sits on the couch.

Am I ready? Palms sweaty and my dry mouth, I take her hand in mine. "I really like you. I want to be more. More than just whatever this is called."

Sasha starts stammering, closing her eyes and taking a deep

breath. "Th—there is so much ab—about me you don't know. If you d—did, you would ch—change your mind."

"I know your secret. I've known since that first night in the bar. Your persuasion doesn't work on me," I reply with a quirky smile, not knowing what her reaction would be.

"So, what am I?" she asks for confirmation.

"You're a vampire."

Immediately, her eyes go to the floor, and the room fall silent.

"Listen," I say, gripping her shoulders and forcing her to look at me. "You don't need to freak out, okay? I have told no one, and I won't. All right?"

She doesn't answer, and panic floods through me. What if she doesn't want me?

"I love you, Sasha. Only you. I'd protect you with my life."

"It'd be more likely I'd be protecting you," she sniffs. "Super strength and all that."

"Then I'll protect your secret with my life. How's that?" I chuck her chin up. She smiles faintly and lifts her hand to touch mine.

"It's a lot to process. And there's a lot to think about. Give me time, okay? Please?" She pulls my hand away from her face.

"There's no need to freak out."

"Let me think about it. There are a lot of things I have to consider," she replies, getting off the couch.

I watch her walk away. Something about her exit makes me feel like this is the last time I am going to see her.

26
Samuel

My humanity is gone. Another puppet for him to use and throw away whenever he wants. I tried hard to hold on to a sliver, to protect Sasha's secret, but it's becoming harder and harder.

"Tell me what you know about their plans? Don't hold back."

He has this effect on me, I can't lie to him. If I did, he'd know it. "Find your weakness and use it against you."

"What weakness is that?"

"I'm not sure. Wasn't around long enough to find out if they even found one. You pulled me too soon."

His hand slams down on the table, "nonsense. You gotta be able to give me something. Anything else that could prove useful against beating them?"

The compellingness of my sire is strong. It was never like this before, but I think it has something to do with giving into the lust. "Sasha's secret."

His eyes bores into mine, "what secret? Tell me now, or I'll rip your throat out."

My eyes close, trying to keep it in, but it's no use. "Sasha is their Savior. Our elder saw her eradicating the Blood Takers."

Without Sasha, will the Guardians be able to take us out? As much as I want to keep her secret, I can't.

"Well, that just won't do. We will need to kill her."

"I think I have a better idea." A smile displays. "there's this boy. She's been getting close to. A human. Let's capture him and use it to our advantage."

"See, this is where you belong. The out of box thinking is a nice change of pace."

I know it probably isn't the best idea throwing Drake under the bus, but if it means keeping Sasha alive longer, then so be it. His life isn't as important as hers.

I might be a Blood Taker now, but I can still prolong as much as I can. This sliver of humanity won't be around long, and once it's gone, I'm afraid of what I might do.

Jakob comes up with a plan of his own for Drake and didn't waste any time executing it. Only a mere hour later we have Drake in our sights.

"Get your hands off me," Drake snarls.

"Believe me, you'll be happy we're here," I say.

"What do you want?" Drake asks, shuffling, trying to get out of my grip around his arm. He'll never win, I'm much stronger than he will ever be.

"Well, let's talk about that inside," I reply again.

At this point, Drake is shaking. Did he think we were going to kill him? I could tell he recognized me from the bar with Sasha.

"I'm sure you recognize me from previous encounters, and that's why I'm here. Jakob and I wanted to pay you a visit. We've been watching Sasha closely and noticed you guys have been spending quite a lot of time together lately. Why's that?"

"We're just friends."

I laugh; he must think I'm an idiot. "Friends? You expect me to believe that. Friends don't leave half-dressed."

"Okay, so what? Why's that any of your business?"

I can hear his heartbeat quicken, and the blood pump through his veins, begging for me to take a quick taste.

"Well, like he said, we've been watching Sasha. We know you've been seeing each other, and we believe you know what she is. Am I right?" Jakob asks.

"What she is. Are you guys drunk? What are you talking about?"

"Don't play with me, boy. I don't have patience for idiots." I scream; my teeth next to his throat.

"Yes, you're right."

"Well, here is some good news. The good news is we would like to turn you, so you can be with Sasha," Jakob replies.

"Why do I have to be turned to be with her?"

I chuckle. "A vampire can't be in a relationship with a human. Hasn't she told you that yet? The minute you ask for more, she'll distance herself. She might be fooling around with you, but she knows the rules. If you're human, she can't *be* with you. End of story."

He didn't even wait a minute before replying. "Can you turn me now?"

I didn't waste a single moment, happy to oblige. His body goes cold and white as I drain him, almost to the point of death where I can choose to crush the fleeting spark that is human life, or give some of myself to him. I lay him out on the floor and watch for a moment as his eyes flick about the room, unfocused. He drinks from my wrist.

"Drink," I command. His hands come up and weakly snatch at my forearm.

He grabs my wrist, and my blood starts flowing into his mouth. Slowly, he regains his sight and strength.

"So, what now?"

"Now, we take you to feed," Jakob says with a smile on his face.

Why am I getting so much enjoyment out of turning Drake? How will this benefit us long term? Jakob hasn't let me in on his plan yet.

We walk out of the apartment building and onto the street. Drake tilts his nose up in the air and sniffs. It's obvious he can smell blood and hear heartbeats. A young lady walks down the street in the wrong place at the wrong time. He chases her down, but we didn't stop him. Instead, we cheer him on. A part of me cringes, appalled at what I'm not only watching, but encouraging. A bigger part, the part controlled by a bloodlust that Jakob forced me to submit to, reveled in it. At first, I tried to hold back, but Jakob didn't accept half measures. And now, my voice is the loudest.

"Drink more! Attaboy, drain her dry!"

It didn't matter because he wouldn't be able to stop. No matter what his brain tells him, he continues to drink.

"AHHHHHH!" he screams as her lifeless body drops on the cement.

"Welcome to the Blood Takers. Follow us!" we say in unison, my hand on his shoulder.

"Nice eyes," Jakob says as we walk off into the night.

27
Jane

"Take a deep breath, because you're going to feel stupid." I say, then takes her own deep breath. "They're right beneath us!"

"Who?" Sasha asks.

"The Blood Takers. They're living right here in Frankfort underground."

"How did you figure that out?"

"Don't worry. Let's just say I got some intel from an inside source."

"What the hell is that supposed to mean? You're hanging out with Blood Takers now?" Out of the corner of my eye, I notice Envio walking in. "What the hell is he doing here?"

I throw my hands up, protecting him. "He's on our side. You must trust me on this. He gave us Jakob's location. He hasn't been beside Jakob for weeks. See?"

I point to his eyes that are fluttering from red to his natural blue color. *Could he really be fighting it? Fighting against Jakob?*

Stephen walks into the house and immediately goes for his throat.

"Stop. Stop! He's on our side, Stephen. Take your damn hands off his throat or so help me…" I snarl.

They take in the pink of my cheeks, how brazenly my fangs borne, how willing I am to fight for this enemy.

Stephen yanks his hands back, and his eyes soar over to Sasha's. I jerk my head to the side, and he follows me to the corner, still glowering at the others.

"Listen, he just gave us Jakob's hiding spot. They've literally been right beneath us this entire time. Did you see his eyes?"

"No." He peers over at Envio, studying him. "Is he…?"

"Yes, his eyes are changing. I don't know if he truly is on our side, but we must at least go check out his information. If he's wrong, we'll kill him," Sasha says, not thinking twice about killing Envio if he's lying.

Stephen and Sasha join Envio and I back in the living room.

"Yeah, we heard. You'll kill me. I got it," Envio says dramatically. "I get it. You don't want to trust me, but all I wanted to do was get away from that scumbag. I didn't choose to become a Blood Taker. If they gave me the option, I'd much rather be one of you. I don't enjoy killing people, unless it's those abusive assholes. In that case, I love to watch them squirm and hear them beg for mercy."

This guy isn't kidding. At least, he's being honest about that.

"Well, with all the recruiting we've done… Do you think we have enough?" I ask Envio. It's his turn to tell us whether we even have a shot.

"Well, I'd say there are probably a hundred that live down there with Jakob. How many you got?"

"Plenty more," I reply with a grin on her face, winking at me.

If we are going to do this, it requires a plan of attack. It must be planned precisely down to a T. Going up against the oldest vampire and the strongest. Jakob likes to keep his attackers feed constantly to make sure they are always ready to pounce. They can't be trusted, but that's why Jakob loves having his followers. They are willing to do things—things not even he is willing to do sometimes.

Sneaky little bastards have been hiding right underneath us the entire time. Stephen sends out a mass alert to everyone to come back to Frankfort as soon as possible. We can hit them with the element of surprise, or they might see us from a mile away. Priority is taking Jakob out. If we can just do that, it will make everything else fall into place. All the other leaders have been neutralized. Thousands of Blood Takers have been taken out over the last couple of weeks. Who will they follow with Jakob out of the picture? Maybe without their leader, they'll stop slaughtering.

All the recruits arrive back in Frankfort for the takedown. We all secretly pray for tonight to go well. Envio tries to follow us, but there is no way they are going to let him lead us into a trap.

"Ian and Gabriel will stay with you to make sure you don't go anywhere. Hopefully I don't have to kill you when I get back," Stephen says, looking straight into Envio's eyes.

Understandably, I know the bond between a vampire and their maker. They will do anything to protect them, even if it means giving up their life most of the time. Envio can't be anywhere near Jakob tonight.

"Are you ready?" I ask Stephen.

"Always."

None of us are prepared to come face to face with Samuel. I don't think I can kill him.

Sasha, Stephen, and I lead the team inside what looks like an abandoned bomb shelter underground. It's dark and smelled musty. Walking deeper and deeper into the shelter, we finally come across some Blood Takers. Luckily, we kill them before they can alert anyone. In front of us are three different pathways. We didn't have a choice; splitting up is the only option.

"You take a group that way, Sasha that way, and I'll take this one," I command.

As we sneak up on some of them, one catches my eye. I stand still, not able to move a muscle.

"It's you," I say, wanting to give him an enormous hug. Maybe he's still him. It isn't like he wanted to become one of them. It was join, or his daughter would be thrown into this life or be killed. I close my eyes tight, trying to keep myself from crying.

"You shouldn't have come here. Now you all are going to die," he says, licking his lips.

I didn't even get time to respond before he busted my lip and flung me into the concrete wall behind him.

"Come on, it's me. What are you doing?" I yell, barely standing.

"Daddy? Is that you?" Amy says, coming out of the shadows behind him.

Samuel turns and looks at her. "That's my name, but I'm not your daddy anymore," he says, flinging her across the room too.

If Amy can't get through to him, no one can.

"Daddy, please. Remember when I was three and terrified of a monster hiding in my closet? You stayed up all night, waiting for that weird noise to appear to show me you had killed it." She laughs. "It was just a rat. You did that for me. You remember?"

Samuel stands up, more poised than before.

"Keep going!" I say. Maybe she can get through to him.

"I — Do you remember when we took our first family vacation? You and Mom saved up for years to take us to the beach. I wasn't a huge fan, but you promised I would grow to love it before we left. On that last day, we spent the whole day walking along the beach, sand between our toes, not worrying about a thing. Do you remember?"

"I—I remember. That's not me anymore. I can't be that guy. I've done unspeakable things. Things I could never forgive myself for. I saved you; this life was never meant for you. The Guardians will protect you. Sasha and Jane will protect you now."

"It doesn't have to be like this, Samuel," I say, speaking quickly and quietly. "Envio—remember him?"

Samuel's head swivels toward me, his red eyes intent and focused.

I hold both hands up and go on. "Yeah, he was a Blood Taker, remember? He's the one who turned me. And you know what? He's the good guy now. If he can fight the bloodlust, you can, too. You're as strong as he is. I know you are."

Samuel stumbles back a step.

"That's right." I keep on. "He fought the bloodlust and won. He's a Guardian. A red-eyed Guardian. You can be, too. Amy's here, Liz is here. You can still bat for the right team, okay? You can."

"I... I..." Samuel stutters, shaking his head—not like a 'no,' I didn't think, more like he couldn't wrap his mind around my words.

"You *can*," I insist. Without another word, he wheels and runs down the dark passageway.

Both of us stand there. He isn't back, but he did resist the urge to hurt us in that moment. That means more than anything. We didn't chase after him.

"We will tell no one. This is our little secret for now," I say to Amy.

Maybe when all of this is over, he can be himself again. I must keep my faith. Poor Liz has been heartbroken without him around. She's not been the same since he left with Jakob.

We veer around the bend, following their voices to find Stephen, Sasha, and Jakob fighting. He caused all of this, the reason we aren't human anymore. Jakob turned these people into monsters. For that, he deserves to die.

28
Sasha

Out of the shadows comes someone very dear from my past in Louisville. Tears flow down my face. It's Drake. *What is he doing here? He has been here this whole time?* I should have kept him safe, away from these slaughterers. I barely recognize him, the illuminating eyes and smug look on his face. My heart drops seeing him like that. I could have halted this, gotten back to him sooner, something. This is all my fault.

"Why the hell is he here with you?" I ask, punching Jakob square in the jaw. My pent-up frustration grows to the surface from all the friends he has taken from me.

"Here's a secret for both of you. Before Drake was your high school boyfriend and first love, he was my son."

Son? Drake is *his* son? My mind starts spinning, taking in the newfound information. How is this possible? Going back years ago, his father left after his accident. His evil father has created a new species and then turned him to spite me? What kind of father would do something like that? Honestly, it didn't surprise me because of how Jakob is. *Sadistic.*

"Drake? You can't do this. You don't have to be like him," I say, reaching my hand out for his. He smacks it away.

"He made me strong. Why did you not come back for me? I only did this to be with you. Am I not worth it? Point taken. My only loyalty is to my father. He gave me a gift," he says, looking over at Jakob with love in his eyes.

His words hurt me. I want more than anything to be with Drake, but now he's a monster. His eyes take me in, trying to gauge my next move. I can't kill him; it's Drake. We used to ride tricycles together, have sleepovers, and he was my first kiss.

Jakob keeps grinning and winking at Drake like he's proud of what he has done. He turned his own son into a monster and is proud of it. What kind of father would want this life for their child?

"Drake, you might not want to see this. Would you go wait with the others?" I ask, hoping there is still some good in there somewhere.

"I'm not gonna let you kill him," he says, swinging his leg around to hit me in my side, which makes me stumble.

"You guys focus on Jakob. I'll deal with him," I say, turning my head up to Drake. There's no way I'm going to let him stop Stephen and Jane from killing Jakob. His life is ending one way or another tonight. Nobody deserves death and pain more than him.

I throw a punch, but he catches it. "Seriously, you're gonna have to do better than that, little lady."

"Keep talking like that, and you really will piss me off, little boy." His demeaning words are getting to me. I didn't want to hurt him, but it appears I might not have a choice.

He jumps on me and starts pummeling. I try to catch my breath, but he's too quick. He's stronger than me.

"Drake, I know you have to still be in there. It's me. Why are you doing this?" I ask, my tears running as it finally hit me he didn't care anymore. "You can run away, far away, and I'll come find you when this is all over. Take the opportunity, or the others will kill you. Please. Listen to me."

His eyes flicker, going back and forth between red and his natural color.

"Go! I'll tell them you got away. They aren't worried about you right now, only Jakob and the others. Go."

He let go of my shirt and ran away.

I gain my composure, dusting off my jeans, and wipe away the blood from my face and busted lip. Running fast into the other room where they are holding Jakob, his face is bloody, and it looks like he's taken several intense blows to the head. My gaze meets a tire iron thrown on the floor.

"I told you I was going to make him suffer. All I needed was a few blows to the head without interference," Stephen says, smiling.

Jane and Stephen both take in my condition, but I wave them off. "I'm fine. Don't worry about me."

Stephen, Alaric, and I held his arms out so he couldn't go anywhere. Jane runs up, jumps on his shoulders, and rips his head off while we tear off his arms. Stephen lights a match, and it engulfs his entire body in the fire.

"You can beg for your life and mercy all you want, but we will not spare you... Thousands of innocent lives were taken at your command, and you created this everlasting life," Stephen explains as he points around the room. "You slaughtered our families, tore families apart all for the sake of your science experiment, and *oops*, you made a new species. You're a sick freak who took advantage of people for the sake of power. Can't be trusted, nor will you be. I won't feel an ounce of sorrow or guilt for taking your life today because by me doing so, so it will save many more lives."

Everything happened so quickly tonight; it leaves most wondering where Drake and Samuel went. When Jane says his name, my eyes water. My heart breaks from seeing him like that. As a human, Drake was gentle and kind, but as a Blood Taker, he had become pure evil. I did get through to him, but nobody knows how he would be once he's out in the world again.

"I tried to talk some sense into him and remind him of us, but he didn't care. Jakob turns him into a monster. One of the few men I have ever genuinely loved is gone," I lie through my teeth, but I can't tell them I let him go. They would immediately go after him.

We have lost so many of our own tonight but successfully taken down the most significant hub, including their leader, Jakob. We could all rest a little easier knowing Jakob will no longer be pulling the strings on his puppets.

After regrouping with the others, the small group heads back to my house.

The Guardians will grieve over the lives taken today, but we will also celebrate the victory of taking out four of the major hubs and their leaders. This is not the last of the Blood Takers, but an excellent start to the change we have been fighting for and the first step to saving humanity.

And maybe not just humanity, I think as images of the ones who were out there fighting their inner demons flickered across my mind's eye: Samuel. Envio. *Drake.*

This is the first step. But there are more Blood Takers out there, although leaderless now. The humans are oblivious, and it would terrify other vampires.

I look out my window as the others' voices continue quietly behind me.

With Jakob dead, he will no longer be a problem for our species, but what's next? What are we going to do about all his followers?

My mind races back to Drake, standing in front of me, fangs out, and not killing him. I couldn't blame myself, but would the others?

I don't understand how Jane could've killed Samuel. If I had been the one to find him, I'm not sure I could've done the same. Samuel was my friend, and he gave me a purpose after my family died. Could I have taken his life? *Not likely.* I would have choked. I had no regrets killing bad people or vampires who take human lives, but Samuel was different. He only joined that side because he had too, and any of us would have done the same if put in his situation.

We need to figure out a plan. What should we do next? There are too many out there, and if we don't figure out something quickly, this won't stay an advantage for long.

Stephen and Liz are talking on the couch. Jane didn't have the heart to tell her, so Stephen takes over.

"We've got something to tell you," Stephen says, taking Liz's hands in his.

"What? I don't like this build-up. It's bad news, isn't it? What happened?" Liz says, tears beginning to stream down her face.

"He didn't make---," He didn't even get to finish before the sobbing started. Samuel had helped her and showed her how to be a vampire when he could have easily just driven right past her. He saved her. "I'm so sorry, Liz."

Most of us knew this was going to happen when he joined Jakob's side. That doesn't mean we didn't pray every day that he would come back to us. The Samuel we all knew and loved deeply.

"What are your plans?" I rub my chin awaiting his answer.

Hell if I know. What do we do now?

TO BE CONTINUED...

FIND OUT WHAT HAPPENS NEXT IN THE *RISE OF THE BLOOD WAR*

Rise of the Blood War Book 2
Blurb

The Guardians have successfully dethroned the leader of the Blood Takers, but what about his loyal followers? With Jakob out of the picture, their plan was simple.

Set rules, reform the Rogues, and ultimately keep their secret.

Rule #1: Only drink what you need to survive.
Rule #2: Register with your assigned Governor.
Rule #3: No relationships with a human.

Their rules aren't hard. You follow them, you *live*. You break them, and you *die*.

When more and more rogues kept creeping up in existence, a *red flag* was raised. Someone was turning humans for personal gain and using them to *expose* their secrets.

Many lies were told on that fateful night of Jakob's death, but *no one* could have *foreseen* who was behind this...

Rise of the Blood War

Rise Book #2

USA Today Best Selling Author
ASHLEY ZAKRZEWSKI

1

Envio

As everyone gets back from the raid, I wonder what my next step will be. Will they accept me into the Guardians now that I proved my loyalty? My overall knowledge of the Blood Takers can prove quite useful to them. However, they didn't have to let me join to get the information.

There is an ache inside, one I never thought I'd feel once Jakob was killed. It isn't necessarily sadness, but emptiness. Hell, he deserved exactly what he got, if not way more. He was a horrible person, vampire, whatever. His reign has ended, and someone else needs to step up to the plate.

The Guardians have been waiting for this moment to change the outcome of fate for both species. How will they make things better? Once word gets out of his death, rogues will split ways and try to take the alpha spot.

Across the cheerful room, Jane is speaking with Sasha, and Stephen with Liz while I sit on the couch, enjoying a beer until spoken to. I am way out of my element here and didn't want to step on anyone's toes. Not one of them thanked me for my intel. I want to say it didn't bother me, but that would be a lie. Something I've never been great at doing except around Jakob. My whole time with him was a lie. I struggled, trying to hold on to my human side as long as I could. And I made it. Here I am, free of his brainwash and puppeteering. I no longer have to be that evil creature.

I walk over to Sasha and tap on her shoulder. "Hey, can I talk to you for a minute?"

She turns and glares at me. "Talking about something important here."

Her hair hits me in the face as she twirls back around to finish her conversation. I put my hand on her shoulder and twisted her back to face me.

"Don't ever do that again. You might think you're better than me, but don't forget without my information, Jakob would still be alive and more of you would have died. Choke on that for a second." I would never have taken her as the rude type, but I guess not all first impressions are good judges of character.

I make my way back to the couch until I can figure out what is going to happen next. It's not like I really have somewhere to be. The room's overall feel should be cheerful, they just killed Jakob after months of trying to figure out where he was hiding. This should be a celebration.

"Hey, what are you doing? You look like a lost puppy. Do I need to call your owner?" Jane says, nudging me.

"No, scotch-free now. See." I say, pointing to my back. "No strings attached."

Her smile gleams, "You can finally be your own man. A whole new look on life now, huh?"

"Pretty much. I can finally be myself. Whoever that is. I guess I have plenty of time to figure that out." I smile, laughing inside. "So what's the word? Why do they look so - uptight?"

"Everyone's upset about the ones we lost. Thrilled that Jakob will no longer be a problem, though. Now we've gotta decide what our next move is."

"You'll need to move quickly. Word will spread about Jakob fast. Rogues without a master, that's terrifying to think about."

"Yeah, see. That's what we're worried about. Those ones," Jane says, rolling her eyes and shaking her head. "The ones that we need to get under control and quick. Jakob's gone; now we need to fix his followers."

"Whatcha got planned in that beautiful head of yours, huh?" I ask, grazing my hand across her flawless cheek.

At my touch, her cheeks redden. Those wide, blue eyes meet mine, and her lips part, just slightly. I ach to kiss the sweet fullness of her mouth, but a bark of laughter from across the room shatters the moment. She blinks, and I pull away.

"Well, I don't know yet. Have to discuss it more in the morning. You gonna stay closer now that it's sorted out? You don't have to hide anymore."

I haven't thought about getting a spot at a different hotel. It would mean I will be closer to the Guardians, and of course, Jane.

"What'd you want?" Sasha interjects, hovering over me on the couch with her arms folded. Hell, did I even want to talk to her after that display of attitude earlier?

"I just wanted to know where I stand. You know, with the Guardians but Stephen's the leader so not sure why I was going to ask you."

Sasha waves over Stephen with a clenched jaw, "He wants to know where he stands. You're the leader."

"Well, your intel proved to be useful. Jane trusts you, but we'll have to work up to that. Maybe over time. We'll see." Stephen darts a look at Jane.

The look he gives her, makes me think she has been rooting for me from the inside. It is going to take time to win them over.

"We understand. You need more time for Envio to prove his loyalty. He'll prove it," Jane says, waving them away and giving her attention back to me. "They'll forgive you eventually. Just gotta give it time. Their tough cookies."

"Understood. Just wish they would see I'm not that person. It was all an act... forced to put on to survive. Believe me. I wouldn't be alive today if I weren't a good actor." I explain but didn't really need to. Jane knows, but the others didn't yet.

"Let's change the subject. Where ya gonna stay?"

"I could stay at the Village Inn. Give me a ride?" I ask, hoping to get some alone time with her.

She turns and looks at Sasha, knowing she heard the conversation, "I'm giving Envio a ride. You need me for anything?"

"Nope, not sure that's a good idea though. Can't he just walk?" Sasha rolls her eyes.

Jane turns her face back to me, "Don't mind her. She doesn't like when someone calls her out."

"I'll be back." Jane and I walk out the door and head to the car.

After getting in, the conversation turns silent. I could tell her mind is on overdrive.

"So, what things were you guys talking about? Just curious."

"What do you mean?"

"What kind of changes are you going to make now that Jakob's dead? Whatever they are, they need to be good and enforced. One thing I know about Jakob's followers is they don't follow unless you're brutal. There must be consequences."

Vampires could be difficult, Blood Takers even more so. They thrive on the thrill of the kill. The sounds of their victims yelling and screaming for mercy. Jakob might have let them kill thousands, but they didn't hesitate to follow his orders when he said no.

"Haven't really decided much yet. It's only been a matter of hours," Jane scoffs.

I know the roughness in her voice means I need to stop. Something happened—something she didn't want to tell anyone. I could feel it deep in my bones.

"So, anything unexpected happen while you were there?" I pry.

She shakes her head, but I know she is lying. Her breathing speeds up, and she closes her eyes as if to hold back tears. It hits me like a train, her sadness. What's even weirder, it's sadness and happiness at the same time.

We pull up to the Village Inn, and she waits outside while I get the room. The door jingles and I approach the pretty blonde at the front desk. Hopefully, the rooms are better kept than this area. The walls are covered in floral wallpaper, but it is peeling off, and there is a faint odor I can't place.

"Hello, a room for the week, please," I say, wanting to get out of this room as soon as possible.

"How many guests?" She asks.

"Just me. My girlfriend might come to visit but won't be staying."

The woman just smiled, "$240, please."

I throw the money on the counter as she slips the key into my hand. "Have a nice night."

Jane turns off the car and follows me into the room, slipping her jacket off and throwing it on the chair. Getting undressed already?

"Maybe I should've picked a better place," I say, taking in the room. It is just as bad as the reception area except for no foul odor. Or at least, yet. Jane sits down, not really paying attention. Her mind is somewhere else entirely. "You feelin' okay?"

"I'm fine. Why?"

"Well, not sure if you know this, but I figure you'd want to. As your maker, I can feel your emotions heavily." I take a deep breath, "I can feel your happiness and sadness right now. What's going on? You can be honest with me, ya know. I'm not one to judge. Look at the horrible things I've done at the hands of Jakob. It's going to take me a while to gain trust with your people."

Jane just sits at the edge of the bed. She didn't seem upset, but perplexed. Her shirt's riding up, showing the small of her back. I have to close my eyes and take a second to keep myself from pouncing on her.

"Oh, like what? What don't I know?" She purses her lips, antagonizing me.

"Did you know about your role in the Blood Takers?"

"Uhh, what do you mean my role? I never joined the Blood Takers."

"You didn't, but you were meant to. When I came to your house, it wasn't by happenstance. I was there for you. You know my - powers. I had seen you helping us to victory. But - you got away."

"You're telling me, I was meant to join the Blood Takers? I just don't believe that. You're out of your mind."

"My visions are usually right. Yours is the only one that didn't bleed true." I stare at the floor for a good minute, giving her time to understand the information. "I'm glad you didn't join and got away. If the Blood Takers had won, our species wouldn't have lasted long."

"Then why the hell would you come and seek me out? If you didn't want me on their side? Makes no sense."

"Jane - I had to do things - many things while with him I despised. It's one of those things that I regret most. You have no idea how much I was rooting for you."

"Why would you even care about me? You turned me so I would become a Blood Taker, that's all I'm hearing. YOU turned me. It was by choice."

I take her hands into mine, kneel down on the floor in front of her, "No - believe me, I had no intention of actually taking you back to Jakob. When I came inside your house, when our eyes met, something inside me awakened. I knew you were gonna be different than planned. You had gone through some of the same things I did - that makes us stronger. We know how to fight inner demons... don't you get it?"

I'm not proud of the things I did at Jakob's hands, but I also had to stay alive long enough for him to get killed. Someone would eventually overthrow him.

"I had to bide my time until the Guardians acted. I envisioned Sasha, but I wasn't going to tell Jakob about it. I never told anyone after you escaped from me. Jakob would have either killed me or sent me to kill Sasha and you." I get on the bed and sit beside her, "I couldn't kill the only chance of me being free. Free from Jakob. If he would have asked me, I'd have to say no, and then I'd be a goner. Jane, I had to do things to stay alive, to be someday free. I was the bad guy for a long time, but now I have my chance to do some good too."

She didn't answer me. Instead, she catches my eyes glancing down to the small of her back again, where her shirt has risen up, showing a good portion of bare skin. Out of urge, I lick my lips and she smiles. Quickly though, the smile is gone.

"What's wrong with you? Huh?" She asks, raising an eyebrow.

I lick my lips again, "Wouldn't you like to know! Believe me; you aren't ready for that. We're talking about you now. All we've been talking about is Jakob, no more about him. He's gone. His name's not even worth mentioning at this point. Tell me - what's going on. I know something's bothering you. Don't forget, I can tell. So just stop lying to me, and spill the beans."

"Let's just say we ran into someone tonight - we should have killed him -" Jane shakes her head, "but we didn't. No one knows, except this other person and me. I don't want anyone to find out."

My face drops, "What? Please tell me you aren't talking about Jakob? Please!"

She laughs, "Nope, he's dead. Burnt to a crisp, that asshole. Someone else."

Who could she be talking about? Who would be there?

"Samuel? Did you see him?" Her head nods, "Why didn't you kill him?"

She starts to cry, "He – just - His daughter started talking to him, trying to remind him of his life with her. You know, before Jakob. It seemed like he was himself for a second. Neither one of us could bring ourselves to kill him. I mean, he could have easily killed both of us, but he didn't."

I have faith that Samuel could fight it. He is a strong man with a lot of willpower, but the urge is a nasty bitch. "I'm glad you told me. He'll need someone that can help him through this. No one else out there can. I'll try to find him."

"I don't know if he'll have anything to do with you. He hated you."

"Well, the circumstances are different now. Don't ya think?"

I brush the loose strand of hair behind her ear and wipe away the wetness on her cheeks. Our eyes lock, and both of us lean in. Her lips touch mine, and a surge of electricity runs through me. I have daydreamed of this moment numerous times since our first kiss, but those didn't compare.

"Sorry—," She says, pulling away. "I don't think we should right now. There's too much going on to start something up. Hell, with our lives, I could die tomorrow."

"Exactly! Even the more reason not to let it stop us from doing what we want. I want you." I say, pulling her in for another kiss, but she pushes me away again.

"I'm not ready. I like you, Envio. I do, but the only man I ever dated was murdered by that maker of yours in front of me. There's no need to rush into anything. Not sure I can go through that again."

I understand her feelings. Seeing your first boyfriend killed in front of your eyes could be traumatic. "Okay, what about we just kick back and watch TV for a bit then? No funny business."

She nods and makes her way up to the pillow, grabbing the remote and turning the TV on.

"Shark week's on. Ever seen it?" She asks.

"Nope." Before becoming a vampire, I never had time for TV, but if it means being close to Jane, it's just what I want to do.

"Well then, Shark Week marathon it is," Jane says, smiling up at me before resting her head on my chest.

2

Sasha

We take a last night off, taking the time to clear our heads, and deal with all the good people we lost over the last couple of months.

"So, after taking last night off... we need to discuss what the future holds for the Guardians... anyone have any ideas they want to throw out?"

"Make rules. Claim territory, just like Jakob did. We won't be as evil as him, but he had that idea right," Stephen cocks his head to the side.

He has a point. That will make it harder for the rogues to hide, and making rules would set the boundaries, which they severely need.

"And by that, you mean...?" I purposely act stupid for him to elaborate.

"Enact territorial rulers. Vampires who make sure others in their area follow our rules. Whatever we decide on."

Like governors of the states? I didn't think that's what he would suggest, but it's not a bad idea. Someone has to be responsible for keeping vampires in their place and inflict consequences on those that break them. Each vampire territory would have what? What should we call it? Ruler sounds to Egyptian. Sheriff sounds human. We will have to come up with something better.

"Territorial rulers? Sounds lame. Weak. We aren't weak," I say, scoffing.

"Okay—what about constables or marshals?"

I look around the coffee table covered in wrinkled papers where he is marking up the plans. He didn't like any of them. "Let's just go with governor." We need to move on to more important things.

"What rules did you have in mind?" Liz asks, intrigued, wiping her face.

"I—don't know. Got anything in mind?" I ask.

#1: *Only drink what you need to survive.*

#2: *Register with your assigned Governor.*

#3: *No relationships with a human.*

"Those are what we need. How did you come up with those so fast?"

"Been thinking about rules for years. At some point, our society would need rules enforced. Glad it's gonna be us doing it."

If Jakob would have done something more like this when he was alive, I'm not sure we would have stood a chance. His numbers were big, but ours were growing too. Once we did more recruiting and the word spread about Jakob's death by our hands, they will fall in line.

"Next up, choosing the Governors. How should we divide it? North, South, East, West? Four states a piece? What?" It isn't really my decision to make since Stephen is the leader, but didn't see any harm in trying to help him out.

"Well, I'm not sure we have that many trusted people to assign someone to sets of four states. Right?" Stephen replies.

"Right, we should probably start small. As we have more trusted individuals, then we can divide it up better," Liz explains.

We have Stephen, Liz, Jane, and myself, but I'm not sure Liz will be up to it. *How do I bring this up without making her feel incompetent?*

"Next item of business. Governors," Stephen says.

Liz replies, "I'd say you, Sasha, and Jane for now."

"Agreed." Stephen replies.

We will also need enforcers, ones that deliver consequences for broken rules. But, we don't have to decide who that would be just yet.

The snow crunched underneath our feet as we trudge to the bar. The pounding of my head overwhelms my views, and I so desperately desire to get out of that damn house. Everyone besides Jane and I set out to travel for recruitment, and we are working to develop a game plan for Stephen when they get back.

This invasion will only work if we act quick and don't twiddle our thumbs. Every day more and more people are losing their lives, and it is finally our chance to put an end to it with no interference from Jakob.

As we arrive at the bar and continue inside, I could tell something is bothering Jane. "What's going on? Spill."

"What do you mean?" Her beer slams down on the table, and her head sways. "Nothing."

Six months ago, maybe she could have lied to me, but not now. I have picked up on a few things since meeting her and avoiding eye contact is one of her tells. "Okay, whatever. You'll tell me, eventually."

No need to pry. Samuel's death might still be upsetting her, and at her hands no less. I still couldn't fathom how she could have managed to go through with it. There isn't any animosity toward her, but if I would have been in her position, I just don't think I could've gone through with it. Blood Taker or not, he devoted his life to help the innocents, and for him not to see what the world would be like without Jakob is a shame. None of this would have been imaginable without him.

"So, when do we take off for our new positions? I know Stephen said as soon as they get back... but I like it here. Gonna miss it."

Jane, Stephen, and I are going to be governors of the states. The rest of the recruits in those states will support us by being given jobs of their own. There are still kinks we will need to work out, but we can figure those out later. "I've always wanted to travel, so weirdly looking forward to a change. We're young, and forever will be. Let's at least enjoy what we can, you know the little things."

One can always notice the negative things about life, but right now I try to stay positive. Sure, we will all have a lot on our plates, but once everything gets established and resolved, things will be better. Eyes on the prize.

"I guess I will be close to the ocean. Always wanted to go."

"See, something to look forward too. Keep that in mind, instead of thinking about all the negatives. It'll help."

After a fast feed, we crunch through the snow, trekking back to Samuel's house to meet the others. Hopefully they secured more recruits, and we can start the transition smoothly. *There goes that positive thinking.*

Stephen's been feeling the pressure since becoming the leader, and even though he probably thought he is doing a good job of disguising it from us, he isn't. Following in Samuel's footsteps will be hard, even for him. Most of the vampires are acquainted with Stephen already and they know he can be trusted. And that will be a huge asset when trying to completely change the way our society operates.

"Y'all got back fast! Hopefully that means it's good news?" Jane asks, striding inside and closing the door behind us.

"We definitely found some interesting recruits." Ian says, his eyes going over to four people sitting on the couch. "Meet Eliza, Malachi, Dr. Kendrick—You already know Envio."

What are they thinking? We can't trust Envio yet, not a smart move. "Gave in so easily, Stephen? Not sure that's a good idea." If we weren't friends, questioning the leader might get me in trouble, but not right now.

"Ian and I actually came up with some ideas while out. Before you jump my ass—let us explain." His hand is out in front of me, in a stop position. "Someone will watch him, but he could be useful in the next stage of this... we need people who will enforce our newfound rules... Envio, Eliza, and Malachi have agreed to do that."

"We don't even know the other two. How do we know their trustworthy?" Stephen brings in newcomers and just throws them one of most essential roles. What the hell is he thinking? I didn't trust Envio, even if he did give us the information that led to Jakob's death.

"I know Eliza and Malachi, personally. You want them on our side, you can bet that." Ian says, giving me a go to hell look.

Right now, I didn't have a choice in the matter, but to listen to Stephen. After all, he is our leader and I could trust him. "Fine, but anything goes wrong, it's on y'all."

Jane sits next to Envio, and you could tell the dynamic between them has shifted. There is something she isn't telling me, but I have a good idea what it could be. The way their eyes sparkle at each other, the sweet touches, and not-so-subtle glances... Envio and Jane are flirting. *You've got to be fucking kidding me.* Out of everyone, she chooses to be with the man that turned her—a man that tried to take her back to Jakob—*what the hell was wrong with her*? *What would Anthony think if he was here?*

Stephen and Ian have found out some things while out of town. Apparently rogues are still following Jakob, even after his death. This will present an obstacle, but nothing our new enforcers can't control, I presume. Some choose to die just because Jakob did and thought it is a test of their loyalty. *Idiots. Die for nothing, whatever.*

We must begin this with optimistic thoughts, wanting to see our world change for the better, but there will be hiccups along the way. It is going to take time and effort to make the rogues see reason. After all, they are used to being cold-blooded killers, and never been told no.

Things with us will be different. They will just have to learn or die. At least they are getting an option, which is far nicer than what

Jakob was doing while he was alive. Sometimes I think we need to be more like him for this to work, but ruthless isn't in any of us.

"Enough about that... let's talk about Dr. Kendrick." The middle-aged vampire raises his hand like he's in school. "He could be of great use to us with his medical knowledge. Under the radar, he's been experimenting on his wife."

"We don't need anymore experiments... look at how the last one turned out... seriously?" What is going on with me? The frustration is churning in my stomach.

"This time is different. Chill for a second." Ian says.

Telling me to chill only makes the fire in my gut want to back-hand him. *Take a deep breath.*

"Maybe, let me explain what he means..." The doctor says, stepping into the middle of the room. "My wife was like us... for a while... until one day the urge got to her. When I found her—she was distraught, realizing what she had done, but not for long. She wanted me to make sure she didn't become a killer—like them—so I locked her in our basement..."

My eyes get big. He locked her up? *How could you do that to your wife?* How would this be useful to us?

"I starved her—and she begged and pleaded—but I didn't give in. My wife wouldn't have wanted to live if she would kill innocent people. After about two weeks—you could notice the change—from fiery yellow back to her beautiful hazel."

"Wait—are you saying that someone can come back from it? How is that even possible?" I ask.

"That's exactly what he's saying, Sasha." Stephen interjects. "We don't know how far gone they can be for it to work—but it's a step in the right direction. What if we could reform the rogues and make them like us?"

The theory makes no sense. How would that work? Humanity can't be taken then restored. "No fucking way that works. At least not for those that have been slaughtering for years.—right?"

"We won't know until we try. That's why he came back with us. Figured it was worth a shot." Ian replies.

He might be some whack job like Jakob. "And how do we know you're even telling the truth? Where's your wife now?"

His posture loosens, and head hangs low. "She was killed by one of them. About a week ago."

Trusting new vampires will not happen easily, and I can't fathom how they believe him with no sort of proof. They might, but I will remain skeptical until he can verify his theory with hard evidence.

Everyday more rogues are choosing death, and maybe we could work this to our advantage. Use some of the ones that declined to side with us and hand over them to him to carry out his experiment instead of just killing them. We could find someplace to house them – form some cells – too bad we aren't sticking around or Jakob's underground tunnel would be perfect. It's got makeshift cells, and plenty of room – but we are leaving tomorrow and this place will be in our rearview.

"Actually— let's think about this..." If we lock them up, the ones we can arrest, then maybe we can rehabilitate them if his experiment really works. "Dr. Kendrick could test his theory out on rogues, it's not like we don't have a continuous supply of them right now."

Stephen rolls his eyes, "I mean obviously – that's the plan. Glad you are on board. Maybe we could do some good, and help them get some of their humanity back. That would be a gamechanger for us."

"How so?"

"We wouldn't have to execute all of them, only the ones that it didn't work on."

Again, if he can confirm his theory true. For all we know, it can be a whistleblower situation, and some nut case who locked his wife up and killed her.

They proceed to converse, but I excuse myself and go to my room, flopping on the bed. Drake, he must be the reason for all my built up irritation and annoyance. Nobody would guess because they all thought he is dead. Probably assumed the reason for my attitude is guilt, like Jane for killing Samuel.

A tap at the door causes me to groan, "what do ya want? Just wanted a sec by myself."

It opens and Stephen settles in my doorway, "what's goin' on with ya? I know everyone is still grieving, but it seems like it's something else."

"Don't really feel like talking about it..."

"I – understand but you can't go act like this around the recruits. We need them to want to help us, and having an attitude and pissing people off isn't gonna accomplish that."

Damn, Stephen must have really grown some balls to have the nerve to speak to me like that. "If someone has a problem with my attitude, then send them my way. The only person complaining so far is you..." Now, I stand in the middle of my room, arms folded across my chest, waiting for some smart-ass remark to come out of his mouth.

"Okay, if this is how you are gonna talk to me, then you definitely won't be heading up tomorrow. We'll end up losing every damn recruit we've built up. Stay behind and work on yourself, and whatever this..." Stephen's hand sways between us. "is."

I swear fire rays shoot at him from my eyes, torching him, but only in my imagination. The door bangs shut, and fumes are coming out of my head. The thing about my anger – it arises from so many things like Samuel's death, Drake's fake one, and now the fact we are willingly letting people fill roles that are very significant in this takeover. Stephen, as much as I hate to say it, is right.

If this is going to work, my trust should be put in Stephen and the others, to do the right thing. *Don't let negativity get to you.* If they trust this Dr. Kenrick and what he is telling us, then I should too. Shit, at this point, what the hell could we possibly lose from experimenting on rogues?

3
Jane

His hands skim over my collarbone, and I swat it off. "Stop. No need to make it obvious." My voice is barely a whisper, but with how our hearing works, everyone heard me.

"Make what obvious, Jane?" Sasha's eyes glaring into my soul as she strolls back into the living room. "Something you need to share with the class?"

Honestly, my fear keeps me from talking to anyone about it. Will they understand? They didn't know him like I did, and even though they are still skeptical of him, I know his true intentions. One day, they will understand. "Nope, nothing."

Sasha will be the one to have the biggest problem, but we aren't an item yet. There is way too much to do, and soon we will be split up on different sides of the country. How the hell will we make that work? *Ugh*. Better to stay how we are until things settle down.

"So," Sasha starts, but then takes a dramatic pause before continuing. "wanna apologize for the way I acted earlier. Our plan will only work if we are all on the same page. Sorry for making shit so difficult. It's nice to meet you guys, and look forward to working with you."

Her hands fall to her sides, and goes back to her room. The tension in the room earlier is chalk thick, and finally it is starting to thaw out.

"So, not to be rude, but she doesn't seem like the same girl you told us about…" Eliza says, side-eyeing Ian with her arms folded across her chest. "Like at all. She's the one that Liz had the vision about saving our species…"

Ian laughs and then shrugs, "same girl. Surprising, huh? She'll get back to normal, just needs time to deal with some stuff."

Envio won't stop caressing me, and it starts to drive me bananas. Currently, his hand is under my shirt, rubbing his hand softly up and down my back. The shivers down my spine are hard to fight off, but he won't quit.

"Jane's gonna take me back to the Inn. Just let me know where you want me tomorrow." Envio says, finally taking his hand off me, and shaking hands with everyone, before heading to my car.

As soon as my ass hits the seat, it comes out. "What the hell was that?" He knows I don't want anyone to know, and yet there he is on the couch caressing my collarbone where everyone can see. Can't he wait until we are alone?

"What—it's not my fault I can't keep my hands off you. The three days I was with Stephen, all I thought about was kissing you there." He points to my collarbone, "and many other places. Shoot me."

The urge to stifle my laugh didn't work, and his hand is now resting on my thigh as we drive to the Inn. As much as he loves to touch me, we haven't done anything besides feel each other up and make out a lot. Mostly because of me, not that the feelings aren't mutual, but a part of me wants to play it safe. Being a virgin can change things, like will he still find me attractive? He isn't that type of guy, not my Envio. Still, I won't bring it up until it is necessary, and that won't be anytime soon considering I didn't plan on sleeping with him right before we leave to be thousands of miles away from each other for an undetermined amount of time.

My heart shattered when Anthony was murdered, and it didn't want to go through something like that again. Besides, the short time I was seeing Anthony, there were no past relationships. Zilch. Until my father took his last breath, then I was free to do all the things I always wanted to, but couldn't. He refused to let me wear makeup, cut my hair, or even have friends. Now, I did them all without hesitation.

The bond we share, it isn't the fact Envio is my maker, but others will see it that way. Especially Sasha, and lately she has been a real bitch. Don't want to hear crap from her right now. Sure, he can tell my emotions, but there is so much more to us. The emotional and physical attraction is booming, but we also can understand each other's pasts. Certain things come out of that, like failure to trust others, and the need to always look behind you. It is a natural thing we will never be able to change, even if we want too.

"Alright, time to go inside and watch something." He gets out of the car, and I didn't move. "You comin'?"

"Oh… yeah," I reply, undoing my seatbelt and turning off the car. "Sorry, minds somewhere else."

Once inside, things get a little awkward. Somehow, all I can think about is being a virgin, and how he probably expects us to sleep together soon. Even vampires have needs, and the fire in my stomach wants him too. Still, this isn't something I am willing to rush into, and if he didn't understand that he isn't the man I think he is. *But, please understand.*

"You can sit down on the bed—you don't have to stand. What's going on with you?" Envio paces next to the bed with a inquisitive eyebrow wiggle.

If only you knew what was going on with me…

"It's like you're nervous to be around me all of a sudden. What gives?" He pats the bed next to him, urging me to sit. "Sit, relax. Did I do something to make you uncomfortable?"

Oh, god. Now, he is going to start blaming himself for this, and I can't let him do that. Envio has been nothing but a gentleman, and put no pressure on me to have sex with him. But, I know it's coming, we are both adults. And most adults have sex, especially when they are actively seeing someone.

"Please tell me what I did so I can fix it..." I can see the wheels in his brain turning, going over everything he did tonight. "Is it because of me touching you in front of them? If so, I'll try harder to keep control of myself..."

Fingers run through my jet-black hair, "There's just so much you don't know about me—As much as I know you want to have sex—and so do I; I think it's best if we wait." The thoughts probably swirling around in his mind right now—like he can have anyone he wants—and he chooses a girl that doesn't want to sleep with him.

"Ok—did I give you the impression we were having sex tonight? Just because I touch you, doesn't mean it requires sex after. You can be intimate without that, you know."

But that's just it. How would I know? I've kissed two guys my entire life, and one of them was with me, without a clue. "Okay, I think we should talk. Maybe if I explain..."

His hand waves, like he's rolling out a red carpet, "the floor is yours, babe."

Envio is looking at me intensely, and right now it's just the two of us. If we are going to be together as a couple at any point, I need to talk to him about stuff like this. "So, you know about intimacy and sex well, I don't." His eyebrow furrows, like he is trying to get my words. "I've never had sex before—and well, besides you—I've only ever kissed one other person. And it never went farther than that." Why do I feel like such an idiot? There is no shame in being a virgin, but there is stigma around it in society.

"Oh—I see." His forefinger touches his lips. "That's not a problem—at least for me. Did you think it would be?"

Of course, I did. "You probably screwed plenty of girls before me and have way more experience. How am I supposed to ever compete with that?" I didn't mean to blurt that out, but it happened. He knows exactly how I feel. Can he blame me? Everyone has had more sex than me, more experience, and terrified isn't even the right word to describe how I feel about potentially losing my virginity to him. What if I suck? He had plenty of girls to compare it to, and what if it makes him lose interest in me? I can now understand why all those girls were so crazy in high school over their boyfriends, and jealous. Not sure how I would react if some girl were to hit on Envio in front of me, probably rip her head off, but that's beside the point.

His hand cups the side of my face, and our eyes link. "Never will I go into how many girls I've slept with—but you don't have to compete with them. If I wanted to be with someone else, then you wouldn't be here, in my bed. Consuming all my thoughts like a schoolboy. I want you, no one else."

Then his lips are on mine, but only for a minute, and then I pull back and stare at him. "don't feel like you have to say these things to make me feel better—I can handle it."

There's a moment of silence, with only the wind howling outside, where I think maybe he isn't telling me the truth. But then his hands grip my hips, haul me forward, and we're kissing. It's intense but gentle the same way Envio is careful, yet all-in. His hand slides from my right hip, up the side of my thigh and then to my ass. I groan into his mouth, parting my lips. And he used this as an opportunity to deepen the kiss.

My hand slides over his biceps, squeezing his muscles, until I am grasping at his shoulders. Right now, I have half a mind to lay myself down and let him take me, rough and wild like I think he might be. But it's me and Envio—and things are too up in the air right now for that to happen, so I break the kiss. Breathing heavily, I hug his neck tight, and he holds me close, his grip firm and secure on my hips and back, until my breathing settles.

"Wow—so now you know what intimacy can be. Not every lingering kiss or touch has to lead to penetration."

The word makes me gawk like a prude, never having used the word before out loud.

"But sometimes it can lead to other places if you want it to... but you have to tell me..." His gigantic hands shift me on my side and his thumb brushes across my nipple. The pressure is ever-so-slight through the layers of my shirt. My breathing hitches, experiencing a coiling sensation between my legs as his thumb makes another pass.

"I—really like you—but," was all I can make out without whimpering. *Who was he? Why had I waited so long to experience something so blissful?*

With no warning, he removes his hand and sits up on the bed, looking down at me. "That's all for tonight. No rush—I'm a patient man."

The bulge in his pants signals he's ready, but didn't want to push past my boundaries, and that only makes me feel better about talking with him about my insecurities instead of keeping them bottled up inside. Envio proves to be the sweet, understanding guy I know he is, and I look forward to whatever our future holds.

"So, what should we watch?" He grabs the remote and turns the tv on. "There's not much on this time a night, but it's your turn to pick."

As I grab it, I snuggle into his chest, wondering how this relationship will work, and if we will ever have the chance to figure out whatever this is—the attraction and bond—maybe someday.

4
Envio

A chime comes through on both of our phones. It must be time to head out. *Fuck!* I pause to pick up my phone because whoever it is can see I read it. *Ugh.* Why did we have to take off today? Couldn't we delay another week? Surely nothing could go awry, right? I snicker to myself, because with rogues on the loose, a number of things can develop in one week. I curl over to pick my phone up from the nightstand and see his name.

Stephen: You'll come with me. Can you be at Samuel's in an hour?

I text back yes, and wrap my arms around Jane, craving to not let her leave. Last night seemed like a serious step for her, as far as being completely forthright with me about her feelings. Sure, me having more experience in the bedroom is accurate, but that shouldn't detract from the fact she is stunning. Jane didn't need to fret about being competent enough to satisfy me, because no matter what, she can. A simple stroke of hers leaves me craving more, and a smile warms me up inside. There isn't a chance in hell I am letting her go.

It killed me to discover all these uncertainties I am absolutely oblivious of, but her mood since tells me maybe they have gone. It clearly has been inhibiting her, and now it is out in the open. She learned where I presently stand, and all her insecurities can go bye-bye.

"So, sounds like we have to report for duty soon… is it wrong I prefer to blow them off and just remain in bed with you?" My hand curves around her face, and a soft kiss placed on her lips.

"Funny—I was just considering the same thing—but we can't. We've struggled to hard to get where we are to let it slip by for some cuddling." Jane declares, scrunching her nose at me. "But maybe twenty minutes more wouldn't hurt." Our heads plant on the bed, twisted in each other, wishing we can just continue like this. But both of us know what our future holds. Long distance, with no understanding when we will see each other again after taking off. The three days away from her killed me, and to recognize that I had to do it again, and for an undetermined amount of time is something I will struggle with for the first several months.

"So, do you think we'll remain in touch… you know, while we are busy taking over the world and all?" Her hands, fingers tangling around in mine.

Her head raises off my heart, and she glances up at me through her darkened lashes, "Why wouldn't we? Just because we won't be seeing each other doesn't mean we can't text or call. They have this feature called FaceTime, you know."

My dirty mind suddenly understands all the things we can do on there to continue to keep the chemistry alive. There is no reluctance in my mind that I will fight to be with her, and if that means being elsewhere for a little while, then it'll all be worth it. We truly have an eternity together, and another month or year won't hurt. Just have to maintain that in my mind. "So, do you think Sasha is ever gonna trust me? Jeez, did she look pissed when she saw me. She wanted to rip my head off right there in that room."

"She'll get over it, someday. Don't mind her. What's significant is Stephen giving you a chance… that's huge. Who expected that would ever happen? Not me, in a million years."

I peer over at the clock, and a groan escapes my throat, "it's time for us to leave if we are gonna make it on time."

"Come on," she reacts, tugging me back down on the bed. "I'm not ready to go yet..."

"If I lay down, there's a chance I may never get back up, and Stephen would murder me. I finally landed an opportunity to prove they can trust me—for real—as much as I would prefer to linger in this bed with you, I can't."

She sulks, and it is the cutest sight. "Fine." Her legs dangle over the side of the bed as she slips her boots on. "Then let's go."

She snatches her keys, but right before she opens the door, my hands grasp her arm, twirls her around to face me, and offer her perhaps the last kiss we might share for a lengthy time. "Something for you to look back on when on the road and missing me." She declines to let go of me, and it's sort of cute, which means our reunion later on will only be that much sweeter. "Seriously, get off me, will ya. We gotta get going." I say, parting our lips, and opening the door jokingly.

We spend the drive over to meet Stephen in silence. My hand on her thigh. Neither of us know what is going to take place once we leave Frankfort, but it is stride in the appropriate direction for the Guardians to safeguard humans. Nervousness is setting in about being their enforcer. Sure, Eliza and Malachi will watch me, even though I don't require a damn babysitter, but for now I will bite my tongue if it makes Stephen give me a chance to prove myself.

My phone beeps.

Stephen: Almost here?

"Seriously? What are we five minutes late and he's already texting you?" Jane says, annoyed.

"Don't want to piss him off... remember I'm the one that's gotta go with him." I add.

"Well, we are here, so he can settle himself."

As we rip up in the driveway, Stephen is leaning against the truck and twirling his keys.

"Sorry, my fault we're late. So, what's the plan?"

He explains I am traveling with him to California, and we will locate a place there first before speaking to any of the recruits. Malachi and Eliza are going with Sasha to New York. *Yeah, not resentful about that. Cold wasn't really my thing.* Jane's going to Texas. *Holy shit*, he isn't joking about being on opposite sides of the country.

"Everyone check in once they get to their destination... our recruits are expecting us in two days. That's when the actual work begins..." He declares, opening the truck door and slipping inside.

I crave to hug Jane, but Sasha is watching me like a hawk, and she has been clear about not wanting anybody to know about us. "Be careful, guys. Safe trip."

Everyone goes to their cars and head out on their various paths. But some of us can't wait until we get there.

Jane: California! No fair... You have to go to the San Monica Pier... I've heard it's glorious.

Stephen glances over at me, "so you ready to prove yourself? This position will not be pleasant for anyone, let alone someone who used to be a rogue."

"I'm ready. Don't worry about me."

"You sure? Probably won't take long before you run into someone you know, from Jakob. You can't offer anyone mercy, they'll eat shit up."

He acts like I've never killed someone, let alone a vampire before. I was fucking Blood Taker, for god's sake. I have spilled plenty of blood on my hands, except now it will be for a good cause. "Believe me, I won't hesitate. Hate for them is as powerful for me as it is for you. They didn't offer me no damn choice to become a monster."

On so many occasions, I have thought how differently things could've worked if someone from the Guardians found me instead of Jakob. I never would have massacred all those innocent people, but that would mean I never would've turned Jane, and I can't imagine how this would run without her.

However long I will be with Stephen, my plan is to show him just how serious I am about wanting to be a Guardian, and how much I hate rogues. It hits close to home, because even I struggled sometimes with giving into the lust, but I fought hard to keep my humanity. All in hope of a different world – a world where vampires didn't have to be feared – but that wasn't possible with Jakob alive.

"Ever been to California?" He asks, slugging me on the shoulder to bring me out of my head.

"Nope – you?" I've heard it has the best weather all year around, but nobody can afford to live there. My cousin once mentioned a hole in wall place called PNG's in a city called Covina. Apparently they serve the best pastrami sandwiches in the state.

"First time. Too bad we won't have time to go sightseeing for fun – we'll be too busy recruiting and finding rogues."

"At some point, all this will settle down, and you can do all the sight seeing you want." I say laughing. "After all, you are the almighty leader."

5

Sasha

Out of all the places he could have sent me, did it really have to be New York? Snow is falling in heaps but the onlookers don't seem to mind. Maybe they are just used to it. The dashboard shows it's 31 degrees outside, and people are still out walking down the streets, heading to their destinations.

The hustle and bustle is different from what I am used to. I have never really been a fan of big cities, and New York City seems as big as you can get.

"Please tell me traffic isn't always this bad?" Eliza mutters from the backseat.

It is a rhetorical question since none of us have ever been here. We have been sitting in almost bumper to bumper traffic for a good portion of thirty minutes, and maybe moved a fourth of a mile. Our view is a cafe' to the right of us, and a boutique shop to the left. To pass time, I sit and watch as the woman comes out of the boutique with several bags full of new items, that surely cost them thousands of dollars. Even with the temperature, they are wearing heels, which seems ridiculous, but I guess in New York City, you must always look your best, no matter the weather.

"If we don't get moving soon. I'll just walk. Screw the snow." Malachi voices his frustration.

Honestly, I can't blame him because at this rate, we wouldn't make it to our condo until dark. We should walk wherever we need to go after this debacle. Lesson number one has been learned.

On the drive up here, most of it is spent trying not to look in my rearview at those two making out, and feeling each other up. The thought of living with them permanently makes my stomach hurt, and god knows they are going to want their privacy.

It takes about two hours to go the three miles necessary to make it to our new home. Eliza and Malachi complain the whole time which only makes it more excruciating. If I have to live with these two, then they need to learn not to complain so damn much.

That leads me to wonder why Stephen sent them with me?

"This must be it." The GPS tells us we have reached our destination. "Let's go check out where we'll be staying."

The outside reminds me of the building the main character lives in from Gossip Girl, doorman and all. I grab my suitcase, and head inside the front door, telling them we didn't need any help with our stuff.

As we head to the elevator, on the right is a huge fitness center, like the size of Samuel's whole house, and the left a pool that could easily accommodate a hundred people.

The elevator door opens, we step inside, and push the button for the ninth floor. Our floor being so high won't bother us, but didn't humans get sick of carrying groceries or shopping bags that high or even higher? Pain in the ass, even if it's superiorly nice.

The elevator opens to our floor, and our door is right across the hall. I enter the key, and the door squeaks open faintly. Please don't let our bedrooms have attached walls or something.

"Holy crap," Eliza says.

When you first walk in, it's a hallway with a bathroom to the left, and a closet to the right. What a weird placement for a bathroom? Further down at the end, is the kitchen, which we won't use, and then it opens up to the living room. It's already furnished, with a dark grey sectional, large flat screen, and a coffee table, and still leaving plenty of open space.

"This is a great size room for the three of us. Plus plenty of room if we have company over." Eliza says, glancing around the living room.

The bigger question looming around in my head's how are we going to afford the rent? This is New York and this place has to be like $2,000 a month or more. I guess Stephen will give us more information upon check in.

"Let's go check out the bedrooms," Eliza winks at Malachi dropping her suitcase to the floor.

Oh god, if I have to listen to them banging every night, I'll pull my damn hair out. This living situation isn't ideal, but it's what Stephen wants, and after the bitch session the other day, I'll bide my time before complaining.

After touring the rest of the condo, the general consensus is our bedrooms are way too close together and the bathroom sits in between both. Not ideal by any means. Whoever decides the floor plans, needs to rethink it. How could this work for humans, having to go all the way by the front door, if someone else is already in this bathroom? Thankfully, we shouldn't have to worry about it too much.

"So, obviously Malachi and I will take this bedroom since it has two closets," she says to me, watching for my reaction.

Not only does it have two closets, but it's also significantly bigger. Before I open my mouth, Stephen's voice pops into my head telling me to be nice. Okay, of course I want the bigger bedroom, but I won't argue with Eliza, instead I just nod.

"That's fine. I like the esthetic of this one anyway." It has a king size bed with black sheets and comforter, but bright red pillows. I didn't mind it, but this floor to ceiling window situation would have to go. I'll have to get some curtains or something, because I don't want people to be able to see me, *ugh creepy*.

My suitcase sits on the bed as I start to unpack my crap into the six drawer dresser in the corner, realizing I really don't own that much stuff. Maybe eventually, I will go out and get some more outfits, but never really cared enough too.

A loud knock sounds at our front door, which carries me out of the bedroom, through the living room, and back down the hallway.

Opening the door slightly, "Can I help you?" A very tall man, probably close to six foot two is standing outside our door in a suit.

"You must be Sasha, I presume?" The man extends his hand. "I'm Kastiel. Stephen said you would be arriving today."

I put my finger up, and close the door, dialing Stephen's number for confirmation we should be expecting company.

"You make it?"

"About an hour ago. Someone named Kastiel is at our door. You know 'em?"

"Yeah, he's the one that secured the condo for you. He'll be one of your constituents. Let him in, and I'll talk to you later once we are settled in." The call drops, and I open the door.

"Sorry, can never be too careful these days. Come on in." I open the door for him to enter, and show him to the living room.

"So, you must be the infamous Sasha everyone has heard about. We are lucky to have found you when we did. Things wouldn't have worked out in our favor."

A couple weeks ago, the vision of Liz's got out somehow, and now everyone is aware of the special role I am supposed to play within the Guardians. It is creepy because some treat me like I am some kind of queen, being held up on a pedestal for all to see. "Yeah, still think the outcome would have been the same thus far. We all played our part in getting this far, and as long as we continue moving forward, things will go as anticipated."

Eliza and Malachi come into the room and introduce themselves, sitting down on the sectional to ask him about New York City, and things they could go out and explore tonight. They can't be serious. I doubt Stephen is going to let us go out and sight see when rogues are out everywhere. The whole point is to move as fast as we can, catch them and send them to Dr. Kenrick to work his supposed magic. Keep your eye on the ball.

"If you've never been here, there are probably plenty of things you want to see. Times Square, Statue of Liberty, and the tourist guide book you pick up will have plenty of suggestions." Kastiel mentions.

He seems like a pretty eye on the ball type of person, trying to get them to focus on the tasks at hand rather than sightseeing. I might already like him.

"Well, I just wanted to stop by, and offer help if you need it. But looks like you guys are settling in just fine. Here's my number if you need anything." He says, handing me a business card, and leaving.

After reviewing his business card, his demeanor makes sense now. He is some hot shot defense lawyer. Why would he be the one to get us this apartment and show up here to help us out? It seems a little out of his wheelhouse. Although, vampires are maintaining everyday jobs and maybe he is just one of those that has lived under the radar even after being turned.

Next time I see him, there are some questions I would like to ask, but after I get to know him a little better. I didn't want to seem nosy right off the bat.

"So, what do ya think?" Eliza says, strolling into my bedroom. "About the Kastiel guy?"

From the googly eyes, I know she is asking if I found him attractive. She has no idea about Drake and everything that happened, so I can't hold it against her. "He's not my type. And my heart belongs to someone else."

She settles on my bed, and pats it. "Like who? Wait, you are seeing someone? Give me all the juicy details?"

Eliza didn't seem like the nosey girl type, but apparently I was wrong in that assumption. Girl talk really isn't for me, and even if it was, she would be the last person I'd confide in about Drake or anything else. "Just my ex. Long story. But really, why don't you go get settled in? I've got plenty to do in here without you asking me a bunch of questions." I try to be nice about it, but sometimes I can't help it. She's in my bedroom, on my bed, asking me about my love life, like go the hell away.

She gets my point, and leaves the room, and shuts the door behind her. Finally, I could get some peace and quiet for a little while. After being stuck in that damn car with them the whole trip, some space away is needed. Maybe prepare myself for whatever is about to come next. Stephen really didn't give us much to go off, besides to come here to this address, and then check in for more details. My assumption is he would send us out to look for rogues, but he also mentioned something about meeting with people before getting into the search, so I will just patiently await my instructions from our leader. Until then, I lay down on the bed, turn on the tv to watch the news to see how much crap happens here, and get a feel for the crime rate. The only way to know what's abnormal is to get to know what's considered normal around here.

6
Stephen

Some might think being a leader is easy, like you just bark out orders and everyone follows them. It's nothing like that, in fact ever since my taking over, the stress has been high. An entire species is looking at me for guidance and that means every decision I make can be ridiculed, or worse. The one decision everyone agrees with, Jakob's death. With him out of the way, we finally have a chance at making our society work under these new rules. If we can get rogues under control, maybe things will fall in line. Yet, we still don't know how many are out there roaming the streets undetected, but that's where Envio, Eliza and Malachi come in. As the enforcers, their job will be to track them down, give them their options, and execute if necessary. As we find more vampires we can trust, the enforcement team will grow.

For now, we all need to settle into our sections, get to know those that have agreed to help, and then I need to come up with an overall plan.

The house Envio and I are staying at is nicer than I expected. Walking in the door, it has high vaulted ceilings, grand staircase, and just looks expensive. Envio shoves past me, and goes to check out the upstairs first. Not me, I take a left to go into the living room area which is close to 1000 square feet itself. Why did anyone need a living room this big? Next, the chef's eat in kitchen, and then a hallway. An adjacent door opens, and inside is a study with the back wall having ceiling to floor built in bookshelves and a desk. I have a feeling I will be spending a lot of time in here.

"Have you checked the upstairs yet?" Envio asks. "Why do we need all these extra rooms?"

"It's what we were set up with, just go with it," I reply, sitting in my new office.

When Samuel left with Jakob, to my surprise they appointed me the new leader, and it feels good they are putting their faith in me. Honestly, I figured everyone would choose Sasha to take over because of her prophecy but no. I never considered myself leader material, but at the end of the daty, I remind myself of all the people counting on me.

Once I finish settling in, Envio reminds me to call Sasha back. They were able to get settled in New York and Kastiel already stopped by. I thought I would have more time to get with them before the recruits show up, but they must be eager to get started.

When out recruiting earlier this week, Kastiel and I ran into each other by happenstance, and he offered to help out in anyway he could. The fact of the matter, I also like the fact he has been living alongside humans in a pretty demanding job without any issue. It gives me hope on how our future can be if we can get the rogues under control.

I dial her number, and wait for her to answer.

"Finally settled in?" She asks.

"As much as I can be for now. How'd it go with Kastiel? He seems like a good one, and really wants to help us get to the finish line."

"He's interesting, I guess. Eliza's over here already trying to basically set me with the guy. What's his role in all this?"

"Just a helping benefactor. He works a lot, but wants to help in some way. He'll cover the rent at your place indefinitely as a contribution to our cause." This helps us out because we can focus on building our new society rather than having to work. It's a win-win.

"So, we have people like him paying for our living situations? How do we know they can be trusted?"

"Leave that to me. I'll check in with details on the next phase soon." I say, before ending the call.

Sasha is an asset to us, but right now she needs to focus on herself and determine where all of this pent up anger is coming from. Until she does, I am worried about assigning anything to her. Like me, our recruits look up to her and since the vision got out, they need to believe in her now more than ever. So sending her around people isn't an option until she gets her emotions in check. What am I going to do if she ends up like this long term? Recruits will start to question what is happening, and what the hell would I tell them? No, I will just give her some time alone, to process whatever the heck is going on, and then we can all move forward.

The one that has surprised me is Envio. As much as we initially thought we couldn't trust him, my gut tells me his eagerness is genuine. He really wants to help build our society and earn our loyalty. We should at least give him the chance, after all, without his intel Jakob wouldn't be dead right now.

On the ride up to San Diego, Envio explained to me how once he found out we existed, he strived to hold on until the right time to approach us. Looking back, I can see his reasoning. If Jakob found out too soon, he never would have lived long enough to tell us his whereabouts.

For now, until proven otherwise, Envio is a part of this team, and those like Sasha who can't seem to trust him will have to get over it. That's exactly why he's with me and no one else right now. It is my decision to bring him onboard, and it only seems fitting that he be with me at first to keep him on the straight and narrow.

My eyes glance at the clock, it's already past seven. We have a meeting at eight.

"Envio, let's go. We're gonna be late." Shortly after, he runs down the stairs, out the door, and we are in the car.

Once we pull up to the bar, I turn to Envio. "These vampires we are meeting tonight represent someone very important."

"Got it, boss."

Alaric and Kieran are waiting inside for us. Why the hell am I so nervous? I'm the leader, and should exude confidence. These two work closely with the Senator on all things vampires related. It will come in handy to have someone on our side like them.

"There you are." Keiran says, standing up and shaking my hand.

"This is Envio. He's one of our enforcers."

The three of them shake hands, and then we get down to business. There has to be a reason they want to meet with me. "So what brings you guys here?"

Kerian explains that the Senator has some things he wants corrected first, like eliminating all the rogues in California, before sending out our enforcers to other states. Refraining from rolling my eyes where they could see, I get he's the Senator, but eradicating rogues is our top priority, and it could take months to track down and find all rogues within just this one state. What about the others? Why are they less important? Maybe working with this man will be harder than I thought. It's my first day in California and already he is trying to push me into something I don't agree with. Not a good sign.

"I don't know if I can agree to that. We can't wait to search the rest of the country for months. What if I assign one enforcer to California and surrounding states? We must reach a compromise because as the leader, I can't agree to pulling all of our resources to just the state of California."

Kieran and Alaric take a minute, looking at each other, before he responds. "I can take this back to him, but he won't be pleased. He thought working directly with you would make things simpler, but maybe he is wrong."

I stand my ground, getting up from the booth we are sitting in, and Envio doing the same. "As I said before coming here, I'm happy to work with him, but not if it means allocating all my resources only to him. That goes against what we are trying to accomplish. Let me know what he decides." Without waiting for a response, I leave the table with Envio following me, and head straight out of the door.

There is the confident leader I know I can be. This is why they put their faith in me. No matter how beneficial it can be to have him on our side, I would not agree to those terms. He has to be insane to think I would agree to that. California is huge, yes, but why should we completely prioritize them over the other states? My integrity as their leader will not be compromised.

"Um, thought you said best behavior, boss?" Envio asks, eyes wide. "Not that I'm complaining, because I'm loving this side of you. Take charge and do what's right. That's what we need."

"I'm not gonna let this guy come in and tell me how to operate. I don't care how much help he can provide."

I will wait around for word from Kerian and Alaric but if the Senator is smart, he would take my offer. He doesn't want to get on my bad side, no matter his title with the human government, because if isn't like he's going to help them find vampires. He wouldn't go against his own kind. So, the only logical explanation is to work together, and rid the world of all the evil.

7
Jane

First off, Texas is not my idea of a great place. Where are all the mountains and scenery? The only good thing is the beach, which I will probably never even get to see because Stephen is going to have me so damn busy. I am past the point of being optimistic being stuck down here, but the faster we can get things handled, the quicker I can possibly get out of here.

The drive hasn't been that bad until I hit Texas. The stretch of solar turbines are cool to see, but the overpowering smell of manure ruined that. The longer I drive, and the closer I get to my destination, I get worried. I'm currently out in the middle of nowhere. As the arrival time on my GPS dwindles down, I realize where I'm staying is going to be out in the middle of nowhere land, away from everything. Did Stephen hate me or something?

When I arrive at the address given, 504 Oak Drive, there is a quaint house sitting in the middle of nowhere, literally nothing around it as far as I can see. *You've got to be kidding me.* Why did I have to be the one sent out here to live like this? He could have at least put me closer to the beach.

Me: Please tell me y'all are staying in some secluded place, because this is where I am.

A picture is snapped and sent as proof.

Envio: Sorry to say, no. This place has like four empty bedrooms alone.

Of course I am the one to get stuck down here, while he's up there at some mansion. Why did I have to be the one to live alone? Why couldn't Sasha stay alone? She prefers it anyways. Hell, after her outburst, this would be perfect for her.

Opening my door, I grab my keys and head to the front door with my suitcase. Maybe the inside is nice, and has stuff to keep me occupied. *Fingers crossed.*

When it opens, what I see surprises me. The house is more roomy inside than it looks. The living room is quite large with a sofa and loveseat, and thank god a tv. The kitchen is small, which I don't mind, and the bedroom is a decent size with a comfortable bed for me to lounge on.

Envio: Have you at least gone inside?

Me: Okay, maybe the inside is better, but I'm still stuck out here by myself. Shoot me now!

The good thing is we are fast, so a trip to see each other wouldn't take very long. So, he can come keep me company when he has any downtime, but who knows when that will be.

Me: Still wish you were here.

As much as I might complain about us being seperated, he is in a great position now. Working directly alongside Stephen will give him the chance to prove how loyal he can be. A huge step in the right direction for him.

Envio: ;)

I get to unpacking and putting my stuff away, and then call Stephen to check in.

"I made it. But I'm not pleased about being this far away from civilization."

He laughs, "you aren't that far. Maybe fifteen minutes. It'll come in handy when you need to handle business. Rogues like the South for some reason, so you will stay busy and won't even notice."

"Okay, so what business would you like me to handle?"

"Settle in, and I'll give you the next phase once I have made my plan. You'll have a visitor later, Cassius. He will be helping you deal with things down there. Everyone is in such a hurry to dive right in, and here I thought you guys would be happy with a day of downtime once getting your stations. Jeez. I'll talk to you soon."

Who are all these new people and how did Stephen know them? Did he have some secret vampire notebook of affiliates or something? I just find it strange, since I've never heard of this person before, and all of the sudden, he's coming to help me. Does he not think I can handle it by myself down here? He should know better.

Envio is with him, and that means I can gain some insider information, like what is going on up there in California? Stephen has to be getting these vampires from somewhere and know that he can trust them. But how?

Me: Able to Facetime?

The silence will kill me. I have never been completely alone in any house. It makes it eerie, and so maybe he can help me pass the time until my so called visitor shows up.

The request displays on my screen and I lay back on my bed. "Hey there, stranger. How are things up there on the East Coast?" In the background I can see his bedroom, which is twice the size of mine. "Dang, you really are living in some sort of mansion, aren't you?"

He laughs, "something like that. Yours can't be that bad. How about a tour?"

As he requests, I walk him around the house, and show him where I would be living for gosh knows how long. "Still not that bad? I mean you're living like a damn king up there!"

"Well - if things - nevermind." He shakes his head, "shouldn't discuss things with you like that. Stephen needs to be able to trust me, and that means keeping my mouth shut unless asked."

"About what? Something I need to know?"

He lays down on his bed, "no. Forget it. What are your plans tonight? Shark week is on."

"Oh, apparently I'll be getting a visitor tonight. Some vampire named Cassius. Ever heard of him?"

"Sure haven't."

I notice the apprehension in his voice, like he might have something to worry about. "Don't worry, I'm not gonna fall in love with this guy or anything."

Like on cue, there is a knock on the door. That must be him.

"Hold on, I think he's here."

"Okay, well keep me on the phone. Just so I know everything's okay since we don't know this guy."

I smile into the camera and then sit it down on the living room table, as I walk to the door.

"Can I help you?"

"You must be Jane. Stephen sent me."

The man outside my house is not something Envio has to worry about. I've never been into blondes, especially the muscular types, but his green eyes were beautiful. "Yeah, come on in."

Even though Stephen trusts this vampire, doesn't mean I do right off the bat. It makes me feel better to know Envio is at least on the phone so he can hear everything.

"So, I take it you have gotten your things put away?" He asks, just inside the door.

"Most of it, yes. I only learned about your visit about twenty minutes ago."

"Oh, sorry for the short notice. Well, I'll be going. Just wanted to introduce myself, give you my number, and tell you I look forward to working with you."

His hand extends, shakes mine, "before you leave. How do you know Stephen? I've never heard him mention you." He might not tell me anything, but it is worth a shot.

"I met him earlier this week, but I knew Samuel from about a year ago. Too bad what happened to him. Really thought he would be around to see us wipe those assholes off the face of the planet once and for all."

"That makes sense. He was a great leader." It's times like this I wish I could tell him he is still alive and out there, but I can't. "It was nice meeting you."

He waves as he shuts the front door behind him.

I go to the couch, pick up the phone, and start chatting with Envio again. "He's gone. Doesn't seem like a bad guy, but who knows."

"There has to be a reason Stephen chose him to work with us. Gotta give him the benefit of the doubt just like they are giving me, remember?"

Okay, so maybe he's right. "Okay, spoken like a true follower. Look at you, already falling into line for him. He'll be happy with that."

I hear his door open, and then his voice. "Hey, I gotta go. Boss needs me. Call you soon."

And just like that I am by myself, and out in the middle of nowhere Texas. Could this get any worse?

8
Envio

Why didn't he knock? If Stephen starts asking questions about Jane, will I be able to keep lying? Sneaking around with her while living with him is going to be harder than I thought, but he might already have a clue.

"Who was that? Jane?" Stephen asks me, glaringly.

"Yeah, she wanted someone on the phone when that Cassius guy showed up. So she called me." I hate lying to people, but I will do it for her. Stephen can't know about us yet. Jane would kill me.

"Alright, well we need to talk and I gotta call the others so come down to my office, please."

Maybe he finally received word from Alaric about the Senator's ridiculous request. I still don't understand how he could think Stephen would ever agree to something like that. If he did, many vampires would advocate for a new leader. We need someone who is in it for all of our best interests, and not about pleasing one person like the Senator, just expecting him to do things his way.

I follow him down the stairs, and into his office, sitting down in one of the chairs. He dials Sasha and tells her to put everyone on speakerphone.

"Alright we are all here, what's going on?"

Stephen explains he has received some leads on two rogues out in New Mexico that are currently up to a kill count of roughly thirteen in two days. He wants Eliza, Malachi and I to meet up, and get them. This would be a perfect opportunity to test Dr. Kendrick's theory.

"You'll be going to Albuquerque, last lead was just a couple of hours ago. Sasha, wait for further instructions."

She didn't seem too happy with his response, but like me, orders must be followed whether we like them or not, right? She should know that better than anyone.

"Alright, we'll leave now." Malachi says, the door closing behind them.

He hangs up the phone with Sasha without even so much as a goodbye, and tells me to be careful. He doesn't know how dangerous they are, but since they recently fed and will continue to feed until they are caught, all three of us will be tracking them down.

We are all in Albuquerque, at a run down bar on the bad side of town, where Stephen says they were last seen. So, we all sit down, order a beer, and feel the place out. There's probably thirty people inside, but none of them are setting off my radar.

"Okay, they must have moved on. So, we should watch for any news alerts in the surrounding cities, and go from there."

Malachi and Eliza head to get a hotel, and hunker down until we get more news. They brought their laptop so they could stay up to date. "We'll call you if we get any hits."

It is our first assignment, and I don't know about them but I am eager to please Stephen and show him I can handle this position. It means a lot that he put his faith in me, and don't want to let him or the others down. Especially Jane. Without her, no one would have ever believed in me and mostly likely would have died alongside Jakob.

We all get rooms at this pay cash hotel, really run down, but cheap. I didn't plan on staying here long, so I didn't really care what it is like as long as I have somewhere to sit and monitor the news. It has a tv, and a bed. Check.

Jane: Got word Dr. Kendrick is coming out to Texas. Too bad you can't come with him.

A smile takes over my face, just like it always does when her name appears on my phone. I don't know why we questioned whether we would stay in touch after going separate ways.

Me: Well, if we catch these rogues, then we might be headed that way. They will be the first ones for him to prove his theory on. So, fingers crossed we find them soon so we can see each other. =)

It isn't always going to be this slow, and we need to take advantage of it while we can. So, if it means getting to see Jane, I'm all for it. Send me on any missions to take rogues back to Texas.

Jane: You actually think he's telling the truth? I mean I wasn't going to say anything in front of the others, but it seems kind of out there. Starvation and suddenly you are back to whatever is considered normal for us?

Like her, I am not going to voice my opinion out loud to anyone but her, but until the good doctor is able to prove his theory, I think everyone is skeptical. Stephen might want to believe it's true, but without evidence, how could anyone really know? This is the chance for him to provide truth to his theory, and then we can start reforming them. This will help our numbers increase without having to kill a bunch of rogues. But, how many rogues are actually going to agree? That will be the problem we run into.

As a former Blood Taker, I know how loyal they are to their way of life, and it's going to take a lot of convincing to turn them into one of us, starvation or not. Once they develop the thrill of the kill, it's not something you could easily get rid of. But if he could, more power to him.

Eliza: Got a hit in eastside Albuquerque, heading there now.

I pack up my backpack, throw it on my shoulders, and take off in lightning speed. Reaching a club, I could feel the presence of another. My eyes search the crowd, trying to pick one of them out, but there are too many humans. It's hard to get a read on rogues when surrounded by hearts thumping.

Eliza and I lock eyes, and she darts her eyes to the left side of the club, where I see Malachi making his way up to what I assume to be one of the rogues. From this far, it doesn't seem like an altercation is taking place until the rogue slams him on the ground, and the other one comes out of nowhere and puts his foot on Malachi's neck.

"What the hell do you think you are doing?" Eliza yells. "Get your filthy paws off me! Or so help me."

We have to get them, back to Jane's in Texas, but we would need all three of us to do it without hurting one of them.

Eliza and I must have had the same idea, we both spring into action, each grabbing one of them, and then Malachi taking over for his girlfriend.

"You guys are gonna have fun where you are going." I say, whispering in my rogue's ear before we all take off to Jane's.

She isn't kidding when she says she is living out in the middle of nowhere. I knock on the door, and the smile that wraps around her face when she opens the door and sees me, makes my day.

"Hey there. Got a package for the Doctor."

She ushers us inside, and downstairs. "You didn't tell me you had a basement."

"Didn't know I had it until he showed up. Guess that's the reason I'm out here in the boonies."

The basement is huge, and already has cells built, and an intercom system.

"Stick them each in one, and then lock it." Dr. Kendrick instructs us. "After that, you're free to go."

That's it? I am this close to Jane and there is no way I would be going back to California tonight.

Me: Already got a hotel in Albuquerque. I'll be home in morning. Cool?

I could see his face now reading that message, knowing he's already picking up on little things about Jane and I testing the waters. Although, that might work to my advantage and he will be cool with it.

Stephen: That's fine. Good work tonight. Keep it up.

Eliza and Malachi head back to New York, and I go sneak into Jane's bedroom.

"So, guess who gets to stay the night?" My hands up in the air.

Jane jumps up and down. "Really? Best news. Come here."

She pulls me down on the bed, and nuzzles into my chest. Sometimes I wish we could have met before we were turned, and maybe we could have led normal lives, got married, had kids, the whole nine yards. "I really missed you, sweetheart. I'll take whatever time I can get with you." I place a simple kiss on her lips, and take a moment to take her in. She really is the most beautiful woman I have ever seen, and from the moment I saw her that night, I knew I would do anything to be with her.

My fingers continue to run through her hair as she nuzzles into my chest, just enjoying the small amount of time we have together, before we are torn apart on opposite sides of the country again. Once Stephen comes up with his next phase, who knows when we will see each other next.

"So, how's the mansion life?" She asks, laughing.

I tickle her stomach, making her cackle, and laugh even harder. Anything to see her smile. "Oh you know, baller on a budget. Living the high life."

We get back into our comfortable cuddle puddle and the next few hours drift away, with us just caressing each other, and exploring our boundaries. Jane isn't ready for sex, but intimacy means just as much to me. Affection is my love language, and Jane has caught on to that. Every single touch, kiss, or caress drives me nuts.

Oh how I wish I didn't have to go back to California tomorrow, and could just stay and spend eternity just like this with her.

We still have not heard word from Kieran or Alaric, and honestly I am not surprised. If he chooses not to compromise, then that's on him. Stephen is doing the right thing.

Today Stephen has Governors, Enforcers, and the Registrars coming to the house to discuss the next phase in the takeover. I have overheard some of it, the registering. This isn't new. If we can get all the vampires registered, it will make it easier to determine how many we have, and where. The human government does the same thing with the census project. We need to get things in order now, so we can have more an idea what we are working with in the future.

The doorbell sounds, and Stephen and both make it to the door at the same time. I can't wait to see this Cassius guy that will be spending time with Jane in my absence. I never expected me to be jealous, but I guess maybe I am a little.

The door opens to Kieran, Alaric, and another vampire.

"Envio, you are already now these two, but this is Cassius from Texas."

"Nice to meet you." I say, shaking his hand.

So, first glance, this guy is solid muscle, which I don't think is her type anyway. It calms my jealousy a bit. "You guys ready for the next phase? I'm ready to get the ball rolling."

Eliza, Sasha, and Malachi show up next, and Stephen introduces everyone, and then finally Jane and a man named Kastiel. Not sure why he is wearing a suit, but whatever.

Everyone mingles getting to know each other and such, before Stephen explains his next implementation. It is important we all work together in this next phase simultaneously, which confrontation. The only person who might have a problem with that is Sasha, but we'll see.

"Alright everyone, let's get to the discussion. Don't want to waste anymore time." The room falls silent, everyone directing their attention to Stephen. "Let's talk about registering. This is where we are going to focus most of our efforts first."

"I agree. It'll help us determine how many we have, that way each of us can come up with a game plan for our areas." Sasha chimes in.

"Exactly. Kieran, Alaric, Cassius, and Kastiel have agreed to be our Registrars. Remember though, they hold jobs in the human world, so they will work on that as they are able, and report back to the Governor of said area. Any issues, they will report directly to me."

Kieran speaks up, handing Stephen a manilla envelope, "off topic, but we brought a list of leads on rogues."

"Envio, Eliza, and Malachi. Great job on your first tracking mission. Keep up the good work. These leads will be assigned to you. From now on, your direct liaison will be Sasha. Leads will be given to her to distribute amongst the three of you."

I try to hide my surprise that he is giving Sasha an actual role in this because of their outburst before we left Kentucky, but at the same time, without something she would just become a bigger pain in his ass. At least this way, the only vampires she talks to are the enforcers, and Stephen.

"Anyone have any questions about their assignments? I'd like everyone to start immediately." Stephen says, his eyes searching around the room for skepticism. "Alright, then let's get back to our areas and get to work."

Everyone leaves immediately which doesn't give me a chance to even say hi to Jane, but work is work.

"So, looks like he compromised. Figured he would." Stephen tells me, with a smile on his face. "He wants to be a part of our new society, then he will have to learn how to play fair."

He goes back into his office, and I await my orders from Sasha for my mission. I must say I'm not thrilled about having to work directly with her, especially knowing the problem she has with me, but if that's what it takes, then so be it.

9
Sasha

After my outburst, I am surprised to find Stephen trusting me as his liaison. I know I need to be better, and I'm trying. Things need to get back to normal, whatever that is.

My phone buzzes on the dresser, and Stephen sends pictures of the leads. Finally, we could start building our new society and get things in order. The longer wait, the more problems we are going to run into.

I knock on Eliza and Malachi's bedroom door, and ask them to come to the living room.

"Whatcha got for us?"

"Well, Malachi looks like you will be heading to Minnesota and Eliza to Pennsylvania. I'll continue to feed you guys any intel I get, but make sure you report back to me with your progress. The files will be sent to your phones."

I could tell they didn't want to be separated, but they will have to get over it. This isn't shaped around their relationship.

"Okay, boss." They exchange a kiss, and head out the door.

Me: Sending over your intel now. Keep me updated on your progress.

Envio still isn't my choice for the role, but Stephen trusts him. So for now, I need to get over it and just do my job.

The house is quiet, and it hits me that I will have the condo to myself while they are gone. Maybe I should take some time to go out and explore. I really need to feed, since I haven't while being in New York. The only problem is I don't know enough about my area yet to determine a good place to go, but I know just the person to call.

The line tills until he picks up.

"Hey, it's Sasha. Got any ideas on where I can go to feed?"

"There's a bar a couple blocks down from the condo. I'll meet you there and text you the address."

"Oh, you don't have to do that."

"I want to. See you there."

Well, I guess I don't have a choice now. He is the only one I know that has lived here and could give me pointers on things. Maybe, it's best to get a feel for him, as we will probably be seeing more of each other after the next phase. Stephen did tell me to try and trust these new recruits, and Kastiel seems like a good place to start.

I change into something more club like and head out the door. When I arrive at the address, this place is more like a club and has a bouncer with a rope and all. Welcome to New York City.

"Hey, you made it." Kastiel says, from the front of the line. "get up here. This is Lakyn."

The bouncer lets us in, and we find a quiet enough spot. "So he's a vampire? Another one holding down a regular job. So interesting to see."

"You will see that a lot around here. You'd be surprised how many vampires reside in New York. Most have jobs, and live a normal life. Being a vampire doesn't have to be a hindrance , at least to us."

Kastiel explains that there are many vampires that have specialty jobs: plastic surgeons, lawyers, and some even within the government itself. When they got turned, they just continued about their normal lives like it wasn't a bother. Things really are different outside of

Kentucky. Would we even know any of this if we didn't branch out when we did? Stephen must be having a ball trying to get a grip on the different things we are learning.

"Now, something you might not know, you are sorta a vampire celebrity. Once everyone got word of Liz's prophecy, everyone's faith went to you. Hoping you would be the one to finally change the outcome we were looking at with Jakob and the rogues. So, don't be surprised if you have some that are eager to meet you and ask questions. I have to admit having you here in New York is great."

Hearing him tell me this is a little bit intimidating that all of these vampires are looking to me to make this chance when Stephen is our leader. They should be looking at him. "I'm not that special. Just believe in what we can accomplish and want to get there. It seems like you do too."

He shows some hesitancy. "Honestly, we have been waiting for this. Just focused on staying off Jakob's radar as long as I could. I knew eventually someone would overthrow him, just took some time. As soon as I found out about his death, I knew I had to find Stephen and offer my help."

It's nice getting to know a little bit about Kastiel and learning a little bit about how things have been for him on this side of the country. I can see why Stephen trusts him and I have to say I do too.

A couple days have gone by, and the leads just keep rolling in. The problem we are running into is we are killing more rogues than reforming. The rules aren't hard to follow. Don't kill humans and don't get into relationships with them. How fucking hard is that? I guess for someone who is used to ripping out throats; it could be. Things need to start looking up, or this isn't going to work. Why would anyone rather die? Like what the hell is wrong with them? That doesn't even make sense. Isn't our instinct to survive? Even as humans? So we do anything to stay alive, right? Why the hell aren't the vampires doing that? Hell, we could live to be who knows how old, so why don't we enjoy it, by surviving alongside humans with an endless blood supply. The stupidity of some of these rogues is beside me. I'll never fucking understand. Ugh.

As much as I hate the Blood Takers, with Dr. Kendrick proving he can bring vampires back to be more like us, my conscience couldn't fathom killing every one of them. We should at least give them the option, and leave it up to them. With Jakob gone and out of the picture, my hope is more would join, but isn't how it's going currently.

Rogues are still out there begging for someone to wrangle them up and give them direction, instead of leaving them out there to do whatever they want. All vampires are aware of the new rules under Stephen's reign, and it is necessary to have a government in place or chaos ensues.

Our enforcers have done a great job at keeping the rogues to a small number, but no matter how much they did, someone is still turning humans. Last week, thousands of deaths were showcased all over the National News, which only brought attention to the odd killings that are continuing to grow in numbers across the United States.

Stephen and I have tried to keep rogues to a minimum, but every time our enforcers track one down, a new one pops up. Somewhere out there, a vampire is working against us, and we just need to find out who that is.

In my little bit of down time here and there, I try to see if I can find Drake. He might still be out there somewhere, but who knows what will happen if he appears on our radar?

Currently, Eliza and Malachi are off tracking down a rogue so I have the condo all to myself, which is how it should have been in the first place. Now more listening to them bang or makeout all night. Peaceful is just how I liked to spend my nights alone.

A knock on the door tells me Kastiel is here with more information for me.

"Come on in." I say, opening the door.

"We found one," Kastiel says, approaching me with a paper in hand.

"Where?"

He looks down at the paper, "New Jersey."

New Jersey? That's odd. We've never had a report of a rogue anywhere near there."I'll let Eliza know."

Crap, they are all three already out on missions, so this one will have to wait until tomorrow. Good thing about our new society, We have hundreds of thousands of vampires at this point running around. Most would call and report any suspicious activity or a rogue if they see one. It is part of the rules.

10
Envio

"Don't move another muscle. I don't want to be the bad guy here. Just register. That's all you have to do." I shout at the rogue, showing my teeth. The corn stalks are swaying in the wind behind him, and if he takes off in those, it will be hard to catch him. "Just register. So we can all go home." It is hard to talk sense into some rogues after they have followed Jakob for so long. Many refuse to live under our new rules, but in reality they must.

Under Jakob's reign, I was the bad guy most of the time, but when I joined the Guardians my hope was that would change. But, being the enforcer is my job now. It started as a way for me to prove my loyalty to them, or well mostly to Sasha. The only person that trusts me fully is Jane.

Oh, lovely Jane.

I have been tracking this rogue for days, but since he left bodies behind leaving a trail across Mississippi, it turns out to be quite easy. He left twenty to thirty dead bodies behind.. This is what we are trying to avoid—innocent people dying at the hands of vampires.

When Jakob was still alive, vampires could do whatever they wanted, but now things have changed.

"You know the rules. Two others are surrounding the area; you won't survive if you try to run." I rub my hands together, trying to contemplate his next move. They always run. This one, in particular, seems pretty far gone, and sometimes a sacrifice has to be made for the greater good. With the new rules, there would be no place for him. His choice needs to be made here and now.. *Register or be killed.*

After Jakob was eliminated, it has been easier to get some of them to reform, and those that did are sent to Dr. Kendrick to see if he could get them back to a normal vampire without the lust for killing.

"Make your choice," Eliza yells out from across the field, increasing her pitch and tapping her feet. "Register or meet your death."

Instead of answering, he takes off into the direction of Eliza through the cornstalks, evidently thinking he could kill and get past her. *Bad mistake.* Eliza is tough and isn't one you want to piss off. Jakob and his crew murdered her parents. This seems to be a running theme with the Guardians. Almost everyone has someone that one of the Blood Takers has killed. Eliza takes complete enjoyment with killing a rogue for not complying with our rules with no hesitation.

Across the field, I can hear Eliza scurrying. The stalks keep me from seeing them on the other side, but I know there is no way the rogue will get past her. Eliza and Malachi, her boyfriend, are an unstoppable team. As soon as I see the smoke, that indicated our job was finished, at least with this one. He didn't want to listen to reason.

Eliza isn't great about offering them the option, so I usually take charge in that aspect. Sasha won't be happy if we are murdering vampires out of spite; that goes against everything the Guardians stand for.

They come out of the stalks with a smile on their faces. Finding a rogue always puts them in a cheerful mood. "Alright, another one dead. Why can't they all just say no? It would make it so much easier." The smile on her face lets me know she isn't kidding in the slightest.

"Just remember, they have a choice. We aren't the bad guys here." I say, shaking my head.

The only problem I have with those two was they are always all over each other. When I see Eliza and Malachi together, it makes my heartache. I can still feel Jane; she is with me wherever I go. I know if she is in trouble or in pain. Our time apart hasn't diminished my feelings toward her. If anything, it's strengthened them. I understand her reasoning for not hooking up or jumping into anything. One day, we will be together again.

"What are you doing? You just gonna stand here looking at corn stalks all day?" Eliza asks.

"Oh— uh, I was just daydreaming. My bad." I laugh. Jane takes over my thoughts a lot.

"Well, Sasha'll be happy to hear about his death. Or well--- I mean that he died instead of registering, I mean." Eliza says, her arms hanging around Malachi's neck.

"Yeah, I'll call and update her and see what's next."

I dial Sasha's number with angst. "Checking in."

"How'd it go? Will you be bringing him back?"

"No- uh, he chose the other option."

The silence on the phone when explaining to her another rogue decided to die instead of joining us kills me. Even though Sasha is the leader now, she cares about vampires and wants even the evil ones to have a choice.

"There's plenty more where that came from. I'll send you some details about a new rogue shortly. You can stay the night there and then resume in the morning. Take the night off."

"Thanks, boss," I reply, hanging up the phone.

One day, the rogues will be eradicated, and we will be the only ones left. It's going to take some time, though. Not all of them are easy to track like the last one. Some are good at covering their tracks. They know we are watching.

"Alright, Sasha said to take the night off, and she'll send us details later. I'll head back to the hotel. See ya tomorrow."

We work closely, but I didn't necessarily like them. Every time I look at those two, it makes me think of what Jane and I could have been."Have fun, lovebirds," I yell, walking back to the hotel. I didn't like to drive if I didn't have to. Walking helps me clear my head, and I need it.

My phone dings.

Stephen: I heard y'all didn't have luck. Hopefully, this streak doesn't continue. We need to reform these rogues, not kill all of them. Dr. Kendrick thinks he's close. Keep up the excellent work.

Back at Jane's house, there is a basement where rogues were kept. We don't starve them, but only give them enough blood to sustain life. This helps them get back close enough to their human nature. Possibly regain their emotions again. We know it can be done.

As I approach the hotel, I turn on the TV to watch Shark week, which makes me think about Jane even more. I can't get this girl out of my head.

11
Eliza

It's been a long-awaited move for the Guardians to take over and make a new society for us. So far Stephen has done an unbelievable job keeping the killing to a minimum, besides the rabid rogues. Are they ever going to stop? Would we always have them working against us?

"What's the plan for today? Have ya heard anything on a new assignment?" He asks, laying down in bed, half-dressed after an ecstacy filled night."Nothing yet. Maybe we can go and do something today that's not job-related. Maybe dinner and a movie?" The smile on my face gets more significant because I miss spending time with him. Sure we work together, but it's not the same. Quality time is rare for us these days, but we still haven't lost our chemistry.

"I was thinking more like just stay in bed and never leave the room." His smile widens, and then he winks his beautiful greyish blue eyes at me.

"I'm good with that," I answer, realizing he just wants to be next to me.

I pull the blanket off of him, revealing his chiseled chest that always makes me want to jump him, but I don't.

His hands splay against his upper body, "How dare you. I'm not dressed."

Malachi is comical, and it is one of the things I love about him. He keeps me laughing, which is great to have during all of this bullshit. I climb up on the bed, making my way up to him. "Maybe I just want to lay with you in the bed." I said, snuggling into his chest, wishing we could stop and do this more often.

Sasha has been sending us out on missions every day. Malachi and I are always on the move, which we love to travel, but we want to be able to stop and enjoy things. Maybe one day. Our leader's actions prove he is in this for the long haul and wants our species to survive, unlike Jakob. They are polar opposites.. His goal isn't to hurt anyone, hell we have to give rogues a choice. They are the reason we are in this predicament in the first place. They chose to follow the wrong leader, and they should each pay for their crimes, but the decision is up to Stephen. I wasn't fond of this because they were the reason we were in this predicament in the first place. They followed the wrong leader, and they should each pay for their crimes.

"Whatcha thinking about sweetie?" He asks, running his fingers through my blonde hair. I love it when he does that, and it usually makes me daydream.

"Just how things are going and how our future looks. If we keep it up, maybe we could have a semi-normal life one day. That's our goal, isn't it?"

He nods, "I wanna be able to settle down and enjoy life with you. Running is fine now, but not forever. You know?"

I understand where he is coming from there. We want to enjoy the life and the opportunity given to us.

My phone buzzes on the nightstand, and his head perks up. The sighs echo off the walls because we both know what that means. I let it ring a couple of times before I finally answer.

"Eliza."

"Good, wasn't sure if you were going to answer. Y'all up for a new mission today?" Sasha asks, not expecting us to say no.

"Where?"

"Cherryhill, New Jersey."

I cock my head to the side, stunned at her response. *New jersey?* "Are you serious? What the heck are they doing out there?"

"Not sure, Rogue M.O. definitely."

"Alright, we're on it."

I throw my head back on the pillow, wishing we could have just let it go to voicemail. "Back to reality, babe. Maybe next time."

He rolls his eyes and leaves the bed, slipping on his pants and t-shirt. "Guess we better get going. The faster we find and kill them, the closer we are to a simple life."

As much as we love killing rogues, our future is what we look forward to and the reason we work continuously. In our mind, the faster we take out all the rogues, the closer we'll be to chill for more than just a couple of hours together.

I slip on my shorts, a tank top, and my converses ready to take on the day like any other. "Me and you against the world, baby."

Malachi takes the lead on driving us up to New Jersey. We could've just ran, but we like to drive and enjoy the views. It is a six-hour drive, and my favorite CD is in ***

As we pull up to the bar, I couldn't wait to stretch my legs. Road trips are fun, but after a couple of hours, my legs begin to feel like weights. "Finally, we're here." I step out of the car, and my knees almost buckle.

"Let's go get a drink and dance. Loosen up those legs of yours," Malachi says with a wink.

Walking into the bar, we are surprised to find it deserted. At most, there are ten people, including the two bartenders. It isn't likely the rogue would venture here because they like crowds. It still didn't make sense. Why here of all places?

We order two beers and take them on the dance floor. A slow song comes on, and I place my hands around his neck as he pulls me in close. I love it when he nuzzles my hair. We didn't necessarily have the time to waste, but stopping and enjoying each other is necessary for any relationship if you want it to last.

When the song is over, it is time to leave. We need to find this rogue. I chug down the last of our beers and head out to the next bar we could find. He has to be here somewhere.

My phone rings as we are walking down the strip of bars.

"Eliza."

"You won't find him at a bar. Just got another alert. He attacked a birthday party full of kids. Eight kids and six adults were found dead in a home on Evernever street."

"That sick asshole. It's one thing to kill adults, but kids? Now, I've got even more of a reason to kill this one."

"We are going to break the rules. No choice, just kill the rogue. I would never allow someone like that into our group even if they wanted too."

"Understood."

No way I will let a sicko like that walk the streets ever again.

"What's going on?" Malachi asks.

"Sick asshole killed a bunch of kids. Let's find him. Like yesterday."

Every wasted moment means one more possible death, and I don't want that on my conscience.

We need to figure out a perimeter around Evernever street. That's where this just happened. He couldn't be too far, especially if he's on a binge.

Malachi pulls out his phone, "That's just a couple blocks from here."

Is he near us? I didn't have any feeling that he is, but maybe I am not focused enough earlier to pay attention to it.

"Should we split up?" I ask. "See if we can sense anything in the other bars around here?"

"Do you think he would be at a bar right now?"

"Not sure. But I don't want to leave here until we are a hundred percent sure."

We split up and begin trailing through the bars to see if we detect anything. The first bar is a bust for me, and so is the second, but the third is right where we need to be.

Me: He's in Low Down Bar.

I wait for him to arrive before going any further. It is dangerous to try to take on a rogue alone because you never know how strong they're going to be.

"Where?" He ask, scouring over the crowd in the bar.

I point over to the corner, where a man is watching us. "There."

The man smiles and waves at us to come over.

"To what do I owe this pleasure?" The man says in a British accent with his arms extends out across the booth.

We look at each other and then back at him. "You've been killing children?" I thought I'd ask to make sure he is the one who did that. Rogues rarely lie about their kills.

"By God, you've already found out about that one. I'm still licking their blood off my fingers right now."

This one is worse than the rest I've encountered. "You don't even care that you just killed a bunch of kids?"

He looks up, scrunches his face, and says, "Should I? I mean, their blood is some of the best I've ever tasted. Why don't we ever explore that more?"

I want so badly to just rip him up in this bar, but I know that is against the rules. We couldn't do anything so public. How are we going to get him to leave the bar?

Malachi and I sit down across from him, biding our time until we could kill this son of a bitch.

"So, tell me about your favorite feed? You've gotta have one."

"Don't have one. I don't feed like you. We don't kill humans."

"Why's that? And don't give me some bullshit answer like because Sasha tells me I can't. Give me the real answer."

"I don't feed like you. Human blood fuels me, yes, but I also understand that without them, we have no future. Zilch, nada, nothing."

He shakes his head, getting frustrated. "Why does everyone keep saying that rubbish? Just because without them we have no future doesn't mean they should get to live normally and we have to hide. Why can't we be the superior ones? Why can't we make the rules?"

He has a good point, but who am I to second guess my leader? He has taken us this far, and I plan to stand behind her until she proves otherwise. "Why jeopardize what we have? War will kill millions, that's millions less for us to feed on. Why do you have such a problem with the way society is now? We don't have to hide; just be careful. There's a big difference there."

"We don't want to jeopardize our species before we even get to flourish. Think about it; we have the potential to live thousands of years if Jakob was right. You want to throw all that away just for some good blood and the thrill of the kill? I'm not. I'd rather enjoy a couple of thousand years on an island with this beautiful woman," Malachi explains.

He has been unusually quiet during this conversation, and it starts to worry me. Either he is having second thoughts or this rogue is somehow getting to him.

"So what's your name? Might as well, since we're going to be here for a while," I ask.

"Felix Twelvetrees. Pleased to meet you." He reaches his hand out to shake mine.

He's a frustrating rogue. The vamp killed a bunch of children, so there's that despisement. The one thing that always gets me fired up, them thinking they are doing the right thing.

I take out my phone under the table and text Sasha and Envio.

Me: Felix Twelvetrees. We have found him. Let you know when it's done.

I still want to find out as much as I could from him before we have to kill him. He might have some valuable information he's withholding and not even know it.

"So do you know Godric?" I ask, trying to fish for some information. "He's been trying to get a group of rogues together."

He touches his chin and then takes a huge sip of his whiskey. "Sounds familiar. What's he look like?"

"We've never met him so that we wouldn't know."

"Can't help ya then. I meet lots of people, as you can imagine. Most of the time I don't ask for names."

He is full of shit, and he knows who Godric is. "What brings you to New Jersey?"

He dances around the question, "It's a beautiful place, that is. Why wouldn't I want to come here?"

I shake my head, "Don't fuck with us. Tell us the real reason."

He rolls his eyes and starts fidgeting with his hands. "Do you know who Blakeley is?"

Malachi and I both look at each other, shaking our heads. The name doesn't sound familiar at all.

Me: Do you know a Blakeley?

"No, name doesn't ring a bell. Should we?"

His face shows his amusement. "Yes, you should. For hunters, or whatever they call you, you aren't very wise."

Sasha: No

Now my interest is piqued, and I need to figure out who this Blakeley person is. "Is she a rogue?"

He laughs in response. "She will be."

So he's hunting to turn her into a rogue. What is so special about her? "She a family member? Ex-girlfriend?"

"None of the above. She related to someone vital. You tell Sasha, she better watch out. I'm not the only one looking for her. Once found, it'll be a game-changer."

Blakeley quickly becomes my top priority. He has given us some pertinent information that we wouldn't have otherwise caught wind of, and that makes this grueling conversation worth it in the end.

"Let's finish this conversation outside, shall we?" Felix says, taking his last sip of whiskey and slamming it down on the table. "Damn, I'll never get sick of the taste."

Malachi and I follow him outside and into an alley. Did he not care about dying, or is he so confident he would kill us first?

"No chance that you could just let me go. Tell them you killed me. We had a nice conversation, I thought."

He is grasping at straws because that is never going to happen. He is dying tonight, one way or another. There is no way we were letting him walk these streets again.

I chuckle in response to his question, and then Malachi is on top of him. "Are you a sicko? Do you like preying on innocent children?" He asks, ripping one arm off and then starting on the other.

Between the screaming, he yells. "I was taught this way. It's not something you can just stop cold turkey. Hell, it's worse than cocaine addiction. I've dealt with that too."

We work together to shut him up, but the banter continues as we tear every limb from his body. Malachi siphones a little bit of gas out of our car and pours it on Felix. I smile as a box of matches is pulled out of my back pocket. "Burn in hell for all eternity. You'll pay for what you've done. Don't think this is the end for you," I explain, lighting the match and throwing it at him. We watch him burn to char, and it is satisfying knowing he is off the streets, and kids would be safe again.

My mind, however, keeps reverting to Blakeley. Who is she? Why is she important to the rogues? Now our mission is to figure that out.

12

Warwick

My eyes gaze upon the beauty of my wife, Tasha, carrying our daughter, Avery, in the nursery. She is a natural and I recognize what a remarkable mother she will be. I remain outside the door, not requiring my presence known, just observing from afar in silence.

"Good, girl. Drink up. You'll need it to grow big and strong someday," Tasha whispers to Avery.

My smile broadens, hearing her talk to our little girl so sweetly. Avery is our very own miracle.

We got married about five years, and we sought to conceive, but no luck. Two years passed, and we reached out to a specialist to identify out why we were having so much trouble becoming pregnant. The doctor advised us that it impedes her Fallopian tubes, causing pregnancy to be impossible without medical interference. It annihilated us. We considered having the operation to unblock them and commenced trying again afterwards. Another two years went by, and our miracle finally arrived.

"Honey?" She yells, not noticing I am right outside the entrance.

I linger a couple of seconds, "yes, sweetheart? Everything okay?"

"Can you run and get some more formula? We're almost out, and with that snowstorm coming in, I don't want to take any chances of running out."

As I clutch my coat and slide my boots on, she follows me to the door. "I'll be back soon. Love you." I

It is freezing outside with the approaching snowstorm and already has three inches of snow on the ground. Our car broke down a couple of weeks ago, and we didn't have the cash to look at a new one yet. So, my boots slosh through the snow blended with grass in my driveway and to the main road. As long as I remain on course, I should be back before the storm hits.

The farther I go, the more the heaping snow is progressing to come down. My body is now shivering from the downturn in temperature, and I need to get inside quickly. A truck slows down beside me.

"Need a ride?" the man asks, all bundled up. "I'm headed into town."

I glance uneasily down the road, pondering the bite of the chill against the threats inherent in hitchhiking.

Another blustery gust makes my teeth chatter.

"You know, ordinarily, I'd say no," I grin, "But it's freezing out here, and the wife says we're almost outta formula. I'd be thankful for the lift."

I jump in the truck and slam the door behind me, holding my hands up to the vent to gain some warmth on them.

"Where ya headed?" he asks, the truck moving.

"That store just up the road." The man is driving relatively slow, which I assume is because of the amount of snow on the ground, but then he continues looking behind the car. "Something wrong? You keep peering out your rearview mirror."

The truck slows down and trails over to the side of the road. "Looks like I have a flat. I must fix it real quick."

As he gets out and leaves the door open, I keep my hands in front of the vent, hoping my fingers would warm up soon. Out of my periphery, I see the man coming toward me and jerk back. "What the hell are you doing?"

He forces a cloth against my face, and, within moments, I could feel myself slipping.

When my eyes flicker open, the first element I notice is a starlit sky through a barred window. The temperature has declined severely, and shivering is the factor keeping my body warm. I struggle to be as quiet as possible, but with every slight movement, the chains around my wrists sound. The man would know I'm awake now. My chances of escaping diminish when a creak sounds and footsteps are heading toward me.

"My, my. You're already awake," he says, gripping my collar.

"Please. Don't kill me." I beg, identifying it wouldn't do any good. "I'll give you anything you want."

"Yes, you will," he responds with a demonic grin, right before he bites into my neck.

The pinching of his fangs entering my neck makes me flinch. I struggle to push him off, the chains are too tight.

"Stop! Why the hell are you doing this?" I ask, panicking.

The creature didn't stop, but pushes my head to the side. I could see the blood dripping down my shoulder, and it hurt worse the more I struggle.

"Please let me go!"

He draws away, "Shut up, will ya? Can't ya see I'm busy?"

"I don't understand why you're doing this?" I ask as he settles up over me, blood spattered across his face, my blood.

"Cause I want to. That a good enough answer for ya?"

"Uh - what are you?" I ask, wishing to know what I am in the presence of because he isn't human. Couldn't be. Instead of acknowledging my query, he leans back in. I scowl at the touch of his long tongue stroking firmly over the puncture wounds in my flesh. I swallow hard, resisting the compulsion to gag. When he concludes, his thumb rubs the wound and then he ascends back upstairs.

Hours later, I could hear rustling around upstairs. Is the creature going to let me go? My Avery is going to grow up without her father. I shake my head frantically, seeking to run the negative thoughts away.

It is essential I remain positive, try to make the man see reason, or maybe even a tad guilty. From what I've observed so far, it'll be a long shot.

"What do you want with me?" I holler, rattling the chains to get his attention.

The creature opens the squeaky door, and with each noisy tread, my breathing quivers. The light provided by the window displays blood smeared across his face. His knees bend, and we are now at eye level. "I want to turn you."

"Turn - turn me?" His answer scares me shitless. My body stills. There is no way he is a vampire? I sealed my eyes. *They're not real, don't be absurd.* There must to be a better explanation.

"Into a vampire. A cold-blooded killer." He snarls, his fangs making a debut. "You might just be the best one yet. We'll see."

"Why are you doing this?" My voice trembles. "Why me?"

He chuckles, "I need to create rogues. As many as I can. Build an army."

My eyes increase, "An army for what?"

"I'm sick of humans getting to live life in the open while we've gotta hide. Or so the Guardians think. They couldn't be more wrong; the vampire is superior. We could wipe humans out easily."

"So, that's what the army's for? To wipe out humans?"

"Wow, you catch on fast," he murmurs.

In one swift move, the wound on my neck reopens from his fangs, and he is sipping from me farther. All the while, I couldn't get the thought of vampires being real out of my mind. He has to be a psycho, one of those crazy fanatics that wears fake vampire fangs.

As he proceeds to consume, an icy sensation passes through my body, and weakness is setting in. "What's happening to me?"

"I'm draining you. You'll soon wake up a vampire."

He must be insane, perhaps an escapee from a psychiatric hospital or something. Why did I have to accept a lift from a stranger? I know better and look where it has me. Here. Stuck in this place.

It isn't long before my thoughts subside. I struggle to hold my eyes open. They are like weights, and soon enough, they get the best of me.

I jerk awake, quickly realizing the chains are still bearing me hostage. My stomach is rumbling, and something unsettling piques my interest. What is that smell? I sniff the air again; it is sweet, like brown sugar barbeque sauce. Boy, did that sound fantastic right about now. I pull on the chains to create some noise, but to my surprise, they break. The cuffs clang to the floor, and I peer in dismay at my wrists. I wiggle them, peering at the expanse of pale flesh-they didn't look any different from yesterday. And yet... I peek back to the iron laying on the ground. How the hell did I do that? I tried multiple times yesterday, and they didn't even budge an inch.

My feet urge up the stairs to the basement door. "Let me out of here. NOW!"

The creature laughs as he opens the door, "Finally, you're awake."

As we near the living room, there the smell is again. Shock takes over me when I curve the corner and see a young woman around age twenty-two hung up from the ceiling. Blood coats across her face and neck. As much as I crave to regurgitate at the sight, it makes my stomach ache worse.

He forces me closer. "I left just enough for you. Don't fight it."

My will is resisting the impulse so hard. The body requires sustenance, but my mind is at a hell no viewpoint. I will not be the killer he calls for. Or anything like him. Whatever that is, vampire or not.

He keeps nudging me closer to her, the young girl whose pulse is galloping. "Nope, I'll pass," I say, shuffling away.

He catches me by the collar of my shirt, "I don't wanna have to force you. That'll take all the fun out of it."

The floral wallpaper covers the antiquated room, and it looks like it's closing in on me. I am hungry, almost to the point of starvation.

My body takes over, and it is no longer attending to my mind, defying direct orders. *You're not a monster. Don't do it.*

Suddenly, his hot breath is against my ear as he hisses, "Do it, or maybe I need to bring your family…"

I didn't even let him finish. "Okay, hold on."

My family. A beautiful family I'd likely never see again after this. If I become anything like him, they will be in danger.

Never in a million years did I expect to come face to face with a fucking vampire. I consider running, but he'd catch me. And then what? Kill me, right? At least if I did what he asks, maybe I'd get to see her again someday. He didn't seem like one to change his mind, and I couldn't let my wife and daughter get trapped in the middle of this situation.

My legs take me closer as the saliva sloshes around my mouth from the marvelous smell. I lick my lips and whispers, "I'm so sorry."

My eyes close, and a moan leaves my mouth as my fangs penetrate the wound in her neck, letting blood stream out into my mouth. Her screams become background noise along with the creature cheering me on. My body wants it so badly, but my mind knows this means I am now a monster just like him. There is no going back. A single tear drops from my eye as her body thrashes around.

"Please. Stop." She gasps out the words, wide eyes frantic.

The thirst takes over, and there is nothing I can do to stop it. The young girl's body wanes, her weight sagging in the cuffs.

"Please." Her voice reverberates in my mind. "I don't wanna die."

Moments later, her lifeless body hangs from the cuffs as I lick the last drop of blood off her neck.

"Good boy. Godric applauds you." He claps, as if I just put on a very enticing show.

"Godric?" I ask, glancing around like there is an audience.

He giggles and points at himself, "Me, idiot."

I consumed this young woman to appease my craving, playing into Godric's strategy of developing into a monster.

"Let's talk business. Have a seat."

The couch is a violet velvet Victorian loveseat, atop a dingy gray rug. This isn't Godric's house. guess this must have been my victim's house. My eyes roam around the living room; her poor lifeless body still dangling from the ceiling. On the stand next to the TV is a picture of a little boy around age two. A child would be without his mom because of my actions.

"Pay attention, boy. We've got important things to discuss." He glares, snapping at me. "Here's the same spill I give the others. Only turn young males, no women. Kill as many as you'd like, as often as you'd like. The more attention you get from the media, the better."

My eyebrow wrinkles. Why can't we turn women? He must have been a sexist human before, and it carried into him now. I bump my shoulders. Instead, I need to concentrate on getting the hell away from him. "Where should I start?"

"Wherever you wanna go. As long as you're killing and turning, I really don't give a shit." He twists his hand at me, gesturing me to take off.

The front door opens, and my feet carry me farther away from Godric. I will leave and never look back, but there is one thing I need to do first.

I trudge across the grassy landscape and could see my home off in the distance. We reside on an acre of land, which could have made this problematic during daylight. She could discover me from a far distance approaching the house. To my luck, the sun went down.

When I reach the house from the side without windows, my chest tightens, picking up her heartbeat rhythm in my ears. *I can do this. Fight it for her.*

I step in the front door after working up sufficient courage to reveal my face. It is as if time remains still, and she didn't move. Her gaze tells me she isn't certain if this is real.

"Is that really you?" She asks, tears spilling down on her cheeks, engorging me in a bear hug. "Where've you been? It has worried me sick." She says, pecking me on the cheek.

"I got picked up by someone. They found me on the side of the road, almost hypothermic." This is the first time I outright lied to my wife.

She asks me something, but it becomes background noise to the music of her throbbing heartbeat and the blood pumping through her veins. The longer I stand there, the tougher it is to control.

Before I get going, I need to see Avery. The nursery is just as I left it, my sweatshirt on the back of the rocking chair, and the book I read to her every night before I went to bed in the seat. Would this be the last time I would get to see my precious Avery? Would she remember me? The thought of her growing up without a father sinks in, and I don't want to leave her, but it's what's best for her and Tasha.

I lean over the crib and pluck her up. Her pretty blue eyes gaze at me, and a slight smile appears, delighted to see her daddy. I place kisses on her cheek as I lay her in the crib, and I leave the room before the urge sets in.

"Can't stay. Not sure when I'll be back."

It flabbergasts Tasha. "You just got back. Where the heck are you going?"

"I can't tell you." I curve to the exit, and she clutches me.

"Please, don't leave. We need you. I need you."

Growing up, I always promised never to leave my child without a father. I despised men who deserted their kids. Never in a million years would I think I would turn into that man.

"I love you," I confess to her, letting her hand slide out of mine as I step out the door. I did the toughest thing imaginable and step out on my family.

13
Eliza

Malachi and I rented a condo and decided to take a mini-vacation while we could. We've been hunting rogues for the last half of the year straight without a break, and we needed some R&R. It wasn't that we weren't faithful to the Guardians and their cause, but we needed to stop and spend some time together. Sasha was a great leader and cared about the longevity of vampires. Jakob, not so much. I wish I could have been a part of the cause back when they slaughtered him and got my revenge for my parents.

"So, this is nice, isn't it?" Malachi asked, nuzzling into my hair on the California king bed.

He was amazing. We were together before we got turned, and he fought to save me. He didn't have to, he could've run, but he didn't. Malachi was one of the bravest vampires I knew, and he was all mine. I'd never let him go; eternal love was true for us. Before all this vampire stuff happened, we planned on getting married and starting a family, but that wasn't the case now. Our priorities had changed. They had to. Our dream of having a family closed, but we still had each other.

When we heard about the Guardians shutting down the Blood

Takers, we immediately knew it was a cause we wanted to take part in. When they enlisted us as enforcers, it became surreal. We were always traveling, not staying in one place too long, and it was just what we wanted. We knew we were essential to the cause but able to do what we wanted, travel.

"Earth to Liza?" Malachi snapped, trying to get my attention.

"Oh---sorry. My mind wandered off dangerously. Go figure. You know how that goes." I laughed because it happened a lot with me. Daydreaming was something that happened regularly.

"You enjoying yourself? Going stir crazy yet?"

I'm not used to staying in the same place for long; it felt almost wrong. We had so many things that we should be doing, but instead, we were lounging around a condo. "We've been here for days. I'm getting there."

"Come on, enjoy it while we can. Let's take a bath in the jacuzzi tub. That'll make you feel better." He kissed me and looked deeply into my eyes. "Maybe one day, we can settle down somewhere when all of this is under control. Hell, maybe even just travel to all the places we've wanted to go but haven't been able to."

We couldn't do anything until we got the Godric situation under control, and the rogues. Who knew how long that was going to take? Years? Decades? Let's hope not. "I'll wait patiently until that day."

His kiss turned from sweet to passionate, and I knew what he wanted. We've always done well in that area of our relationship. I ran my fingers through his coarse brown hair, and then my phone rang. My eyes opened, and I glanced over at my phone.

"Please, just let it ring. I'm not ready to go back yet. I need some alone time with you. Just us."

Reality set back in quick when Envio's name appeared on my phone. I sat there for a moment looking at him, like could I not answer?

"Don't answer it. One more day. Just one." Malachi glared at me. "Come on. They can handle whatever it is for one more day. We deserve this."

"Sorry." I apologized, answering, "Eliza."

"Listen, there's been an attack in Plano. Since you guys are already there, can you check it out and get back to me? I know you are on vacation, but it would be a tremendous help."

Envio knew how important it was to take time for himself, but he wouldn't be calling if necessary. "Sure. Text me the address. I'll go check it out and call you back."

Malachi didn't take his eyes off me the whole time. "Seriously? Are you going? Why couldn't you just tell him you would check it out tomorrow?"

"Because I'm loyal. It's the job I signed up for. So did you. So stop complaining." I didn't want to be rude, but honestly, I was missing the rush of catching rogues. It's something I enjoyed.

"You can go. I'll stay here. I'm taking my last day. Have fun." He said, going to the bathroom to soak in the jacuzzi tub.

Typically, we didn't fight, but apparently, he wasn't giving up his last day of vacation for anything. My phone beeped with the address from Envio. "I'll be back."

I rushed onto the scene, surrounded by police officers. Time to shine. In and out without being noticed. As I rushed in, the smell of dead carcasses was undeniable and rank. Going from room to room, taking pictures of the bodies so I could inspect closer later, one thing seemed odd, no blood. Hell, if I didn't know any better, I would think they died of natural causes. No wounds on the neck, so they closed the wounds when done. Something just didn't seem right here. I could hear officers coming inside, so I bailed. Not that they could ever catch me.

I needed more information before informing Envio and Sasha. I ran back to the condo and grabbed my forged media badge. The officers usually didn't pay close attention when they checked anyways. "I'll be back. Gonna try to get some more information from the officers on scene." I said, rushing out of the room, blowing him a kiss.

I pushed through the crowd emerging outside the retirement

home to the front. "Excuse me, officer?" I waved my hands, trying to get one of their attention.

"Yes, miss. This is a crime scene. Please stay back. A press conference will be later."

"I---just have one question. How many deceased?" I had an idea, but they were already taking bodies out when I got on the scene earlier.

The officer glared at me. "Off the record, seventy-two."

My jaw elongated on the cement below me. It would take a group of rogues to do that kind of damage. A vampire can only drink so much. They'd be sick after five humans if not before. I shoved my way back out of the crowd and made my way to the condo. Maybe I could come across more clues from the photos that could point me in the direction of who or what was responsible for this wrongdoing.

I uploaded the pictures to my laptop so I could look for more clues to this puzzle. I was sure it was a rabid pack of rogues responsible, why would a human drain them? Where were the exit points? Rogues were usually like wolves; they love the thrill of the kill. They like blood. Sure they like drinking it, but they love to see it smeared on bodies or walls. So, this just doesn't add up as a rogue killing unless someone was trying to cover up their tracks, and threw us off. Could this have been Godric and a new crew? Some sort of weird initiation thing?

Picture after picture, I looked over the bodies to see if I had missed anything. Upon completion, I believed this was rogues.

"Bad news," I said, hearing Envio sigh on the other end.

"Shit, okay. Hit me."

"72 dead here in Texas. Retirement home wiped out."

"Okay? And? Rogues?"

"Bodies drained and no marks. Gotta be. But something else I feel I should share with you, there were no visible wounds."

"What do you mean?"

"They closed up the bite wounds afterward. And there was no blood like anywhere. Whatever it was, they were super careful about covering up their tracks to make this seem like natural causes or a plague that hit a retirement home. It's eerie as shit, Envio. Not sure what else to say."

"Okay. I'll call and let Sasha know. Enjoy the rest of your vacation."

I didn't mention Godric because the governors had enough on their plates. Rogues were emerging all over, and there was only one explanation: Godric. Sasha was made aware of his plan to overthrow the Guardians and try to go back to the Blood Taker days, but we would never let that happen. Things were going better than ever with the news. Vampires now had a way of life that they had to abide by, which made our species' longevity protected.

After I showered, the television announced breaking news. "A local nursing house was a scene of an attack today when seventy-two confirmed residents were found dead. There are no leads on the perpetrators at this time, but investigators assure us they are working hard to find the people responsible."

Interesting. No mention of the bodies being drained, although I'm sure that's something they didn't want everyone to know. It could cause panic. I wonder what the coroner would rule once he's had a look at the bodies. There was no natural explanation for what happened.

Something weird was happening, and we needed to figure out fast. Whoever this pack was, they were careful, and that made this even scarier.

Me: Have you gotten anything back on Blakely yet?
Envio: Not yet. Let you know as soon as I do.

14
Warwick

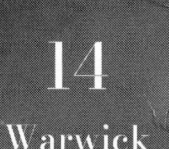

I fell into his trap, and have become exactly what he wanted. A killer. No matter how much blood I consume, my body feels like it's starving. I have been on a binger for quite some time now, and could never get enough. They taste so fucking good.

I search for my next meal, finding a restaurant with three beautiful ladies sitting outside, enjoying a cigarette. "Any chance I could get one?" I flash my smile, and that usually works.

A young woman smiles, "Sure. It's menthol."

My smile gets more prominent, "Just my type." I sit at the table next to them, knowing it won't take long before they ask me to join. I like playing with my food. It only takes a couple of minutes before they are anxiously asking me to join them for drinks. Happy to oblige. We have some meaningless conversation where they mostly talk about men being dogs. I assume they want me to tell them about how good of a guy I am or tell them all men aren't that way, but not worth my time.

When they get ready to leave, I would follow them. My stomach is aching, begging for nourishment.

"It was nice to meet you. See you around sometime."

The girls walk down the street to their cars, and I start to follow them until a van pulls up, and someone drags me inside. "What the fuck are you doing? Do you have any clue who I am?" Instead of giving me an answer, they inject me with something that immediately causes my eyes to close.

―――

I wake in a concrete room, with three vampires staring at me. Where am I?

"Who the hell are you?" I ask, glancing around this room, which only sent me back to my time with Godric.

"I'd like to ask you the same thing. Why have you been causing such a ruckus?" A young vamp asks,Arms folded.

"Ruckus? What do you mean?"

"All the bodies you've left behind? You know the rules, that's not tolerated."

They are the Guardians? From where I am sitting, they don't look so scary.

"Who's your maker?" A young man asks.

"I'll ask the questions here. Who are you?" Did they expect me to start telling them shit without knowing who the hell they are? They kidnap me, throw me in a basement, and assume they would get answers to all their questions. What's in it for me?

"Stephen. Leader of the Guardians."

Oh, so there's my confirmation. Apparently, I have attracted them onto my scent with all the bodies I leave behind. Yet, they still didn't seem that scary or powerful. Nothing like Godric described. They are the reason Godric is building this army.

"Why are you raising suspicion of our kind?"

"Our kind? You guys aren't real vampires. You care too much about humans. Don't give me a lecture." I refuse to sit here and listen to their nonsense. I've heard about the things they've done to rogues.

Some kind of science experiment to turn them back into humans, and I want no part of that.

"We've been living alongside humans for a reason. They're our food source. Without them, we don't survive."

All I could focus on was the clicking of heels coming down the hallway towards me. A woman about twenty-five comes in, with bright red hair and some of the most beautiful green eyes I've ever seen. Godric did mention a little bit about Sasha, but if anyone is intimidating it's her. Could this be the same girl he told me about?

"Where'd you come from?" She asks, throwing water in my face. "Who turned you? I want an answer now." Her spit is landing on my face.

Again, no response. Why would I answer her questions? It would only mean my death.

"I need you to give me an answer. Who turned you?"

She isn't going to stop until I give her what she wants. Information is the only thing keeping me alive at this point, and once I give it up, wouldn't she kill me?

"Just tell me what I need to know, and this'll stop. No one gets hurt."

The little bitch wouldn't put it to rest. "A creature named Godric turned me. I come from Georgia. The bodies, well, I did that because it was fun. Why else would I do it?" I reply with a smile.

"You little shit, you're killing innocent people. Don't you realize that? We protect our livelihood. Humans are our future. Without them, we can't exist. We can't afford to keep killing them. Don't you understand?"

I just shake my head; honestly, I don't care what she says.

"I don't like you. You're reckless. I can't have vampires like you running around free and unwarranted. This could cause an issue, not to mention, it could turn into another Blood Takers situation we can't afford."

"Blood Takers?" I ask. Godric didn't mention Blood Takers.

She scoffs, "The Blood Takers were ruled by Jakob, who we killed for messing with our future. He was reckless and ignorant. A lot like you. Hopefully, we don't have to do the same to you."

Oh wow, she is the one that killed the leader of the last group? This must be why Godric despises her so much, and talks about taking back what is rightfully ours.

"You can work for me, or I will kill you right here," Sasha says. "At least I am nice enough to give you a choice."

"You think I'm scared to die?"

"No, but I know you want your family to live, right?"

She did not just bring my family into this, and if all she has talked about is true, she wouldn't kill them because they are human. "Do you normally threaten families to get people to work for you? Are you that desperate?"

"No, but recruitment is necessary to survive. Plain and simple. We can't let you leave here without it being beneficial for us. So?"

"What do you want me to do?" I ask.

"Well, I'd like you to go through training. It'll help you learn how to control your hunger. You have to change if you want to be out and about."

"Training? You have training for vampires now?"

"Yes, we do. The only people you're allowed to kill are the ones I tell you too. Rogues are at the top of that list."

So work for her or die? The question isn't really a hard decision to make because she isn't killing me."Okay. Okay. I'll work for you. But doing what?"

"You can help us find this Godric. So, we can make an example out of him. That'll show rogues not to mess with us."

Interesting idea. Not knowing much about the guy, I have no idea what kind of impact it would do to the others. Do they realize how hard it will be to find him though? Probably not.

"It won't be that easy. I'll need to play it off; He'll eventually seek me out again."

She cracks a smile, taking seed in my devious plan, and agrees.

"Okay, let Godric come to you. You'll be tracking down rogues once you are more accustomed to our reality."

"What do you mean accustomed to?"

"Dr. Kendrick here will drain you. Call it vampire rehab. It'll strip all the human blood, and then starve you. That'll give you the best chance at becoming halfway normal again. That is if you still want to work for us?"

Could I do that without killing one of her people? I surely would get scorched for that. Probably at her hand, no less.

Sasha leaves the room, and my rehabilitation starts. He puts something inside my arm that will drain the blood from my body.. It didn't take long for me to become irritable, being used to eating every couple of hours.

"Let me out of here. I need to feed!"

They aren't going to let me go, but some self-control needs to be gained or I would end up murdering their precious doctor.

15
Jane

Dr. Kendrick has been having more and more luck with good results, and if I find Samuel, it will be the first place he goes. This would be hard to explain to the others, him being alive and all, but if he could make him better, then it's worth it.

My mission is to find Samuel. He's the person who started the Guardians and the war against Jakob. If anyone deserves a second chance, it is him.

After two very long months of searching for Samuel state to state, I get a lead from Cassius in Little Rock. He has been spotted at You'll Be Sorry Liquor Store. He likes to drink, but it would only be a matter of time before he would show up again to replenish. Stakeout commenced.

Two nights later, he is walking into the liquor store on a stormy night. Almost immediately, I notice his eyes are different. He has contacts in, so he can get around without causing alarms.

"Wait around the corner, and we'll snatch him up when he walks home."

We have to be fast, as not to cause any unwanted attention from bystanders. Once I get into the van, he recognizes me, and things settle down.

"Jane, is that you?" He asks.

I nod as Cassius starts to drive. At this point, he is cordial.

"Why are you doing this?"

He knows precisely why, like every other vampire, he knows the rules.

"I'm taking you back to Sasha and Stephen. They'll be glad to see you." I smile, hoping they will forgive me.

"I don't want to see them. I want to go back to where I was. Can't you just take me back?" He asks, agitated.

"Unfortunately, you know I can't do that. You aren't registered. Once you are and agree to follow the new rules and boundaries, then we can talk. Until then, you're coming with us."

I shoot a quick text message to Sasha and Stephen, letting them know I have a transport coming. Stephen would be in town for their monthly check-in.

He starts becoming very angry, thrashing around in the back of the van. Thank god, we are only an hour away. He in't going to make this process easy, but I didn't expect it. Dr. Kendrick did provide me with a sedative.

They are not going to be happy, but I have to give him a shot at being himself again. They would see it that way, wouldn't they? They never voiced they were upset with me, but I know. Everyone started acting different towards me once they found out I killed Samuel.

I could think of two people who wild be ecstatic to see him: Amy and Liz.

The rest of the drive is full of questions from Cassius wanting to know who he is and why he is so important to catch? Right now, I tell him it's private orders for now.

When we finally pull up to Sasha's place, I am surprised the sedation keeps him out the entire time. I take a deep breath knowing this can go one of two ways, and one way will end very badly.

"Bring him inside."

As I open the door, they both greet me, surprised.

"To what do we owe this pleasure?" Sasha asks.

Her face goes blank, seeing him. Speechless, she can't say a word.

"Whhaa - Is that Samuel? How? Where?" Stephen asks me with tears in his eyes.

"We captured him in Little Rock. I thought you guys might want to test him out with the experiment. Maybe we can get him back." I reply.

"But you said you killed him? How's he still here? Alive? Why the fuck did you lie to us? We could have found him a long time ago and brought him back. Just why?" Stephen asks, cracking his knuckles like he is about to step into an arena.

"I lied because I couldn't bring myself to do it. I didn't want either of you to think I was weak. Everyone was so strong back then, and even Sasha killed Drake. Her lover."

Sasha didn't move, just stammering, trying to find words. I could tell she wants to yell at me, but she can't even bring herself to it.

"How was he not on the registry?" Stephen asks.

"Well, probably because he's smart and knows how to hide from us. He was one of us at one point, remember?"

"Bring him to Dr. Kendrick. We need to keep him sedated until we know what to do." Stephen orders the men while showing them to Dr. Kendrick's lab.

He is surprised as everyone else. "I thought he was dead?" Dr. Kendrick asks.

"We all did," Sasha says, giving me a fuck you look.

I know she is pissed at me for lying, but he's here now. They could save him. That had to count for something, right?

Dr. Kendrick isolates Samuel in a room built out of bulletproof glass, plus tested against many vampires to ensure it will hold. They know that by how old he is and the amount of blood he consumes how powerful he will be.

"Why are you doing this to me?"

"Why? Cause we want you back. That's why. I know you can be good again."

I know he could be a good guy again. He just needs to believe it too.

"Let me out of here!" Samuel screams, trying to get out.

"Save your energy! Getting out of there is impossible. Let's focus on getting you better." Dr. Kendrick informs him.

"I'm fine. Just hungry. You don't have to lock me up."

He isn't the same Samuel we all know. The lust lingering still deep inside him. Dr. Kendrick better work his magic. If we have to kill him, things will get ugly around here.

The glass between us makes things difficult. With the microphone in the room, I can hear him. I didn't know what else to say. Surely there are still Jakob followers out there looking for Samuel.

Walking out of the room to let the doctor do his thing, I dial Amy's number to fill her in on the situation.

"What?" Amy's voice snaps on the other end.

We haven't spoken in years. "It's time."

"Time for? Wait, you found him?"

"Yup. He's at Sasha's place now with Dr. Kendrick. They know he's alive. Have you thought about how you're gonna tell Liz?"

"No, but I'd rather not tell her that I kept it from her. She's been so kind to me."

"You don't have to tell her you were a part of it. I understand. But you must tell her. Can you do that?"

She takes a deep breath, "Yes. How's he? What's he like?"

"Well, he didn't try to kill me, so that's a plus. I don't feel like he's better either. It's going to take time. You know that. We've been waiting for this."

"I know. Just eager, that's all. Once I tell Liz, she won't wait. You know that, right?"

"I planned on it. I think both of you will help him get better quicker."

"See you soon."

Once she tells LIzm, they will immediately head down here, and I hope we can get him better before they show up. Fingers crossed.

16
Samuel

When you don't consume blood, the body goes weak and almost limp. I imagine it's what the body feels like in old age. It's been a week since I have eaten.

"Please, I need it. I'm going to die if I don't feed. Please don't let me die!" I yell, knowing the good Doctor could hear me. Surely, he wouldn't let me die here. Maybe if I pull on his heartstrings a bit, he will reconsider.

I hear the hum of the speaker coming on, "You won't die. Be strong and patient."

Sasha's voice apparent in the background.

They come into the room, carrying chains. "I'm sorry to do this, but it's time for the next phase. Just in case, we must chain you up, so you don't hurt anyone."

I am not a villain, just need to eat. I will be fine once I get some blood in my system.

While Dr. Kendrick chains me up, she sits down in a chair in front of me. She caresses my face, "Are we going to get our Samuel back?"

"Never," I reply. Too much has happened for me ever to be that man again. The darkness in me will never entirely be gone no matter what they do. "I'll never be that same man again. Face the facts. Nothing you can do can make me that man again. But I can try to be better."

She hands me a picture of Liz. *My lover*. Oh, how I have missed her. Next is a picture of Amy. My beautiful daughter."Why are you showing me these?"

"I want you to know what's waiting for you on the other side. When you get better, they'll be here for you."

They are trying to make me feel love again, but I never lost it. Sure, I am a killer, but I still love Liz and Amy. I'm not sure anything will ever change that.

Stephen comes in to relieve Sasha. I can't bear to look at him. Knowing I did so many awful things that could have disrupted everything we fought for in the beginning. Not to mention, he's like a son to me.

"Turn the microphone off, please," Stephen instructs Dr. Kendrick.

Why didn't he want anyone to hear what he has to say?

He leans over and puts his hand on my shoulder, "Hey dear friend, I know this has been difficult, but in just a couple of days, you'll be with the woman you love and your daughter. Just remember that."

"Elizabeth?" I ask.

Stephen nods, slightly closing his eyes.

"She won't want anything to do with me after all the horrible things I've done. I can't ever go back to her."

He pulls out a couple of pictures from his pocket, hoping they would spark a light in my brain..Anger entered my body, and my fists immediately clenched.

"Do you know what happened to them?" Stephen asks.

"That asshole killed my wife. My son. Slaughtered them. Amy, where is she?"

"She's staying with Liz. All is well with both of them."

"Liz is going to be furious, thinking I was dead for all these years. Jane was only doing what she thought was right at the time."

"I was the one that broke the news to her. She was distraught for many years until she found out you were alive. Don't worry; her love for you is strong. You'll get her back."

My brain switches gears and starts going through the days I was with the Guardians. We were fighting for a more significant cause. Yet, somehow I don't feel happy about it.

"The Guardians won. I should be happy about that, but I don't feel anything."

"Don't worry, you will. Give it time. We fought this war for you. For all the people we've lost."

I know the Guardians well, once being their leader, talking them into war against the Blood Takers to save not only humanity but also our species. They have fulfilled the first part of the mission, taking out Jakob. Now, they did the right thing by separating the United States into factions of sorts to keep the vampires in line.

Jane visits next. When she comes into the room, her head hangs low, and I know why.

"No need to feel bad. If you had killed me then, I wouldn't be able to be reformed now. Think about that? I know the others are probably upset, but they'll forgive you. You did the right thing."

She fumbles with her hands, "I know, but I lied to Liz. To everyone.. All this time, she has been grieving your loss. I didn't say anything. I should 've," She couldn't even finish her sentence.

"Liz is a strong woman. I'm sure she'll be upset, but ultimately I'm alive. That means you didn't kill me. She will forgive you, eventually."

Tears form in her eyes, and all I want to do was to hug her, but couldn't because of the chains.

I hear someone over the microphone, "Are you sure it's him? He's himself?"

"I can assure you that he's himself. It'll take work to keep him that way. Since he had given into the Blood Lust already, it will be easier for him to give in again. We need you to make sure that doesn't happen. He'll need to be supervised for the next few months to ensure a relapse doesn't occur. Other than that, you're free to take him home." He explains as he opens the door.

I am dressed and ready to go, but no one mentioned I will be going home with Liz and Amy. Am I ready to see her after all the awful things I have done, even to the Guardians. How could she still love me?

"Samuel? Honey?"

My gaze meets hers, and oh my did she look beautiful. "It's me. Me as I can be."

She engulfs me in her arms and didn't want to let go. Hell, I didn't want her too.

"Daddy?" I turn around to see Amy.

"Sweetie? You've gotten so big. So grown."

She holds me tightly. My love and daughter are now back in my life and I will do anything to keep them there.

"We made up a room for you at my house. Would you like to stay with us?" Liz asks.ed.

"Why would I want to go anywhere else?" I smile. My happiness is back. "Thank you, Doctor. Without you, I would still be that evil creature. I'm sorry for all the awful things I said to you."

He smiles, and standing next to him is Jane.

Liz approaches her, "I can't thank you enough for what you did. You let him go and brought him back to me. I'm so sorry for the way I've been treating you. I'll be forever grateful."

She kisses Jane on the forehead while I give her a big smile.

We leave knowing we have an eternity to be with each other, and that still didn't seem like enough.

The car ride is silent. I'm not sure any of us know what to say. Once we get to LIz's house, everything is exactly the same as I head up to the master bedroom.

"So, I thought you would sleep in a guest bedroom for now," Liz says, startling me as she walks into the room.

Why do I need to sleep in the guest bedroom? Is she still scared of me? Surely, she's not. I'm better now. "You don't have to be scared of me, love. I won't hurt you."

She looks at the floor, "I'm not sure I can trust you fully yet. Until then, I would like you to sleep in the guest bedroom."

She didn't seem to give me any leeway, so I would comply..I want to pull her close, nuzzle into her hair while whispering *I love you*. If trust is what I need to build, then I will start now.

I take my stuff to the guest bedroom down the hall and put it away before heading downstairs to take a look at her bookshelves. Liz has always been a wonderful writer, and I hope she hasn't stopped due to all this crap.

There are new books with her name on the shelves. I skimmed through the first one. These books are about our fight. Blood Takers VS. Guardians.

"What are you doing?" Liz asks, coming around the corner to find me with the book in my hand.

"Looking at your new editions to your bookcase. How are sales going?"

She shakes her head while walking over, takes the book out of my hand, placing it back on the shelf. "They sell better than anything I've ever written. They like the tension between the two opposing groups."

"I'm so sorry for the way I was. If I could change it, I would, but I would do anything to save my family. You know that. I'm not the same vampire I was five years ago. But I'm not completely the Samuel you knew either. I've got this darkness inside me that I can't shake. I wish I could."

"Exactly why I wanted you to sleep in the guest room. I love you, but I can't let you that close to me yet. You could relapse, and I don't want to be in the middle. I don't want your DAUGHTER to either."

I understand Being in the same house as them is a dream come true. I'll do whatever it takes to get in their good graces again.

17

Envio

When Sasha's name scrolls across my phone, I sigh. It's been nice having some down time.

"Who's next?" I answer, waiting for my next assignment.

"Well, actually, it's a recruit and an assignment." She quickly replies, probably waiting to see my reaction.

"Recruit? Who?"

"Warwick. We've already done our side of things. Now it's your turn to contribute. He'll need guidance. You understand?"

"Why do I have to be the babysitter? What about Eliza?"

"You know you would be better for this particular situation. I'll send him over to your location. Don't cause issues, the faster he knows what to do, the shorter amount of time he'll be in your hair."

"Text me details on the assignment," I reply and hang up.

Am I the full-fledged babysitter for the Guardians now? I much rather work by myself if possible.

I turn the TV off, put on my clothes, and repack my duffel bag. I guess this one'll be going on assignment with me today. I hope he's ready.

To my surprise, he shows up rather quickly, extending his hand as I let him into my room. "Hey, nice to meet ya. I'm Warwick."

I grip his hand roughly to show him I meant business. We have work to do.

"Envio. Let's get to work. Did Sasha already fill you in on our mission?"

He looks at me, inquisitively, "No. Was she supposed to?"

That woman irks me. Briefing him means even more time taken away from actually tracking them down. Isn't that our sole purpose as enforcers? To track down rogues?

"Listen. He goes by Jack. He's pretty rough and has been around since Jakob's era. He was a follower. Usually, they are the hardest to recruit on our side."

"Okay. Where?"

I laugh, "if it were that easy, we would be out of a job." Tracking a rogue down is extensive. First, you must figure out their patterns, and then their feeding schedule. One thing about vampires, they love their plans. Most stick to a schedule and barely budge, especially when it comes to feeding.

"So, what should we do first?" He asks, eager to do good on this first mission.

"See if we can find any unexplained deaths lately. Usually, they lead back to vampires every time. It might not be the rogue we are looking for, but we will surely find one if we just investigate."

I have him research articles on unexplained deaths around the United States to see if anything would constitute a vampire. He does this himself to learn the tricks of the trade. It'll be good practice for him when Sasha ends up sending him out alone. Being an enforcer isn't an easy job.

Warwick gets easily frustrated which isn't a good thing if she is wanting him to be an enforcer. How does she expect him to be able to handle rogues shit talking him and still give them the option? Did Sasha think this through? How well did she know this vampire?

"I finally found one in Michigan. Body drained, blaming it on wild animals. NOt likely, though." He jumps up with his hands in the air claiming victory.

Sometimes, it's like a needle in a haystack because no one knows where to start the investigation. Tracking is the best part. I guess because it's a part of our instinct—the thrill of the find.

"Alright. Are you ready to go? We got some tracking to do. He couldn't have gotten too far."

We trek across the country to Oscoda, Michigan. We didn't pick the best time to come here, considering its winter, and Michigan is known for its snow. I drive over the Ausable Bridge that takes us over the river that feeds into Lake Huron. The lake looks to be never-ending, but mostly frozen over. We approach the main street, where many old mom and pop shops still fuel the town with the necessities.

"Good thing we don't get cold, but we need to get jackets anyway. If someone sees us out here with no jackets, it would be suspicious."

I park the car, and we walk inside a storefront. Fashion must not be a priority around here. The clothes in this store were hideous. Both of us pick up a jacket and paid, ready to get out of there.

As I shut my door to the car, "How ya feeling?"

He shakes his head, "Fine. Why?"

He shoots me a look like I am an overprotective parent or something. "It's your first."

He laughs then slaps me on the shoulder, "Yes, it is. Let's get it done."

At the four-way stop, a right would take us to the Lake Huron boardwalk, but I imagine no one goes down there at this time of year. Instead, we take a left and come upon an old abandoned two-story school covered in ivy and an old gray tint.

"Let's go inside. I've heard about that place."

"Calm down." I roll my eyes and continue, "What about it?"

He laughs, "It's supposedly haunted. I know we are on a mission, but I'll most likely never be back in this town. Let's live a little and have some fun."

Not sure what he means by fun. Ghost hunting isn't my idea of fun or blowing off steam. I'd rather lay in bed and watch shark week to do that.

"Fuck it. Let's do it."

I park, and we both get out and walk towards the creepy old schoolhouse. I'm only doing this because I'm not a pussy. My walking slows, and I let Warwick get ahead of me. He's he one that wants to see it anyway. Let him deal with all of it first. This way, I can run if need be.

My older brother used to watch ghost investigations all the time on TV when we visited my grandparents. I guess that's why I'm so terrified. I've seen too much crazy shit to know that ghosts are probably real, hell I didn't believe vampires were real until I became one.

"Why ya slowing down? Let's get in there and check it out."

"I'm sure they don't just leave the front door unlocked. Looters and all. "I said as he tried to open the door, and to my surprise, it did. "Are you fucking kidding me? They leave it unlocked?"

Warwick didn't waste any time going inside, and the door slams behind him. Did I want to venture inside? My gut tells me, no, but I know if I don't, then I'll be a laughing stock.

Inside, it is eerie, and you could feel a presence around you, the moment you step inside. It's quiet, but something is here with us. "Warwick? Where'd you go?"

"In here." He yells.

When I walk inside the old gymnasium, it is dark. "What the hell are you doing here?" He's sitting in the middle of the floor, criss-cross.

"I heard something in here." He points up at the bleachers. "From there."

I sit next to him, knowing he is yanking my chain and just trying to freak me out. It didn't take much when it came to ghosts. A calm energy comes over me, and then a whisper into my ear, "help me." My body reacts. "No fucking way." I grab my ear. My mind must be playing tricks on me, but then I hear it again. "Help me."

"What's wrong?" He asks, staring at me.

"A little girl just asked me to help her. Let's get out of here, like now." I say, heading towards the door.

"You're fucking with me, right? I was kidding about hearing something."

"No, I'm dead fucking serious. Let's get out of here."

Both of us head to the car, without even so much as looking behind us. "Let's never do that again. I don't fuck with ghosts."

Once inside the car, I lock the door and take off toward the main strip's backside. "He's got to be around here somewhere. Look up and see where the nearest bar is."

"Why?"

"It's the easiest place to feed."

Warwick isn't as bad as I thought he would be. Usually, I get stuck with idiots who would never survive doing this job.

"There's one up here. Take a right at the next stop sign and go all the way down to the end. It looks like it's the only one for about five miles."

If my assumptions are right, Jack would be within five miles of the crime scene unless he already skipped town. I park the car and turn off the engine. "Alright, let's talk plan. Act as normal as you can. We're here to get a drink. If I sense him, I'll cough. We'll wait for him to leave, and then follow him."

"Sounds easy enough."

The bar isn't very crowded, probably because it is a Tuesday night. Not many people go out drinking during the week unless it's their day off. I slap a ten-dollar bill on the bar while sitting down on a vacant stool, "Two Buds, please."

Warwick sits down next to me and watches me gazing around the room.

"Nothing?" He asks. "Let's drink these and then try another one."

I haven't heard much about Warwick from anyone. What made him want this job? "Let me ask ya something. Why'd you become an enforcer anyway?"

He shrugs, "honestly wasn't giving a choice."

"What do you mean? They forced you?" This seems highly unlikely of Sasha knowing how important that role is to the Guardians.

"Let's back up. Sasha's hooligans kidnapped me and took me back to wherever. And gave me the option of working for her or dying."

"Wait, you're telling me you were a rogue? Why would they reform you and then make you become an enforcer?"

"My maker, Godric. They seem pretty interested in him. Hell, all I wanna do is see my family again someday. She threatened them, so I agreed."

Fueling with fire, Sasha should not have trusted him with this job so easily. What the hell is she thinking? "Yes, he's high on our priority list to catch. Haven't even gotten close. You know where he is?"

"I wish I did. Maybe then I wouldn't have to do this anymore. No offense."

"None took. Sometimes I enjoy it more than others."

As we take our last sips, someone comes out of the back of the bar, and I get the sensation. That is Jack. "That's him."

"You sure?"

I nod.

Once he leaves, we quickly get up and follow after him. The problem with the sensation is it works both ways. "Stay alert," I say, opening the door to leave.

Right outside, his back leaning against the wall is Jack. "Well, well. What do we have here? Stephen send you out here to do his dirty work? Couldn't handle me himself?" The toothpick twirls around in his mouth like an old western movie. All he is missing was the cowboy hat.

"You know exactly why we're here. Breaking the rules has consequences. Are you ready to pay for them?"

He laughs, "I was expecting you, boys. Knew you'd show up here."

"Is that a yes?" Warwick asks, getting into a fighting stance.

He nods, and then the weirdest thing happened. He didn't even try to run. "What? You want to die?"

"Much rather than be a good little vampire."

Warwick grabs him, and we take him around back where we wouldn't have any witnesses, pulling him limb from limb. No screaming or begging. Jack is silent the entire time until I light a match, and his body goes up in flames.

As we walk off, all we hear is the subtle groaning from a vampire that has paid the ultimate consequence for breaking our rules.

18
Sasha

I sit at my desk, taking a sip of red wine before I start working on my plans. Low and behold, my phone rings with Envio's name displaying across the screen.

"What can I do for you?"

"Jack's dead. He didn't beg or anything. These rogues hate us."

"Well, we don't like them, so it's mutual. Not worried about it."

"So, we got some other things to discuss." He says sternly.

"Oh, yeah, like what?"

"Like the fact, Warwick was turned by Godric. And the fact you threatened his family. What are you, Jakob now?"

"Don't you ever compare me to Jakob. Ever. You fucking hear me? I'm nothing like that piece of shit."

"Really, well, didn't he threaten Samuel's family to make him join? Or do you not remember that little detail?"

How dare he think he can talk to me that way. "Word of advice. I'd change your tone unless you want to be sitting in a cell tonight. You do not get to disrespect me ever." I say, very calmly. "I wouldn't hurt his family. You know better."

"That doesn't change the fact you still threatened them. We're not the Blood Takers. Don't lose sight of the bigger picture here. I know it's stressful, and you want to catch Godric. But we have to do it the right way. If we don't, then we are no better than they were."

I get where he is coming from, but he can change his tone. "I'll consider changing how I've been operating, but Envio."

"Yes?"

"Don't ever come at me like that again. Next time, it won't end pretty. Understood?"

"Got it."

There are more important things to worry about, like finding Godric. We have searched everywhere and still haven't seen him. He's got to be somewhere. Is someone hiding him? I want to believe everyone is following the rules, but there's always some that rebel. Those are the ones we still have to worry about in the end.

If someone is hiding Godric, there will be consequences, but I genuinely don't think anyone would be stupid enough to do that. They all have first hand knowledge of what happens when you break our rules. I wonder if any of the other governors would go along with raids. If we start invading their privacy, things will get out of hand fast. We would be directly violating that and could turn some of them against us. I can't chance that with Godric and his blood puppies out there.

My eyes catch the picture of Drake and me from across the room and draws me to it. I run my fingers across the glass, over his beautiful smile.

Maybe I should take a day and visit Samuel. He would be able to help me put my mind at ease. I need someone who will tell me the truth.

I pull my phone out and dial Liz.

"Hello?"

"How's he doing?" I ask first.

"He's doing good. Something wrong?"

She is usually really good at reading me. My theory is somehow when she had the vision of me, somehow we bonded, but I'll never be able to prove it. "Not at all. Mind if I come to visit?"

"Go ahead. See ya soon." She replies, hanging up the phone.

I grab my backpack and pack a couple of things and then run over to Liz's. I have always loved her Victorian-style house. The doorbell sounds, and I wait on someone to answer.

"What a surprise. I didn't know you were coming." Samuel says, whisking me inside and shutting the door. "What are you doing here?"

The inside looks the same, nothing out of place. "Wanted to come to see you guys and get away for a little while."

"Things getting rough?" He asks, putting his hand on my shoulder. "It'll happen. It's what you do during the tough times that will matter."

Samuel is always good at words. He and Liz should join forces and write a book together. "She still writing?"

"Oh, you don't know?"

"Know what?"

He walks over to the bookshelf and pulls off two books. "You haven't seen these?"

I turn them over to read the back. "She's writing about us?"

"Yeah, I haven't got to read them yet. I'm not even supposed to know."

"She knows how dangerous this is, right?"

"Don't go making this into a big deal. Vampires are a myth, remember? There are thousands of books out there about them every day. We'll be fine."

"But this isn't fiction."

"Humans don't need to know that."

I guess he's right. Who am I to tell her what she could write about? I'll stay out of it. "On another note, how ya feeling?"

"Good. Been feeding with Amy and Liz once a week. Haven't had any issues." His eyes darted. "Have I thought about it? Yes, but never acted on it. I don't want to kill humans. Just gotta have self-control."

I nod and head for the couch. "Where are the ladies? I'm surprised they both haven't come down her running."

"Liz is still writing. Trying to finish her third book. Amy, well, who knows."

Amy never really liked any of us. Of course, It is understandable why. We were with her father every day when she couldn't be. The only person she truly got close to was Liz.

I pick the book off the coffee table and study the cover depicting two groups. She went with authenticity. Some have red moon eyes, and others didn't. I open the book and begin to read only to find out how factual it is to our real lives. After about ten pages, I could already tell she didn't change anything. The vision of me is even in here. I sit the book back down, not wanting to read anymore.

"Don't like it?"

"I'd rather not read about it. We lived it. No need to go through that bullshit again." I try not to let it irritate me, but she is profiting off of us. Hell, she even included Anthony's death in there.

"I understand. No matter what, I try to be supportive of her. Especially now. She needs an escape, and if that's writing a book about all the awful things that's happened, then I'm going to support her on it." He shrugs. "If others want to get offended or mad, well, they can get over it."

It's great she found something to help her escape, but to write down all of our secrets and tragedies for the world to read? That just seems like a wrong move and would probably come back to bite us in the ass later.

"Ames, look who's here," Samuel says.

I receive the most evident fuck you look from Amy. What the hell did I do to make her hate me so much?

He catches sight of the look. "What's going on between you two? Something we need to air out?"

"No, daddy. You can't force me to like your friends."

The hostility in the room is ruining this visit for me. Why can't she just grow the fuck up? "I don't want to be friends. Just cordial, but I see you can't even do that." I say, getting up from the couch. "Next time, you can come to visit me, Samuel." I didn't waste any time leaving and getting away from the negative energy I'm feeling right now.

19
Warwick

Lately, I've been thinking a lot about Tasha and Avery. How were they coping since I've disappeared? Today was my daughter's first birthday, and I couldn't be there. I was going to miss so many pivotal moments like her first step, words, and birthday. I never wanted to become this man, but when Godric kidnapped me, my whole life flipped upside down. It's not like I had much of a choice. When I visited them before I left the state, there was one thing that made my decision to go more comfortably. I had the urge to feed on my daughter.

Even to fathom that killed me. Could I ever actually do that? It was a valid question, but not one that I ever wanted to find the answer too. My job as her father was to protect her, not hurt her. My presence wouldn't have helped her in the long run, and the thought of me hurting my daughter or wife scared me. It scared me enough to walk away. It was one of the hardest things I'd ever had to do, and every day I still think about them. Were they doing okay? Does my daughter remember me? It kills me to believe that Avery won't have me around when she needs me. I'll miss all of her father's daughter's dances, her first boyfriend, graduation, and even her wedding. My eyes closed, trying to keep the waterfalls at bay, but it was hard. I wanted more than anything to hold her and let her know I'm here for her.

"Dude, you okay?" Envio asked, walking in. "Talk to me."

Envio and I had some ups and downs, especially when he discovered that Godric was my maker, and I was a rogue. I could understand his hesitancy, but I wanted more than anything to live a somewhat normal life one day. If that meant I had to do Sasha's bidding for a while, then that's what I would do. "Just processing through some things."

"You need to talk? Listen, I know we aren't like super close or anything, but I hate to see people like this."

I wasn't sure if it's something I wanted to talk to him about, but it's not like I have anyone else. "Today's my daughter's first birthday."

His eyes widened, shocked at my response. "Wow. That's gotta be rough."

He had no idea how rough. I wanted to go over there, announce that I'm still alive, and just be a part of their family again. I'd thought about it several times, but I knew that wasn't the right thing to do. They don't need any part of this world. I'd made enemies doing what I did for Sasha, and I didn't want to give someone any ammo against them. "Yeah, just really missing them lately. Wishing things could've been different, that's all."

"Have you seen them since being turned?"

My mind jumped back to the last night I saw them, my stomach tightening at the sound of their blood pumping through their veins. "Yeah, the night I left. I stopped to see them, but getting close to them meant the urge to hurt them. I couldn't stay very long."

Envio was meshing his hands together, thinking before he spoke. "Have you visited without them seeing you? Maybe just to put your mind at ease?"

"Wouldn't Sasha get upset?"

His shoulders tensed visibly, and he clapped his hands together, "on the contrary of what you might think, you're allowed to make some decisions yourself. If Sasha gets mad at you for simply going there and not letting them know you're still alive, I'll handle it. She's usually not like this, but something has changed since she took over. It's like she's going down a different path or something."

He wasn't pleased when he found out that she threatened to hurt my family to make me join. I never thought anyone would turn on their precious leader, but Envio seemed to have his way of thinking and wasn't scared to call her out on her bullshit. I liked that about him. It wasn't that he didn't trust her decisions, but questioning if she was starting to go down a dark path. The Guardians were trying to get rid of the darkness around vampires, not make it worse.

"No, seriously, though. Why don't you go there, and just see your family? They don't have to know you're there. Maybe that'll give you a little peace of mind."

He was right. There couldn't be any harm in just seeing them. I'd be quiet and not let them see me. "Alright, but I'll need a stiff drink when I get back. Meet me at the hotel bar."

I ran as fast as my legs would take me. It's one of the qualities of vampires I liked the most, being able to get anywhere in the United States within an hour tops. It made commuting anywhere so much easier. When I stopped, my quaint little white farmhouse was dark from the street.

It was dark outside, and the only light was the stars in the sky. The house didn't have many lights on, so it was a perfect time. I peeked into the nursery window to catch a glimpse and saw her peacefully sleeping with Tasha passed out in the rocking chair, clutching my sweater. So badly, I wanted to hold her, kiss my daughter, and go back to normal life, but it wasn't possible. I couldn't endanger my family, that would be selfish. The next hour I spent gazing upon the amazing life I once had, and how nothing could ever come close to this, but it was time for her to move on. Tasha deserved love and companionship. I took a long last glance, knowing I couldn't ever come back.

When I got back to the hotel, the bar seemed a fitting place to be right now. A drink would help me calm my nerves. I scoured the bar, looking for Envio.

"Over here." He said, waving his hand in the air in the back. "Already got you a whiskey."

I took a seat and downed it in the first drink. "Now, that's just what I needed."

"I took you as a whiskey guy. Me too." He said, clanking our glasses together and raising his hand for two more. "So, how'd it go?"

"I think that'll be the last time I go back. It was hard, but my wife needs to be able to move on."

"I couldn't imagine having a family before all this. I'm not sure how you do it."

"Day by day. I just have to remind myself that they are better off without me and this world. You better than anyone understand that doing this job, we make enemies. I can't put that risk on them. They need to be safe."

He nodded his head and raised his glass. "To goodbyes."

I didn't want to think about it anymore; instead, I tried to drown my sorrows tonight and learn a little more about Envio. "So, I don't know that much about you. What was it like before being turned?"

His face went blank, "I... was about to start college. I had taken two years off after high school to volunteer at the local children's shelter. They were low on staff and were on the brink of having to shut down. Someone had to step up."

I wouldn't have taken him for the non-profit type, but I guess that's why I wanted to get to know him a little better. "Wow, I commend you on that. That's a very noble thing to do."

"I never got to start. Jakob got to me the day before I was supposed to leave. Go figure." He said, shaking his head.

"Wait, Jakob, was your maker? I don't understand then why you were so against me?" My mind was spinning, realizing he was a rogue.

"I only killed when I had too. Every day was a struggle to make

Jakob believe I was on his side, but my self-control was strong. I held on until I could join the Guardians."

"So, you never fully gave in to the lust? That must have been hard? I gave in on the first night."

"Many do, especially with vampires that push for that. My mind always goes back to what would have changed if I had left for college a day earlier? Would I still be living my normal human life, oblivious to all of this going on around me?"

I laughed, "Probably. Even though all the evidence points towards us, it's like they are too naive to believe it could be true. It's good for us, but it makes you think what else might be out there that we don't realize."

"I feel ya on that."

"So, any ladies?" I asked, curious to see if he was dating anyone. Do vampires even date?

"There's one I would like to be, but we are on separate paths right now. Maybe one day, when things settle down." He answered, glancing down at the ground, swirling the drink around in his cup. "We'll see."

"Is it a vampire or a human?"

"Well, you know the rules. We aren't allowed to be with humans, end of the story. Sasha knew first hand what implications could happen."

"What do you mean?"

"The man she was in love with happened to be Jakob's son. Neither of them knew he was his father until he found out that he was seeing Sasha. He got turned to hurt Sasha."

"I couldn't imagine that. Jakob sounds like a real asshole. I've not heard a single good thing about him."

"He was one of the worst, in my opinion."

"So, who is she?"

"You might have met her by now. Jane?"

"Oh, she's a beautiful woman. Seems very headstrong like Sasha. Makes sense."

"I'm her maker, but we have a connection outside of that. We talked briefly about being together before we went our separate ways. She didn't want to jump into anything because we didn't know where we would be, and right now, we are both pretty focused on getting rid of the rogues and making this world a better place for both species."

Knowing that someone had found possible love from another vampire makes me wonder if I could find the same one day. If I were going to alive for generations, then eventually, I would need a partner when the time was right.

Something odd happened today. I received a text from Sasha, sending me out on my first mission by myself. What happened that changed her mind so quickly of me not needing a babysitter? Did Envio say something? Hopefully, I didn't cross any boundaries last night, but I just wanted to know him a little better and find out what this life of mine was going to be like firsthand.

My assignment was to find a couple of rogues that had been causing problems and a lot of media attention to their deaths. Hundreds of bodies discovered throughout Louisiana, and it needed to stop. The more work I did for Sasha, the more I realized why they were so gung-ho on making the world a better place. My family was human, and I wouldn't want some blood-sucking monster to go after them. So when I think of humans getting killed, I worry that one day it could be them if I don't help put a stop to it.

It would be weird going back to the state where I did my first binge. Hell, that's where Sasha captured me. Maybe this was a test to see if I could handle this on my own? The rogues were making it easier for me to find them, leaving bodies across Louisiana. If I follow the bodies, I'll find them. It's like they wanted to be found, and asked the ultimate question. Did they want death?

As I trekked across Louisiana, keeping alert on any new bodies found, the search began. The body trails led from Slidell at the edge of Texas to Baton Rouge. They had to be somewhere close. Was I missing something?

I looked up events going on within Louisiana and found that a strip of bars in Alexandria was having a pub crawl. Bar events made it easier to attack without being noticed right away. I made my way to the first bar, getting a beer and finding a spot in the back of the room so my cover wouldn't be blown right off the bat.

After about two hours, two vampires walked into the bar, eyeing the woman first thing. That was them; I could feel it. I couldn't announce myself because that would cause more problems with the crowd. So, all I could do was patiently wait for them to make their move or leave.

Finally, one of them retreated outside, and I waited until the other one followed. I followed both out, waiting for my chance.

"What do you think you are doing?" I asked. "Ladies, go back inside. You won't be leaving with them tonight."

"Why don't you mind your own fucking business tough guy?" The rogue snarled.

"I would've if you weren't trying to kill those beautiful ladies." Both rogues were snarling, waiting to pounce on me. I had been training for this moment; it was my turn to prove that I could do this without a babysitter.

The rogue snarled and showed his teeth again, "Why don't you leave us be? You can't take all three of us."

"I'm not sure why you think I would be scared of you? I can assure you I'm not. Let's make a deal."

"We don't make deals. Not with vampires like you."

"Like me? You mean vampires trying to do the right thing. Keep humanity around so our species can survive?"

All of a sudden, I felt something breeze behind me.

"Come on, fellas. Don't be stupid. Make your decision. You know the drill." Envio explained.

Why the hell was he here? Did he not believe I could do it myself? I'm beyond irritated at this point.

"You can't be serious? Why would we ever register?"

"Is that a no?" I asked, eyes wide.

"Answers a hell no."

Envio and I glanced at each other and knew what had to happen. They made their decision. Their limbs and bodies burned in the fire, and we watched until they were gone.

"Why are you here?" I asked.

"Sasha wanted me to check in on you. It's your first mission, that's all."

"I don't need a babysitter. I was handling this myself."

Envio didn't need to be here. I could have handled this by myself. How was I ever going to get Sasha to trust me if she keeps sending people to check on me?

"Listen, Sasha just wants to make sure you're focused. You could be a great asset to the Guardians if you stay focused."

What? He acted like I didn't know this already. I've been doing nothing but trying to prove myself to her so I could be free if that's even an option anymore.

20
Samuel

Things had gotten a tad better between Liz and me. I was still in the guest room, but I was fighting to earn her trust back. The way she looked at me that night made my heart break into pieces. She was terrified of me. My hope, she never looked at me like that again.

Amy had been by my side since being home. So many years, I was not able to see her, and we were making up for the lost time. She was grown now and ready to make her own decisions. There was no desire for her to be a part of the Guardians. As a father, I wanted to shield her from that life. Seeing me go to the opposite side, most likely didn't help, but she saw the monster inside me. We would need to have a long adult conversation about all of that.

"Whatcha doing, Dad?" Amy asked, plopping down on the couch next to me.

"Catching up on reading Liz's new series. On to the second book now. Not sure if I'm ready to read it."

"Why? Dad, nobody blames you. You had to do those things. You aren't that guy anymore."

A tear fell, "How can you be so sure?"

She moved closer and took my hands in hers. "Dad. What you

did, you did for your family. You paid the ultimate price for us. You couldn't have known that he was going to do that to mom and brother. You couldn't. Stop beating yourself up."

If she only knew all the things I did while being under Jakob's watch. Explicable things. I should have never left my family alone. I was naive to think he wouldn't use them to get to me. He was smarter than I initially gave him credit. "I just wish they were still here. I missed so many years with you guys. I never got to know the kind of man your brother became."

She squeezed my hand. "He became a man you would have been proud of. He kept hope in us every day that one day we would see you again. He never gave up."

I closed my eyes, trying to keep the tears from falling. Jakob had taken away half my family. I wish I could have been the one to take him down. Instead, I followed him like a lost puppy at his beck and call. What an idiot.

"I'm gonna leave you alone for a bit. I think you should read it."

As Amy walked away, the realization that my daughter was now grown and helping me through tough times seemed crazy. I should be doing that for her, not the other way around. She's wiser than her years. I cracked open the book and started with Chapter one.

After many hours on the couch, delving into Liz and how she wrote this book about our actual lives, I wondered many things. She didn't depict me as a villain in the story. I was someone who gave everything they believed in to save their family. Even all the things I did for Jakob, they were to protect the Guardians. It relieved me to see me as she saw me. Not as a monster, but as a hero.

I heard her coming downstairs, and I rushed the book back onto her shelves. She didn't seem to want me to read them. "I was wondering when you were going to come down. How's the writing going?"

She touched her forehead, "Tiring. I just want it to be perfect for the readers. They are so demanding. I still haven't figured out how I want to end the series."

I wanted to shout from the rooftops the ideas I had, but then she would know I read the books. She wouldn't be too happy to know that. "Well, let me read the books, and then I can help ya. I've got a good mind to generate some ideas for you."

The worried look she gave me said it all. "No, that's okay. I can finish it myself. Not sure you need a reminder of everything that's happened in your past. We don't want you to revert."

Seriously? She's still worried that I'm going to go back to that guy. I got close to her and said, "Dear, you needn't worry. I'm not going to turn back into that guy. I want to support you in everything you do; let me help."

Her eyes rolled, and a smile ensued. "Only if you're sure. The depictions in this book aren't the best. I don't want them to anger you in any way."

She was so worried about offending me. Nothing I read in her books did that in any way. If anything, it made me realize I was too hard on myself for the things I couldn't control during that time. "I'll start reading now."

Liz sat next to me writing while I read the first book. Her eyes kept wandering over to the book and then to my face to see my reaction. I couldn't make it seem as though I had already read it, so I took it slow. Savoring every word she had written. It was eloquent, descriptive, and made you want to read the next page to discover what was going to happen next. Liz was talented. As I neared the end of the first book, her eyes wandered more often with every turn of a page. When I got to the last one, she closed her laptop and stared at me, waiting for my reaction.

"So---?" She asked, eagerly awaiting my opinion.

"I---it' s--- good. How you captured our message, and the details are so vivid."

A smile stretched across her face. "You liked it? Not too much? I wanted it to be as realistic as possible. The humans don't know it's true. I mean, would you if you hadn't experienced it?"

She was right. It was all the truth, but no human would ever guess so. Vampires were still not on the radar—all a myth like sparkly vampires. "No---but it's good. You're very talented."

She walked over to the bookshelf and grabbed the second book, "I guess it's time you read this one." I could tell with the worried look on her face, letting me read this book was hard for her. "Just remember. I love you."

She opened her laptop back up and began writing as I read. Page after page, I was still enchanted with her writing, keeping me directly in the middle of the action. I was reliving all the things we went through. Her eyes kept popping over to me, every time I'd make a sound, and I'd reassure her with a smile.

After four long hours of reading, I came to the last page. Tears in my eyes, and knowing how the book ends, I wanted to put it down and kiss her. I closed the book and set it down on the table. "You have to keep writing. The reader will continue to read as long as you write. Why does the one you are writing have to be the last book? You could write three more of these. I can tell you enjoy this."

"I do--- I just don't know if I want to include certain things because if anyone came across one of us, we would be outed."

"Sasha is doing her best to make sure everyone follows suit. Writing is your passion, which means you can't stop." My hand settled on hers. "You can't stop writing. Continue to do what you love. I'll support you a hundred percent." No matter her decision, she had someone who truly wanted her to succeed. I could never sit down and write books. I'd get frustrated and give up after the first chapter, most likely. "Now, let's talk about ideas for the next book. I've got a bundle of them."

21
Envio

Eliza hasn't been able to find the rogue that attacked the nursing home, although we still think it was a group. I took over while she did some digging on to find Blakeley and tracked the killings to North Carolina. Bodies had been found almost in a straight line from Texas to North Carolina, so I knew it was the same rogues because of the pattern they left behind. My only question was why they were closing the wounds and cleaning up the blood? Typical rogues don't do that. It's almost like they had a conscience.

An eerie mist covered the town on Halloween night, and kids dressed as witches, goblins, and vampires. Walking down the main street, stores are handing out candy, while I carefully search for the rogues. They have to be here somewhere. I felt it.

I turn around, and someone almost knocks me down. "Watch where you're going." I look up, brushing off my jeans when I see this beautiful blonde nurse with a smile.

"I'm sorry. I didn't mean to." Her blue eyes meet mine, and thereis a slight pause before I catch myself staring.

"It's okay. Just be more careful. I could've been a two-year-old." I smile at her, jokingly. Her perfume isn't strong, but a nice change of pace from what I've been smelling in this town. I'm not sure if they process meat here, but it smells like manure. I start to walk away when she begins to talk.

"So...there's a festival with a haunted house going on a couple of blocks from here. Maybe you wanna come." She hands me the flyer and shoots me a dirty wink.

I am interested in seeing anyone, I've got Jane, but the flyer she hands me looks fun. I haven't taken a load off much since taking this enforcer position. Maybe I should go just for a bit. Blow off some steam.

There are drunk people everywhere, and this town is known for weird things happening. I mean, Salem has mysterious killings all the time that the cops can't explain, and it isn't vampires. You'd think the humans would be smart enough not to be out partying in the woods on this night.

"Hey, wasn't sure you'd come." The blonde approaches me from behind. "Wanna do the haunted house with me? It's getting pretty scary in there. I don't want to go alone."

I guess the least I can do is escort the lady. No strings attached. As we wait our turn to go in, I hear screams from inside. At first, I ams worried, but it's a Halloween Haunted House; of course, they are people screaming. If they did right, there's probably people inside dressed up jumping out at you. That's the whole point right, the thrill of the scare.

"So, are you even a little scared?" She asks, tucking her arm into mine.

"Nope, not many things scare me. I've seen some pretty awful things."

"Oh. What are you a police officer or something?"

"Well- something like that. Sure."

"I'm a teacher. The scariest things I see are grumpy toddlers."

We are finally at the front of the line, and she grips my arm even harder, and takes a deep breath. I can tell she isn't quite ready to go inside. "You'll be alright. I won't let anyone hurt you. It's all in good fun. Just remember, it's all fake. Just like a movie."

As we get inside, we start navigating through the dust and cobwebs everywhere. I feel a hand on my shoulder, and then hear screams. I turn around to a big Frankenstein looking guy standing over me. Creatures are popping out left and right, causing her to scream in my ear.

"Hold on, it's dark, and there are stairs up and ahead to go up." As we approach the stairs, I can hear her pulse quicken with each creak of the old warped stairs. "It's okay. They're doing it right if you are this scared."

"I feel like I'm in a scary movie. Don't mind me, but I might have a heart attack by the end of this."

This place is huge so that we might be in here for a while. Usually, it's over before you know it, but not this one. After a couple of left turns, we come to a hallway with someone sitting at the end.

"Let's go back that way and make a right instead." She insists, pulling me in the other direction. "I don't like this anymore. Let's get out of here."

Each direction we go, it seems to be a dead end. Surely there has to be a way out of this place. At this point, I am getting a little irritated. I can still hear screams that are closer to us. Where are they coming from? How the hell do we get out of here?

"Alright, I'm freaked out. Can we get out of here?" She yells, hoping someone working would hear her, but no one responds. "Hello? Anyone?"

It becomes ominously silent, and the wind dies down. I can't hear a thing. "Hello? The young lady would like out. Where's the emergency exit? We keep coming to dead ends."

Suddenly, a door opens, and a guy grabs her out of my arms before I can react. He is fast, faster than me. "Hello? I'd like to leave too. Make sure she gets home okay. Hello?"

How can he be faster than me? It's not humanly possible. I kick down the door to my right and find her lifeless body lying on the ground with blood everywhere. They must be here. The humans going through this wouldn't think twice about a bloody dead body on the floor.

I try to find my way outside, trying to find the man that just snatched her up. I an usually sense another vampire being around.

I pull out my phone. "Eliza?"

"What?"

"I'm in Salem. I found something. Get here as fast as you can. I'm at the corner lot of Main street. It's got a huge corn maze and Haunted House; you can't miss it."

With her speed, she'd be here in minutes, depending on where she is in the United States.

"What's all the fuss about?" Malachi says.

"Good, you guys are here." I take a deep breath, "So I was accompanying this girl through the house, someone snatched her, and then when I finally got to her, she was dead. Neck wounds and blood everywhere."

"Rogues?" Eliza asks.

"Obviously. Maybe the ones we have been searching for. I tracked them here. I think it's a group of them traveling together."

Eliza and Malachi will be a great asset to this investigation. They found the first scene in Texas, and we have been trying to track them ever since.

"They've got to be somewhere near here. Rogues used her as a warning. They have no fucking clue who I am. But they sure are about to find. Let's split up."

Our best chances of catching them are to split up and search around. They can't be too far away, they will stop to eat, and that is how we will catch them. We've never been this close to them before; no way am I going to let them get away, not with the enforcers right on their tail.

Leaves crunch as I try to trek quietly through the woods, searching for the rogues. I can hear the humans back at the festival having a good time, but nothing out here. They couldn't have gotten away that quick.

Just like that, I hear faint screams coming from the east part of the woods. I take off, running as fast as I can, and land in front of five rogues; hopefully, Eliza and Malachi aren't far away. I can't take them all on by myself.

"What the hell are you doing here?" One of them snarls.

"I'm with the Guardians. It seems like you have been causing quite the mess lately."

"And? What do you plan to do about it?" He replies, looking at his friends with a grin.

"Well, my job is to stop you. Quite a job." Honestly, I am stalling until Malachi and Eliza show up. Where the hell are they?

"And how do you plan on doing that? You're outnumbered. Those odds don't seem great for you."

"I've overcome worse."

"Last shot. Walk away, and we'll let you live."

There were bodies everywhere, with some still being fed on by his friends. "I don't shy away from a fight."

22

Eliza

As we watch them burn, we are happy that another threat has been eliminated. If we don't get to Godric soon, we could have an uprising on our hands. No one wants to go through that again. We've interrogated rogues but still haven't gotten any viable information about his whereabouts.

"Thanks for the help. Couldn't have taken down all of them without you guys." Envio says.

He is right. Five against one isn't good odds and usually frowned upon for taking such a risk. "No problem. Gotta head back and try to make some progress on my Blakeley investigation."

"Still nothing?"

"Not yet. Hopefully, I'll have something to go off of soon."

I've still been digging, trying to figure out who this Blakeley girl is and why the rogues are hunting her? Maybe she can lead us to Godric?

For the past week, I've been trying to pull anything I can up on Blakeley, but there are eighteen matches within a thirty-mile radius of Cherry Hill, New Jersey. I have to thoroughly go through each file to make sure we don't miss anything. Malachi is helping me skim through the data to see if he can place anything that will lead to someone we know. It is the only lead that Felix gave us.

"We've got to be missing something. Can you think of anything else he said, anything that might be of importance?" I ask.

"He said once found, it would be a gamechanger. Maybe he means that she will help them try to take us down?"

If this is the case, we need to find her before they do. The only problem, they know the reason, and we didn't. The irritation is setting in, knowing that if we didn't get this done fast enough, an uprising could be erupting. "Well, maybe we should take a different approach to this. Maybe pull a genealogy report on each of them. That will show us who they are related too. Might save us some time, possibly." Honestly, I hope it did because we need the answer like a week ago.

I pull out my laptop and start running reports on each of the matches, printing them out. "Here. Start going through these while I'm doing the searches." I tell Malachi. He is trying to be helpful, but he needs to be productive. I hand him a stack of papers paperclipped for him to skim through the names on the list. "See you notice any names."

It is taking about fifteen minutes per match to run the report and then print it off. This is going to take a couple of days to go through all these pages.

"Anything yet?" I ask, urgingly.

"Nada."

Something has to give. We need a one-up and fast. Godric is acquiring rogues faster than we can find and kill them. If this gets out of hand and turns into another Blood Takers situation, it won't be good for us. The country is already trying to figure out who is doing all the killings, and they aren't going to stop until they have someone to pin it on. Most are scared to leave their homes to even go to work in fear of being slaughtered. Some are also stupid and didn't believe all the media. Those are the ones that usually get killed because they are foolish and going out when told to stay home.

"I found something." He yells from the bed. "You might want to take a look at this."

I jump up and go to sit next to him. His index finger points to a name, and my eyes widen. No fucking way. It can't be. How did no one know about this?

The name printed on the paper makes my blood boil. If they get a hold of her and used it to their advantage, an uprising is coming. Now I have a full name to search and find out where she is possibly staying or working that will lead us to her.

Me: Her name is Blakeley Peters. Figured it out, but it's something we should discuss in person.

We need to keep between all of us, and not let word get out. If it did, Guardians could start to worry or tell the wrong person that we know of her. The rogues have no idea we know about her existence, and that's the way we need to keep it.

"I did expect this. Hell, no one did." Malachi says.

Stephen: Alright Sasha's on way. Meet at my house.

Usually, we drive, but this information has a sense of urgency, so our speed could have us there in less than twenty minutes.

Running up to Stephen's place, I am not sure how they will take the news. It can have a devastating effect on what we have been trying to build.

"Let's go into my office. Who knows who could be lurking around."

As Stephen shut her door, all eyes were on me, clutching the file on Blakeley Peters. "Here is everything I've been able to find so far. The second page will be the one you want to look at."

She turns to the second page and immediately stops. "You can't be serious? How is this possible?"

Envio walks over to glance at the name, and even he can't believe what he is seeing. "This makes no sense. He never mentioned a daughter."

"Well, it's something he wanted to keep a secret. It seems

someone knew since the rogues are going after her. They're not smart enough to figure that out on their own."

"So, what do you propose their game plan is?" Sasha asks.

"Just a theory, but I think they are going after her so she can lead the rogues. They have been looking for a new leader ever since Jakob's death." Honestly, I'm not sure why else they would be interested in her at all?

Stephen nods, "I think you're right. So any idea where she's at?"

"Well, I was able to pull some information. She works at a diner on K st in Jersey City and lives a couple of blocks from there. I'm not sure how the rogues haven't figured this out yet."

Stephen is pacing the room, hand against his chin, while we wait for him to tell us our next move. "I'll send Envio to get her. He can maybe persuade her with good looks to come back with him. Or at least keep her safe until we find Godric."

Envio wastes no time accepting and taking off.

23
Envio

The traditional sit-down diner is half occupied, with the waitresses buzzing around refilling drinks. I've been sitting here for a couple of hours, and they've refilled my coffee five times already. Blakeley is nowhere, and I can only sit here so long without being creepy.

"Do you want some more coffee, sir?"

I shake my head because, at this point, it is time for me to leave. Maybe come back tomorrow on a different shift. I take the last sip of my cold coffee and grab my jacket.

The street outside is filled with people shopping for their precious Christmas gifts as the snow falls to the ground. The old main road is away from the city and seems like a tiny town.

When I was younger, Christmas was my favorite holiday. My mother was very chipper around that time of year, and we always baked new things every year to try out. Why did I stop celebrating Christmas? Is it because I am a vampire? Would it be weird of me to celebrate it now? I truly miss the Christmas spirit and am having thoughts about celebrating it again. It'd be nice to have something to take my mind off all the stresses this job brings.

I come to an alleyway and can hear someone struggling.

"Stop. Get away from me." A woman yells, pulling the strap of her purse. "That's mine."

She needs help; there is no way I can just walk away without assisting. My feet stomp against the ground approaching them. "Get away from here." I growl.

The man glances at me for a second and pulls one more time on the purse before running away.

"Thank you. I just cashed my check, and if he would have taken it... Well, I wouldn't be able to pay my rent."

The lighting is dim, but as her face raises from her purse, my smile swept. "No worries, ma'am. I'm just glad you're okay. No telling what he would've done to you."

Blakeley is standing right in front of me, and I just saved her. What a great first impression. "This might be too forward, but would you like to grab a cup of coffee?"

She seems a little on edge still but agrees. "Sure. Uh there's a diner around the corner. My shift starts in half an hour, but I could use a cup of coffee."

She starts walking past me, and I follow after her. "So, I'm new here. Any advice?"

"Carry fanny packs." She says, trying to keep a straight face. "Purses make you an easy target."

"Good thing I don't carry one." I smile.

Me: Found her.

The bell above the door sounds as Blakeley, and I walk into the diner. The waitress looks at me and then her. I'd only left less than twenty minutes ago. The coffee cup from before is still sitting on the table.

"Have a seat. Let me go put stuff down in the back." She motions to the table.

As she walks into the back, my previous waitress follows her. Hopefully, she didn't tell her I am some crazy guy or something. My eyes are fixed on the swinging kitchen door, waiting for her to return.

The front door opens, and a rogue enters. Not yet. Fuck, what am

I going to do? I don't think he will make a scene inside. As long as I keep my eye on her, she will be safe.

Me: Rogue is here. At diner. I'll keep an eye on her

"Hey, what ya looking at? See something interesting?"

I didn't see her come out, but chuckle and takes a sip of the coffee she brings me.

"Didn't know how you liked it, so here is some cream and sugar."

"I like it black, thanks."

I try to pay attention to her, but the rogue is sitting two booths down and staring at me. He knows I am a vampire but isn't sure yet what side I'm on.

"So what brings you here? Especially this part?" She asks, setting her coffee down and chin landing on her palms.

"Honestly, not sure. I like to travel and have never been to New Jersey. Only stopping in. It's not like I'm moving here." I laugh.

"Well, you won't be staying long. Nothing interesting here." Her eyes roll. "I can't wait to get away from here."

"Then why are you still here?"

Her eyes shoot at mine, probably not used to someone being so forward. "I can't afford to go anywhere. It was hard enough for me to find this job. Hell, where would I go?"

I once had the same dream, getting out of Illinois. So I understood. There's a difference between wanting to be somewhere else and doing it. Up and moving to another state is a big decision and can't be taken lightly. Did the new place have a high crime rate? How's the economy? Lots of job openings? "Kentucky has a flourishing economy right now, and lots of open jobs. Ever thought about moving there?"

"Nope. Never considered it. Always thought about California."

"Well, you'd be right then. Unless you are a doctor, lawyer, or have six roommates. It's way too expensive to live there."

My grandparents lived in California and always struggled to pay the bills. They finally left and moved to Illinois to be closer to us. I know firsthand how hard it is to be able to survive there.

"Valid point. Okay, so somewhere else then."

The other waitresses come up and ask if I want a refill. "Sure."

"Oh and you're shift started five minutes ago." She says to Blakeley.

She stands up and looks embarrassed. "Sorry to cut this short. My boss will kill me for being late."

I didn't even get to respond before she is in the back. She is an interesting woman with aspirations. Now, all I need to do is keep the rogue away from her. I couldn't tell if she is friendly or if she is into me. Usually, I'm not the type of guy to string girls along, but I might have to, in this case, for her good.

I watch as she straps on her apron, and starts making drinks for the other patrons.

How am I going to stay here without seeming like a creep? Her coworker already keeps staring at me like I'm a serial killer or something. It does seem slightly weird for someone to be here for three hours, leave, and then come back twenty minutes later. Had she mentioned it to her?

Blakeley approaches the rogue, and he is drooling over her.

"Can I getcha something to drink?"

"Waters fine." He answers.

I have to do something. My hand raises in the air as if I am in a classroom.

"You need something?"

I smile, "Could I get a menu? I'm starving over here."

She nods and swiftly walks away as the rogue gazes at me again. He is trying to figure out if I am a threat or not. I can't give up my position and have to stay close to her.

I look over the menu, and nothing seems enticing. When is the last time I ate human food? Years ago, possibly.

"How's the chicken fried steak?"

"Sub par." She laughs.

My radar goes off and confirms that she is into me. Insulting her place of works food to a customer, that's bold. "I'll take that."

She rolls her eyes, "don't say I didn't give you a fair warning."

Me: I'm not sure how long I can sit here without looking suspicious to the humans. Blakeley likes me, but not the other waitresses.

Sasha: Suck it up. Do what you can. Don't let the rogue near her.

Me: He's inside the diner, and she's a waitress.

Sasha: you know what I mean

I do, but I love fucking with her. It is so easy, sometimes.

Me: 10-4

After pushing around the chicken fried steak and finishing yet another cup of coffee, I have overstayed my welcome and pay the bill.

"Any chance I'll see you again?" I ask, gazing into her hazel eyes.

"I was wondering if I could show you my appreciation for earlier. I get off around 6."

The smile erupts across her face, letting me know she is nervous about being so forward. "I'll be up. Here's my number."

Instead of making it more awkward, I leave and wait for her to go in the back so I can secure a place where I can still see inside the restaurant. I might not be able to be inside, but surveillance is still vital until that rogue leaves.

My phone starts buzzing. The name that pops across my screen makes me jerk my head back. This has to be a joke.

"Hello?"

"Long time, no talk, stranger." Her sweet, sarcastic voice hits my ear.

"What's up? Everything okay?"

"I should be asking you the same thing. Heard your on a mission to find Jakob's daughter?"

How did she know about that? Did Sasha tell her? I thought we aren't supposed to be telling anyone. "Uhh… yeah, I am. Going okay so far."

"I saw a picture. She's a good looking woman. Be careful."

Is Jane calling me because she's worried or jealous? "Always am. Should have taken the chance when you had it." I joke, but my tone didn't convey that.

"I regret that, but it was the right decision. Look at all the shit we've run into."

I've been going nonstop since I took this position, so I completely understood her reasoning now better than I did then. "Agreed. Maybe one day."

"Well, someone's knocking on my door. Gotta go. Catch up soon."

Sasha: More on the way. There's only one thing left to do.

Me: what exactly are you telling me to do?

Sasha: Kill her

Are you fucking serious? There's no way I'm going to kill her. What the hell is she thinking? Are we killing humans now for our gain? I joined the guardians to be on the right side, and it seems like Sasha is going down the wrong path.

Instead of texting back, I pick up my phone, and I call Sasha.

"Why on earth would I do that?"

"Because that's the only thing that's going to keep us from another uprising. If the rogues get to her before you do, all hell will break loose. We can't afford for that to happen again. We've worked too damn hard for it to go south now."

I stay silent for a few moments letting what she's saying sink into my brain. I'm not quite sure how I feel about killing a human for personal gain. Can I disobey her and get away with it? Would Stephen agree with her decision?

"I'm sorry, that's just not gonna happen. I'm not that person anymore, and I refuse to kill a human and go against the rules you set. You made me become an enforcer to carry out the rules, and now you're asking me to break the rules. How hypocritical could you be?"

"Everyone would understand that it's the right thing to do right now. An uprising would mean everything that we've worked so hard to achieve in the last five years would mean nothing. If Blakely gets turned, all rooms will get behind her, and an uprising will happen. And it's not gonna be like with Jacob because now they know what they're up against so it'll be twice as bad."

I understand what she is saying, but I won't do it. Blakeley hasn't done anything wrong. It isn't right to take her life because of her father. She can't help who she is related to, and just because Blakeley is associated with Jakob doesn't mean that she's a bad person. In just the short amount of time I've been around her, she seems like a brilliant woman who has aspirations in life. Who am I to take that life away from her? "My answer is still no."

"Fine. Your choice, but just remember I did give you one. Eliza's on her way. She understands what her death would mean for our future. We can't take the chance, Envio. You'll understand eventually."

24
Warwick

Sasha encouraged me to apply for the police academy so I can keep an eye on the city's crime. My partner, Jenna, didn't care for me much.

"Why are you always staring at me like that?" Jenna asks, walking out of the coffee shop.

"I wasn't. Just waiting for you, that's all." I stammer, lying.

"Well, I'm done. So, stop staring at me now. Thanks." She scoffs and slips into the passenger seat of the cruiser.

We were partnered right out of the academy instead of with experienced partners.

The radio buzzs, "All units, we have a 10-71. 1052 Osiago Avenue."

I haven't worked a shooting since becoming a cop. I've always wanted to take down an active shooter. "Copy. Unit 12 responding. 2 minutes ETA."

"Copy 12." The dispatcher replies on the radio.

I look at Jenna, her blue eyes wide, and make a quick U-turn while turning the sirens on. The traffic is terrible, so we have to weave in and out of parked cars due to rush hour.

Pulling up on the scene, I open my door and stand behind it. We are the only unit here as of now.

"Dispatch. Unit 12 arrived. Copy." Jenna says.

"Copy. More on the way."

Jenna wi now outside of the cruiser with her gun pointing directly at the man.

"Sir, we don't want to hurt you," I scream. Our training covered these situations. *Assess the situation.* "Is there anyone inside?"

He points the gun to his front door, "my bitch of a wife."

"Anyone else?"

"My two kids."

How could this guy be pointing his gun at his home knowing his two kids were inside? "Sir, I need you to put the weapon down. Let's de-escalate this before more cops show up."

He wipes his tears, the gun resting on his forehead. "I can't do that. That bitch has to pay."

I glance over at Jenna, nod, and put my weapon down. "Sir, I'm going to come over to you without my weapon."

"Don't - don't come any closer." He points the gun straight at me. Even though a bullet wouldn't kill me, Jenna didn't know that.

"Okay- I'll stop here," I say with my hands up. "Can I at least go inside and make sure they are alright?" The man just stares at me, didn't move a muscle.

"They're fine. I'm not leaving until my wife's dead."

He's distraught. I don't think he will hurt the kids, but his wife is another story. She did something to him that he thinks is worth killing her over. "Why do you want your wife dead so bad?"

"She cheated on me. With my boss." He wipes his eyes again, "15 years of marriage down the drain just like that. I gave everything to her and my children, and this is the thanks I get. My wife fucking my boss in my bed."

My eyes open wide in shock. I didn't know what to say. How the hell am I going to de-escalate this situation? "Is he inside too?"

He didn't respond but nods.

I could hear Jenna updating dispatch on the radio. "We have two children, the mother and a man inside the home. Threats of killing the wife. Copy."

Where the hell are those other units? It fell like it's been twenty minutes since we arrived. "The others will be here soon. If we don't resolve this now, you might end up leaving in a body bag. I don't want that."

"The only person leaving here in a body bag is my wife. You can bet on that." He replies.

Rushing him is the only way everyone is going to make it out of this situation safely. I need to do it before the others show up. Once Jenna takes her eyes off me. I rush him, g etting the gun from him, but not before he shoots me. The echo of the gunshot catches Jenna's attention right before it goes into my chest.

"Nooooo - are you okay?" Jenna screams, running toward us.

The first thing she did is cuff him, and then come over to check on me. I try to get her to check on the hostages, but she wouldn't.

"Are you okay?" She asks, patting over my chest, checking for wounds. "I don't understand. I saw him shoot you?"

It pierced my chest, but it didn't stay inside. Perks of being a vampire. "He missed, see." I pull up my shirt, letting her take a glimpse at my chest to inspect for any wounds. Her eyes widen.

"But I saw - I saw the bullet go into your chest." Jenna wipes her forehead, staring at the ground, probably wondering what the hell is going on.

"Obviously it didn't. If shot, I'd be dead."

I walk into the home. "He's in cuffs. You can come out now."

The hostages come out of a closet, hugging one another, and glad to see me. "He's under arrest. You're safe now."

Things have been tense since the shooting between us.

"Jenna. Warwick. Before you head out, come into my office." The captain asks.

"Yes, sir. What can we do?" I ask.

"I've got a young lady here that has requested a ride-along. You guys are the last ones out for the shift so, she's all yours."

As I walk out of the station, I see a young blonde leaning up against our car. I didn't expect her to look like that. She is wearing a short enough skirt and a tank top, that's it.

"Jenna's a no-show. It looks like you get to ride up front today."

She slips into the passenger seat, making her skirt ride up, revealing her upper thigh. I try to restrain myself from staring, but it's challenging.

The next few hours, Samantha tells me about her aspirations to be a police officer, and then conversation turns personal.

"So, have a good night?" She asks.

"Watching some TV. That's about it." I answer, making myself seem like the most dull person on the planet. My hands run through my short brown hair. *Stop being so depressing.*

"No woman in your life?"

"Nope. Kind of like it that way." I answer.

We pull into the station at the end of the day, and I really want to get her number. "Well, it was nice meeting you. Would you like to get together sometime?"

"Yeah, that sounds nice."

She writes her number down on a piece of paper, "Here. Call me when you're free."

When I get home, her number lays on my coffee table for a couple of hours while wondering if I should call her or not. Should I wait a couple of days, so I don't seem so eager? I'd been out of the game far too long to know the customary rules on asking someone out.

I dial her number. The ringing kept going until; finally, her sweet voice erupts.

"Hello?"

I perk up off the couch, "Uhh- hey, It's Warwick."

"Oh, wow. I wasn't sure if you would call me or not. Didn't expect it this soon."

I could tell how surprised she is. "Well, reaching out to see if you would like to hang out sometime? With me, of course."

She laughs, "That's kinda why I gave you my number, silly. Just let me know when."

"Are you free tonight?" I eagerly ask. Silence takes over the conversation for a minute. Maybe I'm moving too fast. Stupid. "Or uhh - what about Friday night?"

"I'm free tonight."

A smile sweeps across his face. "Well, what would you like to do? I can cook you dinner."

My mind reverts to the rules, no relationships with humans. Am I willing to break them for Samantha?

"Dinner sounds great. Send me the address. But just a heads up, my best friend will also have your address in case you try to kill me or something. See you in a bit."

Kill her? Wow, she has an imagination. Although going to some guys house after only knowing them a day, it's good to air on the side of caution.

After making a trip to the grocery store for items to cook, I start preparing the food. A rap at the door let me know she has arrived.

"Hey, come in," I say. "You can hang your jacket on that hook there. I'll be in the kitchen."

After hanging her coat up, she follows me into the kitchen. "What are you making?"

"Baked chicken breast, mashed potatoes, and probably a salad. Sound okay?"

No response, only a smile.

I try to focus on preparing the meal instead of staring at her while enjoying some conversation. "So, how's it going at the Academy?"

"I don't start until next week. I didn't apply in time for this round.
"

"Are you excited? Ready for the big bad streets?"

Her look is priceless. "Big bad streets? Come on now. Plus, it's our job to keep them safe, right?"

As a police officer, it's our job to keep the streets protected for everyone. It's sometimes hard to do that. "So many criminals out there, though."

"We work hard to put people like that behind bars. Don't underestimate yourself." She replies, slightly touching my hand on the counter.

I quickly move my hand away and point myself back toward the stove to finish preparing. I shouldn't be doing this. Her lips have been invading my thoughts for the last week. A part of me feels compelled to her, craving her touch.

"Are you okay?"

"Yeah- sorry. I must be getting tired."

I walk over and grab her coat, "You should go and get some rest. We can do this another time."

Instead of slipping it on, she pulls me close and plants a kiss.

After first, I jerk away. "You're tired. Maybe another time."

"This is a perfect time." She smiles and kisses me.

My hands creep up to her hips and then through her belt loops, pulling her even closer.

I know this is wrong, but then why did it feel so right?

She takes off her shirt and then mine. Her breasts are perky, even more than I imagined. A primal growl erupts when she puts her hand on me, and my mouth lands on her neck.

"What the fuck are you doing?" She yells, her hand darting up to her neck.

"I'm sorry. I didn't mean to." Her blood smells sweet and every time I kiss her, it makes me want to taste her even more.

"Please. Stop. It hurts." She yells, but I didn't budge, and before I know it, she is unconscious.

All the times I've been tested since my reform and never once have I strayed until now. What is so exquisite about Sam that makes me so crazy? Crazy enough to risk my immortality?

Her lifeless body is being held in my arms while I weigh my two options: turn her or let her die. If I turn her, she would have to register. Once she did, it would eventually lead them back to me. I rub my forehead, not sure I can let her die because of me. Fuck it. I nip my wrist and hold it to her mouth, waiting for her to drink. It takes a couple of minutes. After taking what she needs, a slumber ensued.

Meanwhile, her phone keeps buzzing, but without a passcode, I can't get in. After turning her phone off, I lay down next to her waiting for her slumber to end.

Soon after, my phone starts to ring.

"Warwick," I answer.

"What the hell are you doing? You've got humans following you?"

"What?' I reply, looking around. "How do you know?"

"Cause my guys have been watching you after your little incident."

"Why? I can handle myself."

"Let's just say when your partner filed a report that you got shot and magically healed within minutes; eyebrows raised. What'd you expect?"

She's been having me followed. "So, who is it?"

"Not sure but their human," Sasha replies. "My guys are MIA after their last report, so watch your back."

Sam starts to move, and I need to get out of here. "I'm leaving. Gotta go."

"Wha- What's going on?" She asks, rubbing her face and looking around the room. "Wait? Did you bite me? I'm not a - vampire, am I?"

Did she know? "We gotta get out of here." The look she flashed me confirmed.

"Their coming for you. Run!"

25

Warwick

We both could hear many hearts beating standing outside the house. I grabbed her, and we whisked away, not stopping until we hit Georgia.

"What the hell are we gonna do? They won't stop until they've captured your kind."

"Remember, now it's our kind."

I want to put as much road between us as possible. Better question, how did I not pick up on being followed? Is Sam that distracting? The critical thing, staying on top of my game. How did she know about me? Is she helping the ones that were following me?

As we get settled in a discreet hotel, I have questions.

"You feeling okay? You weren't asleep very long."

"I feel like a million bucks. Thanks to you."

Her sarcastic tone rumbles through me. "I didn't have a choice. Would you rather be dead?"

"I'd rather be human than a monster."

"Is that what you think of me? That I'm a monster?" I want to know the truth.

I - don't think you're a monster necessarily. I mean, you did just turn me."

Fuck. She's right. Even knowing my secret, she wants to sleep with me, and I end up taking her to my side. "But I swear that wasn't my intention. I've never been intimate with someone since... becoming this way. Now I understand why they don't condone human-vampire relationships."

Sam starts to walk over to me, but I can't face her.

She places her hand on my shoulder "I can tell you feel guilty. I wanted to sleep with you. So it's not your fault. I played a part in this too."

But it is me who couldn't control myself. I've been very tempted but never acted because I understood the consequences. Sam is my soft spot. "So, do you know the people that were following me?"

Her head tilts down, "Yes."

"How?"

"I was working for them."

I try to act surprised. "You were? What do you mean?"

"They've been watching you since you joined the academy. You showed off some remarkable skills that made them obsessed with you."

My feelings toward Sam are all a lie? She is just trying to get close to me. How did I ever think crushing on a human would end well?

"Will you say something? You look pissed."

"Uh - well, it hurts to know everything between us was a lie."

She cuts me off. "No, not everything. There's a connection between us. I can't deny that."

So, I'm not the only one. "But you were going to turn me in? I'm not a monster, no matter what they've seen."

Sam approaches me, lays her hand on my shoulder again. "I know you aren't. You could've ripped me to shreds or let me die. Instead, you turned me."

Not quite sure if she knows enough about our kind. Sam needs to be brought up to speed and make some tough decisions.

"Don't beat yourself up. I should've known better. I practically threw myself at you, even knowing what you were capable of."

I didn't respond but need some air. I run through some scenarios in my head, and she freaks out in all of them. Grow a pair and just tell her.

As I open our room door, there she is on the bed with her clothes strung on the floor. "No, not now." I pick up her shirt and throw it to her. She stands up in all her glory and walks toward me.

"Let's finish what we started. You don't have to worry about hurting me now."

She's right but still doesn't feel like the best time. "Listen, we need to talk. I'm serious." Her hands glide to the hem of my shirt and pull it off. Once the kissing starts, I can't resist any longer.

Something about Samantha is unique, and I just can't quite put my finger on it. As I lay next to her, I wonder what this means for us. It didn't make me feel too good to find out she originally only got close to me for her boss, but things are different now.

"Ready to talk now?" I ask, gazing into her eyes.

"Unless you'd rather have a round two?" She proposes.

"I'd like to get this done first. For both of our sakes."

"Shoot."

My chest rises and falls before I begin. "So - you've got some choices to make. I need to know what you want to do before we go any further."

"And they are?"

"Do you want to be a vampire?"

"I don't understand. Aren't I one already?"

"Yes, but you could choose to die instead of feed."

"Why the hell would anyone choose death?"

"Some have. As I said, it's a hard decision."

"I choose to live."

"Well, hold on. We have rules. I've already broken them by being with and turning you. We have to go about this carefully." If Stephen or Sasha find out about her, it'll be my death.

"Okay. What do you want me to do?"

"Register with the Guardians. Our government."

"You know they are never going to give up until they capture one of your kind. Vampires are a mystery to them, and they don't like secrets. If they ever confirm that you exist, the world is going to change big time."

"It's harder to capture us than you think. I'm not that worried."

Her eyes gaze into mine, and her palm grazes over my chest, "So how about that second round?"

A smile sweeps across my face, "Wow. Are you obsessed already? Going through withdrawals, are you?"

She climbs up on my lap, "You could fix it." Another kiss plants on my lips. "Don't you want too?"

I laughs, "Maybe later. Let's enjoy some time together before we have to go on the run again. We can't stay anywhere for too long. That's what makes it easy to find vampires. No trails of blood or anything."

"How do you know that?"

I look to the ground, "it's a long story. I'd rather not get into that now." She just keeps staring at me. "I am an enforcer for our leader. I track bad vampires and kill them."

"What's so bad about that?"

"I didn't want to be a killer, okay! When I got away from Godric, I thought maybe I could change, but I still became a killer but for different reasons."

"It's the perspective that determines who was the villain and the hero. From me, you're the hero."

"Let's just enjoy tonight. We'll leave in the morning."

The sunrise comes faster than we expect. I stand by my word, and don't plan on staying here any longer than necessary. At some point, Sam will need to feed, or she will become very ill. Feeding would be dangerous right now; they couldn't be too far behind us at this point.

"Ready to go?"

Samantha nods, and we join hands before rushing off to our next stop. Minnesota will be quite far and it would take them some time to catch up to us. We just have to stay ahead of the others.

We make it to Minnesota, gaining a few days ahead of them. Who knows what they will do if they find out that Sam is now a vampire. As we fear, they think we're all monsters. There's nothing we can do to change their minds at this point. I didn't want to tell Sasha and Stephen, but I have too. The Guardians need to be aware of what's going on and let everyone know.

I slap my forehead, not looking forward to this call with her. As the ringing ensues, I naturally hope she won't pick up. Maybe, I'd just leave a message for her. Fuck.

"What the hell took you so long? Why haven't you been answering my calls?" Sasha yells.

I run my hands through my hair, "Uhh - well, I was trying to stay ahead of the pitchforks."

"What do you mean?"

"The people following me work for the human government. They know about our species."

"How do you know this? Who are they?"

"I overheard a conversation between them. They want to find out how to kill us off. I would have called early, but hell, maybe they tapped my phone." What if they did? They could trace Sasha. "I think maybe we should cut this call short just in case. I'm going to keep moving around. I'll call you in a few days from another phone and check-in. Stay safe and warn the others."

As she hangs up, I drop the phone on the bed. "Do you think they have my phone tapped?"

She shrugs, "Wouldn't put it past them. They're never going to stop trying to find you."

The problem is I know she is serious. Hell, what if they get a hold of a rogue? That could be the worst thing imaginable. They want humans to find out about us, and even worse, they'd just kill them instantly. I don't understand how they think they could trap us? Hell, the only weakness we know of is the fire. Burning our bodies is the only way to kill us. I'd be interested to see what they come up with to trap us.

"How long are we going to stay here?" Sam asks, snuggling on my shoulder.

"Probably a day or two. No longer. We will have to keep moving around as often as we can."

"We can't just keep moving around forever."

"Why can't we? Eventually, they get old and tired, and we don't. It's just a matter of time. We have plenty of that."

A knock at the door sounds. "Housekeeping." The door opens, and a dart hits my neck. What the fuck is in this? My mind feels fuzzy, and then everything goes dark.

How did they find us? Samantha's boss captured us, even though I didn't struggle. I could quickly kill them all, but I don't want it to have to come to that. We aren't supposed to kill humans.

The chains are digging into my wrists, leaving cuts, but they will heal as soon as they come off. I just have to buy my time until I can escape. The room is cold and damp. Where the hell am I? Where is Samantha? I focus on my surroundings and can hear her.

"Lori, I tried to get away, but he's too fast. I didn't have my phone to call you. I'm so glad you finally found me." She says sobbing.

What the hell? She's playing the kidnapped card. Surely they will find out eventually that she isn't human anymore. It's not like she can hide it forever. If she didn't feed within a week, it will mean her death. It's a huge leap for her; how will this help her in any way?

"Listen, you're safe now, but I need you to tell us what you have found out. We need to know everything." Lori replies eagerly.

She wouldn't dare tell them anything they can use against us, especially now that she's a vampire.

"Well, his boss, who I presume is the leader, called and knows that you were tailing him now. She doesn't seem like a nice person, either."

"Well they are vampires, so we didn't expect them to be nice." Lori laughs.

They have us all wrong. The Blood Takers have ruined it for us. All those bodies they left in the streets throughout the country are now returning to haunt us.

"She will come looking for him, and when she does, you don't want to be in her way."

Why is she lying to them? Sasha isn't evil, far from it, and she has no clue where we are at so she wouldn't look in the right places even if she wants to find me. Samantha, what the hell are you doing?

"Well, that's why we have you. I guess you've spent a lot of time with him in the past week. Have you discovered any weaknesses while you've been with him? Something that could help us have a one up on them when the time is right? You'd be doing the country a favor and saving countless lives in the process. Anything come to mind at all?"

I can hear her struggle. It is like she didn't want to tell them, but knows she has too or it would be suspicious. "Fire. You can only kill them permanently if you burn their bodies."

Fuck! Out of all the things, she could have told her, why tell her that? Humans knowing this information is detrimental.

"Let's go talk to him and see if we can get more out of him. There has to be more. No one has only one weakness."

They both walk in, and I try to act as if I didn't hear their conversation. "What do you want? Just let me go. I've not harmed you or your people."

"But you have. Or at least your people have. Humans have been dying left and right at the hands of you vampires."

Again, not us but the Blood Takers. Should I even try to explain it? Wouldn't it just be a waste of my breath?

"But that's the rogues. We are trying to eradicate them, but it's harder to control them than you think. Just like criminals. You can't stop all criminal activity in your country, can you?"

"Nice try. Not gonna work on me." She laughs at me again.

"Samantha, what's the meaning of this? Who are these people?" I need to act like I didn't know what is going on.

She smiles, "I work for an organization trying to prove the vampire's existence. They are the reason behind all the lives lost in the last decade. You made it quite easy for them. Really should keep your powers in check."

"But- I haven't done anything wrong. If you've been watching me, then you know I haven't killed anyone. I'm a police officer; I signed on to help people, not hurt them."

"I'm sure that's what you want us to think. Probably waiting around until the time is right." She points to Samantha. "You kidnapped her against her will, that's not something a police officer would do, is it?"

I have to get out of here, and so does Samantha. We didn't have a lot of time.

"Could I have some water?" I cough, trying to appear that my throat is dry.

The lady nods and leaves the room without any hesitation. She might want to hurt me, but I could tell she is still a compassionate person even if she has me chained up. I wait until I didn't hear her near and try to plead with Samantha. "We gotta get out of here. If you don't feed soon, you'll die."

"I know, but if I don't lead them to believe you kidnapped me, I'll be stuck in here, same as you. How the hell can I help you by being chained up?"

I laugh, breaking the chains loose. "You mean these chains? They aren't doing anything. I hope they don't believe chains were going to keep me in here." I open the door, and bolt towards the exit door with Samantha behind me, my hand in hers. "We have to go now while we have the chance."

Samantha looks scared, glancing behind her. "But, what if I stay and help lead them in the wrong direction? I could help you and the others buy some time before they do anything?"

"No, come with me. End of story. If they find out you're a vampire, they'll kill you."

I can feel the sadness erupting through her, "but it will buy you guys some time to figure out how you are going to handle this. She's going to inform the president. Do you understand what that means for vampires?"

I shake my head because all I care about is keeping her safe. I've only known her for a couple of weeks, but my heart belongs to her. I couldn't explain it. There is no way I am leaving her behind.

"That means the world will know about vampires soon enough. You will be hunted, outed, and possibly eradicated. They won't stop until you are all dead."

I can hear the hustling of boots on the cement heading toward us after finding the cell empty. "Please, you have to come with me. You can't stay here; you aren't safe."

"He's trying to escape, this way," Samantha yells, throwing herself to the ground. "Go. Alert Sasha and the others. It's better this way, I promise. I can handle myself."

They are getting closer; I have to make a choice fast. I have to put the cause above my feelings. Running out of that door is one of the hardest things, knowing Samantha will be dead in a week.

26

Stephen

Things just haven't been going right in the last few weeks. We've tried to find Godric, but no luck. Until we catch him, the rogue situation will only get worse. More and more are popping up all over the country, and each turned out to be worse than the last.

Warwick has proven to be a great enforcer, but when Sasha informed me he has been followed, my anxiety begins to flare up. It's been over a week with no communication from him. Did they get him? Capture him? I laugh at the latter because what could they have that would possibly keep a vampire captured?

"Sir, Call on Line 1 from Warwick. He said it's urgent."

My face dropped. It couldn't be good news. "I'll take it. Thank you." Before I pick up the phone, a deep breath is taken to calm my anxiety. "What's going on?"

"I - they know. I was taken and put into an underground bunker but escaped. The group knows our weaknesses. It's bad."

They did capture him, but how did they find out about our weakness? "How? Do you mean fire? The only people who know about that are vampires, so how could they find out that information?"

"I don't know, but it's bad. I overheard them before I broke out, and they were going to inform the President. They are going to try to kill us all. We need to warn the others fast."

I've never heard him so terrified. Surely he didn't think that humans could kill us all. We are much faster than they are, they would have to get all of us in the same space and then burn it down, but even then we can just run out. "Come to my house. I'll call a meeting and have everyone here by five. Can you do that?"

"Yes. I'll be there."

If the humans did try to kill us, what would we do? We can't kill them; it's not only against our rules but how would we survive as a species without them?

I sent out a mass message to the enforcers and governors: *Emergency meeting at my house—5 pm. Attendance is required.*

My phone starts to flood with worry texts, wondering what the emergency meeting is all about. Instead of trying to explain it to a bunch of people separately, the conference will be when everyone finds out at the same time. There is no need to cause chaos before we know that it is going to happen. Maybe Warwick heard them wrong. Surely the President wouldn't just announce the existence of vampires in a press conference, right?

I hear the doorbell ring, and my guys answered it, followed by Warwick's voice. Of course, he's the first one here.

"You made it. Are you okay?" I greet him with a smile, but he looks like shit.

"Yeah, yeah. Enough with the pleasantries. What are we going to do?" He says, brushing past me, heading straight to my office.

"Straight shooter, I've always liked that about you."

"They won't wait long. If announced soon, the humans would have more of an advantage on us."

"Do you think they will announce it that fast? I'd guess it would take them at least a couple of days to come up with how to announce it and proceed before involving the public." I mean, that's what I would do in their situation. I wasn't going to send an email to every vampire, telling them to be careful because humans knew about our existence. That would be jumping the gun and causing chaos. They would become fearful and start killing anyone they suspect was going to try to hurt them. Not the way we want this to go.

"This woman, their leader Lori, she's tough. Her team has been trying to find the cause behind all of the deaths in the last decade. They knew it couldn't be animals or humans. They kept digging and digging until they found me. I ruined this for us."

The blame goes to the Blood Takers and Jakob for causing this affliction between humans and vampires. If he can just keep his pack from savagely murdering hundreds, we won't be in this predicament. "Listen, it's not your fault. Don't blame yourself."

The doorbell rings again, but this time multiple voices are heard. "Shall we go join the others?"

As we make our way down the stairs, Jane, Sasha, and Envio are waiting at the bottom.

"What's with this meeting?" Ian asks. "I have so many things I'm trying to get finished."

"This takes precedence. I'll explain once everyone is here."

"Warwick, please show them into the dining room while we wait for the others."

I run back up to my office and shut the door. How am I going to explain this? Before I can finish my thought process, the doorbell rings again. Eliza and Malachi have arrived.

"Let's all go join the others in the dining room. We have a lot to discuss."

As I follow them inside and sit down, I am still unsure about how to deliver the news.

"So, I called this emergency meeting because I have some news that needed to be shared with you first. Before we get into it, remember we don't want chaos. How we handle this would determine the outcome."

"Just get on it. What's the news?" Sasha begs.

"Well - the humans have finally figured us out."

Everyone looks at each other and starts speaking at the same time.

"One person at a time." I yell.

"What do you mean they know about us?"

"A government agency captured Warwick, and he was able to gather some information."

"What information exactly?" Malachi asks.

"They know we exist, how to kill us, and they plan on telling the President."

"Wait, wait, what…. You mean they are ALL going to know we exist? We can't let that happen." Eliza states.

"That's why we are all here. We need to formulate a plan."

"A plan? Why didn't he just kill them when he had the chance? That would have stopped everything?" Envio says.

Warwick stands up to defend himself. "I follow our rules. Isn't one of them not killing humans?"

"Yes, it is. You're right. Take a seat." I need to get the room under control before it escalates further. "We need to prepare in case this blows up. If the President announces us, then life as we know it will cease to exist. The good thing is humans won't be able to tell that we are vampires unless we use our powers. Rogues, on the other hand, with their eyes, they'd be easy to spot."

The room gets quieter as they process what I just said. The humans could help us eradicate the rogues inadvertently.

"But… my eyes aren't different. They know that's not the only way a vampire can look. So I'm sure they will pass that along to the others. We can't count on that one thing. Let's not be stupid here." Warwick says.

He is right. Who knows what is going to happen once they make the announcement. Would it be an all-out war? Would any of us be safe? I thought we would have more time to prepare for this and get rid of the rogues.

"I think we need to come up with a plan of action to protect our species. We might have to kill humans; that's what happens in times of war."

"I agree, but if we tell vampires it's okay to kill humans, don't you think that might open up for them to go crazy? Becoming rogues, possibly again?" Envio blurts out.

"That's a chance we are going to have to take, unfortunately. We don't have a choice."

It seems like everyone has made up their mind on how to proceed. If it comes to it, we will have to kill humans that stand in our way. War is not how we want this to end, and we will not be the ones to start it. "Governors, you will go back to your districts and notify your people. Enforcers, I need you to keep an eye out for anything out of the ordinary in the next couple of days. If you see anything suspicious, call one of us."

"Sir, you might want to see this?" One of the guards points to the living room where I can hear a TV playing.

Everyone rushes into the room to see what the fuss is about.

"The President of the United States has just issued a National Stay at Home order. The President received word earlier today about a terrorist organization that has made its way into the country and has planned to eradicate. They are asking anyone that would like to join the National Guard to assist on this hunt to go down to your local police station."

Seriously? They tell the world it's a terrorist group? Well, technically, that's helpful because they still don't know about vampires. However, no one will know who they can trust.

"Governors, make your way back home and inform your people of the truth. I'm sure they have seen this by now and are wondering what's going on. They will be searching for us, so everyone stay hidden. I suggest taking your cars instead of using your powers. Anyone could be watching."

27

Envio

I couldn't believe my eyes are finally seeing her. This isn't the best circumstance, but I'll take it. I tried to pay attention as best I could while Sasha was talking, but my eyes keep glancing back to her. Jane has cut her hair into a pixie, and it shows off her porcelain skin. She is talking with Sasha, and her back is to me. *Do it. Now's your chance.* I shake my head, getting rid of the jitters, and just go for it.

I tap on her shoulder, "Long time, no see gorgeous." She leans in for a hug and I take it. "Your hair looks great. Never thought you'd cut it."

She smiles, "Got sick of it. Wanted something easy to manage."

"Understandable. Well, nice to see you." I say.

"It sure has been a long time. How did the Blakeley thing work out?" Her eyebrow raises, and it occurs to me Sasha didn't tell anyone the outcome of that.

"Nothing to worry about. You know I only want you. Do I need to make that clear again? Cause if you want too, I can." My fingers are caressing the small of her back, and so badly I just want to slip the dress off her and have my way.

"I'm aware. Maybe we are getting closer to us being able to happen. Or well, depending on what happens with the humans."

I know she is skeptical about starting a relationship because of everything going on back then and now, but to me it's even more of a reason to do it. We have no idea how long we will actually live, before anything could happen. I just want to be with her. "I say let's do what we want, and forget about everything going on. There will always be something, and I don't want that to stop us from our happiness."

Her eyes fall to the floor, "I just worry. That maybe. You won't like me as much once you have me. I think you like the thrill of the chase. What happens when we finally settle down? Will you get bored?"

I didn't even think twice before grabbing her hand, and whisking her back to my hotel. This conversation needs to happen in private.

"I will never get bored of you. It's been five years and I'm still madly in love with you Maybe even more so. Please stop shutting me out. Just let me in." I beg her.

Her arms goes around my neck and her lips land on mine. Is she ready? Her body is telling me she is, the way she shoves on the bed and gets on top of me. Jane might be a virgin, but she's obviously been doing her homework.

I push back a little bit, "No rush. I didn't mean we had to have sex tonight."

No hesitation her lips are back on mine within milliseconds, and I am happier than a clam. Did I want to have sex with Jane? Of course, but taking someone's virginity is a big deal, and she need to be sure I am the guy she wants to do it. I didn't want her to regret it afterwards. It would break my heart.

Even with everything going on, the job assigned to me wasn't over. Eventually, the rogues will lead me to Godric. I just have to keep following them. They will get sloppy eventually. Once Godric is captured, we can kill the rogues. The Guardians won't have to worry about them anymore. Our species can live alongside humans without any fear if *we made it that long.*

The stay at home order is in place, and people are not supposed to be out and about, which means those that are, they are disobeying direct orders.

I stay in my car, waiting for them to come out or move. It takes three days for them to leave their hotel room. They pile into a car, not to seem suspicious, and head toward Texas. I didn't follow them to close because I didn't want them to spot me. That's when I spot military vehicles entering the city.

Me: Heads up, military vehicles are headed into the city. You might want to prepare for war. Gather everyone you can up.

The last thing we want to do is worry everyone, but it seems like we have almost everyone following the rules, the rogues are again going to ruin it for us. Maybe, we should have killed Jakob sooner? What if I showed Stephen where Jakob was a month earlier, would things have changed? Could we have stayed out of the agency's eyes?

The car pulls down a dirt road, and I know it will be too risky to go by myself. I look around for a mailbox to get an address.

Me: Send twenty to 1504 Sixth Terrace in Alto

I will need backup if I am going to show up where Godric might be. I have no clue how many would be there, and I couldn't take the chance of getting overpowered.

I whisk of air tousles my hair, and before me are more Guardians. "Sasha, I didn't mean you. It would be best if you were back at the house, preparing for war. What the hell are you doing?"

"I'm not going to let Godric get away. If he's in there, then my place is here." She says, shoving me out of the way. "Alright, most of you know the drill. Split up into two teams. Attack from opposite sides, but watch for their master."

Appalled, I scoff. "This was my mission. I should be giving the orders here."

Instead of answering, the groups split up and head down the dirt road into what might be an ambush.

I can hear vampires up ahead, partying, and having a good time. As I follow behind Sasha, my feet carried past her right into the field with around twenty or so rogues. I look around briefly as both groups start to infiltrate. Body parts are flying everywhere, but they make it easy since they already have a fire going. We work together, questioning them, and then pulling them apart to meet their fiery death. I look around, trying to find Sasha, but I didn't see her. My head whips from side to side, hoping to see her somewhere but didn't.

"Where's Sasha, Cassius?" I yell, fighting off a rogue that is about twice my size. "I don't see her anywhere."

As Cassius's head peers around, trying to find our leader. His eyes bulge. "Over there."

I squeeze my eyelids together, making out Sasha but not who she is talking too. As my vision cleared, I see him.

28
Sasha

When I see him across the clearing, my heart sinks. He's alive and responsible for all this bullshit.

"Why are you doing this?" I ask, trying to keep the tears in check. "I never thought I'd see you again."

His grin isn't friendly but sinister. "You knew I'd come for you one day."

"After everything we've been through, why would you choose him over me?"

He is jumping from leg to leg, preparing for an attack. I know he is pissed we killed Jakob, but why can't he see it was our only option to find peace? His father was hurting our chances of survival. A war between vampires and humans could mean the end.

"I knew you would find me eventually. Do you like my new name? It was my dad's choice when I was a baby. Mama didn't like it, though." His sinister grin grows even more prominent. "Why don't you join me? Doesn't look like the leader thing is ever gonna work for you. Stephen stole that spot. We could take over the entire world, humans kissing the ground we walk on. All that can be ours. You just have to say yes."

As much as I'd love for him to be by my side, the answer is no. I couldn't be a part of butchering humans, turning people for personal gain, and the evil acts that he fancies. It just isn't me. "You know the answer to that. The real question is, why won't you join me?"

His smile quickly fades, "That'll never happen. I don't want to keep hiding. This gift was given to you, and instead of using it, you just hide in the shadows, afraid of the humans finding out. Why?"

He never understood, especially since being brainwashed. "We want to live alongside them peacefully. They would never accept us as equals. So, we hide our fangs and just live. What's so wrong with that?" I know his answer.

"If you would have just joined my father, think of all the things we could have accomplished by now. A lot more than your precious Guardians have. Don't you want to be worshipped? Have the power to slaughter thousands on a whim?"

"Never. Power goes to your head. The point of a leader is to stay grounded. Think about what's best for your people. When's the last time you did that?"

"I." Drake starts to say, but Envio is on top of him.

"How are you alive? She killed you years ago." Envio says, glancing back at me, baring his fangs.

"She didn't have the heart back then, and still doesn't now. That's why you're going to let me go. Isn't he, Sasha?" His glance bore into my eyes like he is trying to convince me.

More of the Guardians are now present, and they all stand by waiting for orders. "Let's detain him and take him back to Jane's quarters." I might not be able to kill him myself, but there are plenty of others who wouldn't hesitate.

"Yes, ma'am." Cassius nods, whisking him away as asked.

It is just Envio and me, and his judgment is written all over his face. "Why lie? After all these years? Hell, did you know it was Drake this whole time?"

I turn my back to him, and before heading to my house, I say, "I prayed it wasn't. But, I had my suspicions from the beginning. He was the only one that the rogues would listen to because of Jakob. You have to understand."

In the seconds it takes me to get back to her quarters, the realization he is alive hit me. I hoped and prayed all these years, but now what do I do?

"Ma'am, we put him in the basement detained. He's asking for you." Cassius says.

What am I going to do? DioI trust myself to be alone with him? My theoretical heart shattered in pieces. It is unearthing to see him like that—a monster, created by his father to spite me.

"What ya think?" Envio asks, leaning against the wall with his hands folded with Jane standing next to him. "You gonna go down there and let him out, then tell us he's dead? It's not like you haven't done it before."

His sarcasm is astounding, but I give him a pass with everything going on. "I'm not sure I'm gonna go down there. I've got to think it through."

"I still don't understand. If you killed Drake, then we would have never ended up in this second war. Do you get that? It's all because of your poor decision making." He says, his spit almost touching my face, he is that close.

Jane steps forward, trying to vouch for me, I hope. "Oh - wait a minute."

Before she can finish, "What about Jane? If Jane turned, would you kill her? Don't even attempt to lie to me and say you would cause I know the answer. You couldn't."

Envio's glance diverts to Jane, looking at her intently. "I would do what I have too."

"Seriously? I don't buy it for a second. When it came down to it, you wouldn't have the heart. I've been there. Believe me." The anger inside me is fixing to erupt. "Don't ever question my decision making again. Shut up and do your job."

Could I kill Drake? No. Could I watch someone else kill him? Most likely not, without evoking emotion. I couldn't let others see me as weak. My feelings for Drake should have been null and void when I found out he is Godric. And solely responsible for the deaths across the country. There must be consequences for that, and the result is death.

I pace Jane's bedroom, knowing what must be done, but not having the heart to do it. Drake and I have known each other since preschool, and I'd never imagined it would come to this.

A knock sounds at the door. "Sasha, you in there?"

My eyes roll, hearing Jane's voice on the other side. "Whatcha need?" Honestly, I just wand to figure this out right now. The longer I delay it, the harder it is going to be.

"I've got an idea. Hear me out." She says from the other side of the door. "Can I come in?"

She's always had a clear head and helped me too many times to count. I open the door, and she steps inside, closing the door behind herself.

"So, I know he must suffer consequences. There isn't a choice on that. However, we can use it to our advantage instead of killing him ourselves." She says, her hands moving around as she's speaking, waiting for me to respond. "Well, maybe we can offer him to the humans."

Why would we do that? "They'd just experiment on him. He'd probably escape and we'd be back in the same damn boat. Can't let that happen."

Jane shakes her head, "No, what if we talked to the government, whoever we can, and help them realize that not all vampires are bad. Maybe they'll see the light, and this can all go away. We can hand him over to them as a peace offering."

My mind is trying to wrap around if he is better off being killed by us or being handed off to the humans? So many Guardians would love to get their hands on the son of Jakob, especially once they discovered he is the reason for all the trouble with the humans. "Let me talk to Stephen about it. It's his decision, not mine. It's a pretty good idea to get us out of trouble with the humans, possibly. I don't think it'll be that easy though," I answer, but get interrupted by pounding on the door.

"Come in." I say, walking toward the door to see who the hell is pounding on it like a hammer.

Envio rushes inside with a worried look on his face, "Turn on the news. Hurry."

What could be going on now? We are already going to war with the humans most likely, what else is there? The news is running a story of anguish around the world.

"We are following the story... people have been getting attacked inside their homes, and the military has found them killed, throats slashed, and blood everywhere. We are currently up to 11,000 confirmed deaths around the country like this. Our thoughts are this has something to do with the President's announcement to stay inside our homes. Who's behind these attacks?"

I turn off the TV and slap my forehead. Of course, it will only get worse. Who knows how many rogues are out there? Drake has been waiting for this, a chance to pounce and start taking humans out. We've got to do something. "Let's see what we can do. I'll try to make some calls and see if I can get a hold of a government official. Maybe a governor, so they can spread the word. I still don't think they'll go for it."

"Understood, but it's worth a shot." Jane replies.

I leave the room, heading downstairs to see Drake. The outcome of his fate is not going to be right either way, but I still want to talk to him. Maybe there is a part of him that always loved me. I stop hesitantly on the stairs and look up, talking to myself. "Stand your ground. Don't let him talk you into anything." A deep breath sounds from my chest and I continue down the stairs until I see him.

"Well, well. What took you so long? It feels like it's been hours." He says a smile on his face.

I could tell he has been pacing because his shoes are off and feet are dirty. "You wanted to see me?" I ask, leaning up against the wall.

"When am I getting out of here? Hell, I don't even understand why I'm stuck here? I've been doing vampires a favor, what is so wrong with us being on top? Why should humans get to have everything?" His tone conveys the seriousness of what he is saying.

In his mind, he thinks that to be true. Neither of us can understand the other one's side. His father corrupted him beyond repair. "That's the reason. This war we are facing is because of you. Lots of vampires and humans are going to die. What do you not understand? Without humans, our species wouldn't survive. If they are happy and oblivious to us, then we can live and feed without causing mass chaos. Or well - before your rogues came into the picture."

"They've done nothing but expose the truth. The world should know. Why should anyone have to live in fear?" He replies, hands up in the air.

"Are you fucking kidding me? Without fear? I'm pretty sure you're making them that way. When people hear reports of bodies slaughtered in the streets, you don't think that causes fear? Fear of the Unknown?" I shake my head, getting pissed. He is arguing a moot point. No matter if he thinks he's right or not. "Living amongst the humans hasn't ever been a problem for me or the others. We are fine with it. You're people are only acting that way because you and your father preached that they could hold power. That goes to y'all's head. Peace is all we care about - and ensuring the future of our species."

"Jesus, they chose you guys to lead them? It still amazes me that they think you two would be the best choice to lead them. You're being completely ignorant. What happened when they changed you? Something went wrong."

I am disgusted at his words. They hurt, but I know he is just trying to get a rise out of me, so I stand my ground and don't let it show. "You're right. Different is what I had to be to see things from different perspectives. A leader should do what's best for the entire species, not just her people. The only reason your rogues were getting the option to join before being killed was because of my order. Otherwise, there'd be a lot less out there of you guys. Just choke on that, asshole."

His eyes get huge, "Wow - you got some guts since I saw you last. Do other men let you talk to them that way? Cause let me tell you one thing, you might be cute, but you'd never get away with that if I weren't stuck behind this glass."

The more he speaks, the easier it is to realize he isn't the same Drake I love. He would never talk to me with that tone, or threaten me. Maybe I wouldn't have such a hard time if Stephen hands him over after all. "I've heard enough of your bullshit. Next time you see me, things won't be so pretty for you. Realize that." My eyes mow him down, letting him know I am not one to be fucked with by any means. As I pass Jane, I flick my head to the side, "Come on."

Stephen: Please inform all Guardians to be on high alert. They are bringing troops into the larger cities and searching door to door. Only kill if you must. Remember, we aren't their enemy.

Looking down the hallway before shutting the door, "Listen. Drake's worthless. He's not the same man I loved."

"I could've told you that. What finally opened up your eyes?" She asks, her hands crossed.

"Let's not get into that."

Stephen walks into the room, " We need to prepare ourselves for military infiltration. Eventually, they'll be at our front door, and we need to figure out a plan."

"How do they plan on telling if we are vampires? That's the part I don't understand. What good are sweeps if they can't tell whose one or not?"

"I don't have those answers right now. Nonetheless, being prepared is key. I've gotta feeling it's not going to go well."

Her head nods, and leaves me and Stephen alone in the room. White noise would be a solace right now because my mind is running 100 MPH and couldn't keep up. How could they tell if we were a vampire? Not all vampires have illuminating eyes? Maybe they think that's the common factor? Who knows. If that's the case, then all the Guardians should be fine.

Something has to be done, fast. If this war progresses, thousands are going to die at least. We want peace, not war.

"So, Jane had a good idea. If we can give them the person responsible for all those deaths, maybe we could get along. It's a long shot, but it's better than doing nothing."

29
Envio

Sasha and I have been colliding lately. I'm afraid I have to disagree with her decisions, and I'm not sure I'll ever be able to look at her the same after Blakeley. We are supposed to be guarding humans, not killing them. And that's just what she did. Eliza killed her, just so the rogues couldn't have her. I wonder if she were still alive, would the rogues always be looking for her not that we have Drake? Probably even more so, and that would be bad.

She was a delightful girl, and it sucks that she was drug into this situation by her father without even knowing it. Did Eliza hesitate or even care that she was killing an innocent woman?

There are many things I am capable of, but killing an innocent girl isn't one of them. Maybe five years ago under Jakob's reign, but not now. I am maturing into the man I aspire to be. One that I can be proud of being.

Now we are back in this mess because of the rogues again, and back at square one. Humans are terrified of the unfamiliar.

It's not like they are going to welcome us with open arms after everything that's happened. Thousands of Americans have died because of our kind. They wouldn't see the differentiation between the two groups. That's where things are going to get tricky.

A knock on my hotel door startles me; I walk to the door and open it slowly.

"Hey, I know you're busy, but I need to talk to someone. Can I come in?" Warwick asks, already walking inside my room.

He looks nervous but eager to tell me whatever it is he is hiding. "What is it? Everything okay?"

His hands keep running through his hair while pacing the room. "What's going on? You're worrying me?"

"I don't know how. I need to - Listen, man, I fucked up. Bad. You know the agency that captured me?"

"Yeah, so. What about them?"

"So, they sent this chick Samantha to do ride alongs with my partner and me. I invited her over for dinner, and things got a little out of hand."

"How out of hand? You know what our roles are. We can't tolerate rule breakers. Please tell me you didn't."

He sits down in a chair and puts his face in his palms. "We were getting intimate, you know it'd been such a long time since a woman had touched me. Things escalated quickly, and I started feeding. I tried to stop but couldn't. Suddenly, she was almost dead, and it was all my fault. Do I let her die or turn her? Man, I couldn't let her die because of me."

"You did the right thing by not letting her die. But you still broke the rules. Sasha won't be happy."

"I know. I swear I regret it, but it happened, and I can't change that."

"What happened after that?"

"I found out she was working with them against me. She said she had feelings for me, and that's why she ran with me."

"Where is this girl now?"

"My guess, dead. She was with me when I got captured. Samantha played it like she was still human and hadn't fed yet."

"So she stayed behind to help them? Is that how they found out about our weaknesses?"

"I can't say for certain but doubt it. Samantha stayed behind to save me some time to get away."

Warwick knows what he did was wrong and the fact he has the guts to admit to it when he didn't have to means everything. Hopefully, Stephen would agree and show him leniency.

I put my hand on his shoulder and tell him, "Listen, man, it means a lot that you came forward with this. That in of itself shows that you are loyal to us. I'm not saying there won't be consequences, but maybe she'll let you live."

He just keeps his head down, feeling like shit. Warwick has come along way since being captured by Sasha and coerced into working for the Guardians.

My mind switches gears and comes back to the situation at hand. If Samantha is possibly still alive, maybe she could set up a meeting for us with the humans. It's a long shot, but if it works out could mean a brighter future for both of us.

"Hey man, could you try to call her?"

"Who?"

"Samantha? There's a chance she's still alive. Maybe she could help us out. If she's alive, then that means she's one of us fully. It would be in her best interest."

I doubt she fed, especially with the agency watching her every move, but there's a chance.

Warwick pulls out his phone and calls her. I can hear the ringing repeat and then a voicemail. Fuck, she us dead.

"Sorry she didn't answer. I told you she was dead. No way she got the chance to feed around those people. They're like hawks."

His phone starts ringing, and my eyes grow. "Is that her?"

"Hello?" He answers.

"Why are you calling me? You know how dangerous that is?" Samantha's voice echoes She didn't seem too happy about his call.

"I thought you were dead. You've been alive this whole time and never even bothered to let me know."

"You know how it is with them. What do you need?" She asks like he is a burden to her.

"Listen, you know what's going on. I need you to set up a meeting between our leader and yours. Whoever you can get." Warwick asks, seemingly shocked to hear her voice. "How are you still alive, and they haven't figured it out?"

"I'm good at acting; that's how. Don't mess this up. I've been doing my best at keeping them away from y'all. It's hard to do that when vampires are out killing humans left and right during all of this, but I'll see what I can do as far as a meeting."

"We look forward to your call. Bye."

His face in his palms tells me he has feelings for this girl but did she? Why would she not at least call and let him know about her being alive after he left? Something just doesn't seem right, and I'm not sure if we should trust her.

"How do I tell Stephen? He's gonna kill me. I know it. Why did I have to be so stupid? I knew better, I did."

"Listen, we all make mistakes. Learn from it and don't ever do it again. Alright?"

If she could get us a meeting with someone, then maybe we could work something out. Did I have faith in Sasha not to make things worse? Not exactly, my confidence in her had decreased quite a lot in the last couple of weeks due to her wretched judgment. But Stephen is different.

Jane isn't pleased with me for belittling Sasha about Drake, but come on. The rebellion wouldn't have happened if she would have just killed him that night. He gave the rogues purpose, and that's something they didn't need. It only caused more obstacles for us.

It is a sensitive spot for her since she lied about killing Samuel, but he was one of us first. Everyone knows he only joined the other side to save his family; otherwise, he would've still been a Guardian. I couldn't criticize her for that, but what Sasha did is downright mislead all of us about someone who could potentially disrupt everything we worked so hard to build. To me, that is inexcusable.

30
Jane

Things are getting complicated, and we have to be cautious. No one knows how this will play out or how many will end up dead due to this war. Would this end in war? Could we hand over Drake, and this all be put in the past? I hope so, but never know how humans will react to knowing vampires aren't a myth. Would we have to go into actual hiding after this? Could we live peacefully alongside each other? It is a step none of us foresaw, but it's happening anyway.

Our reaction will determine the result of this war, and the fewer people that die, the better. We aren't like Drake, and we just need to prove that to humans. Show them that we aren't guilty of the deaths across the country. It's a longshot, but if we can communicate with their government, maybe we could reach some agreement. We have been living alongside humans for years without them knowing, and we can go back to that again, but hopefully, that wouldn't be the case. We aren't predators looking to kill their species. The rogues started this war five years ago. Stephen has tried to prevent it, but Drake has been plotting against us the entire time. He knew that eventually, enough attention would come to a head, and vampires would be revealed. There wasn't anything we could've done. Now we've got him in custody, and giving him over to the humans could be beneficial to both sides. It would show the rogues we mean business and give justice to the families of those that were killed by his orders.

I pace the bedroom, maintaining my thoughts, and figuring out how we can make this work. The plan needs to be executed appropriately for this to end correctly.

A thump sounded at my door, "I need to talk to you."

Envio's voice staggered to my ears, "Come in. You don't have to knock."

He opens the door and walks over to me. "I've got some information, but you have to be the one to tell Stephen and Sasha. They'll be pissed because it violates one of our rules. However, it's going to be advantageous."

I wobble my head, "Okay, what is it? Spit it out. The last thing we need to be doing is misusing time. Humans could be here any second."

"Someone within our team had sex with and turned a human. The human in question works for the agency that kidnapped Warwick."

"Are you fucking joking? And we are just now being told this? It'd been nice to have this information hours ago." My hands are darting everywhere, throwing out every curse word in the book. "Can he get a hold of her? Set up a meeting?" If we could, then this could all work out in both of our favors.

"Already set. In one hour. At Topaz Tower." Envio says, eyebrows up high. "He'll be meeting with the President."

That's a lot of stress, but he signed up for it when he became leader. "Alright, I'll go let him know. I can't promise that he won't kill him. He violated the rules, and you should know better than anyone what happens then." Being an enforcer came with a lot of obligation, but he was suitable for it. Envio is a great man, and I wish I would have met him before being a vampire.

"Make sure that she knows he regrets it. He is fully faithful to our cause. Showed us that time and time again."

I acknowledge and exit the room. He can't go solo, just like the President wouldn't show up to this meeting with his security detail. Could this be a trap? If we came out and revealed ourselves, they could use it against us. We have to be vigilant and keep this in mind.

"Do you know where Sasha and Stephen are?" I question Cassius.

"Outside. Trying to come up with a plan. From the clamors, I'd say it's not going splendidly."

This meeting would be a massive leap of faith for us, and there's always a chance it could go sideways, but did we have a choice?

"Hey I need to talk to you guys. Like now. You've got a meeting."

"What meeting? With who?" Stephen asks.

"A meeting's been set up with the President of the United States in like half an hour." My eyes bug out of my head, realizing how crazy that sounds. "And before you ask, no, I'm not joking."

I fill them in on the details, and Sasha isn't thrilled, but can't read Stephen. Warwick has broken the rules, the very ones he made to make our society thrive. How he is going to deal with that is up to him. "You can't go alone. I'll start gathering us up to escort you. We leave in ten minutes."

I walk back inside, to gather everyone. It is a huge opportunity to get a meeting with the President, and we have to be very cautious about how we proceed.

"How'd it go?" Envio asks as I crack the bedroom door. "Are they gonna kill him?"

I wobble my head, "I'm not sure. We didn't dwell on that. I'm sure he will show mercy this once."

Envio moves closer and put his palms around to the base of my spine, "You know, I'd do anything for you, right?"

My feelings for Envio are powerful, and sooner or later, I want to be with him. I deserve happiness, especially after all the shit I went through before becoming a vampire.

"It's time to go. Who is going with us?" He asks.

"Me, you, Cassius and Sasha," I clarify.

"What about Warwick?"

"Probably best not to bring him. Let the wounds heal before we deal with that."

I take one last moment for Envio's arms to envelope around me before we leave for one of the most important meetings of our future. No one knows how this is going to go, and if it ends badly, millions will die.

31

Stephen

My nerves are shot, and I have no idea what to expect, going into this meeting or what I am going to say. My head is wrapping around many things, stuff that could help ease the burden that Drake caused on the humans. Someone will have to answer for that, and it isn't going to us. We didn't endanger any humans, well except Blakeley, and I can't say I agree with Sasha's decision, but she knows better than to do that again.

"Sir, it's time. We have to go, or we'll be late." Cassius says, popping his head inside.

"I'm coming," I reply, my chest rising and falling. My actions are going to decide the result, and I need to be in the appropriate mindset going into this, or it could have significant repercussions.

I walk out of the room, my steps sounding across the house. Jane, Sasha, and Envio are waiting for me. "You ready?"

"Not really, but guess I have to be." Honestly, I never thought this day would come, meeting with the humans to determine our fate. I am perfectly content, living alongside them without them knowing we exist. I think things are better that way, but once again, the rogues fucked everything up.

Everyone piles into the SUV, nervous about what's to come. No one knows if this is a trap, and this could be our last night on Earth. All of this fighting might have been for nothing.

"Do you think they are going to kill us?" Jane asks Envio.

"I have to have faith that they want peace as much as we do," Envio replies, holding her hand.

To be honest, I acted like it surprises me, but it hasn't been hard to pick up on the clues. They both deserve to be happy. I smile at her and wink. They make a good couple.

"Approaching the tower," Cassius says. "I see three SUV's sir."

It's go time and no turning back now.

"Okay, listen, everyone. Before we get out and venture into the unknown, let's talk. Everyone needs to be careful; no one knows what's going to happen. You're not to kill anyone, you understand?" I shake my head, "If we die tonight, we go knowing we did everything we could to be the good guys."

Everyone just looks at me and waits for me to get out. We are the good guys, and as much as they might not see, we need to make them understand that.

Cassius opens my door, and the others follow behind me. People start piling out of the SUVs with guns. "Approach with your hands raised, guys."

The last thing I want is to give them a reason to be scared of us. We need to make them feel comfortable. "We don't want to harm you. Our hands are up, and we have no weapons. I just wanna talk." I say, approaching the guys in black and white suits. "Who's your leader?"

A man with white hair and medium height answers, "that would be me. President Walters." The men are surrounding him, hesitant to let him out in the open. "I was told you had something you wanted to speak about."

"Yes, sir. As you know, many have died in recent days following your stay at home order. We have the person responsible and are willing to hand him over to you. In exchange, we would like peace. Our kind means you no harm."

The others stand behind me, slowly bringing their hands down from above their heads.

"Sir, we have been protecting your kind for years now from what we call rogues. These are vampires that slaughter humans. After taking out their leader, an uprising has begun again, but we caught their new leader and are willing to give him." Envio explains.

Did I ask him to speak? He isn't the leader and has no business speaking right now. I'll deal with this later. "We want the families of the victims to get justice. It would be our peace offering."

The President is very quiet, which makes me quite nervous, unable to tell what to anticipate. The men huddle around him as he makes a phone call.

"I had to say something. He needs to know we aren't the bad guys." Envio whispers to me.

"Do not speak again unless I ask. If this fails, it's on my hands, not yours. Therefore, I should be the only one speaking for our kind right now."

All the others stare at me like I'm the biggest asshole ever. Maybe I am, but whatever happens during this meeting could tarnish my name as a leader, and I am not going to let Envio ruin that.

"Where is he?" He asks.

"We have him back at my house, sir. Are we in agreement then? Hand him over for peace. No more announcements or searches?"

"I can't promise that some of you won't be executed. If my men find them hurting us, then they will be executed without hesitation. If you could bring him to me, we will discuss our arrangements further after I have him in custody."

The President wastes no time getting into his SUV and driving off, leaving me behind in the dust. Drake ss being handed over to the humans to be dealt with accordingly.

Part of me wonders if what he said is true and whether he will hold his end. At this point, I didn't have the hand to second guess. If this is our chance at peace, then it needs to be taken. No matter the cost, even if that costs Drake's life.

After returning to Jane's house, I need some alone time to process what happened. Things are getting complicated, and we have to be cautious. No one knows how this would play out or how many would end up dead if they didn't hold up their side of the bargain. Would we have to go to war with them? Could we hand over Drake, and this all be put in the past?

None of us want to wage war, but if it happens, we will only kill those that are unavoidable: the fewer people that die, the better. We aren't like Drake, and we just need to prove that to humans. Show them that we aren't guilty of the deaths across the country. We aren't predators looking to destroy their species. The rogues started this battle five years ago. I tried to prevent it, but Drake was scheming against us the whole time. There wasn't anything we could've done. Now we've got him in confinement, giving him over to the humans could be beneficial to both parties. It would show the rogues we mean business and give justice to the families of those that were killed by his orders.

The question on everyone's mind tonight is, could I do it and how is Sasha going to handle it?

TO BE CONTINUED...

FIND OUT WHAT HAPPENS NEXT IN THE *RISE OF THE SOCIAL ORDER*

Rise of the Social Order

Rise Book #3

USA Today Best Selling Author
ASHLEY ZAKRZEWSKI

1
Warwick

The residence is mute, allowing the thoughts to take over. The others aren't back from the meeting yet. Should I remain here? After breaking the rule, the likely outcome is death and there's no running from it. Sam is the one that got me into this mess. Why couldn't she just stay away? If she did, death wouldn't be in my future.

Squinting from deep deliberation, I lean forward on the couch, placing my elbows on my knees. Sam's decision to linger behind and proceed to work with the agency seemed odd, but it probably helped her identify how to integrate in and not get detected.

This meeting she pulled together is the make-or-break point. War would erupt if it didn't go well. We don't want to slay them, but if they proclaim war, there won't be an option. The whispers started when I got shot, and that's what drew the agency to watch me and send Sam in for infiltration.

Will Stephen decide to show leniency? If Sasha has any way or forces her two cents in to make Stephen believe I'm this awful beast, then probably not. My stomach's in tangles as I now pace around the living room. Death is frightening, even more so as a vampire. As a human, my faith in God carried me on the right path, but soon strayed after being turned. Even if Heaven did exist for vampires, it's not for ones like me who killed many innocent people. Why couldn't Drake have chosen someone else that day? Vampires turned my whole life upside down, and it seems fitting I die at the hands of one, too.

The front door closes as I trek toward my family. It's been a while since I walked out of the house with no sort of explanation. Did Tasha hope I would come back? If only she knew the truth, things could be different. Yet I'd rather leave them in the dark and keep them safe.

The day I met Tasha resurfaces in my mind. Never really had much luck in the romance department. There was nothing in my fridge after a long day of teaching, so like anyone else, the grocery store became my destination. *Thank God.* There I was, strolling down the meat section, when I see this woman trying to figure out what to get for dinners that week. Stupidly, I chuckled, and she twisted.

"What's so amusing? Not used to people talking to their meat?" Her eyes met mine, and a slight smile started.

"I do it too. The brisket looks good. Too much for just one person, though. Bummer."

"Yeah, that's my problem. It's hard to cook for just one."

"I'm Warwick."

"Tasha," she replied, batting her eyelashes.

"Maybe we could get together and cook for two. I make a mean brisket."

For a couple of days after, I gawked at her phone number written on a piece of paper, wondering how long to linger before calling. It didn't take long for me to give in and invite her over. The night was perfect, and I found myself in awe of how lucky I was to be in her company. Afterward, we saw each other every day and within eight months, I proposed, knowing she was the one for me, and it became the best day of my life.

Our perfect life hit a speed bump when Tasha found out about her inability to have children. All she talked about was becoming a mother someday, and it killed me she could never experience that. It took us a couple years of getting different opinions, and miraculously she was pregnant with Avery. I remember making sure she didn't lift a finger since she was so high-risk for miscarriage. We made a promise the night we found Avery was coming that we would never leave each other, no matter how hard things got.

Coming back to reality, I approach the home, hearing Avery giggling in the living room. *Boy, do I miss that sound.* She's in the middle of a blanket on her tummy, with Tasha right beside her cheering her on.

"You can do it. Mommy's big girl," Tasha says, a big smile on her face. "Just a couple more minutes, and then we'll get ready for bed."

I try to get the negative thoughts out and focus on the time I have, but my mood shifts when I think about missing all of her firsts. I cheer Avery on quietly, wishing I could be right there on the other side, but knowing it will never happen. The rogues make that impossible, and we haven't seen the possibility of wiping them out completely. There are just too many and the way they multiply, it's just not feasible right now.

"Alright, it's time to get ready for bed, silly girl," Tasha says, picking her up and hoisting her on her hip.

Our nightly ritual had always been snuggle time in the living room with mom and dad. Then I would read a bedtime story in the nursery. Bonding time was important to me, especially after a long day at work. They always say that girls are closer with their daddies and until recently I would say that's a hundred percent valid, but now without me in the picture, the bond with her mother will only grow stronger in my absence.

What will she tell Avery when she gets older? That I abandoned them? Just left one day, and never came back?

Tasha sets her down and walks over to the bookshelf. "So what do we want to read tonight? *Princess and the Frog? Cinderella?* Maybe

Dumbo?" She pulls the book off the shelf and sits in the rocking chair, turning to the first page.

The next hour is spent observing them, reveling in the time I get before my punishment is decided. They are better off without me now, and they already think I'm dead. I'll never see my little girl grow up, get married, or become a mother.

A sound alerts Tasha and her eyes dart toward the window. *Shit, did she see me?*

"Hello? Is someone there?" Tasha rushes over to the crib, picks Avery up, and dials 911.

"I think there's someone outside my house. Can you send an officer, please?"

After getting farther away from the house, I check to see who called. *Envio*. Probably to give me the heads-up about Stephen's decision. It sinks back into my pocket, and instead of returning his call, I decide to go to the bar and have a couple last whiskeys before heading back to Texas.

2
Envio

Why the hell isn't he answering his phone? It doesn't look good when he just takes off instead of confronting Stephen. *What the hell, buddy?*

His voicemail picks up. "Answer your damn phone. We're back and Stephen wants to talk. Why are you making it look worse? Get your ass back here!"

I scratch my forehead, wondering what the hell could be going through his head that he thinks running is a viable option. He realizes who they will send after him, and unfortunately, I have to follow orders.

"Where is he?" Jane asks, watching me pace around her bedroom. "Sasha is already hounding Stephen about his decision on his punishment."

"He won't answer his fucking phone. What the hell?"

"Can you blame him, though? I mean, surely he knows it could be death, and who sticks around and waits to die?" Her hand is on her hip, like I should already know the answer.

"Still, you know it doesn't look good." I dial his number again, and still voicemail. "Okay, I'm going after him. I have a good idea on where he would go. Try to stall them for me."

Not everyone knows about Warwick's family, yet he confided in me in the bar that day. If he thinks he's going to die tonight, the most logical thing is for him to take off and see his family.

I sneak out without Sasha or Stephen seeing me, too busy talking about the meeting, which is a good thing. Maybe I can get there and back before they realize I even left.

Showing up on his property, he isn't outside anywhere and I know he wouldn't go in. That would only put his family in harm's way. He must be somewhere in town.

Me: *You're not with your family. Where are you? Let's get you back to Texas so you can explain yourself before your punishment is decided. Don't run. It'll only make things worse.*

Honestly, I didn't think he would run, but when death is on the table, you can never be too sure. As an enforcer, I know this all too well. Warwick is a friend, and I didn't want to be the one to kill him. Stephen knows that good vampires make mistakes, hence me. He, even after everything bad I've done, gave me another chance to prove myself. I can only hope he will do the same for Warwick.

Warwick: *I'm at the only bar in town. Come have a last drink with me.*

I head there, knowing he's already fearing the worst. We don't know Stephen's decision yet, and until we do, nothing is concrete. He needs to man up and confront this head-on. We are aware of how guilty he feels, and he needs to tell Stephen that. Running isn't an option.

The bar is almost empty except for a couple of patrons, the bartender, and a jukebox that sits in the far corner playing country music. Warwick sits a couple stools down from it, beer in hand. "Thanks for texting me back. I was worried you were running."

"I know what happens when you run. We both do. No matter where I'd go, you'd find me. No use."

He's right. It might take me a while, but I'd find him, eventually.

"Stephen hasn't decided yet—but I don't think you being gone makes things look good. We need to get your ass back there so you can defend yourself. It's the only thing that's going to help."

"We both know Sasha will never let him show me leniency."

"Well, good thing she's not our leader. The final say so is Stephen's. Who gives a shit what Sasha thinks?" I get she is the Savior or whatever they say, but ever since she found Drake in that underground lair turned, she hasn't been the same. Her decisions are flawed, and I'm so damn glad Stephen is our leader. Who knows what things would be like if she had his power?

He knows I'm right. For a while, I almost thought those two had a thing, but it's more of a brother-sister relationship. "But he listens to her. That in itself isn't gonna help me."

"He listens to Jane and me too. Come on, let's get back and find out. No more moping around."

"One more whiskey. It could be my last. I'm in no hurry to speed up my execution."

I hate that he doesn't feel like he has a chance. Sasha must fool vampires into thinking she's got all this say in decisions when she doesn't. If she had that power, we'd be even more screwed right now.

Warwick downs his drink and slaps it on the bartop. "Let's get this over with..."

We make it back without them noticing I ever left and with Warwick in tow.

"They've been down there in the basement. Wonder what the hell they could talk about for so long." Jane says.

"I have an idea." My eyes focus on Warwick. "Sasha has a strong opinion, and I'm sure she's doing everything she can to voice it right now."

Warwick takes a seat on the couch, head in his hands, waiting for Stephen.

"How about you just figure out what you're going to say to him, and that's all," Jane says.

We go into the kitchen to give him some space to think. Hopefully he can come up with something good.

"I feel bad for him… you know."

"What do you mean?"

"He might die because he accidentally got carried away and turned a human. And that human just worked for the very people that know about our existence."

"Yeah, he doesn't have very good luck. Literally how could he have known?"

Oh wow, actually that makes me think of something.

Stephen and Sasha walk into the living room with the door slamming behind them. Warwick stirs a little and stands up. A bead of sweat trickles off his brow as he rubs his hands together.

"So I see he came back," Sasha says, folding her arms across her chest. "At least he's being a man about it."

God, why does she have to be such a bitch? What is her problem with Warwick, anyway? She's the one that recruited him. Even threatened his family. So what gives?

All attention goes to Stephen, waiting for him to speak.

"Okay, Warwick. I've had some time to think about the situation you put us in…"

I butt in. "Actually, I have something to say real quick."

Stephen nods, and his hand sweeps, giving me the floor. "Go ahead."

"If it wasn't for his action, the agency would have never been brought to our attention. And because of him, we have an insider. Yeah, he did some stupid things, and he regrets it—but it also helps us too. Don't you think so?"

The look on Sasha's face is priceless. She turns to see Stephen's reaction. "You've got to be kidding me. So just because the girl he turned is working with the agency, that means all else should be wiped clean like he did nothing wrong?"

Now my anger is bursting at the seams. She needs to be put in her place. "I'm not sure why it concerns you so much. The only person who gets to decide on what happens to him is Stephen. He's our leader, not you, remember? Or have you forgotten?"

Sasha walks toward me, and Jane steps in. "He's right. You need to take a step back."

Her eyes go wide. "Oh, so now you're defending your boyfriend?" She scoffs. "Figures you'd take his side. Pathetic."

"When you're acting like a complete bitch, yes. Bring your ego down a notch, precious Savior. You aren't our leader."

"You all need to calm down," Stephen says, raising his voice. "This is my decision, and I've made it. Anyone that doesn't like it, well, I don't really care."

"And what is your decision?" Warwick asks, a bead of sweat trickling down his forehead.

"Well, first, I know others that have made mistakes, and after a chance, they changed for the better. The last thing I want to do is kill someone because of a stupid mistake. You will no longer be an enforcer; in fact, you'll work directly with me in California from now on. If anything like this ever happens again, then I will show no leniency."

An audible sigh comes from Warwick's throat, realizing he's going to live to see another day. Surely he has learned his lesson and will do nothing like this again.

"Stephen," Sasha speaks.

His hand flies up. "I need no more from you right now on this topic. The decision has been made."

Jane and I exchange a glance, while Sasha storms out of the house like a child. I don't know why Stephen hasn't removed her from her position with the way she's been acting. How can he trust her to make sound decisions, even at that level?

"I've got some business to attend to in California. Envio and Jane, I need you to monitor Drake while I'm gone, and Warwick is coming with me. I'm not sure how Sasha is going to handle us turning him over to the humans, so she's not to be left alone with him, even for a second."

"Of course, sir," Jane replies.

Once they are gone, Jane and I have a lot to discuss. So many things have happened in the last few days, things we never thought would. She's the only person I truly trust.

"How do you think the handover's gonna go? You think Sasha might do something crazy to stop it?"

Her head shakes. "Honestly, I'm not sure at this point. She's not the same Sasha from Frankfort. People do crazy things for love all the time, but surely she realizes he isn't the same Drake as before. She can't be that damn naïve."

At first, Jane pushed back when I tried to explain the change in Sasha I'd seen while she was my direct supervisor while out enforcing, but I think she is finally seeing what I did. Her stepping in just a bit ago, proved that she is doubting Sasha's abilities too. "Do you think Stephen is noticing how broken she is? Even worse than he thought before we left Frankfort? It really isn't a good idea for her to be someone making decisions for our kind. I've thought about talking to him about it, but I didn't want to overstep."

"Oh, in the last few days, I think he has realized plenty about her and others. There will be changes coming. Especially after the meeting with the humans. They have to."

The only way we are going to come to any peace agreement is if we hand over Drake. I see different outcomes to that scenario. The first one, we hand him over, everything goes back to the way it was before, and this is over. The second one, after handing him over, they experiment more on him to find more of our weaknesses, and then use it against us, starting a war they can't possibly win.

"I'm just wondering if handing him over is our best option. He deserves to pay for his crimes, but there are so many things that could go wrong."

She gets closer and puts her hands around my neck. "We have to trust Stephen to make the right decision with the information he has. No one can foresee what might happen in every scenario. But I think handing him over is a show of good faith from us and will show them we don't mean any harm. Peace is the end game here."

She's right. Stephen will make the right decision with the information he has, and that's all. I wouldn't want to be in his shoes right now. As a leader, there will always be someone who questions your decisions, and all he can do is justify them the best he can. What he decides will not only impact our future but also the humans.

The front door opens and Cassius walks in. "Everybody already headed back to their posts?"

I don't know why but he irritates me, but only because he gets to spend so much time with Jane. He's not a bad-looking vampire either, but I try to keep my jealousy under wraps. "Yeah, it's just us right now. Stephen will be back."

Cassius makes his way to the couch and sits down. "Well, that was an interesting ordeal. Honestly, I thought it would end in a blood bath. Glad it went down civilly."

The looming question on everyone's mind is when and if Stephen is going to hand Drake over.

3
Stephen

Things are heating up between crucial members of the Guardians. Animosity has begun and as their leader, I need to come up with a way to stop it. Many things have gone awry in the last couple weeks and some without my knowledge. A certain someone did not get my permission to murder an innocent human, and for that there will be consequences. Things need to change around here if the peace with humans is ever going to work. Who the hell can I trust anymore?

Sasha is the last person I'd expect to disobey me, yet she's done it multiple times now.

Warwick being with me in California helps me keep an eye on him, but more importantly makes it easier for some changes within the organization that are absolutely necessary for the survival of our society. I can't have someone that jeopardizes everything we stand for giving orders.

Sasha has a lot going on because of the discovery of Drake being Godric, and him playing her like a flute to get her to let him out, but I don't care. Her feelings for Drake should have been left behind in the underground bunker the night Jakob died. She lied to everyone about killing him and she still awaits punishment for that. No matter if it was for the sake of love or not. This alone proves she's not competent enough to do the things necessary in her current position of power. My only choice is to ask her to step down. Things might get ugly, but that's the way it has to be. Friend or not.

Sasha's coming over to discuss some things, but she has been kept in the dark about my decision and it needs to be kept that way. With her erratic behavior lately, we don't need something else to go wrong and bring us unwanted attention. There's no telling what she might do when I tell her. Do I think she would sabotage things with the humans? No. But I can't trust her either.

This opportunity we have with the human government right now seems like a win, if they are being upfront with me. I don't like the fact we have to hand Drake over before any type of agreement can be made. It could all be a setup and they'll come after us anyway, but my optimism prevails. Let's show them we're the good guys, so we don't have to murder half their population for them to understand that they can't win.

The what-ifs are hindering my ability to make a concrete decision. Whether or not he's handed over, there's a chance for a bigger war to erupt, and even more lives to be lost. Can I really believe that the humans are so willing to just let it all go because we hand over one vampire? It just seems a little too easy. However, from my side, it's a sign of good faith in our agreement to reach peaceful cohabitation. And right now, that's all we can do. It's up to them to keep their end of the bargain.

"Sir, I've got Kieran here to see you," Warwick says from the other side of my office door.

What the hell does he want? I've got enough going on without having to deal with this asshole. "Bring him in, but get Envio here as soon as possible."

Things have been dicey since our last discussion, and I'm sure the governor has heard about our recent run-in with the president. With his position, he knows things that might be advantageous to our kind. Maybe we can work together to ensure the peace agreement. It's no secret that having him on the inside is helpful in many circumstances. I'm trying to play nice with him, but Kieran makes that difficult.

"Where've you been? I came by earlier and you were nowhere to be found. Something you should fill me in on?" He leans against the doorframe with his arms across his chest, like he is catching me in a lie or something.

He isn't someone I like, but for now, it's beneficial that we continue to work together to gather information. Not that I have to notify him anytime something happens. "I was at a meeting. I'm sure your boss already heard. That's why you're here, right?"

"He isn't pleased. He wants to know what your plan is. You captured Godric or Drake? Whatever the hell his name is. The one that has been causing all these problems?"

"Yes, and the president said if we hand him over, then we can work on arrangements for a treaty but only after."

"Do you think that's wise?"

Of course, he thinks he's qualified to question my decisions. Another vampire that needs to be knocked down a notch or two. "I'm deciding and whatever that is, everyone will stand by it. Even the governor. You can be sure to tell him that."

His eyebrow arches. "Really? He's a powerful man. Maybe you should consider all the outcomes…"

Kieran seems to think I'm intimidated by him and the governor. The duty I have is to preserve our society and try to make it to where we don't start an all-out war. I don't need to take advice or hindrance from anyone. Maybe Kieran and the governor need to rethink their role and step back a bit. They have no say in what decisions I make. I'm the damn leader, and it's time they recognize that. Treat me with respect and don't talk to me like a puppet.

"Let's just say he wants some answers and would like them within two days. We both know the population of vampires in this state, and things will need to be carefully executed in order to keep his inhabitants safe," Kieran says before slightly nodding and leaving my office.

Every time I have to interact with that macho jackass, my blood boils. He's the embodiment of men I despise, and I can only imagine what kind of asshole he was prior to being a vampire.

"Get ahold of Envio?"

"Yeah, should be here any minute. What was that all about?" Warwick asks.

I forget some don't know about the governor. "Let's just say I've got someone working from the inside for us."

Warwick's eyes dance. "Smart move. He didn't seem happy."

"His boss is never happy. You'll see that. But he's not our leader, and soon he'll understand where his place is."

The outcome of my conversation with Envio will determine some very important decisions. He has adequately earned my respect since leaving Frankfort, and he's shown he's a very valuable asset to the team. My hope is he's ready to move up and take another position. Some might not like my decision, but it's not up to them.

"Now a bad time?" Envio says, peeking his head inside my office.

"Not at all. Been waiting for you." I gesture for him to take a seat. This might not be a short conversation. "As you're aware, there have been some judgment calls made I didn't agree with and without my permission."

"Yes, sir," Envio replies, looking away from me.

"I know you're not the one responsible, and Eliza was just following orders. Were you aware of what Eliza was going to do?" The question is only to gauge what he knows, and what he's willing to tell me.

"Sasha gave the orders, and I refused. After all the horrible things I've done in my past, it's not a road I ever want to go down again."

This says a lot about his character, and how much he has changed since becoming a Guardian. Things need to change and that starts with the structure. "I've been thinking of changing some things. Seeing the way the three of you acted today toward Sasha, I think we can all agree that she hasn't quite been herself in a while, and it's having a negative effect on how our society might be perceived."

"That's a fact, sir. It scared Warwick to face you because he thought Sasha held the power of his consequence. She acts like she's our leader and that infuriates me."

Maybe I've been too relaxed with her and need to tighten the reins a bit. She seems to overstep, and that needs to be combatted. "Well, I'm going to be dealing with that shortly. Before I can, there are some things I need to ask you."

"Like what?" He stops slouching and sits up in his chair. "What do you mean, sir?"

"If I were to make Sasha an enforcer, we would need someone to oversee her position. With all of your expertise in tracking and your rapport with the team already, you were the first person I wanted to offer the opportunity."

"Me? Are you sure?"

Envio has done nothing but prove himself since Jakob's death, and he's never gone against my orders. I don't see him as a Blood Taker, and I won't fault him for his past. People deserve second chances, and I'm glad Jane talked me into it back in Frankfort. "You've done nothing but prove yourself since I brought you to California. Do you need time to think about it?"

He shakes his head. "Do I need to be in New York?"

"Sasha will most likely want to keep the place in New York, plus then we'd have all the enforcers under one roof. Seems more logical anyway."

"Let me know once everything on that side is handled. I trust you will notify the team of the new arrangements?" Envio asks, getting up from the chair to shake my hand.

"Yes. Now get back to Jane. You might want to enjoy some downtime while you can."

Envio leaves, and I set it up for Sasha to be here within the hour. Things will get heated even more so now that Envio will take her position. This should be interesting.

4
Sasha

Frustration is coursing through my veins, and the struggle to calm myself down is real. How could Stephen let them talk to me that way? Not even say a word in my defense? In these last few days, things have been changing and not for the better. People are starting to turn against me. For someone like Envio to talk to me that way, fuels my rage even further, knowing he hasn't always been on our side. Since being turned, I've been there for the Guardians without hesitation, even when they lied to me. Yet now, they're letting amateurs displace me in front of lackeys? Stephen and I will talk about this, and before I leave his office, he'll understand my rage.

I lay my keys to the condo down in the glass bowl and take a seat on the sectional in the living room. There are so many things we need to figure out before meeting back up with the president. My biggest concern is how do we know if we can trust him? Yet did we really have a choice? Things are heating up, and everyone wants to avoid all-out war. Too many lives will be lost if that happens, and that's not the Guardians intention. It goes against everything we have been working toward.

Ever since Samuel decided to take a step back from the

Guardians, things have been hectic. We all understood why he did it. After losing so many years with his daughter and Liz, he just wants to spend time with them and not focus on the logistical side of things. He trusts Stephen to handle things. After all, there's no way he would be elected to be leader again. I want to call him, ask for his advice, but I think it will be better to leave him be. If things do go south, then at least he can live in his fantasy world a little longer. Who am I to take that away from him?

A knock on the door startles me for a second; I didn't hear the person approach since I'm stuck in my head. "Who is it?"

"Kastiel," he says, clearing his throat. "Sorry for stopping by unannounced. I wasn't sure if you'd be home."

Opening the door, he greets me with a smile, and then walks past me to the couch, wearing his normal attire, a suit. It still shocks me that he's been able to hide within the human world for so long.

"Listen. I just came to check up on things. I heard about a meeting? Is there anything I can do to help?" he asks, rubbing his hands together, his blue eyes pouring into mine.

What did he think he could help with? He's a defense lawyer and has money, but neither helps in this situation. "Nope. Nothing with your expertise. Plus, I don't think Stephen has even formally made up his mind yet."

"He's actually questioning it? Why on earth would he do that? He did unspeakable things against us and the humans. Hundreds if not thousands of lives were lost because of him. He should be handed over and let them do what they want with him."

Kastiel probably has no knowledge of Drake being my former lover, and so he's not quick to bite his tongue before speaking in my presence. My feelings about the exchange are deluded. Of course, the vampire responsible should pay, but it's Drake. None of this would have happened if I would have kept an eye on him. If he never got captured and turned by Jakob, then he would still be human. "I'm sure he's considering all scenarios and outcomes before making a final decision. Trusting the humans can prove to be disastrous for both species if they don't hold up their end of the bargain. Can you imagine how many more lives will be lost if a war erupts? We won't have a choice."

His index finger hits his lip, dragging across it. "Good point. Let's just hope it doesn't come to that. The world would be over as we know it. There'd be no going back unless there is a complete surrender from the other side."

He has some good points, and now I'm starting to understand why Stephen puts trust in Kastiel. Sure, he's embedded in the human world, which is always helpful, but he also cares about the outcome of our society. We need more vampires like that. Ones that don't want to just tuck away and try to be the most human they can. I understand why so many want to do that; it's what they know. Yet trying to make a change and keep things running smoothly is also a huge part of why they get to live oblivious like they do. Because of us.

"I'm surprised you're back so soon. I figured you'd try to stay out of New York for a couple days. I can tell you don't really like it here. Is there somewhere else you'd rather be?"

"Actually, yes. Somewhere where the weather is seventy-five and sunny year-round would be great." I snicker. "I couldn't stay in Texas. I needed to come back and cool down. Some of our members aren't too happy with me right now—but they'll see I'm right eventually."

"Well, sometimes people don't see eye to eye with their superiors. That's normal. The thing is how they handle it. Well, if you need to blow off some steam, we still got that sight-seeing I promised you whenever you're ready. You got my number. Or did you wanna go tonight?"

"I'm not really in the mindset to do anything." Something tells me that this would be more like a date than just the two of us going as friends.

Don't get me wrong, he isn't bad-looking, but right now I'm trying to muddle through my feelings with everything surrounding Drake, and the fact he might very well be dead for good tomorrow or the next day. Yet I find myself wanting to spend time with Kastiel. Eliza seems to think there's chemistry there; she even said so that first night in New York when he showed up on our doorstep. *Slow your roll. One thing at a time.* I don't have the time or the energy to start anything up with Kastiel right now.

"I'm gonna be honest here... There's too much going on for me to even think about seeing New York or seeing someone."

"Oh, I— No rush. Just thought it would be nice to do before the world might go to shit," he says, hands in his pockets.

I move my hair behind my ears. "Thanks for the offer though. I've got to get to Stephen's. He'll kill me if I'm late."

Kastiel nods, and we both head for the door, ride down on the elevator, and say goodbye.

My feet carry me as fast as they can to California until I'm standing at his front door, ringing the doorbell.

Warwick answers with a look of disgust on his face. *Feeling's mutual, buddy.* "Where's Stephen?"

He responds by pointing his finger toward the office. *Wow, not even a verbal response.* Obviously I don't like him, but we're going to be working together regardless, so we have to at least be able to verbally communicate on some level. I'll give him some time, but there would be no apology. I still think Stephen made the wrong decision, and Warwick should have been given the final death. We don't want other vampires to think they can get away with breaking the rules or see that we're providing leniency. It only takes one wrong person to find out.

"Stephen, I'm here," I say, making my way to him.

He stands up and greets me, but not happily. "We have a lot to discuss. Shut the door and take a seat."

My eyes squint, wondering why he can't discuss it with the door open; surely he's had words with the others by now. So what's the big secret? I shut the door as he asks, "So, let's make this quick. I've got things to do since the world might be going to shit any day now."

His palms intertwine and lie on the top of his desk. "Well, we have some issues that need to be addressed. And answers from you. The time it takes is up to you."

"Okay, stop being so weird and get to the point," I say, rolling my eyes. What fucking issues could he possibly be talking about? This better not be about Warwick.

"Well, before we get into the big things, let's discuss Drake. Only out of respect and courtesy for our friendship, am I letting you know my decision has been made and he'll be turned over to the agency. I think it's our best chance at preventing an all-out war. I know you two have history, and this might drudge up your past, but it's got to be done. He's not the same man you loved all those years, and he has proven that to you, hasn't he?"

"I know he isn't the same person since he got turned, but a part of me wishes he could be. That'll never change. That doesn't affect my knowing he deserves the punishment he'll get for the actions he chose to make after being turned."

He nods, not saying anything.

"Is it possible for me to accompany you on the exchange?" I ask, wide eyes.

"Of course. That'll be fine. I'll let you know the details once they're arranged. Now that that's out of the way, we've got other things to discuss."

"Like what?"

"Let's start with Blakeley."

Oh God, not that again. Is he seriously questioning my decision on her? Would he rather we let her live and possibly be turned against us? He can't be serious. "What about her? She's dead."

"And why is that?" His head slants.

"She was a threat to our cause. If the rogues found her and turned her, they would have a new leader to follow. That would mean big consequences and complications for what we're trying to do."

"So you think because it might happen, we should murder innocent humans? That makes us no better than them, Sasha." His tone rises, and he slams his fists down on the desk.

"You seriously can't be trying to justify her being alive?"

"Actually, I'm doing just that, and you would have known… yet you failed to consult me before making the decision yourself, which in fact, wasn't your choice to make."

"You put me in charge of the enforcers, Stephen. You did! So, in fact, it was my decision. I didn't realize I needed to consult you on every single damn decision I make."

"That's the problem. You're obviously not capable of handling your duties with the judgment I thought, and that poses a huge problem. So effective immediately, you're relieved of your duties."

Oh no, you fucking don't.

"You will stay in New York except for when you're on an assignment."

"Assignment? What fucking assignment is that?"

"You will be taking Envio's spot as enforcer."

My jaw tightens. "I didn't agree to be a puppy. You're not seriously considering giving him my position? I've put in years of work for you and the cause… What will people think when they see their Savior being a lackey?"

"At this point, he's proven to be able to have good judgment. Far better than yours. If you would've listened to him, we wouldn't be discussing this right now. Plus, it's not just about her. You've been acting like you're superior, above everyone. Maybe this will make you understand that you're not and never will be the leader. You don't have what it takes, Sasha. Savior or not."

I want to get up from this chair and rip his fucking throat out, but I refrain. Stephen will figure out that Envio is not capable of being in my position, and he'll be begging for me to come back.

"We're done here. Envio will be in touch," Stephen says, getting up, opening the door, and gesturing for me to leave. "Oh, and if I find out you're misbehaving in any way or making your own decisions about things, the next chat we have won't be so pleasant."

5

Stephen

The sheer fuck you in her voice really makes me want to take away all responsibility from her, but I know that'll only make matters worse. Demotion will give her a chance to earn herself back into a role in the future. For her to start acting right, she'll need something to keep her motivated to do better, and this might be just the kick in the ass she needs. It sucks to be so harsh and blunt, especially after getting so close, but my job is to do what's best for our society, and right now that's not having Sasha in any place of authority.

The door closes behind me as I search for Warwick to see if he can set up the exchange through Samantha. We could get this over with and hopefully be on the road to some peace after all the awful things Drake did. No one will ever forget his or his father's name, it's engraved in our minds, but he will pay for what he's done, whether it's by our hands or theirs.

Warwick is found outside on the deck, admiring the waves hitting the sand, and most likely how lucky he is to be alive after what he did. As a vampire, we aren't as human as we'd like to be, but mistakes are still made, and sometimes second chances are warranted.

"I need you to alert Kieran that we're going with the exchange, and then set it up with Samantha as soon as possible. We need to get this done and over with. The longer he's in our possession, the more likely his goons will come for me."

"Final decision, then?" he asks.

I nod and head back to my office. "Let me know the arrangements. I'll update the others in Texas so they're aware."

Envio and Jane are back in Texas keeping an eye on Drake with Dr. Kendrick. It won't take long before the rogues catch wind of his capture and try to retaliate and rescue him. They are given strict orders—no one in or out without my permission, and that includes Sasha. My faith in her to make rational decisions is gone, and with all their history, if he says the right thing, she might try to prevent this, and then things could get ugly. Hopefully, she has come to peace with my decision and understands it's for the best, and what the maniac deserves.

"Boss. He wants the exchange to happen tonight. He said no more waiting." The phone is on mute, but still in his hand. "They want an answer."

"Okay, can they give us two hours for the doctor to get him ready for transport?"

He gets back on the phone. "Two hours? Does that work? Okay, I'll let him know."

"Two hours, and she's texting me the exact location. You better get going."

Sasha will meet me there at Jane's to go with us on the exchange. As a friend, I couldn't deny her request to be with us when we handed him off to the president.

"We weren't expecting you so soon," Jane says, as I walk through the door.

"The exchange is in less than two hours. Sasha will be here any minute. Let's make this exchange as cordial as possible. I know there's bad blood right now, but we can't let that affect tonight. Okay?"

Nods from both Jane and Envio are exchanged, and I head down to the basement to talk to Dr. Kendrick. He'll have one hour to get him ready and heavily sedated, and then the location is almost a one-hour drive away. Only because we want the best outcome possible, which is Drake not escaping, Dr. Kendrick has opted to provide a day's worth of extra sedative in case they need it.

When I get back upstairs, the air is thick. Things will be this way for a while, until Sasha accepts my decision on her demotion. It's not like she can never move up again, but she will have to prove to everyone she deserves the chance. Maybe now she can see why second chances are so important. Might help give her a different outlook on Warwick and Envio. Yet she's so stubborn, so probably not.

Envio follows me to the side. "I haven't had a chance to reach out to Eliza or Malachi yet."

"How'd she take it?" His head flicks over to Sasha.

"Better than I thought, but time will tell."

My watch goes off, and it's time to load Drake and head to the meeting site.

"Jane and I will go get Drake. Today might be the first step in the right direction. Who knew this day would ever come?" Envio says, shaking his head.

Sasha and I make our way to the sedan and wait for them to arrive. They put him in the trunk, and we head to the exchange site. So many things go through my head. The offer for a peace agreement on their side is hopeful, but we can't know for sure until it actually happens. Something could backfire, or this all could be a ploy to get their hands on one of us. Maybe me. After all, if they execute the leader, then vampires would have no one to follow, and they could march in and try to take out most of us. I'd like to say they aren't that smart or stupid, but we'll see.

Sasha sits in the passenger seat, fiddling with her fingers, and everyone knows their history goes back to early childhood. Bad guy or not, she'll have a hard time with this. No matter the bitterness between us, I can understand how big a part of her life was spent with Drake. She blames herself for him becoming this awful vampire;

it's shattered her in a way that I don't know if she will ever recover from or forgive herself.

"Listen, this needs to go smoothly. Everyone on your best behavior," I say and wait until I get a nod from all three.

Sasha, Envio, Jane, and I pull up to the meeting spot and as hesitant as I am, this has to be the right decision. Drake killed thousands of humans, and they deserve justice on their side too. I know what they're going to do to him, but in the end, he deserves it. Yes, I have a conscience, but it's not struggling with this. The evil creature is off the deep end, and there's no going back. Dr. Kendrick couldn't help him even if he tried. Drake is a goner.

"You ready?" I ask, reaching for Sasha's hand, seeing her shaking next to me. No matter what, she is still having slight trouble with this. "You want me to do it?"

She shakes her head. "It should be me."

A deep breath is taken as we all step outside and three men meet Sasha at the back as I pop the trunk, finding Drake starting to wake up already. "There he is. The serum is wearing off, but there's more in the bag. It's enough to last you twenty-four to thirty-six hours. Remember he's a sweet-talker, so only trust your best men around him."

The guys nod and carry him off, Drake struggling to get out of their hold.

"You're doing the right thing," President Walters says. "He's a disgrace to your species. Don't lose any sleep over this scumbag."

"After what he's done to our kind and yours, I have no regrets about handing him over to see some justice. My only request is that you make him suffer. Like all of our people did," I tell him, rubbing my hands together.

"Don't do this. Sas—please. I love you," Drake screams as the servicemen take him inside. "You can't let them do this. This isn't you."

"Don't listen to a word he says," I take Sasha's hand and lead her to the car. "Let's get out of here."

Everyone gets back in, and I wait a minute before leaving. Even though I'm not happy with Sasha's actions lately, she's still a close friend. Seeing her like this hurts. "You okay?" I ask. "I know it's hard, but it's the right thing."

"Doesn't make it hurt any less." She shoves her face into my chest as the tears start coming. "Even after all the awful things he did, I still love him. How is that?"

"Love doesn't conquer all. It's hard to change the image you have of him from when you were younger. Understandably. You've just got to move on."

She sits back in her seat, and we head back to Jane's and wait for the next meeting. There are so many things to discuss with President Walters, and the next few days will be crucial to brainstorming ideas and having them ready for him when he calls.

6
Envio

Once we get back to Jane's from the meeting, so many things are running through my head. Could this work and peace truly be obtained between vampires and humans? Even more so after all the casualties Drake and his father caused? Things are up in the air at this point, but hopefully President Walters keeps his promise. Peace will be beneficial for both our kinds, because war will only cause more bloodshed and hundreds of thousands of lives potentially lost. Surely, the agency working for him would make him aware of the dangers.

"Do you really think he's going to sign a peace treaty? That he's going to tell the world about vampires' existence? The world would never be the same," Jane says, pacing the bedroom while I sit on her bed.

"No clue at this point. Gonna have to wait and see how this pans out. Right now, we just wait to see what his next move is and go from there."

Jane sits on my lap, her legs dangling off the side of my legs, her arms around my neck. "Can you imagine not having to fight anymore? All this running around and drama just poof, gone? We might actually get a normal enough life if this goes well."

I'd love nothing more than to be able to spend all my time with her, but something always goes wrong. Plus, we would have to get rid of all the rogues for us not to have to worry. How the hell are we going to do that? They turn humans faster than we can track them down. Numbers are just getting larger every day. Yet I continue searching in theory that one day maybe it'll all work out and I can get my happy ending.

Speaking of tracking them down, I haven't heard back from Eliza and Malachi. Maybe they aren't too happy about me being their new boss, but we have to continue like normal. There are still rogues running around out there, and the more we can keep them contained, the better it will look when the chance for peace comes. I try their cell phones again, but no answer. Usually, they would have checked in by now.

"I'm gonna have to go track down Malachi and Eliza. They aren't returning my calls... Might be nothing, but I'd rather be safe than sorry," I say, kissing Jane on the lips before heading out of the bedroom.

Everyone is on edge right now, waiting to figure out what the humans are going to do with Drake. We have no knowledge of what all they know about vampires, and Drake is a good sweet-talker. If he's able to escape the humans, it'll take us months or longer to find him again. Hopefully, they kill him fast before he even has the chance.

As I make my way to the front door, Stephen and Sasha are on the couch, and he's trying to calm her down. This makes it easier to leave without either of them questioning me. I don't want Stephen to think I can't handle my new position, and my enforcers being MIA on me isn't a great start. Sasha would have a field day about this one.

First stop, the condo in New York. I text Kastiel so he can meet me there to open the door. No need to bust in and screw up the place.

When I make it off the elevator, he's standing outside the door, but it's open.

"Thanks for coming. You could've gone inside..." I say, making my way to the door. Only now I see why he didn't. Even from the entryway, I know something is wrong. We inch inside, looking for anything that could lead us to what happened. The living room shows they put up a fight. Who would come after them? Rogues, maybe? Yet were they really dumb enough to seek out our enforcers instead of hiding from them?

"How can I help?" Kastiel asks. "Where should I start looking?"

He means well, but he isn't exactly trained to track people down, especially wearing a two-thousand-dollar suit and leather shoes. "I'll alert Stephen and the others. Thank you though."

I've only been in my new position for less than two days, and already two enforcers have been kidnapped or killed. How could I let this happen? I should have come and checked two days ago when I couldn't get ahold of them. This is all my fault.

My legs carry me fast back to Jane's house. As I stand outside the door, preparing myself to explain this to the others inside, I think of something. Is this just a coincidence that they are kidnapped around the same time we hand over Drake? Seems like an unlikely quick turn of events to me.

The door opens and I find Sasha and Stephen still on the couch. "Eliza and Malachi are missing."

"What the fuck do you mean missing?" Sasha spills out. "I'm sure they are somewhere, probably just on strike or something."

Stephen glances at her. "Stop."

"The condo shows evidence of a struggle, so something definitely happened. Question is how long have they been missing?"

"I talked to Eliza last night about your position change. Everything seemed fine," Stephen replies.

So, between last night and tonight. A struggle implies this must have been done by vampires. Humans wouldn't have the gall to approach two vampires like that, at least I don't think so. "So, we need to come up with a game plan. Who would take them?"

Jane stands silent on the opposite side of the room, pacing. Her anxiety is high, but that's when she does her best thinking. I swear she would have been an investigator if still human.

"Well, if it's vampires, they obviously want something or they would have just killed them at the condo. So if they took them, they will reach out."

"Seriously, are we talking like a ransom or something here?"

"I can think of one thing they could want," Sasha chimes in. "Drake."

It suddenly crosses my mind that this could be a bad situation. If they are to ask for Drake's safe return, then Eliza and Malachi would have to pay the ultimate price. Everyone in the room knows that handing Drake over is not an option. Especially now that he's with the humans, but maybe whoever took them doesn't know that yet.

"We could tell them where he's being held. Maybe they would give us back our two in exchange for Drake's location."

"Sending vampires to extract Drake from the agency's possession isn't a smart idea and could provoke war. As much as I don't want to see Eliza and Malachi die, we have to think about the whole picture. Sacrifice a few, for the safeness of the masses."

It's one of those decisions I'm glad Stephen has to make instead of me. We all hope in foresight to be able to make the hard decisions, but it's much different when they actually arise.

"Now, let's stop assuming what happened, and get out there looking for them. Maybe we can find a way to save them. Any ideas?" Stephen asks.

They could be anywhere with anyone. How the hell are we going to find them?

7

Jane

What the hell is going on? Is this vicious cycle ever going to come to an end? It's been nothing but one thing after another since being turned, and yet we are still battling rogues. Maybe we need to accept the fact that there will always be vampires like them. We kill one, ten more pop up on the radar.

I guess that's the thing. Someone else is always going to want to be on top. Think they can do better and the rogues believe that person is Drake. Honestly, if they are responsible for this, why wouldn't they try to kidnap Stephen instead? You know, leader for leader. Something just didn't seem right, and I can't quite put my finger on it.

"I'll take Jane and go looking. Not sure where to start really," Envio tells Stephen. "Don't you think it's best that we go in pairs if we can? Under the circumstances."

He has a good point. They could pick us off one by one until Stephen or someone else has no choice but to give Drake over to save all of us.

"Yes. Okay, let's start now. Once they find out that we don't have

Drake anymore, then they're dead for sure," Stephen says before heading out the door with Warwick following behind him.

Everyone leaves except us. "Where should we look? I mean they weren't on an assignment, and the apartment's empty. I guess we start looking for rogues?"

"Exactly what we do. Just try. There's no tellin' who has them."

Envio takes my hand and leads me out the door, and then when our feet stop, we are in Virginia. Why the heck are we here of all places?

"This is the last assignment they were on. The last rogue they killed. Maybe the rogue wasn't alone, and his buddy followed them back to the apartment or something..." He stumbles over his words. "I don't know. Grasping at straws here..."

We find a bar, which is where vampires tend to feed because of the crowds it attracts. After finding a table and ordering a beer so as not to look weird, we begin scanning the room. No vampires in here yet.

"So, with everything going on, we really haven't gotten to discuss arrangements," Envio says, rubbing his hands together.

"For?"

"Well, he gave me the option to stay in Texas. I'd like to be close to you. Unless..."

His face shows signs of hesitancy. I didn't realize we were going to take that next step already. "Like living with me?"

"Yes, why do you sound so put off by the idea? It's not like we aren't in the same bed when I'm over now... What's the big deal?"

That's a big step in a relationship, especially in my first ever adult one. It's not that I didn't like the idea of having him around. I'm falling in love with him and have been since the day he turned me, but things change. What if he gets sick of me?

"You're scaring me. Hello? Are you having second thoughts about us being together or something? I know we said we would wait until all the chaos was over, but that will be never. If I die tomorrow, I wanna do it knowing I got to show you how much I love you every day."

When he says things like that, it makes me melt. Envio really is a sweet guy and things have been going so great between us. Could I really blame him for wanting to take the next step?

"Listen, I'll give you some time to think about it. If it's really that big of a deal, then I can find somewhere else to stay."

We break eye contact and focus on the mission at hand. It's more important than our love life right now, and lives are at stake. I don't know Eliza or Malachi too well, since I've never really worked closely with them, but he has.

"I never really got to know them. How are you dealing with all this?" I ask, sliding my hand in his. Sure, he might not show too much emotion right now, but that didn't mean anything. I'm sure it's bothering him.

"It just doesn't make any sense. Eliza is quick on her feet. She'd be hard to capture or track even for me. Whoever did this is good. Like really good."

Goosebumps shift up my back, and I look to the door. It's one of them. He peers across the bar, making direct eye contact with me. "He knows we are here..."

We watch him to see what he does next. What his reaction will be. Will he try to run? Approach us? I sit quietly and let Envio take the lead on this because after all, he has been an enforcer for years, and I'm a little rusty.

The rogue begins to walk toward us, glancing around him, like he's looking for someone.

"What the hell are you doing here?" he snarls.

Envio laughs. "I should ask you the same thing, but today I'm not here to kill you. Only get some information."

He laughs. "Information? What makes you think I'd tell you anything, scumbag?"

Did they know each other? It seems like there is lots of hostility between them for strangers.

"Two of ours have been taken. You wouldn't happen to know anything about that, would ya, Tate?" Envio's eyebrow rises.

Wait? Tate? I remember him mentioning someone with that name before. He was under Jakob, when he was still alive, that is. He tried for a long while like Envio to stay as human as possible, but it didn't last.

"Two of yours sounds like a little cost compared to the thousands of ours you've killed. Let's call it a fair trade and let it go, huh?"

I could feel the testosterone building up and spewing over. We need to stick to the reason why we are here: answers. Someone has to know where they are. Tate would be my guess on who would know, only because of how close him and Jakob were in the end. Some would say he was his right-hand man, and surely that only bled over when Drake took over.

"We did the world a favor by getting rid of as many Blood Takers as we could. Jakob had no right to be a leader of any vampire," Envio screams, causing the bartender to look our way.

"Careful. We don't want to draw attention, remember."

"Don't you dare talk about him. He took you in and gave you purpose and you betrayed him. You make me sick," Tate says, then spits on the floor. "He would still be alive if you didn't help the other side."

"No one cares about that right now. We just need information. Do you know who has them or not?" I ask, trying to cut the tension in the room. We are here to find out information, not start fights. Eliza and Malachi are our priority right now, not killing rogues. As much as he might want to get it over with while we are here, we have bigger things to worry about than killing Tate.

"Oh... who is this beauty? Surely she would rather be with a real vampire." His eyes scan my body. "I doubt you can keep her pleased..."

This throws Envio over the edge and he slams his fist into Tate's jaw. "Don't you dare even look at her. She'd never go for you."

"So, is that a no? I really don't have time to be standing around all day while you guys argue about who is bigger and better..." I say, hands on hips.

Tate laughs and shakes his head, and that's my cue to get out of here. We don't have time wasting false leads, and even though torture might get results if he does, in fact, know anything, we don't have the time to waste. Every minute that passes is another opportunity for them to find out Drake is with the humans.

"Come on, we can't stay here too long. He doesn't know anything," I say, grabbing Envio's arm and leaving the bar. It's understandable the hate he has for Tate, but someone has to keep him in check before we waste any more time.

"I wanna know how the fuck he's still alive? He should have been in the tunnels that night."

We will find him again, and then Envio can have his way with him, but today is about finding our people. Nothing else.

8

Stephen

Where do we even start the search? None of us are dumb. Rogues are still out there all over the country, and we don't have enough time to track them all down. The probability of us finding anyone that knows anything before they find out Drake is with the humans is highly unlikely. The likelihood that they make it out of this alive is almost nil.

I can't hand Drake over just to save two of my people. It would cause an uproar, and we don't need anything else going wrong right now. My mind is blurred, trying to figure out what the best thing is to do in each situation, and I feel like I'm failing everyone. How could two of my people get kidnapped and go unnoticed? It was while Sasha was being demoted, but still. She lives there. How did she not notice? Has she not been home or something? I don't want to blame anyone for this, except for myself. With everything going on, I haven't really had time to think about the rogues, and usually we are one step ahead of them. Of course this is something they would do. Their almighty Drake is captured and they will want to keep from being executed at any cost. So coming after us makes us the middle man, and forces me to make the hard decision. Maybe they are trying to prove to my people that I'm not competent enough to be their leader. Sometimes the thought runs across my mind, that things might be different if they had chosen Sasha or Jane back then.

My mind switches course and Kieran comes to mind. There might be some way they could help me find our people. He has human and vampire connections, so it is worth a shot. Not that I want to ask him for any sort of favor, but it's the right thing to do. I can't let them die because I hate the bastard.

"Hello. Finally decided to think about the best way..." Kieran says before I cut him off.

"No time for idle chitchat. Eliza and Malachi are missing and we believe rogues have them. Yet to be confirmed. I need you to see if you can get any information from your side."

"Well, look who's calling for a favor... Never thought I'd see the day. Can you at least say please?"

"Can you help or not?"

"I'll see what I can find out," Kieran responds and hangs up.

The more vampires we have out searching for information, the better. Yet my mind is trying to wrap around the fact no one has called to ask for Drake. Wouldn't they call and let us know what they want in return? Did they expect us to just know? This whole situation just seems awry, and I don't know what to think. We would have to know who to give him to, if that's what this is all about. Maybe the humans took them, and somehow they got on their radar. It's possible they aren't being quite as honest as we think.

"Came across some rogues, but no information. We'll keep looking. Someone has to know something. I assume no one has reached out yet?" Envio asks.

"No, no one. It might be too late at this point."

"Don't say that. They are fine. We'll get them back, boss."

I want to believe that, but the longer they are missing, the more my optimism fades. Rogues aren't necessarily known for being nice, only slaughtering. Malachi and Eliza are responsible for many deaths of their fellow rogues, and they would want revenge for that. Plus, the fact is, they just enjoy killing, whether vampire or human.

"I haven't heard from Sasha. Tried reaching out a couple times, but no answer. I'm starting to get concerned that something has happened to her now," I tell him, checking my phone to see if maybe she texted me back.

"Okay, well, what do you want us to do?" Envio asks.

My attention is taken away from him when Warwick busts into my office, a state of panic on his face. I know that look; something else is wrong.

"Hold on, Envio," I say, setting the phone down on my desk and giving my attention to Warwick. "What happened now?"

"I'm gonna put the phone on speaker," he says, looking at me. "Sam, he can hear you too. Go ahead."

Why the hell would Sam be calling? We did what they asked when we handed over Drake; what more could they possibly want?

"Okay, listen. I'm not sure what kind of game you guys are playing here, or if you truly have no involvement, but Drake is gone. Somehow, he escaped, and he's been under heavy surveillance. The cameras were destroyed so we don't have any clue how he escaped or who helped him."

You've got to be fucking kidding me. How could they let this happen? Maybe this is all a distraction. Surely they knew we wouldn't hand him over and would be out looking for where Eliza and Malachi are. They gave themselves an in to get him right under both of our noses. *What fucking idiots!*

"We had two of ours kidnapped, we believe. We assumed they wanted Drake back in return, but it wasn't feasible for many reasons. We have to find him," I tell her, pacing my office, trying to figure how the hell we are going to pull this off. We don't have enough resources to be looking for three people, especially with two of our enforcers being the ones missing.

"Walters isn't happy about this. He thinks you double-crossed him. You better get him back or I'm not sure this possible peace is going to happen. He's giving you one day to bring him back to us. Good luck," Sam says before disconnecting.

Fuck. Why does he keep ruining things for us? Like father, like son. If Drake escaped, he had help. But how would they have known where he was being held?

"What the hell do we do now, boss? If he goes on a binge, the humans aren't going to talk to us about peace," Warwick says.

I pick up my phone off the desk. "You still there?"

"Yes, I heard everything. Tell me what you want us to do," Envio asks, waiting for his orders.

"Drake is our priority. Head back to Texas and we'll meet you there."

He is a strategic vampire, and maybe he knew that once we handed him over it wouldn't be long before his lackeys busted him out. Rogues are willing to give their lives for him, and for what? I'll never understand their philosophy.

9

Sasha

What the hell is taking so long? They aren't back yet. Did they get captured? *Fuck!* Maybe this wasn't the best idea. I acted on impulse and selfishness, but can you blame me? Things are getting out of hand, and I just want a way to change the outcome. Don't I deserve a little happiness or am I destined to be miserable? Is that my fate? Maybe there's nothing I can do to change it?

My phone rings and I press ignore again. I didn't want to speak with any of them right now. I am running out of time.

The door swings open, and Tate carries Drake inside. He must be sedated still.

"Let's take him downstairs." He has no clue about my idea of trying to reform Drake. If he did, they would have never broken him out and brought him to me. Surely, they have to know I have an ulterior motive.

We make it downstairs, and things need to happen fast. There's only so much time before they show up looking for me since I've ignored all their calls.

"What the heck is going on? He's supposed to be with the humans," Dr. Kendrick asks.

"Yeah, what are we doin' here? Should be at our house. What the hell are you thinking?" Tate asks.

"Reforming him. One last chance to be the man I love again."

I can't let him die. If he could be reformed, there would be no threat. I've tried to talk sense into the others about it, but no one wants to listen. Yes, he's done awful things, but that doesn't mean his life should mean any less. It's my last chance to make things right.

"What are you doing? We didn't break him out for this! You lyin' bitch," Tate screams, crouching like he's going to pounce on me.

"I have to at least try," I yell, not caring what he says.

Drake hasn't eaten in days already, so the process should take less time than normal. Hopefully, we can get this done before they realize Drake is gone and I had anything to do with his escape. I couldn't live with myself if I didn't at least try every option to keep him alive. Whether Stephen and the others hate me for it, it's something I have to do. He wouldn't even be a vampire if it wasn't for me.

"You really think you can change him? God, you really are fucking stupid," Tate says, walking out of the room.

The rogues hadn't a clue what my plan was when I suggested this, only that they could get their hands on him. I let them know where he was being held, and everything I knew about the complex. Personally, I couldn't help with the escape because of the risk of one human recognizing me, but the rogues had no problem breaking him out.

"We won't let you do this. Hand him over to us, so we can take him home. Where he belongs," Tate says after returning with two of his lackeys standing beside him.

"Not gonna happen. All I need is a couple of hours to see if it works." I look away, and I shouldn't have. "Get off me!" I scream, trying to fight off the two goons holding my arms.

"Did you really think we would let you reform him? He's no good to us that way," Tate whispers in my ear. "He's a cold-blooded killer, just the way we like him. Leave it to some woman to want to change him. Typical."

"He was never meant to be one. Jakob would have never turned him if it wasn't for me. His whole life was ruined by my stupidity. I just want the chance to fix it," I say, pleading with him. The more he talks, the more I see why he is Drake's right-hand man. It's almost as if he idolizes him. He is the one Stephen and the others are going to need to watch out for in the future. If, in fact, Drake does end up being slaughtered by the humans after this failed attempt of selfishness of mine.

"What do ya say? Can we kill her?" one of the lackeys asks.

"No. Drake will want the pleasure of doing this kill himself."

Himself? These vampires sure do know a lot about me. Does that mean that Drake talks about me? I shake my head, realizing the predicament I'm standing in. My first love might be the very person who ends up taking my life. What a way to come full circle after everything I've been through.

"Wake him up." Tate nudges his head to the doctor. "Now!"

"Okay, okay," Dr. Kendrick responds, grabbing a needle and shooting him up with some adrenaline to please my captors.

"He won't kill me. There's still a sliver of the man I love in there. You'll see," I screech, fighting back. Oh, how I wish this to be true. I am not ready to die, but if it's my fate, then there's nothing I can do. I chose this path tonight, and that means the consequences are mine to be dealt with accordingly.

"We'll see about that..." Tate chuckles.

Drake's eyes pop open and he sees me in a hold by his followers. "Did you catch me a present? Aw, guys, you shouldn't have."

"We know how much you've looked forward to killing her. Now's your perfect chance, boss. Put her pathetic life to an end," Tate says, gesturing my way.

The look in his eyes is terrifying. Am I wrong? Has he lost every part of his humanity? I close my eyes, remembering some of the good times I've had with him. When we were eleven, he used to come over every day after school and we would ride our bikes up and down the street until our parents expected us home for dinner.

One of those days, I fell and skinned my knee, and instead of going to get my mother, he held my hand and told me everything would be okay. Or when we were eighteen, freshly graduated from high school. He was due to leave to make it to campus for his first semester of college, but we wanted to spend one last day together before everything changed. I'll never forget the anguish I felt that day when I kissed him before he left. I wasn't sure if I would ever see him again. Drake was supposed to be my future husband, father of my kids, and then my whole life got ripped apart in that damn tornado. Wrecked and thrown to pieces, scattered around in many different places. Yet here we are, with my death resting in his very hands.

"You remember all those years we pined over each other? Or the night we finally made love?" Drake's hot breath hits my neck.

"Yes, of course I do. I love you." Tears are streaming down my face, hoping this is a glimpse into the Drake I used to know. He's got to be in there somewhere. *Please. Show yourself.*

"None of it was real. I just wanted to sleep with you. You didn't actually think I was in love with you or anything, did you? Pathetic."

He is just trying to get me fired up. I wouldn't give him the satisfaction. Once he kills me, there is no going back. The others would slaughter him, whether or not the humans want him. They would get revenge for my death. "Go ahead, say what you want. I don't believe a goddamn word coming out of your mouth right now. If you're going to kill me, just get it over with already."

The sly smile that takes over his face tells me that's exactly what he plans to do. The man I love is gone, completely. And though my life is going to be cut short, at least I'll go knowing I did everything I could to make him *Drake* again.

"You don't think you're going to get off so easy, do you? You killed my father, their leader. You're going to feel pain before we put you down. Let's see what things the good doctor has lying around here, shall we?"

Torture? Seriously? Why am I so stupid? I should have never believed I could save him. Love makes you do stupid things—and right now I'm learning the hard way.

Drake walks around the basement, picking up different objects, trying to find his weapon of choice. We heal fast, so I'm not sure what torture is really going to do. Sure, I'll feel the pain, but only briefly.

"Actually, I have a better idea. You say you love me, right?" he asks.

I nod like an idiot while Tate's guys are still holding me.

"Then this seems more appropriate," he says right before his hand breaks through my chest cavity and rips out my heart. "There. How could you love someone that would do this to you? Huh? You still love me?"

More tears stream down my face, leaving tracks, and I nod. Is he trying to prove to me I shouldn't love a monster? Does he think I don't already know that? It's clear—but he's my Drake. I can't give up on him. I just can't!

He takes a knife and cuts into my stomach three times. I wince, feeling the pain, knowing it will go away in just a few minutes.

"Now?"

"Nothing you can do will make me stop loving you. The real Drake. Not this imposter your father made you into. This isn't who you are," I scream at him.

He shakes his head and looks at Tate. He paces around for a minute or two and the rest of us are silent. "This is the problem. Women are so darn naïve. Exactly why my father never wanted us to get involved with any. Vampire or not."

"And you think your father knew what was best for everyone? He's the damn person who made our species. None of us would be here if it wasn't for his fucked-up way of trying to save you after your coma incident."

"Don't you talk about my father that way, Sasha. I'm warning you."

"You're already going to kill me, so what? At least I'll get everything off my chest before you do. Your father made a mistake and caused a creation of cold-blooded murderers. Killing innocent people left and right just to please himself. That's who your father was."

I could hear the door open upstairs, and Stephen's voice. They are here to figure out why I haven't been answering them. Surely, they know by now that Drake escaped and are looking for him. Hopefully he brought the others.

I try to call out—but Tate covers my mouth.

"Don't you dare say a word."

10
Envio

It's pissing me off that we have no idea where Eliza and Malachi are. They could be dead already. Not exactly the way I want to think, but it's been a couple days with no word. How did I not notice they were missing earlier? Maybe then we could have picked up on something.

"So where to next? He didn't seem to know anything. What about Michigan? I know you said they found a bunch there a couple months ago," Jane says.

"We killed them all. Unless one was good at hiding their killings since then, I doubt it."

I know she is just trying to be helpful in finding them, but honestly, we have no idea where they could be. Or the reason anyone would take them besides Drake. He's the only reason why they would be taken instead of just killed in the apartment.

"Hello?" I say, answering Stephen's call. "Wait. What? How is that possible? Okay, see you there."

"What is it? Did they find them?"

I end the call and look at her. "Drake escaped. We've got to get to Texas. Back to your house."

Just what we need. The humans are going to be furious and

assume we have something to do with it. There goes our peace down the shitter. This will never stop until he's dead. They should have just killed him already. What the hell were they waiting for?

"Let's go."

Getting back to Jane's house, we hear a struggle from inside, but don't want to raise an alarm so we try to keep as quiet as we can entering the house.

"What the hell do you think is going on down there? Surely Drake isn't dumb enough to come back here after escaping? I mean he'd be a full-blown dumbass…"

Same thing runs through my mind, which is why I doubt it's him. He would run as far as possible away from us and try to skimp under the radar for as long as possible. He knows the humans will be looking for him too. They've got the vampire to torture, and they are not about to let him get away. Definitely not now.

"We need to get down there before getting noticed. Shhh…" Jane says, tiptoeing dramatically, waiting for the stairs to squeak like in the movies, giving away their position.

The screams begin, and the snaps of flesh being removed, torn. What the hell is going on down there? That's when I hear his voice.

"You really are so naive. Maybe now you've learned your lesson. Goodbye, Sasha."

My eyes go wide, and I run down the rest of the stairs as fast as my feet will carry me. Not only did they tear her apart, but she is already on fire and almost burned to a crisp ash on the floor.

"Why? She loved you." Jane's voice cracks. "What the hell kind of sociopathic asshole kills the only thing that truly cares for it? Your father really did fuck you up in the head when he turned you."

Tate, Drake, and two rogues are standing over her ashes with maniacal grins. Dr. Kendrick is cowering in the corner, probably thinking he is next.

"Why would you come back here? You had to know it's the first place we would look," I ask, wanting to know how fucking stupid he can really be.

"I was brought back here by your precious Sasha apparently. She had my guys break me out."

"She wouldn't do that," Jane interrupts.

"Oh, there's more to your precious Savior than you think. This whole escape was her plan to try to reform me. Make me into her lover again." He laughs. "But something she just couldn't seem to grasp... I want nothing to do with her. Too bad she couldn't get that through her fucking skull or she'd still be alive."

I want to rip his head off and watch him beg me for mercy. Feel his flesh tear, tendons rip as we pull him apart. "Well, looks like we have you right where we want. You aren't getting out of here."

Jane is trying to stay strong and focus on the anger of her death, but tears are still forming in her eyes. "You really think these guys are gonna protect you? Guess you're all dying down here tonight. I don't give a fuck what the humans want."

We can't do anything until we get some answers about Malachi and Eliza. Tate knows more than he's letting on, and it's only going to make killing him even more satisfying. "Where are our people?"

Drake laughs and then turns around to Tate. "Do we have their people?"

A smile creeps up on his face, one that I didn't want to see. "You actually think we'd keep them alive?"

He could be trying to play us. "Why would it benefit you to kill them? Go through all that trouble to capture them, just to kill them. Is this one of your cat and mouse games?"

"Actually, this game"—he uses air quotes—"is all set on by Sasha. She said we had to do something to distract you while we broke Drake out. It worked flawlessly."

"Except you're here with us. And he isn't going anywhere," Jane butts in. "So, yes, I do think you would keep them alive in case you needed any sort of leverage."

"You're a smart girl, Jane. But no, we didn't need them alive. We took care of them quickly. Who is going to be responsible for coming after us now? With both your—what do you call them again—enforcers dead?"

"Me," I say.

"I'm quivering in my boots over here. When we get out of this house, you'll never catch us. Killing them only made sure of that."

The door closes upstairs and it isn't long before Warwick and Stephen are coming down the walkway. Their eyes focus on the piles of ash on the floor and then dart to Drake.

He pounces on Drake, and I do the same to Tate. It will be my pleasure to put him out of his fucking misery. He's stronger than me, having recently fed, but I'm faster. My hand catches his leg mid-kick and throws him across the room into the wall. "Do you really think you can take me? You've seen what I'm capable of."

"You drained humans then. Now, you're nothing but a weak, pathetic wannabe."

He runs toward me, but my feet charge me toward him, then my hand grips his throat. "Who's weak and pathetic now, asshole?"

He struggles to breathe, but I don't stop. Jane tears him apart and then starts the fire. The only one left standing is Drake.

"What are you doing?" I ask Stephen. "Kill him."

"We can't. The humans want him back. There can't be a war. You know that."

He's not serious. After killing Sasha, he's actually thinking about letting him live. Handing him back over to the humans again for the chance he will escape again? Normally, I wouldn't make a fuss, but this time is different. "What if he gets out again? What's to stop rogues from going and breaking him out? Think about that."

Jane hasn't said a word, but I know her. She's just as irritated as I am. Sure, Sasha hasn't exactly been on the list of our favorite people recently, but he killed her. Justice needs to be served.

"I've made my decision and it's final," Stephen says sternly.

He demands Dr. Kendrick to sedate him and lock him up until they can arrange transport with the humans again which he follows.

"What exactly happened before we got here?" he asks, staring at the ashes on the ground.

He couldn't believe Sasha would orchestrate something like this. Maybe none of us knew her as well as we hoped. For her to plan something like this, execute it, and use our people to distract us is disturbing. Malachi and Eliza's deaths are on her. If Drake hadn't killed her, I'm afraid Stephen would have had no choice but to do the same after finding out about all this.

The four of us stood around for a moment, taking in the fact we just found out we lost three people from our immediate group tonight. Things within will have to change because we can't go too long without enforcers or rogues will think they have free rein now. We can't let them think they won.

"I guess we need to discuss the next steps here. There's more where Tate and the other two came from. We need to bring in some fresh eyes and track them down," I suggest.

"Let's take a couple hours. Process this. And then come to the house," Stephen says, turning to Warwick and heading on his way.

11

Warwick

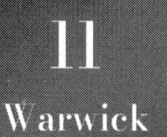

I didn't particularly care for Sasha, but her death still hurts. It impacts our society, especially with her being known as the Savior. Vampires are going to riot when they find out Drake killed her. I'm not sure if Stephen is going to reveal that she put herself in that situation by working alongside the rogues to break him out from the humans. Why would she do that though? Did she really think they were just going to sit around and let him be reformed? He would be no use to them then. Surely, she had to know that. Or maybe her love blinded her from being able to think straight with his impending death looming over her. Everyone knows she still feels guilty for him being turned in the first place, but it's not her fault. Jakob would have found him eventually, and that's not on her.

We need to make sure after this handoff that he doesn't get out again. The humans need to take more of a precaution this time. I need to warn Sam about this. Maybe she can keep a closer eye while there, and since she's a vampire, then she will know when and if they are present. Not that I want her to blow her cover, but Drake can't get out again. Next time, we won't be so lucky to find him. And if he gets out and ghosts us, things will get monumentally worse for all of us.

The killings will skyrocket again, and a chance for peace will be out the door.

I need to meet up with Samantha before this all turns to shit. And that could be any day now. Stephen wants to keep an eye on me, but surely he will understand. They are things that she might be able to fill me in on, things that could help us in this with the president.

"Listen, I know you want me in California, but I'd like permission to meet up with Samantha. Nothing sexual, but I really need to get some answers."

"To what? Do you have feelings for her or something?" he asks, hands folded across his chest.

"No, nothing like that. Isn't anyone wondering how she is still working for them, and they have no idea she's a vampire? I thought she was dead when I left her behind. The guilt was killing me." For weeks, it consumed me, thinking I was the one that got her killed. I didn't think there would be any way she would survive this long, let alone feed. It's whatever if she wants to stay on that side, but she's a vampire and can't hide forever. At some point, the secret's going to come out. She must realize that.

"You can go, but see if you can get some answers about this whole handoff, and maybe what the agency is thinking. You might be able to get some information out of her... That would be beneficial."

"I'll try."

I text Sam to see if she's free to meet up. Too many questions are left unanswered, and it might help us understand more about her and the agency. Did she give them any more of our weaknesses? She couldn't be that stupid. When they find out about her, they would be able to use them against her.

Stephen leaves, and I stay behind, waiting on her response. It might be weird to see her after all this time, to see her alive. At some point, I might have been confused about my feelings for Sam but not anymore. I never should have strayed from my wife, and it will never happen again. My assumption is since she didn't reach out to let me know, that her feelings are gone too. That will make this meeting that much easier, without having to worry about her trying anything.

"So, things are going to be weird around here. Without her," Jane says, pacing around the living room.

"Once they don't show back up with Drake, things are going to get bad. They will come after us, avenge the deaths of tonight," Envio says, running his fingers through his hair. "We need to be prepared for that."

"I'm trying to set up a meeting between me and Sam to discuss some things. Maybe I can get some inside information... We will see."

"Yeah, right. She's not gonna tell you shit. I'm surprised she's even setting up meetings for us in the first place," Jane responds.

Good point. There must be a reason why she is being so nice to us. Wouldn't they ask how she has been in touch with us? Maybe I need to be more leery.

Sam: *If we make it fast. Meet me at Hunts Park in twenty minutes.*

"She might be working for the enemy, but she's a good person. Remember, I knew her before she got turned."

"Oh, I'm sure you did. Doesn't mean anything. She was using you, Warwick. Just like she's still using you. I don't think it's a good idea to stay in contact with her. Stephen can reach out to the president himself and cut her out," Jane says, stopping in the middle of the living room, peering at me.

"I agree. You once had feelings for her. Staying in touch isn't a good idea. And might send her the wrong impression." Envio glances toward Jane. "We don't need any drama, especially between the agency and us."

Why is everyone doubting my ability right now? I don't have any feelings like that toward her anymore. If anything, it's anger for not letting me know she had been alive and not dead. Animosity is more like it. It's not like she didn't have a phone or my number to reach out briefly.

I understand not wanting any drama, but that's not going to happen. Things are taking a different direction.

Me: *See you there.*

We have plenty of other important things to talk about, like who the hell are we going to enable as enforcers? How are we going to prepare for the rogues to come after us and the humans again? It's only a matter of time before they realize Drake and his right-hand man aren't coming back to them. Once they do, the shit show begins. That means we need to be ready and soon.

"We will meet you at Stephen's. Good luck at your meeting, lover boy. You can take my car," Jane says before walking out the door with Envio.

On the ten-minute drive over, I think about what my future might have in store. Would Stephen ever trust me again? I don't really enjoy being his personal pet but it's better than death. He's not going to hear me complain out loud. Will I ever be an enforcer again? I know he says I can go visit my family from afar anytime I want but being in California makes it a little more difficult.

Stephen: *Everyone is headed here. ETA?*

He's already bugging me. I've only been out of his sight for thirty minutes. Jesus.

Me: *Just pulled up to the meeting spot. Thirty to forty-five minutes? Not sure how long. Depends if I can get her to talk.*

I park the car and turn it off, waiting for Sam to show up. I'm a couple minutes early, and there are no other cars around. If she is trying to play human, then she will be driving here. Maybe she got stuck in traffic or something.

Stephen: *Don't keep us waiting too long. We have a lot to discuss.*

A blue Mazda pulls into the parking lot, but I can't see the driver. I sit and wait for them to get out, but nothing. Should I go over there and see if it's her?

Sam: *Here.*

I open my door and close it behind me while taking a deep

breath. It's the first time I'll be seeing her since leaving her behind. My palms start to sweat as I approach the driver's side window.

"Hey there. You gonna get out?" She looks at me, wide-eyed, and I open the door for her. "It's been a while. You look good for someone who is supposed to be dead."

She chuckles at first. "Yeah. Didn't think I'd make it this long, but it's easier than I imagined to fool them. Horrible to say."

Her eyes are drilling into mine, like she wants to ask me something but is scared. I'm not going to push it because I don't know if I want to know. "How did you do it? Newbies, especially on their first feed, almost always come close to killing. We usually have to pull them off. So how?"

Her hands flail around in the air. "Came close. I just kept the thought of death in my mind. My death. I wasn't ready to die."

"Who the hell is? I came close to death too. Made me reevaluate everything."

"What do you mean?"

"Well, when my superior found out about my turning you... It's against our rules as you know. The normal punishment would be death, but Stephen likes to give second chances sometimes. Lucky me."

Here we are, having a normal conversation when she starts it in a different direction. One that I'm not prepared for at all.

"I'd have missed ya. Been wanting to see you but before that first initial call, I was too nervous. You know, just in case they have my phone bugged or something."

"That's your excuse for not calling me all that time? You ever heard of a burner phone? Or borrowing someone else's? I don't buy it." I have to be careful on how I word things now because maybe she still has feelings for me. If that's the case, I have to make it clear that they aren't reciprocated.

"We are on different sides, Warwick. And maybe always will be. Who knows if this peace bullshit is going to stick. Although, I really hope it does. For both our sakes."

The way she words that is almost like she knows something. Why wouldn't the peace stick? Are the humans planning on backing out of our deal? It's not our fault that they let him escape out of their custody. How can they blame us for that? Fuck! If word gets out that Sasha was a part of that escape, we will be fucked. They've met her, and know she is a part of our group, not Drake's. That will look really bad.

"Seeing anyone?" she asks, her eyes focused on the ground. "Not that it's any of my business anymore."

Be clear. Don't lead her on. "Nope, I'm staying faithful to my wife. If all this works out, I can be with her again." The sadness shows in her eyes, hearing me talk about my wife. She knows I'm married. Whether I'm vampire or not, Tasha and I are still considered married. My heart belongs to her.

"I understand. I've got a guy that I was seeing before all this happened with you. Never got a chance to see if it would've gotten serious. But maybe one day I'll have the chance to find out."

I can't leave her without trying to get some information for Stephen. She's being amicable so maybe it'll be my lucky day. "The humans aren't going to screw us over, are they? I know you are working for them, but what happens to us will at some point affect you too."

"Let's just say, they are like a teeter totter. They don't want to trust you, but they realize it might be in their best interest not to wage war against a species like vampires."

"They wouldn't win, you know? If they did start a war."

"They have things that would level the playing field, so don't be too cocky."

"Like what?"

"I've already said too much... I'm gonna go. It was nice seeing you. Good luck," she says before getting back in the car and speeding out of the parking lot.

12
Jane

My heart is still numb from the loss of Sasha. I never would have wanted this. Even if she did betray us. I don't know what I would have done if put in that situation. If Envio went rogue again, and then was handed over to the humans to be killed. I don't think I could let it happen either. It's not that I agree with what Drake says she did, but love is a crazy thing. Sometimes it makes you do things out of character. She had been acting out of character since the night Jakob was killed and never really got back to the old Sasha.

Envio and she have had their fair share of confrontations, but we both will mourn her. She did a lot to help the Guardians get to where we are today, and we can't forget that no matter what she did in the end. She deserves to be remembered for the good things she did too.

"We can't tell anyone about what they said... They could be lying," I say.

"Do you really think they were lying? Their story makes sense. I hate to say it, but I think they were telling the truth."

"Still, we can't tell anyone. It will overshadow every good thing she ever did for the Guardians. We can't let that happen."

His arms go around my shoulders, and he pulls me into an

embrace. "Honey, Stephen will let us know what to tell people, but I agree. For now, we don't mention it to anyone."

I think back to the first mention of Sasha. It wasn't long after I became a vampire myself, and I lived with Liz. She had that weird vision and saw that she would be our Savior. Meeting her for the first time, well, that was kind of intimidating. Liz made her sound like some sort of god, but she was just a girl like me, with issues. Once I went back with Samuel to Frankfort to stay, our relationship grew every day, and by the end of my stay there, we were like sisters.

Things have changed a lot in the last year, and we have grown apart. A lot of that has to do with her guilt over Drake, but also some on my part. Once we were assigned to our regions, I never reached out to check on her, and maybe if I did, she would still be here. She didn't have a shoulder to cry on or a friend to talk to. Things could have been different.

"I'm heading over to Stephen's. You comin'?" Envio asks, putting his hand on the small on my back. "He said an hour."

My eyes are brimming with tears, feeling horrible for not realizing that I let Sasha down. She never verbalized it, but I know. But it's too late to make it right.

"I'm going to make a pit stop. I'll meet you there," I say, planting a kiss on his cheek. "There's someone I need to go see."

We part ways, and I'm now standing in front of the beautiful Victorian house, wondering how I'm going to explain this. They have been kept out of the loop on purpose; Samuel asked it to be that way, so he could focus on his family. Yet I think he would want to know about her death. They were close, and he deserves to find out from one of us, not a stranger.

Knock. Knock. Knock.

I wait for someone to come to the door, hoping it isn't Amy. She didn't care for her in the slightest so a tear wouldn't even be shed.

The door opens and Liz is standing in a nightie with a notepad in her hand. "It's late. What are you doing here?"

"We're vampires. It's not like you were sleeping." I laugh. "I need to speak with you and Samuel."

My throat begins to itch. How the hell am I going to break this news? They were so close, and this is going to break his heart. His grief might consume him, but Liz will be here to help him through it.

"We don't want to know. Remember, we don't want active roles in this," Liz says, hand now on her hip.

I couldn't blame them for not wanting any part of an active role. It's been nothing but batshit crazy. One thing after another, and sometimes I feel like a chicken with my head cut off, not knowing what to do next. "That's not why I'm here. Can I come in?" I ask, making her realize I'm still standing on her porch.

"Oh, sorry, of course," she says, opening the door more, and then closing it behind me. "Samuel, Jane is here."

I start to sweat, not knowing how they are going to take the news. I'm trying to keep it together myself, not wanting to scare them. If anyone was going to end up dead, the last person I'd suspect was Sasha. Especially at the hands of Drake. Like her, I always wished he would become better, and she might get her happily ever after. She deserved it.

Samuel comes down the staircase in a hurry. "It's late. What's wrong?"

"Why does something have to be wrong?"

"It's late, and we haven't seen you in months," Samuel says, giving me a stare. "Out with it."

I begin to talk, but then I can't find the words. "It's Sasha."

"If you came here to talk to us on how to handle her, we can't be of any help. She just needs time. Stephen came by too."

"No. She's dead," I blurt out, my hands flying to cover my mouth.

Samuel and Liz glance at each other, taking in the news. The shock doesn't wear off for a couple of minutes before they start asking questions. I explain that Drake killed her, but I leave out the other details. Stephen hasn't let us know exactly what all he wants us to be telling people.

"Why would she be alone with him? She knows he's not the same. Sasha's smarter than that," Liz says.

"You gonna kill him?" Samuel asks.

He has no idea what's going on with us and the humans or the arrangement that's been made. It's not my place to tell him either. So I have to lie, or I'd be disobeying Stephen. "We haven't discussed that yet, but I'm sure his death is coming regardless."

"If I didn't promise Liz I'd stay away from all that, I'd kill him myself," Samuel says, head in his hands.

It isn't exactly the way I want to visit them, but it had to happen. "I hate to cut this visit short, but I've got to get to California. Figure some stuff out with the others. I miss you guys."

"We miss y'all too. Tell Stephen we said hi."

I nod and make my way to the front door, but I turn around before leaving. "Listen, maybe we can all get together soon. Even though you aren't active in the leadership anymore, you are still like our father. It's nice to see you doing so good again. See ya soon."

13
Stephen

I refuse to sit around and babysit anyone like a child. They are all grown-ass adults and can make their own decisions whether good or bad. It's up to them to face the consequences. The only one I have to be more concerned about is Warwick. But really, I shouldn't be either. I made it clear what would happen if he broke any of our rules again. Surely he isn't dumb enough to do anything stupid. Meeting with Sam didn't seem like a good idea, but I can't keep him on a leash like a pet. I need to know he can still make smart decisions.

"Where the hell is he?" Jane asks, pacing my office. "We all have better things to do than sitting around waiting on him."

"He should be on his way back. Chill. While we are waiting for him, let's discuss our plan."

"Don't you mean your plan?" Envio asks.

"This is going to be talked among us. Enforcers? We need to fill those roles but I only know one person who would even be remotely interested that we can trust."

"Oh yeah, who's that?"

"Cassius. He's been loyal and was upfront about wanting to do something more. Jane hasn't really needed his help all that much and he's getting restless."

"You know him better than we do. So if you think we can trust him, it's ultimately up to you."

The bigger problem is we can't only have one. Even with three, they were constantly tracking down rogues. I think it's better to have them go out in pairs after the incident. Don't want that happening again.

My mind flutters back to seeing Sasha's ashes on the ground, knowing if I would have left just mere minutes before maybe I could've prevented her death. I just can't believe she would do something like that. Drake and they could've been lying. You know, trying to get a rise out of us or something. Well, it worked. No matter what the truth is, her involvement in Drake's escape can't become public knowledge, yet I have to figure something out to tell everyone. It's only a matter of time before someone starts asking questions.

"Sir? Are you okay?" Warwick asks, standing only a couple inches from me. "You don't look so good."

Maybe because I have so many things on my plate right now and not enough time to deal with it all. Or even an idea on how to. "I'm fine. Good to see you made it back. Find out anything useful?"

His eyes tell me there's something to tell. "I- I'm not sure what she meant by it, but she said they have something to level the playing field if we go to war."

"Like equipment? What the hell is that supposed to mean?" I ask, forehead wrinkled from thinking too hard. "They find weaknesses we don't even know about?"

"I don't know. As soon as she said that, there was a total shift in her demeanor and then she left in a hurry without answering me. She didn't seem scared for her sake, but maybe ours. Like she was trying to discreetly warn me."

He can't be serious. What could the humans possibly have that could level it out? We are faster, stronger, and heal quickly. No bomb, gun, or anything else is going to kill us. And even if it did, each one of us could kill ten or more beforehand. "Let's not worry about that right now. We are doing what they ask so no war is coming. When is the handoff?"

"Tomorrow at two," Warwick answers.

Let's handle these problems before jumping into anything else. Cassius will become an enforcer, but who else? Trusting vampires is hard because it's becoming harder to tell who is on our side or not. That means we have to be careful. The only other vampire is Kastiel but he has a lot on his plate from his job in the human world. He can't tackle something like this too. Or maybe he could short term until we can find another candidate. "What about Kastiel, Envio? We could at least ask. You never know. Maybe he will want to after he hears about Eliza and Malachi."

"I doubt it, but I'll talk to him once we are done here."

Okay, that's settled for now. Next is Sasha. We will leave out her helping Drake escape and just say she was killed by Drake and his hoodlums. I doubt anyone will ask questions.

"We don't mention Sasha helping Drake to anyone. No one else needs to know besides those of us in this room. Understood?" Everyone agrees. "Now let's get this going. Envio, go and see what Kastiel says and let me know. I'd rather not send Cassius out anywhere without a partner for a while."

He nods and heads out the door, leaving Jane behind.

"And what do you want me to do?"

"Jane, you can go back to your house. I'll have Cassius come over and you can explain the situation. Fill him in on what we discussed. That way if Kastiel agrees, we can start searching for those responsible as soon as possible."

I'm going to have to call upon Kieran and tell him the bad news. It's literally the last thing I want to do, but we all need to stay amicable right now. Too much shit going downhill.

When he answers the phone, Kieran sounds pissed. It takes me only a few seconds before realizing he already knows most of it. Question is how? It's still swirling around on how he knows. What really frustrates me is when he asks how I could let this happen. Let it? Is he seriously trying to blame me for this? I didn't ask for two of my people to get kidnapped and then killed. There was no way for me to know Sasha was going to go off and do something fucking crazy. He's not going to blame any of this on me.

"You can go fuck yourself. It's nobody's fault."

"You sure? Aren't you their leader? It's your job to protect them. You failed. Hopefully you do a better job next time."

Did he forget that he's a vampire which means I'm his leader too. Dumbass. I can't wait until the day I can knock his ass out cold. Every time I talk to him, I hate him a little more. "This conversation is over. Since you already know everything before I tell you, I'll stop calling."

Warwick is still in the room, and his eyes are the size of Texas. I assume Kieran was so loud that he heard both sides of that conversation.

"Wow, where does he get off talking to you like that?"

I don't respond, but instead focus on trying to calm myself down. Who gives a fuck what that imbecile thinks? He has no idea what it is like to be a leader. Everyone is always counting on you to figure out the best for the society as a whole. I can't let my personal feelings get in the way of any decision, or I'll get torn apart. Even more so now with Kieran watching my every move, which I still don't get. He's not my superior and has no say in anything that involves decision-making. Though he sure thinks so.

"Listen, we need to figure out more on what Sam said. I don't like not knowing. We need to be prepared for all our enemies and the humans are still our enemies. Until peace is finalized."

My biggest concern right now has to be this handoff of Drake and keeping him imprisoned until they kill him. We can't have another escape, and without knowing the true details of what happened with Drake and Sasha, it could happen again.

14
Envio

Stephen seems to think Kastiel is a good choice to be an enforcer, but I'm not so sure. Yes, he has proven to be loyal to the cause, but this requires you to kill. Has he ever killed another vampire? Doubt it. He seems too chill to be capable of that, but I guess I could be wrong.

I go to the apartment in New York and wait for him to meet me. Being here only reminds me of my failures. Not even a day as the new head and two of my people are kidnapped. I didn't even notice they were missing. Maybe I could have prevented their deaths. Stephen doesn't seem to place any blame on me for that, but maybe he should. I should have noticed sooner that they were missing, no matter what was going on at the time.

I make my way through the apartment, seeing the furniture upturned, and things broken on the floor, reminding me of the struggle they both had before ending up dead. Down the hall to the left, I end up in Sasha's room. The room is dark, black and red, and very little around to make it personal. Maybe she didn't think she'd be staying here long. My eyes glance to the wall, and fuck. If anyone ever came in here, they would have known her plans. She hadn't even been trying to hide it, or this wouldn't be here. Anyone could have walked in and seen it. It looks like she has been tracking the rogues closely and waiting for the perfect opportunity to help them get Drake out of our custody. But then we handed him over and the only thing she could do is to involve the rogues. The things love can make you do.

Fuck! How did we all miss this? It's like she had an obsession. It reminds me of the boards you see on cop shows when they are tracking a perp. I snapped a picture and sent it to Stephen confirming that Drake was indeed telling us the truth. Not that we want to believe it.

A knock at the door has me running to it before he sees the wall. "Come on in."

"What's going on? Did you find them?" Kastiel asks, walking fast inside, wanting some answers.

Not only do I get to deliver bad news about Eliza and Malachi, but also Sasha. I don't know how well he got to know her while she's been here. "No... actually it's not good."

"Okay, just tell me," he says, hands going into his pockets.

"They were killed," I say, waiting a minute before hitting him with more.

"By rogues or humans?"

"Rogues. But there's more. Sasha is also gone." I say this, and immediately realize I should have worded it differently.

His eyes go wide, and he starts pacing around, rubbing his hands together. "We need to find her. Where should we look? Just tell me and I'll go..."

"No, not kidnapped. Murdered." His hand flies to his mouth. Were they close? "I'm sorry. But that leads into what I need to talk to you about."

"There's more?"

"Stephen would like you to fill in as enforcer for a bit. We have no one left and need to find the rogues responsible."

He didn't even hesitate. "I've got vacation time I can take. Where do I need to go?"

Maybe he wouldn't have a problem killing if he knew what they were responsible for. I have a feeling there was more to his and Sasha's relationship than we knew about. Although, I doubt Sasha reciprocated those feelings with everything she did for Drake. Her heart still belonged to him until the end, when he took her life.

"Michigan. You will have a partner, Cassius. We don't want anyone pursuing this by themselves. It's too dangerous. You must stick together."

"I want to get started immediately."

Jane is catching Cassius up on everything. Hopefully, she has prepared him.

Me: *Is he caught up? Kastiel is ready.*

"I'll give him the address and he will meet you here shortly. Please keep me informed on anything. And be careful. Watch each other's backs."

Jane: *Yup. Ready.*

Envio: *Send him to the New York apartment.*

I didn't have high expectations for those two, but will do what Stephen wants. We'll know soon enough if they have what it takes to be an enforcer. It's not something for every vampire, especially one that has never killed before or didn't have something to avenge. Eliza and Malachi lost family to the rogues. Me, I did it because I know firsthand how rogues operate, and each one I killed saved innocent lives.

Stephen doesn't budge when I get back to California and update him. All he wants to talk about is what I found in Sasha's room. I still can't get it out of my head that she has been plotting something like this for a while, and no one even noticed. Not even Eliza or Malachi who lived with her. This only leads me to believe all of us need to be more careful and watch everyone closer. If Sasha could hide something like this from us, anyone could. How do we know who we can trust after being betrayed by her? We need to be extremely careful from this point forward.

"I want you to keep in communication with Kastiel and Cassius. I trust them, but at this point anyone is able to betray us," Stephen says, slumping over his desk, hands on his forehead. "We can't let something like this happen again. It's going to be hard enough to keep it under wraps, especially if any other rogue knew about Sasha's plan."

We didn't know who knew, and that could prove to be disastrous. If word gets out about her having a hand in his escape, all hell will break loose. The humans wouldn't trust us at all. Not that they trust us fully now anyway. They would never believe that we had no hand in it, just her. Right now, they are lumping all vampires together, and still don't understand we aren't a threat unless they make us one. "Got it, sir. They'll call if they find anything. Right now, I'm more worried about the exchange."

The handoff is scheduled in an hour, and Drake is being sedated as we speak with an even bigger dose than before. None of us know how long they plan to wait before killing him this time, and we aren't taking any chances of him escaping a second time.

If it were up to me, he would have been killed a long time ago. Somehow he keeps cheating death and seems to find it amusing. He used Sasha like a puppet, knowing that she wouldn't be able to handle the thought of him getting executed. And she fell right into his little trap.

"You and Warwick are coming with me to the handoff. We'll be leaving shortly. Let's hope this time works out better than the last."

"What about Jane? Don't you think the more, the safer we are?" I ask, wondering what his reasoning is behind not wanting her to come. We don't have any idea what they have planned, and every time we meet up with them, I fear it could be a trap. The agency hates vampires and literally formed to find and kill us. I'm supposed to believe that now, they want to combine forces and have peace? No, they could be trying to get us on their good side, so they can kidnap us or Stephen, and use us as experiments or examples.

"No, this time just us three," he replies.

I want to speak up so badly, tell him that's a horrible idea, but I don't. It's not my place and he has enough going on without him worrying about me defying him. Let's just make it through this exchange, and then I'll talk to him. Explain my doubts fully. He'll understand.

My phone slides out of my pocket, and I text Jane to let her know where I'll be. Don't want her to worry. Yet I'm not sure what's going on with us. She seemed distant when I brought up moving in together, like she was totally against the idea. I've been in love with her since the moment I laid eyes on her in my vision, but maybe it's dwindled on her side. I thought our relationship was solid, but if it is, why would she be against it? Of course, I'm not going to force the issue and do something stupid like give her an ultimatum or anything, 'cause that would end badly. We have been around each other a lot more lately; maybe she's getting sick of me. All relationships are tricky, and before becoming a vampire, I hadn't been in many. Maybe a handful and none that were serious. Once things settle down, a heart-to-heart might do us some good. I love her, and always will, but I deserve to be with someone who sees a future with me, and right now, I'm questioning whether she does or not.

15

Stephen

Dr. Kendrick is certain he should be sedated for at least a couple of hours and packed two days' worth in a bag. We aren't taking the chance of him waking up before they are ready to execute him. I'm not going to be responsible for him getting away a second time. Right now, we've got our people out looking for the rogues in Michigan and Virginia where Tate ran into Envio. There has to be more there; Tate would never be running around alone. If they find any, they can lead us to the ones responsible, and we can get some justice for my people.

I've not had the proper time to grieve or even really process the fact that Sasha is dead, and had a hand in the entire escape plan. Hell, it looks like she has been planning something like this for a while. She was my friend, our Savior, and her death will have an effect on each and every vampire. Her actions resulted in the death of Malachi and Eliza, and all I can do is hope she didn't mean for that to end in that manner. She loved Drake, to a fault, but I can't believe she would knowingly have two lives taken just to possibly reform her former lover. No matter how much she changed since the night of Jakob's death, she couldn't have gotten that far gone. Could she?

"Alright, boss. Doctor says he's ready for transport," Warwick says, walking into the room. "Let's get this exchange over with so we can deal with everything else."

Envio and Warwick grab him and carry him out and place him in the back of the truck. Let's hope this sedative is strong enough to keep him out.

"Not sure how things are gonna go there. Don't do anything unless I say."

Fingers crossed this goes smoothly, and we can reach an agreement. I'll need to set the president's mind at ease, but how am I supposed to do that without outright lying? We know that Sasha had something to do with his escape, and if he found out that I lied, any chance at peace is gone. I'll have to tread lightly.

The drive over is silent; no one really knows what to say or expect. It could all be a trap to take us out. Sam did say they think we had something to do with it. At the time, we didn't have knowledge of Sasha's traitorous plan or we would have stopped her. But even then, they wouldn't believe that.

"I'm glad this asshole is finally going to get what he deserves." Envio breaks the silence, popping his fingers. "I don't care what Sasha did; he killed her. She was one of us. All the innocent lives he's taken, people he's turned, lives he's ruined…"

"They'll execute him, and then he'll be out of our lives forever. Sooner or later, without a leader, the rogues will either join or be executed themselves." We can't let revenge consume us, or things will be done that we can't take back. Of course, I want him dead, but we have to be smart about it. If the humans take care of it, it kills two birds with one stone. Both species get their justice, and we get our peace agreement. That's the focus here, and it's my job to remind everyone of that.

We pull up to the building and park a little ways away, not seeing anyone outside. My window rolls down, and I stick my hand outside, the summer breeze warming it up. "We're a little early." The doors open and four men walk out, including the president. He strides over toward us, the others in formation in case we try to do anything while he approaches the truck. Do they really think we would try to attack him here, with hundreds just inside the building? We aren't that stupid.

The three of us get out and meet them behind the truck. Let's keep things amicable. I have no reason to believe they want to do us any harm.

"Thanks for bringing him back. He killed five more of my men in his escape. I won't be waiting any longer. Execution will be today as to not waste any time or allow room for error or escape," President Walters says, flicking his head to the back of the truck. "I take it he's sedated since it's quiet. How long can we expect for him to be out?"

"Only a couple of hours, but the bag contains another couple of doses to be safe," Warwick says, handing the bag to the bodyguards.

"He's responsible for three deaths of our people recently. We want him dead just as much as you do. Justice will be served," I respond.

"My condolences. I think it's time we discuss how this peaceful coexistence is going to work. No more lives need to be lost. There's already been too many. Yet, of course as you can imagine, the threat lies on both sides of this. Would you like to come inside?"

We follow behind them, and as we get closer to the door, it opens, then shuts behind us. People are walking around, some with clipboards, others with earpieces in. This must be the headquarters for the agency that kidnapped Warwick. I eye him to see if he recognizes it. A bead of sweat is trickling down his forehead.

"You okay?" I ask. He's not looking so good. Is it possible for vampires to have PTSD?

"I have a bad feeling, boss. What if he invited us in here with no intentions of a peace agreement? Or he's planning to kill us down here and we just walked right into his trap willingly?" Warwick replies. "I've seen these people, and the hate they have for vampires is great."

We continue following them, down multiple hallways and through corridors, seeing more and more agents. There must be at least five hundred here. Are they all trained with the knowledge of vampires? I'm not getting any weird looks from them, until eyes lock on us by a blonde.

"That's her," Warwick whispers, and Envio and I both stare. "Don't acknowledge her."

Finally, we come to a door with a keypad requiring retina recognition. President Walters gets closer for it to scan, and the doors open. That's some high technology just for a conference room.

"This is as far as the others go. Only you and I will be going inside. No outsiders to distract us. It's up to us as leaders to come to a decision." He winks at his bodyguards who take off down the hall with Drake.

"Sir, I think it's better we stay with you," Warwick says, eyes wide.

"I'll be fine. Just stand here and wait for me."

We both step inside, and the doors close behind us. A long wooden conference table sits smack-dab in the middle of the room with about fifteen chairs around it, and a TV on the wall that had to be at least a hundred inches. He sits down at the head of the table, and I grab one a couple chairs down.

"So, let's get down to business. Things haven't exactly been going how I imagined. His escape proves you can't keep your vampires under control."

"With all due respect, that's like me saying you can't keep your people under control. How many murders and rapes happen every day in the United States? You have hundreds of police officers in each city…"

"Fair point. You still need to get them under control. We can't have peace if my people are worried about being slaughtered by your kind. How many are there?"

"We don't have a precise count, but we find more every day. My enforcers are working on finding the rogues that helped aid in Drake's escape."

"So, you can't guarantee my people are safe?"

"Can you guarantee the safety of your people?"

His eyebrows rise, probably getting sick of me calling him out. He can't expect me to do anything he can't do himself as a leader. We can't make sure nothing ever goes wrong, it's impossible.

"My bigger concern is how we're going to co-exist. Humans will never feel safe, no matter what. Can't you kill Drake without telling the public he's a vampire? Who knows, they might not even believe you."

"If the only way to end the suffering of our people is to co-exist, a level of panic is justified. We just have to be cautious on both sides. Either side could turn on the other in a second."

If he would just kill Drake, and not mention the vampire thing, then we can continue the way we have been, and just live alongside the humans in secret. With all the killings, I don't know if it's the best decision to out us. There are so many things that would need to be addressed like how would we feed? I doubt any human will be comfortable giving us their blood. Without it, we can't survive. Now isn't the time to bring up all the questions looming around in my mind. I'll save those for another time.

"I think we've discussed enough here. We'll have another after Drake's execution," President Walters says, getting up and scanning his eye to open the door.

"You okay, sir?" Warwick asks, looking around the room.

I nod, shake Walters' hand, and head back to the truck.

"His execution is today. We can calm down knowing he won't be alive much longer," I tell them, opening the truck door and climbing inside. "One less thing to worry about, and maybe it will flush rogues out once they find out their precious leader is dead yet again."

16
Warwick

The handoff goes smoothly, and now we're back in California at the house, and Kieran is standing on the porch waiting for us. Is he ever going to leave Stephen alone? "Want me to ask him to leave?"

He shakes his head. "Come inside, Kieran."

I give them their privacy in his office and head out to the deck to enjoy the ocean breeze. The sound of the waves is calming, and with all the drama going on, it's needed. They'll be executing Drake today which will end one of our biggest problems. Since Tate's dead, who will take over leadership? The rogues will have to make a choice, and that can be beneficial to our side. If we can reform them, that means better chances at keeping peace with the humans. I wonder what the president and Stephen discussed back there. How would it work? It's not like they're going to come to accept us overnight. These things take time, and some backlash will happen. We have to be prepared for the humans not to take the news well, and Stephen knows that. I'm sure they discussed that. My phone vibrates in my pocket, and I pull it out, noticing Sam's name on my notification bar. What did she want?

Sam: *Prepare yourself. Watch your back.*

My eyes peer at the screen, trying to decipher the message. What the hell does that mean? Is this a warning? It must be the humans or why else would she be so cryptic.

Me: *Why? What's going on?*

The phone stays in my hand as I stare out at the ocean, wondering what bullshit drama is coming next. Would we even know what to do if things ever settle down? Since being forced to join them, it's been nonstop without a real break. There are always more rogues to track down, or something needing to be done. I haven't been able to visit my family in weeks, and if things turn sideways during this, they could get hurt. Even though I'm a vampire, my mind is always on them, wanting what's best for their well-being too. A war could mean their death.

Me: *Answer me.*

My anxiety gets high when there's no response, so I go inside and stop at Stephen's office door, hoping he and Kieran are close to being done. This isn't something I want to bring up in front of him. He's always in our business as it is. Instead of just walking in, I knock.

"Come in," Stephen calls out.

"Sir, could I show you something real quick?" I ask, walking over to him and placing my phone in front of his eyes. He reads the message and strokes his chin, then looks at me.

"Kieran, I think it's time Warwick and I head to Texas. We're done here."

"I don't think so. We have important things to discuss."

"Come back tomorrow; they can wait until then." Stephen smiles, gesturing him out of his office.

Kieran gets pissed and refuses to leave. I start to hate this guy even more every time he shows up. The disrespect he shows Stephen is ridiculous, and someone needs to teach him some manners.

"You need to leave. We won't ask you again, or I'll throw you out," I say, folding my arms across my chest. It's not that I think I'm intimidating, even though I have about five inches and fifty pounds on him.

Kieran stares at me, then at Stephen, and walks out. "Whatever. You have no respect for my boss. I'll be sure to let him know."

Neither one of us cares what his boss thinks, to be honest. We have more important things to worry about on any given day.

"What the hell did that message mean? Have you been able to get ahold of her?"

"No response."

He runs his fingers through his hair and starts pacing the office. "Guess we'll find out soon enough."

I continue to try to get ahold of her, calling and texting for two hours and nothing. My anxiety is only getting worse with every passing minute. What did we need to watch our backs from? Or only specifically me?

The television is playing in the living room; we keep it on for noise and to keep an eye on what's going on in the human world. It makes it easier to track rogues that way. I hear his voice and wander in to watch it.

"This emergency address will not be suitable for children. Please have them leave the room," President Walters urges his people.

He's not going to do it, is he? Right now? "Stephen, you better get in here," I yell.

"What is it?" His eyes catch a glimpse of him on the TV.

"We are all aware of the horrendous murders that have swept our nation over the last few years. As your president, I have fought to find the individuals responsible and put an end to it. I'm happy to report, we have captured an individual responsible and have him in our custody."

This is it; vampires are fixing to be outed, and the world will never be the same. Once this is known, things could never go back to normal. A part of me wishes we could just stay in the dark; why do they need to know we exist? Then my heart takes over and knows that until everything settles down, there's no chance of being able to hug and kiss my wife or child. I'm at an impasse.

"The American Justice System has always stood to protect an

individual's rights; however, given the amount of murders that he has committed, there will be no trial. All of your elected officials have agreed instead to execute him."

The camera pans out further so we could see the entire room, including Drake, sedated enough to where he couldn't run or hurt anyone. President Walters' finger points to him. "He is responsible. There is more to this individual than meets the eye. My fellow Americans, this is going to shock you, but I ask that you not panic. He may look like an everyday ordinary man; however, he isn't. Vampires walk our streets during the daytime and slaughter our families. The vampire you see before your eyes is their leader."

That's it. No going back. My eyes shift over to Stephen. "It's happening."

"I thought he wasn't going to say anything about vampires yet. This isn't what we discussed," Stephen says, cracking his fingers.

Our eyes can't believe it when a man pulls out a gun, fires it, and Drake hunches over. He's not dead. They know only fire kills us. What the hell are they doing? We wait for his eyes to open and the slaughtering on national television to begin, but nothing.

"I think we got our answer," I say.

"What?"

"On the thing that levels the playing field and why we should watch our backs."

What the hell are we going to do now that they know something that can kill us, that we didn't even know about. The better question is, what the hell special bullet can kill us?

"This vampire escaped at the hands of the people who we thought were helping us seek justice. Effective immediately, a state of emergency is initiated and everyone should stay in their houses until my next address. Our troops will be deploying to find each and every one of these vampires and give them the same death," President Walters says before cutting to the presidential seal.

How did he find out? He had to be talking about Sasha's involvement. Why did she fuck this up for us? All because of some stupid childhood crush. If she would have just let Drake alone, we wouldn't be going to war. Drake just got exactly what he wanted. At this point, we'll have no choice but to fight against the humans to save ourselves.

"I've got to warn the others," Stephen says, pulling out his phone. "Hell, we've got to warn everyone."

When I agreed to walk to get Avery more formula, this is not how I imagined it going. Ever since that choice, my life has been turned upside down, too many times to count. Drake may have turned me, but the Guardians showed me a better version of living as a vampire. Once I joined, I never thought I'd have to kill innocent people, but then again, if they're coming after me, then are they still considered innocent?

The doorbell goes off, and both our heads turn toward the door. We aren't expecting anyone. My job is to protect Stephen at all costs, even if that means giving my own life in the process.

"Are you guys going to let me in?" Kieran's voice sounds from on the other side of the door. He continues to ring the doorbell until I open it. "It's about fucking time. Have you..." He stops when notices the TV on with the presidential seal. "So, you do know. What the hell happened there? Did you know he was going to do that?"

"No, we discussed not saying anything yet. Definitely didn't know he was going to declare war in front of all of the United States either."

"My boss is being asked to hold a press conference. People are already panicking."

He doesn't need to do anything that would cause them to question his loyalty or bring attention to himself. If they even have a suspicion, it won't be hard for them to confirm.

"He's really going to play a role in their side of this war? Stand by while innocent vampires are killed when they have done nothing wrong?" Stephen asks.

"He'll do what he has to. As the governor, it's his job to make an address."

I've never met this so-called governor, but he sounds like a real dick. He can't play both sides in this. Eventually, he'll have to choose.

"All I know is, we are officially at war. The deaths from this moment forward are on Walters' hands, not ours," I say, trying to reason with Kieran. Maybe he could talk his boss out of it. Or at least maybe if he is going to make an address, speak about peace instead.

"The war has already begun. There's no stopping it now. It's too late. Get the idea of peace out of your head and start thinking about how you're going to stay alive," Kieran says before leaving us standing in the living room contemplating just that.

17

Jane

The comfort from being in his arms, lying in bed, and just watching TV for an hour without any interruptions can't be beat. Who knows how many of these opportunities we'll have? Things have been nonstop lately, and it's nice to be able to slow down and enjoy time together.

He kisses my forehead as my head lays on his bare chest, his arms around me. "I couldn't ask for a better afternoon."

"I know something that could make it better." Envio winks at me as his phone starts to ring.

Of course, we'd only get one hour.

"Hello?" he answers.

I could hear Stephen on the other end, freaking out. He's talking so fast, I don't catch all of it. *Drake's dead and the president knows we had something to do with his escape.* How the hell did they find out about that? *The president declared war on national television.* My eyes ram shut, knowing this is the end for our peace. The United States has declared war against our kind, and the only way it ends is with bloodshed. The rogues are going to have a field day with this and kill as many as they can. Revenge for their precious leader and try to take over. Jakob and Drake have been selling them on the fact vampires should be the gods of Earth. Here is their chance to make that happen, or at least try. How the hell are we going to keep all of them in check? Should we? The odds of humans winning this war are slim to none, especially against rogues. I almost feel sorry for them.

Envio gets off the phone, and I put my hand up to let him know I heard. "What are we going to do? Everything is going to shit."

He texts Cassius and Kastiel to report in, because they're busy searching for the rogues and probably haven't seen or heard about the conference yet or they would've called. "I need them here. Once they are, we'll come up with a game plan."

"A game plan? I say we let the rogues fight it out with the humans. We need to keep as many of us as we can. We are the leaders of this society, and losing any more of us might hinder our progress. Sooner or later, the humans will realize they can't win. They have to."

We all knew this could happen, and most of us are somewhat prepared.

I turn the TV on to the news, so we can watch anything that unfolds. It's everywhere, replaying the moment they kill Drake, and it's brutal. All the humans watching, he's instilling fear in them, which is exactly what we try to avoid. Has this been his plan all along? Did he ever actually want peace or was it just all a load of bullshit he told us to get us to hand over Drake?

Envio's phone rings loud again, taking me out of my thoughts. Cassius reports that they've found three rogues in Virginia where we ran into Tate, and they are tailing them to see if they take them back to more before they act. Those two have no clue the crapfest that is going on, until he tells them.

"For right now, we need to abandon this mission and send you back home. Kastiel needs to go back to work and you come back to Texas. We can't lose any more good people. Understood?"

Losing our three really puts things in perspective, and maybe I want him to move in. I mean, if we live long enough for it to happen.

Right now doesn't seem like the right time to bring it up, it's so miniscule compared to what else is going on.

"Breaking news," the TV anchor says. "The governor of California is holding a press conference in five minutes. We will be covering it live here on *HBN News*. Stay tuned."

Envio's head turns, hearing the anchor, and rushes off the phone with Cassius. "Did they say California?"

I shake my head, wondering why he cares. "Why?"

"That's the man that is working with Stephen. He's one of us. Why would he be speaking out about this?"

"Well, I imagine most states will. If he's the only one that doesn't, wouldn't that be suspicious?"

He nods, taking my words into consideration.

We wait until the conference starts, and I turn it up. Both of us are not looking away from the TV as a middle-aged man takes his spot in front of the podium, in a suit, and begins to speak.

"We have just found out some very alarming news from the president. I can imagine you are all panicking, but let's try to stay calm. If you stay in your homes, everything will be fine."

I could tell he's reading from a teleprompter or something, because it's almost like he doesn't want to be saying these things. As a vampire, he knows we wouldn't do anything to intentionally hurt the humans.

"As the governor, I've been thinking a lot about what this could do to us. And each and every one of you is sitting at home, wondering what's going to happen next. The vampires have asked for peace, before anymore killing happens. Elected officials should take this under consideration, as we the people don't want another war. Until then, stay inside."

The TV cuts back to the news, and we look at each other. Why would he do that? The agency is going to be all over him about suggesting that, and it won't end well.

"That didn't make things any better... If anything he just painted a target on his back. We need to go to Stephen's. Protect our leader.

They'll go after him, and it won't be that hard to figure out where he's staying, especially if they get their hands on the governor," Envio says, pacing the room. "We should go now."

I grab a couple things from my room, and we end up at Stephen's. He isn't expecting us when we knock on the door.

"What are you guys doing here?" Warwick asks.

"He needs protection. It's only a matter of time, you know," Envio says.

We go inside and take seats in the living room, finding the news still on.

"This just in, the governor of California has been murdered," the anchor says, pushing her earpiece further in, getting more information. "Murdered by a vampire just minutes after leaving his conference. Stay inside folks."

We all look at each other, knowing their next stop would most likely be here. They already killed the rogues' leader, and they probably think with Stephen gone, we'll submit easier. I laugh. *They got another thing coming.*

Video of military vehicles going through the cities, looking for vampires, is on replay, and things are heating up. What are they going to do when the rogues start attacking? It's too late to rescind the war; it's already begun.

18
Envio

I hold Jane in my arms, knowing our deaths could be coming. There are only two people I would put my life on the line for, Stephen and her. "I love you. If anything happens to me, I just need you to know that."

Her hand grazes my jaw line. "Nothing is going to happen to you. I won't let it."

A quick kiss is planted on her lips before we go back to the conversation going on between Stephen and Warwick.

"Have you warned Cassius and Kastiel?" he asks me.

"Cassius is back in Texas and Kastiel is safe doing what he's been doing before he joined us. They'll never suspect him."

My mind keeps thinking about all the vampires out there, just living their lives, not causing any problems. They work regular jobs, pay taxes, everything a human does. They must be scared and will be looking for guidance. Someone needs to address this with them so as not to cause panic among vampires either.

"You need to go warn everyone. We owe them that," Stephen says.

I can't leave him alone. He must be protected. Plus, without me here, if they do show up for him, Jane could die. "What if I have Kastiel and Cassius go?"

"I know you want to protect me, and I'm grateful, but if they want me dead, it'll happen whether you're here or not. You could even end up dead. I don't want anyone else's death on my hands right now."

He might not like the idea, but I can't follow his orders on this. Who would take over if he gets killed? It's just not feasible. I walk out of his house and go to New York to convince Kastiel to go warn others. Right now, we need his help, and he doesn't get the option to refuse.

The internet gives me the information I need, the address to the firm Kastiel works at, and it's massive. No one would ever suspect him, because he became a vampire after becoming a lawyer, and has never skipped a beat. No weird disappearances. He's good.

I open the front door and walk inside to the receptionist desk where the young lady is turned with her back to me, going through a filing cabinet. Her hair falls to the middle of her back in waves. Something about her seems familiar.

"I'll be just a moment."

It can't be.

When she turns around, our eyes lock, and my heart drops. "What the hell are you doing here?"

She looks confused. "I told you about wanting to come to New York. Why are you so surprised I finally did it?"

"Not surprised, just... How long have you been here?"

She looks up. "I don't know. Probably about a week after seeing you last. Quit the diner and moved before talking myself out of it."

This doesn't make any sense. Out of all the places, she is here, in New York, working for him. How did they even know each other? How is she still alive?

Kastiel walks out and notices me. Secret's out, and my blood is boiling. Why the fuck would anyone keep this from me? I'm the one that begged for her life to be spared in the first place. I would've protected her.

"Good afternoon, Envio. I can see you now," he says, gesturing me toward his office.

"It was really good to see you, Blakeley. Take care," I say with a smile, trying not to show my anger toward the situation and saving it for Kastiel.

Once inside his office with the door shut, I shove him back. "What the hell is going on? Why is she here, working for you? How?"

"Favor for a friend. I offered her a job here, and she took it. Even offered her a relocation bonus."

"But... she's.... Supposed to be dead. You're telling me she's been alive this whole time right here in New York?" My voice rises.

"He asked me to watch out for her. It's not like I could say no."

"Who? Who did?"

"Stephen."

He kept this from me? Even after bringing her up when offering me Sasha's position, not mentioning she was alive and well right under my nose? Why would he want me to believe she is dead? Drake's out of the picture now, so no need to keep her hidden. We can protect her from the rogues.

"What are you doing here? In case you didn't notice, there's a war going on. We aren't supposed to leave the office."

Fuck the war right now. All I want are answers. "You've been given an assignment. At the apartment, there is a list of registered vampires. You'll need to pay a visit and make sure they know we aren't fighting in this. The rogues will take care of that for us. We want as many of us to withstand this as possible."

"What am I supposed to do if I get caught outside? They are doing sweeps everywhere."

"I don't know. Make something up. You're a hotshot lawyer. Isn't your job all about persuading others to believe your story?"

He doesn't object. "Once you are done with that, check in. I've got other things to handle."

It doesn't take me long to be back at Stephen's, standing outside the house, contemplating how to handle the situation. My anger is getting worse, but maybe he has a good reason for keeping it from me. I shouldn't just assume anything.

The door opens, and I head inside to find him. He's alone in his office.

"Is there something you want to tell me?" I ask.

He looks around the room. "Like what?"

"Like why Blakeley is alive and well? Working for Kastiel. She's supposed to be dead."

"The only people that knew she wasn't is Kastiel and I. Better that way. It kept her out of harm's way. Somehow things are being shared with our enemies and I have to be careful until I find out who is or was responsible."

"Didn't we already figure that out? Sasha. She was probably working with Drake the entire time. Wrapped around his finger like a lovesick puppy." My voice rises. "You said you could trust me, so why not tell me?"

"With everything going on, it just slipped my mind. I was going to tell you when the time was right and it wouldn't cause a threat to her."

"How am I supposed to trust you now knowing you've been keeping things from me? Everything I've done for you, for the cause..."

"Don't overthink this and turn it into something it's not," Stephen says, his chair sliding on the hardwood floor, standing up to come toward me. "You're like a brother to me. I wouldn't keep things from you. But for now, this needs to stay between us."

My eyes don't avert from his, wondering if he's telling the truth. We have been busy dealing with rogues, the agency, the president, and then the escape and murders. Maybe I should give him the benefit of the doubt. He did it for me once, and I should return the favor. "Don't ever do it again. I'm on the front lines fighting for this society every day, and I think I deserve to know these things."

I storm out of his office and go back into the living room where Jane sits, still watching the news. More and more reports are coming in about attacks across the country with videos of streets lined with bodies. It's happening and we are just sitting idly by watching it happen.

19

Stephen

Envio stomps and seethes as he walks out of my office. I shouldn't have kept it from him, but at the time, no one could know. Without knowing who is giving our information out, I didn't want to take the risk of telling anyone she was alive, for her safety. Blakeley deserves to live a normal life, and the easiest way to do that was to bring her to New York and watch over her. Just because she is Drake's sister, doesn't mean either side should take advantage of that. The rogues would just want to turn her, and possibly make her their leader, and we couldn't have that either. So, I kept her close enough, under Kastiel's eye, so that he could make sure nothing happened to her.

A part of me always wondered if Sasha was the leak—too many factors led to her—and after seeing the picture of her room, it confirmed it for me. Maybe she was playing both sides, but for how long? How was Drake getting her to tell him information and still treating her like utter shit? Since they are both dead, answers will never be given.

I let out a forceful breath, then grind my teeth. I want to hit something, destroy everything. My memories are being tainted because of this new information, yet I need to remember she wasn't always like that. A traitor. In fact, she wouldn't have even been part of this if we hadn't sought her out in the first place. She did so many things for our cause, and that shouldn't all be diminished. Her being part of Drake's escape can't get out, or no one will remember her as our Savior, only a traitor to our kind. I don't want to take that away from them or her. Everyone always needs a little bit of something to believe in, and that was Sasha for us for a long time. Before she came along, Samuel had no clue what to do. Things were only getting progressively worse week after week with Jakob, and then Liz had that vision. One of a red-haired beauty that would lead us to victory. Word spread fast once recruitment started, and vampires had something to believe in, to get behind. Without her, I'm not sure Jakob would be dead right now. Sasha played a huge part in the early parts of building up the Guardians, and we should always remain thankful for that. I close my eyes, knowing the right thing to do is to let the good memories outweigh the bad.

Every choice we make can have rewards or consequences. Like most, we don't have a clue which choice is the best at that moment, but once we make it, there's no going back. I know I've made a couple of horrible decisions and regret them almost immediately after. Maybe she truly believed he could be reformed. Unfortunately, that led to the consequence of her death by the very person she set out to save.

Most don't think about how their choices affect others. Sasha's resulted in two deaths of our own, plus deaths on Drake's side too. The consequences don't only affect the decision maker, but those around them. Did she know the rogues would kill Eliza and Malachi? Probably not, or she just didn't want to think about it. Yet it happened all because of poor choices and trusting the wrong people. This is why it's so important for me to be careful now and keep people at arm's length. Even the closest person can betray me.

Kieran and the governor are prime examples. I didn't know them before coming to California, and who knows if their "help" was for the right reasons. They could have had a different agenda. With the governor being dead, Kieran will need someone to report to, and that falls to me. He might expect a role within the top, but he hasn't earned that right. No matter what he did before. Things don't work like that with me.

A knock sounds on my office door, but I don't really want to talk to anyone right now. "Go away. I don't really have time to chat right now." Whoever is at the door doesn't listen and knocks again, then opens the door uninvited.

"I know it's not the best time to show up, but it's long overdue," Samuel says, closing the door behind him.

My ass is out of my seat, and then I'm engulfing him in a hug. "I didn't know it was you. What the hell are you doing here? Does Liz know?" I haven't seen him since he decided not to involve himself in the higher things, just to enjoy being with Liz and his daughter. It's not like anyone could blame him. He wanted to make up for lost time.

"Liz and Amy are here too. We couldn't stand by and watch this unfold without at least offering our help. Is there anything we can do? How did this happen?" He takes a seat and leans forward, placing his elbows on my desk.

Samuel might have brought us all together for the cause, but with him being out of it for so long, there are some things that he doesn't need to know. It's better that way, for him to stay out of it. It will keep him and his family safe. "It's a long story, and we don't have time for that. You should just go home and stay inside."

"So you aren't going to fight?" he asks, eyebrow raised.

"The rogues will take care of that. If we look at it this way, the humans will take care of some of them, without us having to lift a finger. Eventually, they will realize it's a lost cause, and the war will end. Or at least I hope."

Samuel's eyebrows scrunch together and the wrinkles on his forehead are more prominent. "So that's how you're playing this? Can't say it's not a good plan, but you might want a Plan B in case it backfires."

I nod and gesture him out of my office. Amy and Liz are sitting in the living room on the couch, and I say my hellos and goodbyes. It's enough to have Warwick, Envio, and Jane here.

If they do come after me, I don't want to worry about them getting murdered. Plus, as the leader, the decisions I have to make are rough, and I don't need anyone else around trying to talk me into or out of my decisions. I really need to send them out to warn others, and that will leave me here alone. They won't like it, but it doesn't matter.

"Each of you needs to take a region and head out. It'll go faster if there's more than just Kastiel and Cassius out there."

"Are you serious? We aren't leaving you," Envio says.

"You don't have a choice. That's an order. Do as I say. You can't sit around and wait for them to show up." They all look at me like I'm crazy, and maybe I am, but as their leader, they have to listen to me. "Go now. Some time alone will do me some good. I have too many things to figure out right now, and it's easier for me to plan when alone."

After some more pushback, they finally leave, and I go back to my office. As much as they want to keep me guarded, our people deserve to know what's going on. Keeping them in the dark won't do us any good, and we don't want them to think they have to fight. Just stay inside, and don't do anything stupid. They are going to have questions, and someone needs to be out there to put them at ease. It's not like they have a way to look at one of us and determine if we are human, except the rogues, because of their eyes. They won't go around hurting innocent people to see if they heal. As long as everyone stays calm, and does nothing out of the ordinary, they will be safe in all this.

Something comes to mind, sitting here in this quiet room. Who will take my spot if something does happen to me? If the agency wants me dead, they'll be coming after me sooner rather than later, and I need to be prepared. Who did I think would be a good leader? Warwick is still facing the consequences for his mishap, so that's a hell no. Envio will be too controversial, even though he's been on our side for longer than Warwick. My mind comes to Jane. She's tough and levelheaded for the most part. Although I can see it being a problem because she's a woman. Even as vampires, our guys can be sexist. Yet she's the best candidate. I believe she will lead us as good as I can.

I take a pen and paper out to write her a letter, for her to find if something does happen. At first, she will be against it, thinking she couldn't possibly be a leader. I did the same thing, but with Envio by her side, she'll do great things.

My ears detect footsteps coming up the walkway, and whoever it is isn't alone. It sounds like there are about eight people, and only one is a vampire. I get up from my desk quietly, but I'm not going to run. Fear will not be shown. If I'm going to be killed, then I'll go out strong, not weak.

They kicked the front door in and were upon me. I recognize Sam is with them and can't blame her. Right now, she's safely blending in with the humans, her life not in any danger. I won't out her because she's done her due diligence by warning us ahead of time to watch our backs.

"Leaders don't hide from their enemies; they confront them. Get your ass out here." The woman says, standing in my living room.

"Maybe he's not here, Athena," Sam says, trying to get them to move on.

She is trying to cover for me because I know she can sense that I'm close. Sam could've easily thrown me under the bus or come and brought me out to Athena herself, but she didn't. Instead, she tries to get them to believe no one is here. Maybe she isn't completely on their side and could be swayed in the future. If we can get her alone.

"No, he's definitely here. Do a sweep of the house. Find him and bring him to me."

The others split up, half going upstairs and the others heading in my direction. This is exactly what they were so afraid of. If Envio and them were still here, they would give their lives to protect me, and no one else deserves to die.

The office door opens, and four men come at me with force. I could easily take them out, but if we are wanting peace at any point, then my fighting would be seen as pushback. Instead, I put up my hands. "No need for force. Take me to your leader." Instead of listening to me, one of them injects me with something that makes my knees buckle. They must have figured out the right amount of dosage to weaken us.

"Not taking any chances with your kind. Let's go."

They put my arms over their shoulders and carry me out to the living room where Athena stands. Her eyes dance over me. "Not what I was expecting from their leader. What are you, like twenty-one? They trust a kid to lead them? That was their first mistake." She moves closer, walking in a circle around me. "I'm here to get some answers. If you cooperate, then maybe I'll make your death quick. None of that ripping limbs and burning you crap you do to each other."

"Answers to what?" I say groggily.

"Well, the president said you have a list of registered vampires. We're gonna need you to hand that over. It'll make our job a lot easier and faster. Why don't you help a girl out...?"

I laugh; she can't be serious. Even with my death coming, there's no way I'll hand that over. Plus, who would be stupid enough to keep a list of all the registrants in one place? She probably already knows that. "There is no list. I'm not sure what you've been told, but whoever gave you that information is wrong."

"You wouldn't be lying to me, would you? Or did you just lie to him? Where's the list?" Her head flicks to the goons holding me and they break my arms, and I scream from the pain. "What the hell is wrong with you? I don't have any fucking list here."

"I'm not going to ask you again. Let's not make this any more difficult or painful than it has to be," Athena says, arms crossed and nostrils flaring.

As a leader, sometimes we have to sacrifice ourselves to save our people. I'm not giving her shit. No amount of torture or broken bones is going to make me give up the location of the lists. If they do get ahold of it, then our kind will be decimated without even seeing it coming. Slaughtered in their homes when they have done nothing to humans. "You'll never find all of them. Do you really think I'm stupid enough to have them here? All in one location? That's suicide."

"Oh, so it's going to be like a treasure hunt. I loved those as a kid. Game on," she says, gesturing to Sam. "Shoot him. We need to find those lists now. Let's not waste any more time."

Sam draws her weapon and locks eyes with me. She takes the safety off and points it at my heart. Her hesitancy is going to get her killed.

Athena's attention is focused on her. "What are you waiting for? Shoot him, or I'll shoot you." Her gun is pointed at Sam's head.

In one fluid motion, Sam shoots Athena, and then the others in quick succession. She saved my life.

20
Warwick

I walk into the beach house and stop when I see Sam and dead bodies scattered across the living room. "What the fuck happened here?"

"Sam saved me."

"Are you okay?" she asks, picking Stephen up off the floor.

He shakes his head as she sits him on the couch. "Why did you do that? They will figure it out now. You won't ever be able to go back."

"Why are you weak? What did they do to you?" I ask, knowing I should have never left. He could have been killed, and that's exactly what we are trying to avoid. Losing more people during all this. How did they figure out where he lives?

Stephen asks, "Why did you do that? Once they find out you killed them, you can't ever go back."

"It's time I stop working for them and fight for my own livelihood. I'm no longer safe with them."

"Oh, so you're only switching sides because it's convenient. We don't need people like that. How do we know you won't go right back to them if given the chance? Or use anything you learn against us?"

"Stop! She tried to get them to leave before they knew for certain

I was here, and then she killed them. She saved my fucking life. We aren't going to give her the third degree right now. So back off!"

He can't be serious? Who cares if she saved his life; it could be part of a bigger plan. Even the other agents' deaths. They could be sending someone in to infiltrate and get information. He must at least be contemplating that.

Sam throws her hair up in a ponytail and gets up off the couch. Her finger runs along the TV stand. "Where are the others?"

"They're out warning the others. Somebody's gotta do it."

The agency isn't going to stop until he's dead. He can't be left alone again. It's like they knew we left. "How did they know he was alone?" I ask, staring at Sam. "They had to have known."

"The house is bugged. They can hear everything, but no visual."

"So they can hear everything we are saying right now?" I reply, wondering why she didn't tell them this sooner. Now, they know the others are out warning our people.

"So they know you've betrayed them... They'll be coming after you too. Painting you as a traitor." I stop myself from saying what I really want to say, that she's a vampire and they never even caught on to it. It makes me laugh to think we have had a vampire inside their agency for this long without them figuring it out, even if she isn't working for us.

"I'm aware. But Stephen has done nothing but try to make peace with us, I mean them, and they declared war. The president isn't making decisions based on what's best for his people... or else he wouldn't put them in harm's way."

Can we even reach a level of peace after this? They tried to assassinate our leader. How could we? Both sides have lost many lives, and it's hard to just let that go even knowing that it's better for both species to peacefully coexist in some fashion.

"We've got some things to take care of," I say, not elaborating, glancing at Sam. "Cassius says he's found the ones responsible for Malachi and Eliza's deaths in Michigan."

"Then what the hell are we still doing here?" he responds, trying to get up.

"We can't go anywhere until that wears off."

I pull Sam into another room, wanting answers. She's been with the agency and might be able to tell us how to beat them. Or at least how to protect Stephen. "I don't care if you did warn me about them being here; it doesn't make me forget that you've been working for them for years. Even after being turned, you decided to stay with them, fight with them. I'll never be able to trust you."

"I might have been with them, but Stephen doesn't deserve to die," she says. "I thought you would beat us here and get him out of here."

"He sent us away. After this, I'm not leaving his side."

"They won't stop until they find that list or every last vampire is dead. And it's not in their nature to give up. Attacks will keep happening until they get what they want."

Right now, the only vampires they are killing are the ones we are wanting to get rid of anyway. They are actually doing us a favor, and not even realizing it. The number of human lives taken far outweighs that of rogues. Yet humans are only seeing them, savagely ripping people apart. The public has yet to see one of us. Maybe that's what we need to do. Find a way to get Stephen on the television, give our side of the story, and maybe something can tip in our favor.

"They aren't going to give up until they find the list or lists… The agency is very persistent when it wants something."

"They are scattered across each state. It'll take them a while to figure out where they're located and retrieve them. None of us are going to give that up. Death or not." I don't say anything further because she can't be trusted. Until minutes ago, she was playing for the other team. Vampire or not, her loyalty has been to them, not us.

It takes about an hour for the sedative to wear off and Stephen to be back to full capacity. "I've alerted Envio and Jane. They'll meet us there."

Once in Michigan, Cassius meets us at a bar downtown. The same bar Envio and I visited when we were here together during my training. It's the only place I knew here.

"What are we going to do to them? Just so we are clear, still giving them the chance to reform?" I ask, wanting a clear-cut answer before we go anywhere. It's best to have these things ironed out before heading into enemy territory.

"What is she doing here?" Cassius asks, walking up and sitting down at our table. "Isn't she working for the agency?"

"Not anymore. We've got more important things to worry about. Where are they?" Stephen asks, not wanting to waste any time.

"Let's head there and I'll show you."

We follow him into the middle of nowhere, a dirt road surrounded by trees, the nearest neighbors being miles away. Cassius explains there's a house at the end where there are about ten rogues living.

Envio and Jane show up, just in time to help.

"About damn time," I say.

Their eyes go straight to Sam. "What…"

"Long story, not getting into it right now. Let's take care of this," Stephen replies, not even giving them the chance to finish.

"Wait…" I put my hand out. "I never got an answer. Are we still giving them the choice like the others?"

"No, we kill every last one of them. They don't deserve a choice."

We head down the road, trying to be as discreet as we can, knowing how good vampires' ears are at picking up on sound. If we catch them off guard, we have a better chance of us all making it out alive.

Once we get inside, it's not what we expected. The rogues are on their knees, a human behind each one, with a gun to their head. How the hell did they know we were coming? They must have been following Cassius, hoping he would lead them to more. It's a trap and we just walked right into it.

"Nice of you to join in for the fun. We were hoping more would show up." The woman's eyes lock on Sam. "What the hell are you doing with them?"

She hesitates, looking around the room, and then her fangs appear. "That's the least of your worries right now."

The woman stops and takes notice. "You've joined their little club, then. Well, I'll enjoy killing you just as much as them. But first, where's the list?"

"You'll never find it. But you won't even have the chance. Did you really think you could take on a bunch of vampires?" Sam responds.

"These weren't so hard. Quite easy actually. Imbeciles."

The rogues have been injected so they can't fight back, but we still have a chance. Jane runs toward an agent, doing a swift kick that sends her flying across the room, hitting the wall so hard that surely her back is broken. Yet she stands right back up like it didn't even faze her. What are they, super soldiers? There's no way a normal human being is able to just stand up after taking a hit like that.

"You want some more?" Sam yells, rushing toward her, knocking her feet out from under her. "You've always been a real bitch. No one's gonna miss you."

Envio is on top of another, pulverizing him, hit after hit, blood everywhere. His fangs make an appearance, attracted to the blood, adrenaline coursing through his veins. Humans can only take so much before their bodies give up. They lose the will to fight.

The other woman is left for me. She's the one from that night I was kidnapped and taken back to the agency's bunker. Payback is a bitch. I jump on her, pushing her down on the ground, getting her in a headlock. Yes, I could tear her throat out, rip her to pieces, but instead I keep my position, her struggling to breathe. Her legs kick and nails bite into my skin, but after a couple seconds they stop as she struggles to take her last breath.

My eyes fall on Stephen, his body lying on the ground, a bullet wound in his forehead. "Stephen?" I run over to him and pull his head in my lap.

"Is he...?" Jane asks.

"He's dead."

21
Jane

The rogues are still unable to move, affected by the sedative. It's their fault Stephen is dead. They killed Eliza and Malachi. I think it's time we stop giving them the option of reformation and just kill them. It seems like every time we try to do something good, bad things happen. Envio and Warwick help me one by one, pulling their limbs and setting them on fire.

Hate and anger is filling me up. What the hell are we supposed to do now? I land on my knees next to Stephen's body and lay my hand on his chest. *How could we let this happen? Why wasn't anyone protecting him?*

Envio kneels beside me and whispers, "We can't stay here. More will show up when they can't get ahold of the agents."

Where are we going to go? Surely they will be at the house in California waiting for someone to come back, but there are things we need to get before they get their hands on those lists. So many vampires have died to protect our cause. When is enough enough? "We must go back to Stephen's. He has one of the lists and if they find it, all vampires in California will be hunted down and killed. We can't let that happen. Not after everything he's done to protect them."

Warwick and Envio nod, pulling me off the ground.

Walking back into his house only makes it seem more real. We will never see him again. When I first joined the Guardians, I came from a rough family. My dad used me as a punching bag, and my mother wasn't a mother at all. I never had the sense of family until I met Liz and the others. They took me in and showed me what a functional family could be like, and Stephen was like my brother. I'd cry more over his death than my parents'.

Warwick and Envio know where he keeps the list hidden in his office. "Go find it, and let's get the hell out of here."

I pace the living room, trying to figure out what to do next. He was a great leader, even though he didn't think he could do it in the beginning. How long until word gets out?

"Jane, you might want to take a look at this..." Warwick yells from the office.

As I approach, I see a piece of paper in his hand. "Oh, good. You found it. Let's go."

"Yes, but we found this too," he says, handing an envelope to me.

I sit down in the office chair, and my hands rest on his desk, opening the letter. My chest rises and falls, preparing myself for what the note could say. Anyone could challenge me to become the leader, and that terrifies me. Would anyone step up?

I open the envelope and there's a letter inside.

Jane,

I know exactly what you are thinking right now. Why the hell would he choose me? I thought the same thing when I became leader when Samuel left. You are strong, intelligent, and can hold our group together. We share the same thoughts when it comes to things, and I need someone who can stay levelheaded under stress. 'Cause let's face it, being a leader is the most stress you'll ever have. Don't let anyone tell you you aren't good enough.

Now, I don't know what caused my death, but if you are reading this, I'd assume something went wrong with the humans. Don't fault them for this. If there comes a time where peace can still be initiated, take it. No matter how many of our people have died, it's better in the long run for our species to survive.

Envio will be the second-in-command, and he's earned that spot. Between the two of you fighting for us, I think we have a good chance at survival. Just remember, keep your personal feelings out of things. You must.

If anyone challenges you, make them and everyone realize why I choose you. Show them your abilities. You are a warrior, Jane. A survivor.

Good luck,
Stephen

Envio and Warwick stare at me, not saying anything. They are both as shocked as I am to find this out. He had confidence in my abilities, and I will do the best I can to make him proud.

"What did the note say?" Warwick asks. "What should we do?"

Overwhelmed by the newfound knowledge, I need to take a minute and process. As the new leader, some things need to be decided firsthand. The war needs to be stopped. Rogues have become even more like savages, going house to house, killing every last human they encounter. If this continues, both species will not survive. It would be advantageous if we call peace on both sides. I can't let Stephen's death affect my decisions going forward. Even though I'd love nothing more than to take revenge against the agency for his death, we all knew this could happen. A backlash because of their inability to trust us. We need to show them they can, even in war.

Warwick leaves and Envio kneels beside me, taking my hand. "Are you okay? It's a lot to process."

"He chose me, and I owe it to him to give it my best. What if I fuck up?" My hands fly up to my face, covering it. "Why if I fail our people?"

He reaches up and takes both my hands. "Don't even talk like that. Even though vampires can live forever, eventually they die.

Especially leaders. I'm sure he's had this in mind for a while now. All you should feel is honor that he picked you."

"I do, but what happens next? What if no one agrees with me taking over?"

"Then you do exactly what Stephen did when people doubted him... Go on about your business and prove to them exactly why they shouldn't."

The one thing everyone in our society agrees upon is living alongside the humans, without chaos, and right now we are at war. With Sam on our side, we can use her to get into contact with the agency. Try to make them see reason so all this can come to an end. No more killing. We've lost enough people.

I join Sam and Warwick in the living room. "Do you still have your cell?" I ask.

She nods, pulling it out of her pocket. "Why?"

"Can you dial the agency for me?"

"They won't talk to you. Not if they don't know Stephen is dead. They will only talk to the leader."

"And they will," I say, grabbing the phone from her hand when I hear ringing. "I'm the leader now."

My first act as the Guardians new leader is to request a meeting with the president. The casualties are in the hundreds of thousands now, and it needs to stop on both sides. Peace is the only way both our species survive this.

I explain to Envio and Warwick what I'm going to do and tell them to go track down as many rogues as they can.

"We can't leave you here by yourself... Look at what happened last time," Warwick says.

"She won't be by herself," Sam says.

"I mean with someone we can trust," Warwick responds. "No offense but you've been on our side for what, like five minutes."

"I'll be fine. Get out there and kill as many of those fuckers as you can. It'll make this easier when he accepts my request to meet. Go."

Envio's eyes are just fixed on mine. He wants so badly to stay and protect me, but he knows that I have to do this.

"We must follow her orders."

He isn't happy about it, but he can't go against me. It doesn't matter that I'm his girlfriend, and he wants to stay and protect me.

"What do you want us to do when we find them?" Envio asks. "Where do we take them?"

"You don't. Execute every last one of them. No more choices. They've lost that right."

They both nod and head out the door.

This will only work if the rogues are out of the picture and the number is already dwindling down because of this war. The humans have actually helped us eradicate most of them, because of their newfound bullet. I'll have to thank them for this later.

Someone finally answers, "Hello, Jane. What a pleasure."

"How did you know it was me?" I look around the house. *Are they here?*

"Guess they forgot to mention the house being bugged."

Shit! "Listen, I want to talk to the president. You can have him call me back on this number." I hang up, and we leave, knowing it's only a matter of time before more agents show up.

The next hiding spot is the New York apartment. I doubt the agency knows any of us lived here, not with it being in Kastiel's name. He's never been on their radar before.

He meets Sam and me at the apartment, and I have to explain to him that Stephen has been killed. Of course, the next question is who will be our leader now? When I tell him about the note the boys found in his office, he doesn't seem surprised.

"You'll make an excellent leader. Good choice on his part," Kastiel says.

I wonder if everyone will be as nice about the newfound leadership as him. "I've asked for a meeting with the president to try and work something out. We've lost too many people on both sides; surely he will listen to reason."

"Good luck. How could you ever know if he could be trusted at this point? I feel like we would always be waiting for the shoe to drop on us. Constantly living in fear."

"Well, think about it from their side, they'll probably feel the same way. Remember they think it was someone inside our society that helped Drake escape. They feel just as betrayed as we do."

"I won't go against you, but how can we expect them to just want to live alongside us now, after all the killing? The president might agree to peace, but will billions of people?"

"That's for him to worry about, not me. All I need to do is establish the agreement. If people break it, then that's on him. There will be consequences for both sides if rules are broken."

Kastiel doesn't understand yet, but he will soon enough. A death, whether vampire or human, will be treated the same. Sentenced to death. If someone is inclined, then they do so knowing the outcome.

Nobody is going to sign up for their own death warrant, will they?

They still haven't called back, but that's not surprising. I'm sure they didn't want to seem desperate. I know they'll call me. Even if it's not to surrender, we have things to discuss.

"So, do you really think you are going to be able to talk them into ending the war?" Sam asks.

"Maybe. I gotta at least try. It's what's best for both sides."

"I don't think he'll go for it. Not with so many of us out there."

"Envio and Warwick can handle tracking down rogues. If they need help, we have others."

"Like who?"

"Cassius and Kieran."

Sam's eyes practically jump out of their sockets. "Did you say Kieran? Stalky, kind of asshole-ish?"

"Wait, how do you know him?"

"He works for the agency. They must have sent him in to watch you guys. You can't trust him. Anyone around him now is in danger."

Is this a trick? Why would the agency send him in to watch us? He's a vampire and worked directly with the governor. How could he keep that hidden from us? This raises so many questions. "Why would they trust a vampire?"

"They turned him. He hates your kind. Being turned took everything away from him. His family, his wife."

"The rogues did that, not us."

"He only sees one kind of vampire. Kieran is psychotic. The agency found him shortly after he gruesomely murdered his wife. He was still covered in her blood when he got to the building."

Fuck. I have to warn the others, but first we have to go somewhere else. If Kieran really is working for them, then they will know about this place and Kastiel. He could be next.

"Where are you going?"

"Kastiel might be in danger. If Kieran really is who you're saying, then they will go after him. Come on."

I wait outside, listening for anything or anyone inside. We don't need to walk into another trap. My eyes close and I focus on the sounds. The only sounds I hear are breathing and a TV.

"Kastiel, if you can hear me, meet me at 2584 West Rd. You're not safe here anymore." I open my eyes, and signal Sam it's time for us to leave.

We meet at an old abandoned factory with Kastiel not that far behind us.

"What do you mean I'm not safe? I've been careful to cover my tracks."

I explain the situation about Kieran, and he seems just as shocked as me. The things he might know, no telling what Stephen told him, thinking he was working with the governor not the agency. He could have been telling them things all this time. That's how they found out about us having something to do with Drake's escape. He must have seen Sasha's room or been there. It doesn't take a genius to put two and two together.

"So, let me get this straight. We don't know what he knows, and he's spying for the enemy? I'm not feeling very optimistic right now," Kastiel says.

He's not the only one.

22

Envio

I didn't want to leave my girlfriend behind, but the fact is she's not just my girlfriend anymore. As our leader, when she gives me an order, I must follow it. No one better touch her or the wrath I'll invoke on the humans will be like nothing they've ever seen. My knuckles turn white just thinking about it. If being out here and hunting down rogues gets us one step closer to being able to settle down and enjoy each other without all this killing, then I'll do it happily.

Maybe we need to call in some reinforcements. The more of us we have out there tracking them down, the faster we can get this done. I text Kieran and Cassius. They can cover Mississippi while we cover Florida. I anticipate at least twenty in each state, maybe a couple more if they've turned anyone recently.

"Are you sure that's a good idea? How do you know we can even trust Kieran? He did nothing but make Stephen's life a living hell..." Warwick says.

"He needs someone to look up to, to take orders from. That person is going to be Jane and I now. Don't forget his last boss was assassinated by the humans. He knows better than anyone, peace is the only way for this to work."

Florida is a big state, so coming up with where to look first is hard. They could be anywhere, but they are most likely sticking together since the military is on every corner. Just like them, we have to be fast and discreet unless we want to be caught.

Pensacola is the first place we end up. The streets are empty besides armored military vehicles sweeping the streets, and others going house to house checking the residents. It's martial law in the United States. I never thought I'd live to see the day.

We stay in the shadows, not going on any major streets, only alleys and dark areas. The one thing that works in our favor is the lack of working streetlights.

"How the hell are we supposed to find them? Just hope and pray they show up on the streets that we're on? This is a suicide mission."

I laugh. "Sooner or later they'll be out. They won't miss the chance to kill."

The farther we walk, the more I start to doubt myself. Maybe he's right. Us being out here is like easy bait, and if caught by the humans, we won't be able to get away fast enough.

Screams begin to echo, not far away, and my instinct takes over, and my feet take off. I see the armored vehicle and three guys in military uniforms being savagely slaughtered. There they are.

The humans scream, beg for their lives, but the rogues don't listen. All they have is a thirst for blood. Warwick and I take a look around, hearing a vehicle that will approach any second now.

"You might be lucky this time, but next time you won't be," Warwick says, running behind the building.

The SUV approaches and all we hear is four shots, and then the screeching of car tires leaving the scene. Once I could confirm they're gone, we peek out onto the street to see all four rogues dead.

Wow, that could have been us if we waited even a second longer. Let's hope Jane can work out an agreement with the president. All around me are cries from people inside their homes, wishing this would stop. They could stop living in fear that today is their last day on Earth.

"We have to keep going; the others can't be that far," I say, leading him back into the alley that stretches along the business strip. "They've got to be close."

We both focus, using our hearing, trying to catch a sound of anyone crying out in pain or worse. Nothing. Where the hell are they?

"Wait... do you hear that?" he asks, finger pointing to the very end of the alley. "I heard a low growl."

I put my finger to my lips, trying to catch the rogue mid-feed so we can kill him, but to our surprise it's not one, but three.

"We are so not prepared for this..." I say before they head right toward us. "Run!"

My stupidity has caught up with me, and seeing three rogues reminds me we haven't fed in like a week. There's no way we can take on multiple rogues each without eating. Yet where the hell are we supposed to get it? There are military vehicles everywhere, and no sane human is going to let a stranger inside their home.

Our legs keep going, until we even have to slow down to catch a breath. "We need to feed. Being out here like this could get us killed."

"Where are we supposed to do that? They're watching all the streets."

I look down the road and see a sign that makes me smile. "There."

"Okay... but how are we supposed to get in and drink from someone without being noticed?"

I shake my head and take off. The more time we stand around, the better chance of us getting caught. He follows me inside the hospital and down to the basement.

"What the hell are we doing down here?" The lights flicker and begin to creep us both out.

"Little known fact, dead bodies still have blood for a little while,"

I say, looking at the tags on the door to find the most recent death. As long as they haven't taken out the organs yet, then we can feed. "Here, this one. Only a couple hours ago. Should be enough for both of us."

"No way. I'm not feeding off a dead guy. You're out of your fucking mind."

I shrug and bite into the left side of his neck. Sure, it might be disgusting, but if it's what I have to do to survive and kill the rogues, then so be it.

It only takes a couple of minutes, and I'm done, feeling refreshed. "We can only do this if we are both at full capacity. You have to feed. Don't make me force you."

His head twitches. "Force me? What the hell am I, five?"

He bites into the body's left side and feeds, probably hating every second of it.

Warwick gags. "That was disgusting. Tastes like sour milk or rotten eggs."

"Well, good thing we never have to do it again." I laugh. "Let's get out of here."

We head back to the alley, knowing the rogues couldn't have gotten too far. Too many humans around for them to kill. We search the alley and find none, but just have to follow the screams.

The military is still doing sweeps house to house and finding bodies. The weird thing is they aren't even doing anything with them, just leaving them inside the homes to clean up later.

My phone vibrates; it's Kieran.

"What? I'm a little busy here."

"We've hit twenty. Where do you want us next?" he asks.

Even as an executioner, this guy's an overachiever. How the hell did he find that many so fast? I don't have time to question him. "Virginia." I hung up and overheard the humans talking.

"By the time this is over with, half our population will be wiped. I'm sick of seeing dead bodies of children."

They are close. We can't be too far behind them. They go inside another house, and we sneak past them to the next street where we can hear somewhat of a struggle inside a home. The door is broken, and we walk in to three rogues about to have a family as a snack.

"You don't have to do this. There's another way," I say, knowing we aren't supposed to give them a choice, but I want them to think we are. "No need to kill innocent children."

The woman laughs at me. "If it isn't the high and mighty Envio. Don't forget you were once like us. Enjoyed the blood just as much as we do."

"That's before I found a way to control it. Have a somewhat normal life instead."

"You call hiding normal?" she asks. "We're done with that. Now is the chance to show them why they need to fear us."

If we cause enough of a ruckus, then the soldiers on the street will hear. If they can get in here fast enough, maybe we can save this poor family from being slaughtered.

"We want to hear them scream and cry. Take notice of us." Her fangs grazed the mother's neck. "Go ahead, scream. Tell me why I should let you live."

The woman is crying frantically, her eyes locked on her daughter's. She didn't answer the rogue, so her head is pulled back to make biting easier.

"No reasons to let you live?"

The mother screams and I can hear boots running toward us. I eye Warwick, hoping he understands and hears them coming. Right before they get to the broken door, we slip out the back of the house, and we can hear the sound of shots being fired. I take a deep breath, listening intently to see if they were accurate enough to take out the rogues that fast. All I can hear is the mom and dad asking their daughter if she's okay.

"That was close. Maybe it's time to move on," Warwick says.

"There's plenty more where that came from."

Thirty-four is the number of rogues we tracked down in Florida by the time we are done, and it's time to move on.

"I don't know what the hell is going on... Cassius isn't answering for an update. Like five times," I say.

"Call Kieran. They're together so maybe he'll answer," Warwick replies.

No matter the circumstances, I still hate the guy. He's an egotistical asshole, and I hate that he has been pulled in to help us, but we need all the vampires we can get to make this work right now.

The phone rings.

"Yes?" Kieran answers.

"Why the hell isn't Cassius answering his phone? You were supposed to check back in."

"I don't know. Probably on silent or something. Who knows."

"Where the hell are you guys?"

"Richmond, Virginia. Couple more here, and then we can move on to wherever we are going."

When we get to Richmond, and I try to call Cassius, he still doesn't answer. I'm going to kill him when we get there. Kieran doesn't answer either. I attempt over and over until Kieran finally answers.

"It happened so fast... he's... he's dead."

"What do you mean? You're supposed to be watching his back. How the fuck could you let that happen?"

"There were too many of them."

"Where are you now?"

We make our way to an alley in the downtown district, and Kieran seems distraught. Almost too much so. He barely knew this guy, yet he's shedding tears for him? Why? He doesn't strike me as an emotional type of person. Maybe we've just had him pegged all wrong.

"What happened?"

"We went inside this house. We tracked three of them there.

Once we got inside, there were more. Like five more. We tried to get away, but not both of us did. They pulled him apart like savages."

This is the problem when you bring in people who didn't normally do this kind of thing. You always stake out how many are inside, before you go rushing in. We should have taken the time to properly teach them, but we didn't have it. Right now, it's a ticking time bomb, and Jane is trying to stop it.

23

Warwick

None of us really knew Cassius as well as Stephen, but he was still one of us. The rogues that killed him will suffer, but right now we need to get back to Jane. Maybe we don't need to be out here. Why not just let the humans do it? They are searching for them anyway, and that means less of our people will die. We can't afford to lose anymore. Weird thing is now that we've lost Eliza, Malachi, Sasha, Stephen, and now Cassius since our first meet up with the president, it kind of puts things in perspective that maybe that wasn't the best choice. Not that I blame Stephen for trying. It's not like he could have predicted it was going to end in war. He's been fighting for peace since Samuel found him and gave him something to believe in and look forward to.

"Let's head back to New York. Check in with Jane and see what to do from there," Envio says.

New York is somewhere Tasha always wanted to visit. I wish I could've taken her for our honeymoon, but I just couldn't afford it. Instead, we ended up spending it locked in our house, just enjoying each other's company.

"Wow, who can afford to live in this palace?" Kieran says, looking up at the tall condo building.

As we go inside, he makes more comments about the amenities and how fancy everything is. On the ride up, he questions how we could afford something like this. None of his business and right now he's not so inclined to be given any answers. Just because we need his help right now, doesn't mean he's a part of the team. His first mission and his partner dies, not looking good for him. The elevator dings and opens, but we do a double take when we see the door open, looking to be broken in. *Oh no, they got to her.*

"I'll check inside. See if you can get ahold of her," Envio says to me with Kieran rushing inside with him.

How did they know about the apartment? It's under Kastiel's name, and as far as I know he doesn't have any ties besides this apartment to vampires. If they suspected him, wouldn't they have come after him a long time ago? Did they know our people were staying here? That Jane had been here?

I pull out my phone and dial her.

She answers on the third ring. "I take it you've been to the apartment by now. The humans are tracking us with some help."

"You okay? Envio's freaking out. Where are you?"

"We're fine, but we had to go to a different location. One we've never been."

"The humans come after you?"

"Long story. Listen, is Kieran with you?" She whispers, like she doesn't want him to hear what's coming next. The shakiness in her voice worries me. Something is obviously going on.

"Yes."

"Can he hear me?"

I look around and move farther away from the door just in case. "I don't think so."

"Okay, listen carefully. Come to 2584 West Rd in New York."

Envio comes back out, sweat dripping from his forehead, sadness in his eyes. "She's not inside. Please tell me you got ahold of her."

"Yeah, she had to go somewhere else. Wants us to meet her there," I reply.

He hesitates before all three of us get back on the elevator and head to the given location. Envio knows something is wrong. Why would Jane need to go somewhere else? How did they find out about the condo in the first place? No one even knew about it besides Kastiel, him, and me. I might not know Kastiel all that well, but he doesn't seem like the traitor type. So, it's got to be someone else. They have to be getting their information from somewhere.

We go to the address and it's an old abandoned industrial building, equipment still inside, looking to be an old bottling factory. It doesn't appear anyone has been here in years. No signs of any squatters, no graffiti, or sleeping bags on the floor.

"Why the hell is she hiding out here?" Kieran asks.

"No fucking clue," Envio answers, looking around for her.

A bead of sweat runs down my forehead. I hate keeping things from Envio, but whatever it is Jane didn't seem to want Kieran to know. Right now, there's no way for me to tell him without Kieran overhearing. Sometimes I hate our hearing capabilities.

"Jane?" We walk around, and Envio raises his voice. "Where are you?"

She comes out of the shadows and he runs to her, engulfing her in a hug. "What's going on? I was scared shitless when I found the apartment ransacked again. I thought they had taken you."

"No." She pushes him off her. "I'm fine. But we do have other things to talk about. Follow me."

Waiting for them to be back, Sam and I are standing next to each other, and she keeps side-eyeing me. I don't know if I can ever trust her fully. Switching sides came too easy for her, and she could easily switch again at any time if the humans give her the option. How will we know if she is loyal to our cause? I suppose that might be up to Jane now, but we all should tread lightly. Who knows what the humans could have up their sleeve? Maybe we shouldn't underestimate them.

"Been back to see your wife lately?" she asks.

I shake my head, knowing it's long overdue, but things keep coming up. With us at war now, it's not in either of our best interests for me to be seen out there. They know what we look like, especially from the meetings, and I don't want to lead them to my loved ones. If something happened to Tasha and Avery because they are trying to get to me, I would never forgive myself. When I left that first day, it was to give them a better chance at life, and I can't go back on that now. Not until I know it's safe.

"Not to sound too forward, but you know she will grow old, and we won't. One day, you will want to fall in love again."

"Well, it won't be with you. So don't even start thinking that. I told you, the feelings I once had for you are gone." How dare she talk like that? Even after my wife is gone, I'll still love her. Will I ever be with another woman? Maybe. But right now isn't the time to be thinking about it.

She scoffs at me and moves away. "Wow, quick to think I'm talking about myself. You're an asshole."

If Jane can strike a deal with the agency, then I might be able to go home to my family at some point. We could have a somewhat normal life. That's what I'm working toward every day supporting the Guardians' cause. It will give me exactly what I want, my family back.

"I need you to tell me what happened with Cassius exactly." Jane asks Kieran, walking back inside the building.

"Tracked some rogues, ended up being more than we anticipated. He didn't make it out." He shrugs his shoulders, giving a completely different reaction than before. Where are the tears?

"He didn't make it out? Or was it your plan all along for him to get left behind? Or maybe you didn't find any rogues at all and you gave him up to the humans?" Sam interjects.

Envio and I look at each other, trying to follow the conversation. Kieran gets on the defensive side and starts stammering through his words.

"No. Why would you say a thing like that? I'm on your side, remember? Why would I do anything for the humans?"

"You must not recognize me," Sam says, putting her hair up in a ponytail. "What about now?"

His fangs eject, and he crouches down like he's going to attack. "What are you doing here? Don't you work for the agency?" He looks around at us. "You trust this girl? Probably telling all kinds of lies. She's the one that has been on their side since day one."

Wait, how do they know each other? It finally comes together with everything that's going on. *He's the traitor.*

"It's been you," Envio says. "This whole time."

"I don't know what you're talking about. I've been on your side, so was my boss. He died trying to help establish peace for us."

Sam moves closer to Kieran. "Are you really still trying to cover this up? I've told Jane about your dealings with the agency. How you hate vampires, even more so because you are one after going home to slaughter your wife. No need to lie anymore."

Envio and I rush him and grab his arms; he won't be going anywhere. Jane begins to ask him all sorts of questions. How did he know Sasha helped the rogues with Drake's escape? How did he know we had meetings with the humans before anyone else? We should have caught on to this a long time ago, but it's never too late to weed out a traitor.

"I suppose you're going to kill me now? Just believe that bitch over there over me? How long has she been on your side? A day? How do you know she's telling the truth?"

"Everything she's telling us adds up. I wish Stephen were here to see you being caught."

It's like the darkness inside him takes over, and his demeanor changes. "Well, I wish I could have been the one to kill that asshole. All high and mighty. Thinking he was better than everyone just because he was the leader. After the agency is done with you, you'll all be dead."

Jane smacks the shit out of him. "Don't speak about him like that.

He was one of the best men I've ever known. You'd be lucky to be even ten percent of the man he was."

I still have questions. "How did the humans find out that silver bullets could kill us too?"

Kieran laughs. "That was all me. They brought me vampires and I got to experiment with different things to see what could kill you besides just fire. They needed something faster, something that put them at an advantage. Just got lucky and found the silver bullet."

"Last question, is there anything else we don't know about that could kill us? Anything you found and told the agency?"

He starts laughing. "You're going to kill me either way, so I think I'll keep my info to myself, thank you very much."

Jane nods her head to us, giving us the signal it's time to execute him. Too bad we didn't have any silver bullets. We hold him as she jumps on his shoulders and tears off his head, and then we take his arms. They are all thrown into a pile, and then Sam pours gasoline on him.

"In our society, there are consequences for the things you've done. I'll be sure to let the agency know about your death, but I doubt they'll even care. You're just another one of their lap dogs doing their bidding," Jane says before throwing a match on his limbs.

The flames engulf him, and it only takes a matter of minutes for there to be nothing but ash and black scorch marks on the concrete floor.

24
Jane

Sam's phone echoes across the building, and her eyes grow. "It's them."

A part of me wants to not answer and make them wait, but I don't. "Well, well, well. It's nice for you to finally return my call."

"He's a busy man. There's a war going on," the agent replies.

"I don't want to talk to you; where's the president?"

"He's on another call and will be getting on shortly."

"Your lap dog Kieran is dead. It took us a while, but we finally figured out how you were getting so much intel. We don't take too kindly to traitors on this side."

"Why would you kill him if you're trying to promote peace? Doesn't look good."

"Would you let a traitor live?" We all know they would have done the same thing, and they were probably looking for Sam for that exact reason. She won't be safe now, with them knowing she's now with us. Even though she hasn't always been loyal, giving us the information on Kieran saved our lives. We owe her for that.

"The president has accepted your plea for a meeting. I'll patch him in now," the agent says, before I hear some clicking noises.

"Well, if it isn't Ms. Jane. I take it you're the new leader with poor Stephen dead?" he asks.

"Yes, but let's get down to business. No small talk, neither of us have the time. Call off your military."

We can't move forward with anything until the military isn't perusing the streets, making everyone on edge. Don't they realize it's only giving the rogues what they want? Easy bait. Humans are scared and locked away in their homes, and they feed off fear. It's like a buffet now.

"Why would I do that? It's not over."

"But it can be. The rogues are the only ones fighting you right now. We want peace. To save humankind. It's a mutual agreement; without you we can't survive. It does us no good to kill off everyone. If you don't back off, there won't be anyone left." He doesn't seem to grasp the concept. Stephen tried to explain this but apparently he wasn't paying attention. "Once the rogues are eliminated, there won't be a reason to be at war."

"Not sure that's the case. What about when you decide you want more?"

"All we want is to be treated fairly, the same as humans. No special treatment. Most of us live alongside you every day and you've probably never even noticed."

"Oh, we've noticed. Didn't act until now, but we did."

"The rogues are still running around slaughtering. It won't look good if we just stop pursuing that. How about this? You take care of all of them, and then we talk."

Much easier said than done. Doesn't he remember that half our squad is now dead because of this bullshit? How the hell are we supposed to track down and kill every single rogue? That could take months, years even. We don't have that kind of time. "The only way you'll agree is if the killings stop?"

"Yes, are you able to do that? Stephen said it would be taken care of, and it hasn't been. They are still running around, killing my people in their homes and out in the streets, causing panic across the country."

We only have Envio, Warwick, Sam, and Kastiel now. If we can get others to join in the eradication of the rogues, we might be able to make this work with the government. I tap my index finger on my chin, but who will that be? Samuel, Liz, and Amy did offer to help, but not sure if he's willing to get out there and kill again. Amy's never killed and not sure her dad would be interested in adding that burden. "I'll see what I can do with my people. We'll need leniency to do this. I can't send my people out there knowing they'll be slaughtered."

"What are you suggesting?"

"The world needs to go back to normal, no more curfew. If we're going to catch and kill them, then we need to be able to walk the streets and track them down. We can't do that with military vehicles everywhere."

"I'll give them the orders to stand down on anything that doesn't have reddish-yellow eyes."

So the agency does know about the eye color. So, the military is looking specifically for rogues. They have no way to know who is a vampire except for that. As long as our people don't do anything stupid, they'll be fine until we can get this resolved.

"We'll get started. You'll hear from me again."

"I hope so. Good luck, Jane," President Walters says, before hanging up.

The others standing around ask me what he said, and I explain the agreement he's willing to make, but only if we take out every single rogue. They are as hesitant as me in knowing if that's actually possible. The problem is for every one we kill, they can turn five more. It's like a never-ending cycle. We must find a way, and that's only going to happen if we all come together.

Do we even know how many rogues there are out there? There could be hundreds or thousands left. How the hell are we supposed to know when they've all been eliminated? I think we're going to have to expand and bring more people in. If we're going to keep this peace, we will need someone for each state to watch out for our people and the humans.

"Envio, call Samuel and have him meet us there. I'll need him for what's coming next."

Samuel might know some people that we can trust to help us. Society is going to have to change, and we are going to need more governors if this is going to work in our favor. Someone for vampires to report to in each state, track down rogues, and make sure everything goes smoothly before and after the agreement is in place.

"Anyone else here that has vampires they can trust to help us, give them this address. We need to get this going as soon as possible. Every hour we waste is more lives lost."

I make a call to bring Ian on board; I haven't seen him since the takedown in Arkansas years ago. His military experience will help, and if his wife comes, well, she's just a badass. I wouldn't want to stand toe-to-toe with her.

Within two hours, we have thirty vampires that someone in this room knows and trusts. Everyone has seen the war and how it is playing out right now. If we don't do something to change it, then our species will be screwed. There will be no one to feed on, blood to be consumed, and the immortality we have been given will be cut short.

"Thank you all for coming today. I'm not going to give some big, long speech about overcoming the enemy because we truly don't have time for that. If you haven't noticed, Stephen is not here, because he was murdered by agents. He selected me to take over in the event of his death, and I intend to do everything in my power to make sure we don't all die. For this to work, each of you will be assigned a state. It will be your responsibility to find and eliminate any rogues within it, and keep the registered vampires upholding our society's rules. Envio or I will be coming around and assigning you shortly."

It might not be the way Stephen or I originally thought this was going to pan out, but at least I'm not giving up.

"So, how do you want to do this?" Envio asks.

"Well, have Sam get a list going with names and the states they live in first. Of course, we want to try to send them to wherever they are already living. Don't want to place someone hundreds of miles away from home."

Many come up to me and speak great things about Stephen and all he did for our kind. They seemed to really like him, and I wish he were here to hear the kind things being said. He might have had those that didn't think he could've been the leader, but this would have meant something to him.

25
Envio

The only thing we can do is try and make this work. Who knows, maybe if this peace thing works out, I can see my mom again. Keep her out of trouble and maybe get her away from that asshole of a husband that beats her. I haven't visited her since I got turned, and I didn't want to. My anger will get out of hand, and there is no telling what I could do. If given the opportunity, I'd protect her from him and show him that real men don't hit women or children.

She didn't exactly have the best luck at picking men to be in her life. My father was abusive too, and I think that's why me and Jane get along so well. Our childhoods fucked us up, and some things are just harder for us. Trusting people is one of them. Yet I completely trust her with all my being.

If she thinks this is the best way to get the outcome we are wanting, then I'll play along. Besides, someday I hope her to be my wife, and to live a long life with her. Without some kind of agreement, that can't happen. Humans will be wiped off the planet, and then what would we do for sustenance? It wouldn't take long before we start to wither away and then die.

"You'll take Oklahoma," she says, looking at the list. "I'm going to go with Texas since that's already where I'm staying, and maybe I can keep a close eye on the agency too."

Wait? We are going to different states? Shouldn't I be going wherever she is? I don't like this, not at all. I thought the whole point of this is to bring us closer together, but maybe not.

"Everyone else is off to their assignments. We will need to make sure we keep communication open. Sam wrote down every governor's phone number so we can reach them if needed. They have been instructed to check in with you at least once a day to keep you updated on their progress. I am going to focus on my assignments, but if anything urgent comes up, let me know."

She is acting like I'm just one of her fellow vampires, not her boyfriend. It didn't seem like us being apart bothered her. Is this how it's going to be now that she's the leader? She forgets all about me and us? My heart's already breaking, noticing the shift in dynamic between us. "Oklahoma? At least it's still close to you." I smile and then lean in to give her a kiss before we part ways for now.

"We need to focus and get this done. There will be plenty of time for that after. People are still dying and it's our job to stop it. Go do what you do best. Hunt. Track."

She disappears and leaves me behind, still standing in the old industrial building. Why is she acting this way? It's a total shift from just yesterday, and the only thing that's changed is her status. It surely can't already be going to her head, can it? I never took her to become egotistical, but maybe I'm reading it all wrong. It could be she is just really focused on fulfilling Stephen's wish to have peace and will do anything to get it. Even if that means pushing me away.

I run my fingers through my hair. I guess it's time to head to Oklahoma and get started. Tracking down rogues isn't easy, but now it's different. They didn't cover up their tracks like they used to before the president declared war. They are enjoying the thrill of the kill. The fear that is bursting out of humans. It's what will keep them going. That's what I'm counting on.

I get a hotel in Tulsa and remember that Jane was once in Tulsa with the others when they were trying to hunt down Jakob. If my memory serves me correctly, there were a couple of hubs here, and the rogues are probably still holed up in the same place as a force of habit.

Me: *So, you remember where the hubs were around Tulsa? I know it's been a while, but could make this go by a lot faster...*

The phone lies on the nightstand while I turn on the news to see if anything new is being broadcasted. President Walters has announced the curfew has been lifted, but military personnel will still be out to protect the citizens. The media is still showing reels of the slaughtering and bodies being found but nothing new. It's all the same shots from yesterday.

My phone rings and her name scrolls across my screen. I hit the green button and answer, "Hey. You didn't have to call. I know you're busy..."

"Faster this way. I'm going to send you some locations on Maps around where I remember. You'll have to check them out."

"Good, thank you. It's gonna help this go by faster so I can get back to you."

"Don't you get it?" she says, irritated. "We have no future if this doesn't work."

"Jane..."

"No, I gotta go." She hangs up, and I'm left wondering why it's bothering her so much now.

Before leaving Frankfort with Stephen to pursue making a new society once Jakob was dead, Jane and I had doubts that we would be alive much longer. Things just weren't looking great then either. The night before, we spent time talking about everything, including our future, what that could look like if we were able to stop the rogues and live alongside the humans. I still want that, more than anything.

My phone beeps and the first location is not far from my hotel. I zoom in to see the building; a small strip of apartments remain there if this is still accurate. Who knows how often they actually update this.

Me: *Thx. Heading there now.*

It's only a short walk before the apartments are in front of me. Everything seems to be quiet, so they must not be here right now. Probably out chasing their next kill. Or worse.

The window remains unlocked on the first apartment so I go in instead of using the front door. Papers are scattered all over the floor, and it reeks. How long since someone has been here? I notice it's part of the newspaper everywhere. Different dates, different sections. Someone is following the killings closely. Maybe whoever is staying here wants to keep track of the human casualties. Or are they keeping them as trophies of each kill?

I go apartment by apartment, and it's the same thing. Newspapers all over the floor of each. Why would they care enough to keep these? My mind comes up with this crazy idea that maybe it's a pattern. If I can figure out why they were keeping them, then it will lead me to where they are now. The amount of dust inside the apartments makes me think they haven't been here in at least a couple of weeks, and who knows if they will ever be coming back. I can't stay around and wait for them to show up; Jane would kill me. She wants me out there, actively tracking down rogues, and right now I'm just standing around inside some apartment.

The next location is a bar in downtown Tulsa that is still open and packed with humans. President Walters should've known the first thing they'd do is go to a bar. Humans have some weird tendencies, and drinking is a normal way to deal with stress or chaos. It makes sense for them to flock to a place like this.

Rogues are here. The hairs on the back of my neck begin to stand up as my eyes search around. No one stands out to me, but they must be close. I can't get a grasp on how many, but at least multiple.

Me: *I need backup. Sending you a location. Meet me here. Be careful.*

Dying isn't something I want to do, so calling in reinforcements is much needed. I'm not going to try to take on multiple rogues by myself even if I've fed in the last couple of days. Leaving Jane behind alone isn't something on my list to do. So to prevent it, Samuel can help. He's been out of the game a couple months, but it's like second nature. As long as he doesn't get carried away, we should be good.

As to not draw attention to myself, I go up to the bar and order a drink. When there are this many people, it's hard to decipher exactly who is vampire and who's not. This will work to my advantage for the moment. When the shot hits the bar, I take it, fast and easy. The music is loud, so I strain to focus, not being able to concentrate to see if I can hear one of them talking.

A hand clamps down on my shoulder, and I elbow them in the gut.

"Jeez, it's just me. Calm down, will ya?" Samuel says, holding his stomach. "Not usually how I'm greeted when asked to help."

I laugh. "Sorry. Didn't know it was you. Thanks for coming. Can you feel it? There are multiple here, but I can't get a lock on who it is. Too many people and the music is too loud to hear anything clearly."

He pans around the bar, attempting to see if he can figure out who we need to go after. His experience might be helpful in this scenario. Samuel has been a vampire longer, which means he is better at homing in on his skills than I.

"Anything?"

He shakes his head and starts to walk away. "Let's walk around and see what we can gather. We aren't doing any good standing around waiting."

You would think that after everything that has happened to him, he would be more inclined to stay on the sidelines and play it safe, but that's not the vibe I'm getting. It's like he's missed being a part of the action, like he craves it.

I follow alongside him, cutting through the crowd, trying to come across one. Women keep stopping me, trying to grind against me, but I shrug them off. We continue forward until we come across the VIP tables in the back. Two women and men sit, chugging alcohol like it's water, and don't even look up as we approach them. The sense works both ways, so they know vampires are here too. Yet they don't even seem fazed.

"Excuse me?" Samuel says, trying to get their attention. "Mind if we have a word with the gentleman, ladies?"

They are human, but the men are not. I've never seen a rogue play with their food like this. Wine and dine them before going into a feeding frenzy isn't exactly typical. They are lucky to be alive being that close to rogues without seeing death.

"Just who the hell do you think you are?" a rogue asks, standing up big and tall, like that is supposed to scare us.

"I've seen scarier things than you, buddy. Sit down, let's talk."

Samuel and I join them at the table, trying to get them to go outside, but they refuse. Rogues are smart; they know we will do anything not to cause a scene, and ripping their throats out in a bar surrounded by humans is something we will avoid. Yet we have to get them out of here, save everyone's life in here without them even knowing it.

"How many of you are there around here?" I ask, seeing if maybe they will answer some questions.

"You want us to help you? Pathetic. The president doesn't even realize that he just opened the country up for more murderous rage. Rogues like me, like him, we don't like chasing down our prey. We like when they come to us. Ready and willing."

Come to them? These women must have approached them, making it easier to prey on their weakness.

"Those women... They are fans. Begging us to bite them. Guess we have a fan club we didn't even know about. They expect Edward, but they'll get Dracula. Poor things don't even realize what they're signing up for."

Oh God, so now we not only have rogues to worry about, but a fucking fan club of people who want to become vampires? He should have never said anything about our existence, because things are going to get ugly. How are we supposed to stop these humans?

"Just because they are willing, doesn't mean you should do it.

The burden of being a vampire isn't something I'd want to give anyone," Samuel says, looking down at the table. "Everyone I've turned is dead. By your late leader's orders, or the humans. Sooner or later, we will all die. The question is when?"

I sit by and idly watch as Samuel tries to offer them some insight from his perspective, but they aren't seeing reason. Jane didn't want us to give them a choice, but he didn't seem to care. Maybe being on the other side, seeing things happen that he couldn't stop, has changed him in a way that none of us will ever understand, not even me.

I didn't reocgnize the two rogues so they must've been turned recently. They probably know nothing about the hubs. Asking them again would be a waste of breath.

"You scared of us?" I ask, trying to get them to think going outside is their idea. "A real man would go toe-to-toe with us. But I guess you've gone soft since taking advantage of younger women."

Both their eyebrows heighten, and one speaks. "We could take you with one arm behind our backs."

Samuel knows what I'm trying to do. So he tries to egg them on. "Unlikely, but I'd love for you to try. It's been a while since I've got to kick someone's ass."

Samuel might be in his late forties, but I've seen him in action, even fought against him, and I know how good he is.

"Well, now's your chance old man." They start to walk outside, and we follow them, laughing internally.

It might have taken a little longer than we wanted, but we still get them to leave the bar so we can kill them in the alley behind the bar instead of causing a scene inside. They both quickly notice they challenged the wrong set of vampires.

26
Samuel

The swift move of my body, the adrenaline coursing through my veins, all the things I've missed these last few months while sitting on the sidelines, trying to focus on family. At first, I didn't think I could go back to the way things were, so I locked myself away at Liz's, scared to come out. Now I know I just need to trust myself again. Inevitably, there will always be a little bit of the dark side left inside, but as long as I continue to be strong and in control, then it won't be a problem.

When they called me asking for help, my instinct was to say no and stay hidden, but Jane is family too, and it seems we've lost too many family members lately. I couldn't just run and hide when this is the big catalyst. After this, peace will be granted, and we won't have to worry about this bullshit anymore. After all, all of us just want to be human again. So many of us lost so much after being turned, that most wish they could go back. If we can pull this off, then just maybe, everyone can be reunited with their families or loved ones. Neither species will have to live in fear of the other.

As the new acting vampire governor of Kentucky, I'm protecting everyone. Not just us. Humans are still cowering in fear even though the curfew has been lifted and things are getting back to a new normal. They can't pretend vampires aren't real anymore; they've seen proof. So now they are finding new ways to cope, like drinking, drugs, and some even picked up overspending. If we kill all rogues and the killings stop, then it's possible they might believe there are good vampires too. We don't all want to slaughter. It won't happen overnight, but it can be the end goal for us.

Arriving back at Liz's house, my body seems different, stronger than I've felt in months. Ready for anything. Liz and Amy might want to stay out of this, but I can't. Too many people are counting on me, us to protect our society. This is how we do it.

The door opens and closes behind me, my footsteps sounding through the foyer, alerting Liz of my arrival. "Hey, sweetie, I'm back." When I walk into the living room, there are papers scattered across the floor, a laptop on the table, and highlighters everywhere. "What the hell is going on?"

"I- It sucks. Going through it again only proves it. Why can't I write the last damn book and get it over with? I'm gonna pull my damn hair out…" Liz says, sitting on the floor, some papers still in her hand, covered in red ink. "If I don't finish it soon, they'll cancel my contract. That means I'll never be able to publish normally again."

Liz's series is based on real-life events, but since we stepped away from that world, she hasn't been able to write. Being out of the loop, away from the actions and decisions has hindered her in such a way that I'm not sure she realizes. "I'm telling you, just come help. You never know, it might give you some inspiration."

Her hands fly up in the air. "All it takes is imagination. I've written plenty of books. Why is this one so hard? Huh?"

I've learned that when she gets like this, it's best to walk away and let her calm down. Although, it seems to happen more often and getting out of the house might do us both some good, but she won't listen to me. When Jane called asking for help, Liz was against it, and so was Amy, not wanting to have anything to do with that anymore. After all, for Amy, vampires took her father, brother, and mother from her. And, well, Liz lost me for a while too. Neither wanted to lose me again, and as understandable as that is, I'm not one to run and hide.

Before joining the Blood Takers to save Sam, I was on top, leading us to build a new society, free of rogues. I need to be a part of the change, the making of a new world.

"You got a minute?" Amy asks, joining me in the kitchen.

"Of course. Need something?"

She paces the room, beginning to talk a couple times but stops herself.

"Whatever it is, just spit it out."

"I took the pretest for the GED. Got a decent score."

I didn't even know she has interest in taking the GED. Good for her. A diploma will help her get a better job, and most things require a diploma besides fast food. "When's the next test? I'm so proud of you."

"In two days. Just figured if I want to do something with my life... however long that may be... then I need to at least get my GED. Maybe go to college."

"I had no idea you were even interested in college, honey."

"Just because I'm a vampire doesn't mean my human life has to stop. The next step in my life before all this was to finish senior year and then go to college. I'm sick of sitting here and going to that dead-end job."

"I say do it! No time like the present, baby girl."

My relationship with my daughter has gotten better, nothing like before I was turned, but someday it possibly could be. She's made it clear what she wants, and that's to be as far away from vampires as possible. When she found out I would be helping them again, that's when she started to distance herself from me. Even in the three days since being back, I've noticed a shift. I know she's scared to lose me again, but we must take risks in life, especially for good causes. The world will never change unless someone has the balls to do it.

Amy heads out the door to her job at the Pizza Shack, trying to save up enough money to get her own place and car. Once we settled into Liz's, I explained that to live in the human world, she must do everything like a human, which means having a job. The only place that would hire her without a high school diploma is Pizza Shack at the mall. It's good for her to know what it's like to work and pay taxes. Kids these days want everything just handed to them, no work ethic, and definitely no motivation for their future. I might have missed years of her life, but no daughter of mine is going to sit around and be lazy.

Liz yells at me from the living room, and I question whether I want to go in there and heed her craziness right now. Her deadline is in two weeks, and she's only written half the book, but the half she's written isn't that great. Her words, not mine. For the past week, every time I come in here, this is what it looks like—a disaster.

"What, sweetheart?" I ask.

"Maybe I'm going about this all wrong. Instead of trying to come up with cool new ideas of things, what about calling Envio or one of the others and get some stories about their time out there in the last couple months?"

Honestly, if doing that will get her to calm down and finish the damn book already, I'm all for it. "Go ahead. Don't know if they will have the time right now though. Remember, on deadline."

She shakes her head and picks up more papers.

I've never seen her this frustrated before. The woman has over forty books published and suddenly she can't seem to write a cohesive story. Maybe she's just being too hard on herself? "It can't be that bad... Can I read some of it?"

Instead of waiting for her to answer, I pick up a couple pages and begin reading. *Angst. Tension. Fighting. Murder.* In some ways, she's still writing about real-life events, but also adding some fluff in there. She depicts that the war with the humans doesn't end until there are only a few of both species left standing. Only then do they finally come to an agreement and repopulate the world a little at a time. "It's good. Why are you freaking out?"

"Harsh critic, I guess."

"Did you even send this off to your editor yet?"

"No, I hated it and wanted everything to be perfect."

"Send it now. Instead of attacking yourself, let's see what he says. If he doesn't like something about it, he'll tell ya," I reply.

My cell phone rings and I answer without looking to see the name. "Hello?"

"Dad, get to the mall now."

Instead of asking for details, I jump in the car and head straight there. The parking lot is almost full. I had forgotten that it's spring break here. Teenagers love to be mall rats. After finally finding a parking spot, I go to the Pizza Shack to talk to Amy.

"What the hell is going on? You okay?" I ask, observing her for any injuries.

"It's not me." Her eyes avert to the shop across the way. "It's them."

Being so worried about Amy, I didn't even notice the sensation of other vampires being so close, but there they are. Three of them. It's getting harder to tell them apart because of the contacts they wear now. "They could be like us. What makes you think they are rogues?"

She looks around. "I dont know, just a feeling."

A text is sent to Warwick with the address, asking him for help. I promised my family that I wouldn't knowingly go up against more than one rogue at a time, and I intend to keep my promises.

Warwick: *On my way.*

Amy isn't used to having rogues this close and I can tell it's freaking her out. I agree to follow them and make sure everything goes okay, to put her at ease. She did right by calling me since it's now my job to kill any and all rogues found in my state. These are just kids though, maybe twenty-one at the most.

Warwick: *I'm here. Standing outside the food court.*

Me: *Stay there. They are headed in that direction.*

I follow them outside and get cautious when they start walking toward the alleyway behind the mall where the trucks unload.

Teenagers like to have sex in weird places, no need to panic yet. Instead of following close, not wanting to accidentally see them fornicating, I keep my distance and just listen. Warwick joins me. All we hear is lots of kissing, giggling, and then fangs into flesh. I know that sound all too well. What I didn't hear is screaming.

We look at each other, then peek around the corner. They are vampires, but not savages. Just like us, they are taking advantage of a pretty girl to feed off of and have a good time. I can't fault them for that.

We head back inside, and I apologize to Warwick for having him come for nothing, but better to be safe than sorry.

"No worries, man. Don't need to lose anyone else. Call me anytime."

He doesn't stick around, not that it's needed. Warwick has a state to protect just like I do.

"So? Did you kill them?" Amy asks, my palms resting on the counter.

"No, they weren't rogues. You can't get jumpy anytime you sense a vampire around. If this goes right with Jane and the others, vampires will be walking around without having to hide soon enough."

"Yeah, I'll be even more worried then."

"Why? You're a vampire."

"I've seen what happens. They were killed right in front of me, remember? I would do anything not to be this disgusting creature." She wipes tears from her eyes. "Go on. Get out of here. I've got to get back to work. And you have vampires to kill."

If my daughter is so scared of vampires, even the good ones, does that mean she's scared of me?

27
Warwick

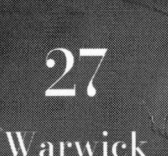

Things have quieted down in the last couple of days, as far as the media coverage goes for the killings. We owe this all to Jane who worked out a deal with the president. When I first arrive in Missouri, the tracking didn't stop, they are everywhere. What is it about this state that they like so much? Personally, I have never been here before, but apparently there is a tourist attraction in a city called Branson. It's called Screamville. Envio catches wind of a crowd coming here for a massive slaughtering. The worst thing about this, it's spring break, which means everyone and their kids from the surrounding states will be coming here right in the middle of it. We have no idea how big the crowd will get, human or rogue, so Jane has summoned everyone there for the week to keep an eye on things.

"The humans got over the vampire thing fast. I didn't figure they would be traveling at all," Envio says, sitting on my couch.

"Think about it. They were stuck in their homes, and that made them miss everything they normally get to do. Now, they can go and do stuff. Of course they are going to do something fun with their kids. Too bad they don't realize they are making matters worse. Good thing they have us," I reply.

"The rest should arrive this morning. Jane said all hands on deck to keep the human casualties to a minimum. If they get what they want, it'll be one hell of a statement to the country. The one thing people care about more than themselves is their kids' safety. You start messing with that, and shit will hit the fan fast."

Since being split up, I haven't talked much with Envio besides this morning. I don't want to pry, but I wonder how we are doing with tracking rogues. Is there a chance we can actually get this done? My mind just keeps picturing being reunited with Tasha and Avery. I want this to work.

"I'd say it's going better than I expected. The South is definitely worse off with rogues, since the North is basically already free of them now. If we focus all our resources on the South, then we might be able to get this done sooner than we thought."

Music to my ears. "The humans took care of a lot of them for us too. How many would you say there is left?"

He scratches his chin. "If I had to guess, probably a hundred or two. Number goes down every passing day."

A deep sigh of relief washes over me, daydreaming about reuniting with my family, being there for my daughter's first day of kindergarten, graduating high school, and walking her down the aisle. All this I'm doing is to get back to them.

"I'm going to dip out for a bit. Be back in an hour, tops," I say, heading out the door.

Next thing, my feet are taking off and they stop at the end of our driveway. A black sedan is parked in front of the house. She finally got herself a car. For the longest time, we couldn't afford one after ours broke down. Babies are expensive and first priority. I get to the side window without being seen and peek in. My heart sinks.

A man is holding my daughter; they are smiling and laughing, and then Tasha and kisses him. Who is he? Why is my wife kissing him? My daughter liking him? My knuckles turn white, and my teeth grind. I've been gone too long, and she is moving on without me. Can

I blame her? Have I given her any reason to think I'm still alive out there? At some point, she has to move on and find someone. I guess in the back of my mind, I always hoped I could come back to her before any of that happened, but now it's too late.

My phone vibrates with a text from Envio, letting me know Jane has arrived at my house. There is no need for me to stand here, gawking at my family, but I'll be back. If she has moved on, I want the peace of mind to know that he's taking good care of them.

I walk in the door. "Sorry. Figured you wouldn't be here for another hour or so."

"I wanted to make it here before anyone else, but it looks like Samuel and Envio beat me," Jane says.

"Not my fault you took forever," Samuel jokes around.

Everyone else should be here soon. Screamville opens in two hours, and we need to be there first thing to keep an eye on things. I have a feeling the rogues are already here, but I have no idea how many.

"Let's remember why we are doing this. Peace. Only make a scene if it's absolutely necessary. Otherwise, kill them away from the humans. Everyone has a cell phone and knows how to take a video. We don't want to end up all over the news and ruin our chances," Jane says.

Over the course of the next two hours, we talk about how different our lives would be if we never became vampires.

"I would've been in college, hopefully with friends, and on my way to becoming a doctor or something," Jane says.

"My wife and son would still be alive. Amy wouldn't be so scared of the world. I would have never become a monster," Samuel shares.

"My wife wouldn't be sleeping with another man, and my child wouldn't be getting held by another man," I say. "What about you, Envio?"

"I'm not sure. Was on track to possibly go to med school."

The conversation gets heavy, Samuel sharing with us he thinks

Amy is terrified of him, and her innate fear of vampires. Granted, apparently the first vampires she met kidnapped her and then killed her mother and brother in front of her. That would make anyone scared of us. Yet she knows we are different and still fears us.

"Oh, it's time to go. Park opens up in twenty minutes," Jane says, stopping the conversation to get down to business.

Over the next several hours, rogues enter the park, looking for their next victim, while we track them. As Jane said, no scenes unless absolutely necessary. I drag mine behind rides and into bathrooms to get away from the crowds of families swarming the park, with no clue the danger that lurks around every corner while they are here.

By the end of the day when the park closes, when we regroup, about thirty are dead between all of us. We know more will be showing up, and the park will be packed all week.

"Listen, I know it was a long day, but look at the progress we are making. If we keep it up, we could be rogue free by the end of the week. Something we've worked toward for years. I'll see you all back at the park tomorrow," Jane says, and everyone disperses back to their hotel rooms.

Back at my house, I can't get the image of Tasha kissing that man out of my head. I'm not going to kill him or anything, but who is he? Surely, he's asked where Avery's dad is, or she's mentioned that she is married. Although, technically, are we? Is there a limitation on how long someone is missing before they are considered widowed? Poor Tasha must really think I'm dead if she is seeing someone. My feelings aside, Avery deserves to have someone who can be with her every night, and Tasha someone who can provide and care for her without limitations. It kills me to say it, but it's true.

The rest of the week goes by in a flash, killing around seventy more rogues between all of us. If there are any more rogues out there, it'll only be a few that are very good at hiding from us and the humans. Yet we will keep our eyes out for the stragglers. If they are smart, they will keep low-key and not kill anyone. But they aren't.

Everyone goes back to their states and starts cleaning it up, hopeful that the agreement with the president will withstand, and both sides can follow the rules set forth.

All I think about is how long will it last before someone fucks up and breaks a rule?

28
Jane

I head back to my house in Texas to prepare for my next meeting with President Walters. We did what he asked, so now he can follow through with his side of the deal. Nothing is expected to go smoothly at first, and won't, but over time it will get better once they see we aren't their enemies.

Sam lets me know that Walters wants to meet in an hour at the same building as the drop-off. Envio and Warwick will come with me, just in case they want to cause any trouble. They shouldn't since we took care of all the killers on our side, and their people can now live without fear. Hell, I know our lives will be much easier now that they're gone.

"You think he's actually going to keep his word? Now that it's here... I'm not sure I can even picture a world where humans are okay with living alongside us," Envio says, pacing my living room.

"It's not going to be easy. And we will have people that break the rules on both sides—it's inevitable—but I think maybe if they actually see no killings, then they will understand we aren't here to hurt them."

"I know you have always been more optimistic than me, but it seems way too easy. After y'all working for years to eradicate the rogues and now they are just gone? Seems like a dream and I'll wake up any second."

I pinch him. "No dream. See?"

I don't know why he's complaining because this means we can finally be together without constant battles. Something always comes between us to where we are separated, and this is finally our chance, everyone's chance, at having normal lives. He could finish college and go to med school if he wants, and I can get a degree if I desire. The world will be ours, and everything will go back to the way things were before Jakob created vampires.

He stops and sits down next to me, clutching my hand. "As long as I'm with you, nothing else matters. Whether we are at war or not."

Warwick comes into the room and clears his throat. "Sorry to interrupt but we'll need to leave soon."

I look at my watch and it's a quarter til. *Crap. We might be late.* We haul ass to the car and then drive as fast as we can without breaking the speed limit to the agency headquarters. The closer we get, the more nervous I become. I've only been a leader for a little over a week and now I'm fixing to make a peace agreement with the president of the United States that will affect both of our species for a long time to come. *Don't fuck this up.*

Stephen would want me to believe in myself and to walk in there with my head held high. We haven't done anything wrong to warrant a double cross, and my hope is this goes smoothly without any complications.

As we pull up to the headquarters, Envio and I take a quick glance at each other before getting out. Warwick hasn't said a word on the ride over, which tells me he's just as nervous as we are. The last time they were here, Stephen was alive, and an agreement was being made. Shortly after, things went downhill fast. This time, no one is dying.

Guards escort us inside, and me to a conference room where President Walters sits at the end of the table.

"Glad you could make it. I was starting to wonder if you were having second thoughts."

"Let's get down to business. We need to discuss what this agreement will mean for both sides, and the expectations we are upholding on each side too."

"You are very demanding. Stephen wasn't that way. I admit, it's in both our best interests for peace to be had, so many lives have been lost, and my people are sick of living in constant fear. However, if we can establish rules that will make them feel safe again, then I think this will benefit both of us."

"Agreed."

Over the next several hours, we talk about everything. Our agreement is he's in charge of the humans, and I'm in charge of all vampires. We must be documented and carry it with us at all times just like humans and their IDs. No retaliation on either side, or they will serve jail time. In the event of death, the person or vampire at fault shall be sentenced to death.

"You will be treated just like humans. Work jobs, pay taxes, own homes, and get married."

"There is something we haven't covered yet."

"What?"

"How are we supposed to get nourishment? Feeding on a live human is against the rules we've established, so how?"

"We can establish blood banks, but we have problems with donors already, so that could be a potential problem in the future. That's something we'll have to figure out as we go," he replies. "This is going to take many meetings and possibly some adjustments after we see how things go after a couple months."

President Walters wants to hold a press conference announcing the new agreement before I leave. I've never even taken a speech class, and he wants me to stand up beside him on live television in front of millions, possibly billions of people. It's terrifying, but that's part of being a leader, and it's time I own up to my role a hundred percent. Instead of doubting myself, maybe it's time I start noticing that under my command, we eradicated the rogues, and are finally making peace with the humans. Something many of us never thought would happen. Some sort of pipe dream for us to work toward, but never actually achieve, but in just a couple of minutes, it will be official for all of the USA to see. We are fixing to make history, and my name will be in future history books about this treaty.

"Are you ready?"

"As I'll ever be."

We leave the conference room and go to another with a podium in the middle with the seal in the background. "My fellow Americans, today I come to you with some good news. The killings are over, and the bad people are dead. The Guardians, a rebel group of vampires, have killed them all. Because of this act of good faith, they will receive pardon to live among us without fear of being killed. Anyone who tries to retaliate will be sentenced to two years in jail. In the event of a murder, the penalty is death, without exceptions. I'd like to introduce you to their leader, Jane."

I step up to the podium, never having given a speech on TV before, and almost freeze. I hear Stephen's voice in my mind telling me, *You can do this*. "Good afternoon, ladies and gentlemen. I want to thank President Walters for the chance he's given us to prove that not all vampires want to kill. We have and will remain peaceful. Many of us have lived alongside you for years without any issues. We hope to continue that trend for many years to come."

The press conference was short and sweet, and we didn't take questions at the end. It's finally here. The end of the fighting. What we have all worked so hard to achieve. If only Sasha and Stephen could have been here to see it. We've lost so many great people along the way, but everyone knew that fighting for our cause came with risk. Yet they still fought alongside us, giving up their lives for our future. The future of humanity.

29

Envio

The bed creaks beneath us as I turn over to face her. It's been a week since the press conference, and things have been better. Jane has been back to visit with the president multiple times since that night, just to go over more things and the future of our country. As we assumed, not everyone is on board with his decision, but he still has two years left on his term. If we can convince the ones doubting us, then we might be able to make this work long term. If not, there's no telling what the next elected president will do.

So many vampires aren't sure that we will survive, but what they don't understand is we are at their mercy. Literally. They are our source of nourishment, and without that, we will wither away and die. Their blood might be what keeps us alive, but that doesn't mean they have to fear us, and it's up to us to prove that, but it will take time. The president is giving us two years, with strings attached, to prove to the American people that we aren't vicious like the others, and just want to live in peace.

"What are you thinking about?" Jane strokes my face and looks longingly into my eyes. "We haven't had this much time together in, well, forever. Yet it doesn't seem like you are here with me right now. What's going on?"

"Maybe now is the right time to talk about our living situation..." I see her stiffen, and then she sits up in the bed.

"Aren't you practically living here already?"

"But you never agreed officially and seemed kind of leery. I just want to make sure we are both on the same page about our future."

Jane rolls her eyes and grabs my hand. "I couldn't imagine it with anyone else, Envio. Ever since I met you, even when I doubted you could be trusted, my body was telling me that you were different."

"Different?"

Things with Jane have always been complicated. I mean, we met under harsh circumstances, with me murdering her father right in front of her, and then turning her for Jakob. Thankfully, Samuel stepped in and messed that up. Who knows what would have happened if he had gotten his hands on her back then? If she had fulfilled my vision and joined under Jakob's reign. Our bond has always been so much more than me being her maker. Sure, I can sense her emotions, but it's much more than that.

"That you weren't like all the other guys... I've never really been with a man, besides the couple dates I had with Stephen's brother before he passed, so all I could go off was TV and overhearing girls from school."

"Is this about the sex thing? We've made love..."

"No, it's about being leery about promising the rest of my life to someone when I've never really been with anyone else. Not that I don't want to be with you, but forever is a long time, especially for us. We could live to be a million years old, and along the way, we could get sick of each other, and I'm deathly afraid of losing you."

Wait, I'm not sure how I should take that. Is she wanting to experiment with other people since she's only been with me? Emotions aside, it makes sense for someone to wonder, but it's another thing to do it while in a committed relationship. This makes me even more worried that something is wrong. I noticed it when I brought up moving in and she seemed so surprised by the request. It's the next logical step in our relationship, which I don't want to stay stagnant. Someday, I hope to call her my wife, but not forty years from now. Maybe we are drifting away, and I need to pull her back to me.

"I'm sorry. It's not that I want to hurt you by telling you these things, but dishonesty isn't my thing. Never has been."

"Listen, I'm glad you said something because I've had this feeling that something is going on but I didn't know what. At least now I know. You are the only woman I want, and if you were going to lose me, don't you think it would have been when we went forever without seeing each other?"

"Possibly, but..."

"But nothing. Stop putting negative thoughts in there." I tap on her temple. "It never does any good. It only causes problems, and no one needs any more of those."

Jane has had so much on her plate the last couple weeks, taking over leadership of us, and dealing with the president that her stress level has been through the ceiling. I can see that coupled with us getting closer could scare her, cause her to question things, but there's no need. I'm right here and not going anywhere unless she makes me.

"I love you," she whispers, lying back down. "Forget I mentioned anything."

Lying there next to her, it reminds me of something she mentioned a couple days ago about visiting my mom. The problem is, what if she's still with that asshole that beats on her? I can't promise I'll be able to hold my anger back and not pummel him right then and there. She might be naive enough to believe he loves her, but I know the truth. The man just likes having someone cower beneath his touch, and still come back day after day. My mother deserves to be happy, and she might think happiness is with him, but she has never had real happiness. I wish her something like me and Jane. Something real, an emotional and physical connection, without being beaten and treated like a pet. Maybe one day she will come to her senses, before her life is taken because of her so-called happiness.

"So, I'm thinking about going to visit my mother today. Just buck up and go, before I change my mind. You know." I push a stray piece of hair behind her earlobe. "But I'd like you to come with me. In case he's there."

She shakes her head and starts moving to get off the bed.

"Where you goin'?"

"Going before you change your mind. Come on." Her eyes don't leave mine until I'm off the bed and getting my shoes on.

"You really are something, you know that? What would I do without you?"

"I've sometimes wondered the same thing, but hopefully you never have to find out."

Ain't that the truth, baby. A world without Jane in it, is a world I wouldn't want to live in.

We stand down the street from her house, and I'm seriously questioning whether this is still a good idea. She hasn't seen me in years, and now I'm just going to show up on her doorstep? She'll have so many questions, and one thing she's always been able to do is tell when I'm lying. If it comes up, then I'll have to tell her about me, you know, being a vampire. How will she react? *Fuck.* I start to turn around to leave and Jane catches my arm.

"Listen, she's your mother. At least let her know that you're alive. She must be worried sick after all these years without any communication."

We walk hand in hand up to her door, and she knocks. My mother opens the door before I can run away.

"Son? I've been worried sick." She opens the door wider and leans in for a hug.

I peer inside. "Is he here?"

"You'd be proud of me, son. I left him a year ago. Couldn't take it anymore."

There are no signs of any beatings. No bruises or cuts. Maybe she's telling the truth this time, and I can finally stop wondering how long until I find her beaten to death by that prick.

"It's just me living here now. Your room is still just as you left it," she says, gesturing to the back of the house. The home I grew up in, watching not one but two men take advantage of mother to a point where she couldn't even think for herself but she was too worried about what they would think or do to her.

"I'm not here looking for a place to stay, Mom. Jane and I actually live together."

Her eyes take note of the woman standing next to me.

"I'm Jane. It's nice to meet you, ma'am."

We are still standing on the porch, the awkwardness seeping through all of us. I didn't think about this being the first time she has met my mother, or the magnitude of it, but it's nice she came with me for moral support. When talking about coming here, my anxiety flared up, not knowing how it was going to go, and I don't think I could've done this alone. Without her, I never would have made it up to the doorstep.

"Would you like to come in? I can make us dinner, maybe some coffee..."

"No, we aren't staying. Just wanted to stop by for a minute. We've got somewhere we have to be soon. Maybe next time..."

Jane looks at me and walks inside, going against my wishes. "We'd love to, actually. Another half hour won't hurt."

Damn it, girl. I shook my head and followed her. Coming in means she will ask questions, and that's what scares me. The question is bound to come up sooner or later, or the subject of the recent revelation of vampires being real. What the hell are we supposed to say then?

My mother goes to the kitchen, leaving us alone on the couch. "Why'd you do that?"

"Give her a chance, babe. She just wants to see her son, and you want to run off after being gone for a couple years... Give her a break."

My mother hands Jane a cup of coffee. "Thanks, Mrs. De Luca."

"Please dear, call me Josie. After all, if my son brought you here, it must be serious enough."

My head hangs back on the couch, knowing where this conversation is going. She asks how we met, and Jane makes up some lame-ass story, not even close to the real one, to appease her. It goes on and on and she keeps answering, knowing that my mother can tell when I'm lying.

Mother's eyes glance to the clock. "You guys better get going. Don't want you to be late to whatever it is you're doing. But come back anytime. I'd love to get to know your girlfriend more." She hugs us and sends us on our way.

How could my life get any better? I've finally gotten everything I prayed for... my mother to be safe, a woman that adores me, and the chance at my life finally getting back to some type of normalcy since being made vampire. What else could I possibly ask for?

About the Author

Ashley Zakrzewski is known for her captivating storytelling, sultry plots, and dynamic protagonists. Hailing from Arkansas, her affinity for the written word began early on, and she has been relentlessly chasing after her dreams ever since. She also writes under the Pen Name Kaci Bell for clean romance.

To sign up for her newsletter when deals are coming: Click to Sign up for newsletter

If you like to save money and support the author, she offers Buy One Get One Free eBooks on her website and bundles that save you even more $$$. No coupon code needed. All discounts will be applied in the cart. Just visit www.ashleyzakrzewski.com

Made in the USA
Columbia, SC
22 February 2024

5b7ccc43-9af3-4dc3-ad4b-a48734448699R03